Her Triplet Alphas

A PARANORMAL NOVEL

written by

JOANNA J

AUTHOR'S NOTES

When I first began writing on the Dreame/Stary Writing App, I wrote on the weekends and weeknights. I spent my days swabbing patients for Coronavirus. I became a doctor because I genuinely wanted to help people feel better, but I was struggling with my own inner turmoil.

Writing was therapeutic for me. It was my escape from reality, especially during the pandemic. I made a little fantasy world, one where immortality was within reach, good always triumphed over evil, and true love always prevailed. I wrote because stories demand to be told. They wind their way into my mind and trickle out through my fingertips.

I hunched over my desk every night, writing about werewolves and witches. My curious cats and my loyal little dog were my honorary co-writers: Noddy, Winky, Dobby, and Minnie, respectively. They were there every night while I wrote this book. They dutifully kept me company throughout the night. They were silent sources of comfort and inspiration. Now, it's just me, Minnie and Dobby, and we miss Noddy and Winky dearly everyday. We love them and we thank them for their never-failing companionship. May they always be blessed and remembered.

The newest addition to the family is a rambunctious tortoiseshell kitten named Zoey. The support from my parents remains steadfast. They have always been there for me at every stage of my life, the little and the big. My editor at Dreame/Stary Writing, the wonderful Mona, is always there to assist and motivate me. Above all, the readers make every minute, hour and day spent worth it. Each and every single reader means so much to me. I am so grateful to everyone involved in making this possible. I am grateful for the many opportunities made possible by the entire team at Dreame/Stary Writing.

Please note that this book is a work of fiction. All the characters, places and names are fictional and derived from my imagination. Any similarities between this book and any true life story are merely coincidental. This book is not based on real events from my life or anyone else's.

Joanna J.

TABLE OF CONTENTS

Chapter 1: ChaSity the ChaRity Case

Chasity

The blanket of pure white snow outside seemed to sparkle in the early morning light. The Pack House was buzzing with excitement about the upcoming festivities. Tomorrow was my birthday, not that anyone cared, or even remembered, because it was also the birthday of the Thorn Triplets. The Thorn Triplets were the pride and joy of the Winter Moon Pack. They were the sons of Alpha Romeo Thorn. They were filthy rich, devilishly handsome and disgustingly arrogant. All the young she-wolves adored them wholeheartedly and stroked their egos on a daily basis. I was cursed to share a birthday and a home with them.

At the tender age of nine, my drug-addicted parents left the pack to go rogue, and they had not been seen or heard from since. They left no instructions regarding their wishes for me, so I was taken into the pack house, and placed under the care of Alpha Romeo and his wife, Ronnie. As if I had not been devastated enough, I was then met with three twelve-year old tormenters. The identical triplet sons of the Alpha were, in order of birth, Alex, Felix and Calix. They despised me and ensured that I knew I was beneath them. Due to their drug seeking habits, my parents had incurred a huge debt, which had been paid off by the Alpha. Thus, I had to earn my keep and repay my debt by doing as many chores as possible, while the triplets enjoyed an idyllic childhood in the very same house. The

1

past nine years of my life had been devoted to the repayment of my parents' debt.

In some packs, the new Alpha ascends at age eighteen when they first shift, but in mine, the age for ascension was twenty one. Thus, tomorrow, on November eleventh, the triplets would turn twenty-one and take over the pack, while I would turn eighteen and experience my first shift. Eighteen was also the minimum age at which werewolves could recognise their fated mate, but I did not care about that. All I wanted was to come of age so I could leave this hell behind.

At least, the pack house had beautiful scenery. We were close to the north pole of Wolf Country, so snow was an everyday affair, though there was no sign of Santa Claus. I certainly did not expect any birthday presents this November or Christmas presents come December. The pack leaders made it clear that I owed them money and they were subtracting my "wages" from the debt, so I was never given any money. I was allowed food, clothes, and shelter, the basics.

I slowly got out of bed. The sun was just peeking out from behind a snow-covered horizon. Everything glistened. I gazed out my window at the wintry terrain. I sighed. I had to start making breakfast for everyone. Despite the huge size of the pack house with its luxurious bedrooms and bathrooms, I was given a small empty storage room to stay in. I had a cot, a shelf of second-hand books and a single drawer full of second-hand clothes. The other drawers contained extra cleaning supplies as I was responsible for the housekeeping at the pack house.

I used the common room's bathroom, showering quickly. I looked at myself in the mirror. My parents had name me Chasity but everyone in the pack called me Charity. This was started by the triplets as a joke, and because they said it so often, even decent pack members thought it was my real name. I had been so shy and scared as a child that I had never bothered to correct them so it had stuck.

I detangled my waist-length dark blonde curls and put them up in a huge bun. Whenever I left them down, the triplets would pull my hair ever since we were little. They had not grown out of this habit even in adulthood. I sighed. There were dark circles forming under my large brown eyes. My light brown skin looked sallow. I had been overworking myself, or rather, the Thorn family had been overworking me. They used to have a maid and a cook with me as the sole assistant of both, but they had fired them last month after numerous conflicts between the staff members and the spoilt triplets. For the past month, I had been drowning in work while attending my final year of high school. I had seven more months of high school before I could leave this place. That was the deal. At eighteen, after high school, I would get my freedom and whatever I had paid off by then would be the end of it. The current Alpha and Luna seemed to think they were being extremely generous.

The pack house had a really good heating system, so despite the fact that outside looked like the frigid tundra, inside was pretty warm. I put on a long-sleeved white babydoll top that covered my behind as I was just wearing black leggings underneath. I started on breakfast. As it was the Triplets' "birthday week" and they would soon be Alphas, everyday was a feast day. I made waffles, pancakes, bacon, scrambled eggs and sausages. I put the butter and maple syrup on the table. I made coffee. I quickly drank some sweet, milky coffee for some energy and started setting the table.

Luna Ronnie entered the dining room, eyeing me, scrutinising my handy-work. She was a tall woman with dark brown long straight hair, pale skin and green eyes.

"The table looks nice," she said, a rare compliment. "But have you washed all the wares? Wash them all before you eat!"

Alpha Romeo sauntered in. He kissed his Luna gently. He gave me a nod of approval regarding the breakfast spread. I smiled feebly at him.

Suddenly, I heard heavy footsteps on the stairs and I took a deep breath. The Triplet Terrors were coming. They towered over me at six feet and four inches each, exactly a foot taller than me. They resembled their father with their shoulder-length thick shiny black hair, chiseled faces, baby blue eyes, dimples and chin-clefts. As they were Alphas, they were all broad-shouldered and muscled, blessed with super speed, and super strength, even beyond what was considered extraordinary for most werewolves. They were perfectly identical and perfectly heinous, or, at least, they were to me. Their deep voices boomed as they shouted excitedly, shoving each other playfully. They would be twenty-one tomorrow, but they still acted like they were twelve.

Alex was the eldest and the most serious and severe. He would surely rule with an iron fist and a surly demeanour. Felix, the middle triplet, loved being the centre of attention and was naturally filled with wise-cracks, jokes and quips. Classic middle child. The youngest, Calix, was the charmer, a professional sweet-talker and Mommy's favourite. He *almost* treated me like I was human.

"Did you make all of this, Charity?" Asked Calix, immediately trying to pull my hair out of its bun.

I nodded, dodging him, only to bump into Felix, who smirked and slipped my hair tie off. My curls tumbled down all around me. Felix and Calix laughed.

"Stop!" I implored them, reaching for my only hair tie.

Felix held it high above my head. He threw it to Alex, who caught it and put it in his pocket. I tried to lunge towards Alex, but Felix grabbed me. Felix and Alex started shoving me back and forth between them, like I was a ball, and they were playing catch.

"I give up! I give up!" I said, while they snickered.

Calix said, "All right. Cut it out. Let her go wash the wares. Mom wants the place kept as clean as possible, so there'll be less to do tomorrow."

The elder two relinquished me. I ran into the kitchen. My heart was racing. I started on the dishes. By the time I was done, the family of five hungry werewolves, four of them from Alpha stock, had devoured literally everything I made, except for one pancake. The dining room chairs were all empty. I went to get the last pancake, but Felix snatched it up. He had zoomed in out of nowhere, fast as a cheetah, and quiet as a mouse.

"I haven't eaten anything," I told him, my eyes wide.

"Good, you're fat enough as it is," he said, sneering.

He ate the pancake in two bites. I sighed. I refused to cry. I had not cried in front of them since the first year of torment when I was nine. My tenth birthday marked a very important vow I had made to myself after crying almost every single day at aged nine. The vow was that I would never let the Triplets make me cry ever again. I would be strong. I had kept that vow successfully for eight years come tomorrow. The comment stung though. The Triplets were widely regarded as the most handsome eligible bachelors in the Pack. They constantly attacked my weight though I was not overweight. Even if I *had been* overweight, it would be wrong to consistently insult me. I had a curvy hourglass figure. My waist was slender. I wore about a size 4 in clothes, which was petite in my opinion, but all the Triplets had stick-thin size 0 girlfriends.

I had to take the bus to school. I had thrown on a hand-me-down black coat over my white top and leggings. I managed to find another hair tie, but this was truly the last one. The pack high school was called Winter Moon High after the pack. Our pack colours, and therefore, also the school colours, were white, blue and silver. The whole school was decorated with streamers and balloons in celebration of the new Alphas, the Triplets.

"You're so lucky, Charity," said Mina Toros, the most popular girl in my senior year. She tossed her long dark hair back and pursed her plump red lips, as she gazed into the mirror inside her locker. She was wearing a pink skirt short enough to qualify as belt. Thank goodness, she had opaque tights on underneath. She usually ignored me except for the occasional pronouncement of how "lucky" I was.

"The things I'd do to those Triplets if I lived in that house," Mina said, licking her lips.

"You'd have to drop out!" Squealed her best friend, the second most popular girl, Tina Gregory. "You'd get pregnant the first month there."

Tina had flawless dark brown skin with curly hair. She was tall and waif-like, and she was also wearing a pink skirt short enough to be a belt with opaque tights underneath. Mina and Tina usually matched as though they were twins. Mina cackled at Tina's joke.

"You know, Charity," said Mina suddenly. "You're not totally hideous."

Gee, thanks.

"Ok," I said, clutching my books.

The girls were blocking my locker, which was sandwiched between their two lockers. Lucky me, indeed.

"Yeah," agreed Tina. "Your hair is actually pretty. You're like a biracial Goldilocks."

I smiled. That sounded like a real compliment.

"Thanks, Tina!" I said.

"Ohhh! And those Triplets are the three bears!" Shrieked Mina. "If I were their Goldie Locks, I'd make sure everything was just right, get it?"

"Or too big," said Tina, giggling.

"That means one of the triplets has to be too small," I said softly.

Being werewolves, Mina and Tina heard me, and they burst out laughing. Wow. I was actually getting along with them for five minutes.

"That was a good one, Charity, surprisingly," said Tina, looking at me like she was only just seeing me for the very first time.

"Yeah," said Mina, giving me the same strange appraising look. "You know, if you had the money, imagine how cute you could look."

I fidgeted uncomfortably, suddenly hyperaware of the patches in my clothes. Mina and Tina strutted off, and I hurriedly opened my locker and got out my Math book. Mr Johnson, who coached football and taught Math, looked like he should be an Alpha too. He was huge and really attractive for a teacher. He was married though to his mate, the Art teacher, Mrs Johnson. He handed out our graded tests while Tina and Mina made flirty faces at him. Those flirty faces were not doing them any good. I noticed they got an F and an F minus respectively. I did not know F minus existed before today. He smiled at me and winked. My heart skipped a beat.

"A plus as usual, Math champ," he boomed.

Mr Johnson was one of the few people in my life, who was nice to me.

"Mina and Tina, see me after class," Mr Johnson said.

After class, Ashton Peters, a tall buff redhead, who played football and was well-liked in the pack, pretended to knock into my desk. The stack of papers on my desk went flying all over the room. Mr Johnson spotted it.

"Stay and help her pick those up, Ashton, my boy," boomed Mr Johnson.

"Aww, coach, I'll be late for football practice," he whined.

"And we'll be late for cheerleading practice," said Mina and Tina in unison, pouting.

"I'm the coach, Ashton, go ahead and be late. I'll explain to your cheerleading coach, okay, girls," said Mr Johnson.

Ashton grumbled. He glared at me as if this were my fault. He started picking up papers at werewolf speed, which caused the ones I was picking up to fly around due to the displaced wind. I eavesdropped on the meeting with Mina and Tina.

Chapter 1: ChaSity the ChaRity Case

"Mina, Tina, I'm giving you a homework assignment to make up those grades. If you don't ace it, there won't be any cheerleading," he said.

The girls gasped. He handed them a stack of papers each and told them they could work on it together and that he set the questions himself, so they would not find the answers online. I snatched up the last few papers from the floor and took the stack Ashton was handing me without looking at me.

"Thanks," I said softly to him.

He glanced down at me, surprised by my thanks. He looked a little guilty all of a sudden. Mr Johnson left the room, leaving Mina and Tina looking dejected. Ashton grabbed the hair tie from my hair, just like Calix had this morning. My curls came tumbling down again. I shrieked. I was so fed up. Ashton laughed and ran away to football practice. There went my last hair tie and my birthday was tomorrow.

"Aren't you going to cheerleading?" I asked the girls, actually feeling sorry for them, as they had been sort of nice earlier.

"No," said Mina.

"What's the use? We'll never ace this homework, so we'll fail the class and be banned from the squad anyway," explained Tina.

I walked up to them and looked at the homework assignment. I snorted. I could get one hundred percent in this in my sleep. I was suddenly struck by an idea.

"Remember how you girls said I had... potential," I said, looking at them.

They shrugged.

"I'll do the assignment, and you can copy it in your handwritings and ace it, okay," I offered.

The girls squealed. They jumped up and down, hugging each other and then me.

"Wait!" Said Mina, relinquishing me and raising her eyebrows.

"What's the catch?" Asked Tina, narrowing her eyes.

"I'm turning eighteen tomorrow, too," I said.

They gasped.

"You have the same birthday as the triplets?" Mina asked.

"Wait, that means everyone ignores your birthday like every single year," said Tina.

It was my turn to shrug.

"And they will this year too, but I at least wanna feel...special. I'm gonna shift for the first time at midnight and who knows...I might see my mate at the big party...not that I care..." I rambled.

"You wanna look hot? Is that it?" Mina said, smirking.

"Yeah, you want us to make you over?" Tina asked, smiling.

I nodded.

Chapter 2: Makeover!

Chasity

I was supposed to go home immediately after school to help with the preparations for the huge birthday party tomorrow night for the Triplets, but I had to do the assignment for the girls, *and* they had to make me over. I knew I would pay for it later, but whatever. The Thorns had hired a party planner. They should be okay for a few hours without their werewolf Cinderella.

I did the assignment for the girls literally in the car on the way to the mall. It was that easy. Math was my thing. I was a nerd in general, and I was proud of this, even though werewolves prized brawn and beauty over brains any day.

The girls were impressed. They quickly copied it, sitting in the freezing parking lot with the heater turned up. Mina drove a sports car. I did not know what kind, but I knew that Mina and Tina were almost as rich as the Alpha and his family. They dragged me into the mall, squealing excitedly, as though I was doing them a favour, even when it came to the makeover. I reminded them I had no money. They rolled their eyes and ignored me. I guessed I could consider the stuff they bought as part of the deal.

I tried on outfit after outfit. Mina and Tina rated each one and seemed to be having a blast. This was actually kind of fun. They encouraged me to pick out a lot of miniskirts and mini dresses. They said I had "great legs" and "nice boobs" even though the Triplets called me fat. Honestly, the clothes they picked for me did suit me. I had some trouble walking in heels, but the girls made me practice in the store like it was a runway. They pretended to be on a catwalk too. They were so confident. I had to marvel at them. Next, they showed me what makeup to wear and how to style my hair at Tina's house. They did a test run. I looked in Tina's floor-length mirror and my jaw dropped.

I had on high heeled black ankle boots with a mini pleated black skirt. I was wearing black stockings, as it was cold out even for a werewolf. My long-sleeved white top had a sweetheart neckline that was really flattering. My hair looked so shiny styled in loose bouncy curls down my back. My skin glowed, and I had cat eyeliner and red lips, that surprisingly suited me. I hugged Mina and Tina. Did I just make two friends?

They drove me to the pack house, hoping to catch a glimpse of the triplets, but they were not at home yet. I started helping the party planner sort out all the decorations and the food. It was tomorrow night, and there was a lot to do. I did my own homework in between all of this. I was a master multitasker. I heard three cars parking. It was the triplets. Alpha and Luna were out shopping for even more gifts, despite the fact that I had already wrapped about a dozen gifts.

The party planner was a bleached blonde in her thirties, who was obsessed with the hunk-i-ness of the triplets. She seemed to dislike me, even though I was the only one helping her. She had been over everyday this week and always tried to make me look bad in front of the triplets. I wanted to tell her that they already hated me, so she could relax. Her name was Ronda Something. I kept forgetting her last name.

The triplets walked in. Each had their arm around a girl. They changed girlfriends every two months or so. It did not make sense learning the girls' names. Contradictorily, the triplets were anxious to find their real mate. They were not sure if they had three separate mates, or just one mate to share. Sounds crazy, but when it came to identical multiples like twins and triplets, they usually shared a single mate, since they had been one egg and one sperm, that split to form the multiples. Thus, theoretically, identical twins and triplets were naturally occurring clones. Every girl wished she was their mate. That was so crazy to me. The triplets were handsome, but they were awful, and *three* mates sounded so complicated.

Ronda glared at their girlfriends, jealousy evident in her beady eyes. The girls did not stay long, and when they left, Ronda told the triplets I had showed up really late to help her. I sighed. I had been under the table literally, while I wrapped tiny presents for door prizes. All the pack members got to pick a mystery present from a huge box tomorrow.

I crawled out from under the table to make myself known, before they had to look for me. Hiding from them would just set them off. The triplets stared at me, their eyes wide. They exchanged a few glances. I remembered my makeover. I did not think they would notice or even care. Alex licked his lips, trailing his eyes from my head to my toes. I took a step back. Felix looked flabbergasted, and Calix smirked at me.

"Leave it to us, Ronda," said Felix, recovering his usual haughty sneer, "We'll punish her."

Ronda smiled maliciously at me. She was the most immature adult I had ever met, including the triplets, and *that* was saying something. The triplets had me backed against the kitchen island.

"I'm sorry," I said, "I had to do some extra math for Mr Johnson."

It was not a complete lie. The triplets knew Mr Johnson, because they had been his football stars back when they went to Winter Moon High. They also knew I had won Math competitions before. They had really enjoyed making fun of me then.

"Okay," said Felix simply, taking a step towards me. "What's all of this?" He gestured to my outfit, makeup and hair.

"My eighteenth birthday is tomorrow. I'm just trying out how I wanna look," I said, looking down, waiting for them to insult me.

"Do you have a boyfriend, is that it?" Asked Alex, anger rising in his voice.

Why did he even care?

"I'm too fat to get a boyfriend, remember?" I said, repeating one of their classic insults.

"Don't play games with us," said Felix softly. "Is all of this for your mate? Have you figured out who he is?"

"No!" I said.

They were acting so strange like I had done something underhanded.

"You'll only know for sure tomorrow. Your inner wolf will tell you who your mate is," said Calix.

"I don't want a mate," I said honestly.

I had never had a guy be nice to me, and I could not picture it happening.

"Why the hell not?" Alex asked, acting like I was crazy for saying that.

The Triplets were so eager to find their real mate, that they would visit other pack lands, hoping to get a whiff of their mate. They assumed their mate was younger than them. That would explain why they could not pick up her scent. Only mates who had come of age could be discovered.

"Because he'd just be mean to me and call me names, and I get enough of that from you," I snapped.

I should not have snapped. I was a little frightened now. The triplets had not hit me since we were little. The last fight happened when I was eleven and they were fourteen. I had punched Calix, breaking his nose for calling me a "fat nasty slut" with "dead druggie parents". My parents' whereabouts had never been confirmed, and I always liked to think they were alive. Calix had let out a blood-curdling scream, alerting his elder brothers. Alex had slapped me and then Felix. Calix had been reluctant, but they made him hit me. They had dragged me out to the frozen river behind the pack house. There had been a hole in the frozen river for ice fishing. I had been small enough to dip in the hole. They had held me under the water until I blacked out. Their parents had been furious. I had been taken to the hospital for hypothermia. I never knew what their punishments had been, but, after that, we never got physical with each other, nothing more than a shove.

"Are you stupid?" Asked Alex.

I shrugged.

"No werewolf would insult his own mate or be mean to her," said Felix, rolling his eyes.

"Don't you know anything?" Added Calix.

"Okay, thanks, I get it now," I said simply.

"You dressed up for us, didn't you?" Said Felix, smirking and rubbing his chin.

Chapter 2: Makeover!

The other two grinned. My heart leapt a little at the sight of their dimples. I shook my head. What was wrong with me? The triplets were monsters and good looks did not absolve them of that.

"Don't make her admit it," said Calix. "She's embarrassed, Felix."

"Admit it! You did this for us!" Felix exclaimed, grinning wickedly.

He kept coming closer. My back was pressed against the kitchen island now. Alex was quiet, smiling faintly, and watching me closely. I just wanted them to go away. I was so frustrated with my whole life. There would not be a single present for me tomorrow. No one had counselled me about my shift at midnight, and I was scared. I knew it would be painful, and I did not need this from these three privileged assholes, who did not deserve the title of Alpha. They were physically Alphas, but they had no integrity. They could not lead this pack. What a joke! I decided to play along.

"Yeah, okay," I said softly, hugging myself tightly and looking down to feign embarrassment. "I dressed up for you. I asked two girls at school to help me. I really did have a math thing, but I went to get dolled up after, so that made me late as well. I'm sorry."

I hid my face in my hands, stifling my laughter. My shoulders were shaking slightly, so they seemed to think I was crying.

"Hey, you know, we aren't the stupid little boys we used to be when we would fight with you," said Alex gently. "We're taking over this pack tomorrow, and as you're part of this pack, we just wanna know what's going on with you. That's all."

Huh?

"Don't cry, stupid," said Felix exasperatedly.

"Don't insult her when you're trying to cheer her up, stupid," said Calix, turning on Felix. "Chasity," said Calix, using my real name for the first time in nine years.

I dropped my hands. I was shocked. I just stared at him.

"You look pretty, okay," said Calix, winking.

My heart skipped a beat. He was bending down. His face was really close to me.

"Thanks for dressing up for us. I hope you wear an even shorter skirt tomorrow," he said softly, smirking.

I rolled my eyes. Alex and Felix burst into laughter. I tried to brush past them, but Felix grabbed my arms and put my back against the island. My breath hitched in my throat.

"Did I say you could leave?" He asked, his nose brushing against my nose as he bent towards me.

I squirmed in his arms.

"You need to have respect for your Alphas, Charity," Alex said, using my awful nickname.

The spell that Calix had cast on me was broken.

"Fuck you!" I screamed. "Let me go! Three Alpha males against one omega female is insane. You have no honour," I cried, struggling against Felix.

He released me.

"We were just playing with you, Charity!" Said Felix "Good grief! Go! Run upstairs!"

I ran upstairs and to my room. I locked the door. I sat on my cot, hugging my knees to my chest.

When darkness fell, the Alpha and Luna came knocking on my door. I went out to them.

"We almost forgot, you have your first shift at midnight, same birthday as the triplets," said Alpha Romeo, rubbing the back of his neck.

I smiled. Were they going to counsel me, or give me a gift?

"Yeah, so make sure and be out of the house, at least, by 11:45pm, so you don't break anything, or make any mess when you shift," said Luna Ronnie.

I nodded. I supposed that was one piece of advice. I left the house at half past eleven, wearing my old clothes. I crunched through the snow. It was pitch-black. I sighed. I was nervous. I was scared of the pain. I wished my parents could be here. For the first nine years of my life, they had been in and out of rehabs. They were inconsistent, but they actually seemed to love me a lot. They would always make my birthdays and holidays special, no matter how high they were. They were deeply in love with each other as mates, and, back then, I almost looked forward to having a mate of my own. It was almost midnight. I did not want to rip my clothes, so I removed them and stood in the snow naked and barefoot, my curls covering me to my waist. If I had not been a werewolf, I would have frozen to death.

Chapter 2: Makeover!

Midnight came, and I felt my bones breaking.

Chapter 3: Shift and Sniff and Squirt

Chasity

The pain shot through me. It was excruciating. I screamed. My bones lengthened and rearranged themselves. Sandy-coloured fur enveloped my form. My eyesight and hearing became so sharp. I stood on all fours. I howled. I was a wolf. I ran through the night, white snow beneath me and black sky above me. I practically flew. When I had tired of running, I made my way back to my clothes. They would probably so cold after lying in the snow. I focused on what I looked like human, and my bones started breaking again. It was painful, but not nearly as bad as the first time. I put on my clothes and headed inside.

The triplets had gone out to ring in their twenty-first birthday with some of their friends at a bar. I passed by their rooms. The house had three floors. The Alpha and Luna slept on the top floor. The Triplets and I slept on the middle floor. I had a tiny converted storage room, whilst each triplet had a master bedroom and bathroom. There was the most delicious smell coming from Calix's room. I snuck in. He was the least scary of the triplets, so I did not mind if he caught my scent, when he came home and realised I had been in his room. His room literally smelled like freshly baked chocolate chip cookies. I looked around. Maybe he had pot cookies hidden somewhere. I did not find anything. Ugh. I had put my scent all over some of his stuff for nothing.

I walked out and caught another scrumptious scent. This one was coming from the middle master bedroom that belonged to Felix. I dared not go in there, but I sniffed the doorway. The smell reminded me of sweet coconut shavings. There was a tropical edge to it. I breathed it in, wondering why I had never picked it up before. My heart started to race. I was afraid to go near Alex's room, but I had to know. If all three rooms suddenly smelled great to me, then...

I refused to think about it. I walked over to Alex's door. I picked up the scent. The strong smell of coffee and cocoa hit me. My mouth watered a little. Did Alex smell that good? The window blew open suddenly and all three scents wafted down the hallway. Their combined scents hit me and moisture pooled in my underwear. I was in big trouble. I went to my tiny room and locked the door. I tried to fall asleep, but I kept tossing and turning. Those scents were plaguing me. Would they smell me when they returned home? Would I suddenly smell different now to them? I did not want to analyse it too much. Maybe my enhanced sense of smell was just picking up a lot that I hadn't noticed before. Maybe everyone smelled this good.

Third Person

Calix, Felix and Alex sauntered into the house at around three in the morning. It was Saturday. Later tonight, they had their official birthday party and alpha ceremony. Celebrating with their girlfriends and their "bros" had left them exhausted and a little tipsy. It was difficult for werewolves to get drunk, no matter how much alcohol they drank, but the triplets had really done their best. They said "good night" and "happy birthday" to each other and parted ways.

Calix stumbled into his room. A familiar scent greeted him, but there was some unmistakable new element to it like a new ingredient enhancing an old favourite recipe of his. Someone had been in his room. A girl. She smelled like roses and honeysuckle. He shivered. That scent was driving him crazy. He could not sleep. It was all over everything. He felt as if he recognised the smell, but he could not say exactly who it was. Surely, he would have noticed and remembered someone who smelled this good.

He could not take it anymore. When the sun came up, he banged on his brothers' doors. They greeted him still half-asleep.

"What's wrong, little bro?" Asked Alex, concern evident on his face.

"It better be good. It's six o' clock in the morning. We partied last night, and we're partying tonight," said Felix, doing a little dance and yawning.

"Smell my room," said Calix.

His brothers laughed. He walked away from them. They followed him.

"Enough bullshit!" Said Felix, storming into Calix's room.

Felix stopped in his tracks. Alex entered and his eyes widened.

"Oh my God," said Felix. "What is that?" The Alpha started sniffing about his brother's room.

"Little Bro, who was in your room?" Asked Alex sharply.

"You've been with our mate!" Said Felix, growling. "You're keeping her all to yourself."

"No, I don't know whose scent it is and it's driving me crazy," said Calix with tired eyes.

"Our mate's been in this room," said Felix gleefully. "*She* found *us*! Oh I can't wait to get my hands on her." Felix growled again.

"What about Sandra, Tonya and Avery?" Asked Calix, mentioning their current girlfriends.

"We've only been dating them for a couple weeks! They know they're not our mates, so it was a temporary thing! I'm gonna end it with Tonya," said Felix dismissively.

"Yeah," agreed Alex. "If we can find our mate in time for the party, we don't want the girls showing up and harassing her."

"Yeah, they'd be jealous," said Calix. "And there's one of her and three of them, so we better tell them before tonight."

The brothers were in agreement. They were now all sitting on Calix's bed.

"Who would be in my room?" Calix wondered.

"There's something familiar about the smell," said Alex, smiling. "It kinda smells a little like…" Alex paused, frowning.

He got up and ran down the hallway. He stood in front of the door to Chasity's little makeshift room. The same smell hit him. It made him shiver. Honeysuckle and Roses. He sighed. He found her door unlocked and opened it eagerly to reveal an empty room with the cot in the corner made. His face fell.

It suddenly dawned on him just how small Chasity's room was, compared to the other bedrooms in the house. There were empty guest bedrooms bigger than this room. Why hadn't his parents given her one of those?

His brothers came up behind him. Felix looked dumbfounded. Calix walked into Chasity's room and lay in her cot, hugging her pillow, deeply inhaling her scent.

"I'm gonna wait for her to come back, right here," he said, curling up on her tiny cot. It was comically small for the six-foot-four Alpha.

"I wanna go get her right now," said Felix, his eyes worried. "We have a lot of talking to do."

"Relax, Felix," said Alex. "Our mate already lives with us, so we're good," said the eldest Alpha grinning.

"No, we're not good, you idiots!" Said Felix, staring at them. "Our mate is Charity. Charity!"

"Don't call her that!" Snarled Calix, his blue eyes turning black.

"Sorry! Shit! It's a bad habit. Chasity," Felix said. Her real name felt good to say out loud.

"What's your problem?" Asked Alex.

He was looking through Chasity's things, thinking of all the stuff he was going to buy her. She hardly had anything, so she would be easy to surprise. It was her birthday too after all.

"We have to go to the mall as soon as it opens," he told his younger brothers. "It's Chasity's birthday too, and I'm sure Mom and Dad didn't get her anything."

"Are you hearing yourself?" Asked Felix.

"Again! What is your problem?" Alex asked Felix. Calix opened his eyes to glare at Felix.

"Chasity is our mate! We had no idea, because she was not of age until today!" Felix said, waving his arms around like a mad man.

Calix and Alex were not following.

"We've treated Chasity like shit! When she realises she's our mate, she's going to reject us!" Said Felix.

Calix shot up into a sitting position. "No, she's not," the youngest said. "No, she can't. We've been waiting three years for our mate."

"Chasity said she didn't want a mate, remember?" Said Felix, spelling it out for them.

"Yeah," said Alex. "But when the mate bond actually hits her, she'll be putty in our hands."

Calix beamed, grinning at Alex. "Yep," Calix agreed.

Felix rolled his eyes. "Do you remember *why* Chasity didn't want a mate? She said it's because he'd be mean to her like we were. Her mate is literally *us.*"

Calix and Alex were starting to look worried.

"She's going to freak out!" Said Felix. "She's going to try to leave. Remember, she's been talking about turning eighteen, finishing high school, and leaving!"

Alex smirked. "She has seven more months of high school. It's November. We have until June or July with her to convince her otherwise."

Felix calmed down a little, thinking it over.

Calix grinned wickedly, his dimples showing, mischief in his baby blue eyes, "Chasity might hate us now but by next summer we'll be making her squirt."

His elder brothers burst into laughter.

Chapter 4: Dangerously Cute

Chasity

I had to wake up at the crack of dawn as usual on the day of the party, despite going to bed after midnight. I was so tired. I passed as far away from the Triplet's rooms as I could, so I would not have to smell those delicious scents. I had to keep away from them. I could not bear to look them in the eyes if just their smell was driving me wild now that I was eighteen. How could fate be so cruel? I wondered if they would be horrible abusive mates. I would not let it reach to that. I had never even had one boyfriend before. Now, I had three mates. What would I be expected to do? How would I handle that? I felt overwhelmed just thinking about it. There was a heat in the lower part of my tummy when I thought about all three of them and me. They were all so big, and with three of them I would not even know who was doing what to me. I bit my lip. I was getting aroused again. I quickly pushed those dirty thoughts away.

Maybe they will reject me outright? I thought.

My heart threatened to cleave in two, or maybe three, when I thought about that. My inner wolf whimpered. I hushed her. My wolf kept pushing thoughts of the triplets into my mind as I worked on all the last minute party details. Felix would be the roughest. Calix would be the gentlest. I was not sure what Alex would be like.

21

He would probably boss me around, telling me to have respect for him as his fated Luna.

A chill crept through me. Luna. The current Luna hated me. She would not want me as her successor. I did not think the current Alpha would care much. Around half past five in the morning, Ronda, the party planner showed up to help.

"Where are the birthday boys?" She said excitedly.

I rolled my eyes. My inner wolf growled. She was possessive. I looked at Ronda's micro mini skirt and tiny tube top. I was surprised she had not frozen to death on the way here. She was holding three identical baby blue gift bags.

"They're asleep," I said, frowning. "They usually don't wake up until noon on weekends,"

"Oh," she said. She looked crestfallen. She put a coat over her tiny outfit, probably to unveil it at noon. Around six o'clock, I heard heavy steps. It couldn't be! The Triplets woke up early! I ran out of the house without thinking. I shifted. Ronda ran out after me, her eyes wide with shock. I went bounding through the snow. I had ripped my clothes shifting suddenly like that. I needed to clear my head and stay clear of the Triplets until I decided what to do.

Third Person

"This is stupid!" Said Calix. "I need my mate, right now. I want Chasity!"

He stormed out of her room and down the stairs with his brothers on his heels. He was surprised to find Ronda in the kitchen.

"Where's Chasity?" Asked Calix, still sleep-deprived and grumpy.

"Hey, sleepy head! Good morning!" Cooed Ronda.

"Have you seen Chasity, Ronda?" Asked Alex.

"I have presents for the birthday boys!" She squealed.

"Is she here?" Felix asked, getting annoyed.

"Who?" Asked Ronda, handing each triplet a gift bag.

Ronda frowned. "She shifted and went for a run," Ronda said.

"Oh, yeah!" Said Alex. "She can shift now," he said, grinning. He was excited to see her wolf and go running through the snow with her.

Chapter 4: Dangerously Cute

"Ok," said Ronda, rolling her eyes. "Since when do you guys care about Charity?"

Calix snarled. Alex glared at Ronda. Ronda was taken aback.

"It's Chasity," corrected Felix, though he was the one who originally gave her the nickname.

Chasity

I had been running for a few hours all around the pack lands. I began to tire. I knew I would be in pain when I shifted back. My wolf was strong, but my human form was weak. I had never been athletic. I could not shift back without going home, because I did not have my clothes. I was stealthy on my way back to the pack house. I saw that one of the Triplet's cars was gone. Hopefully, they had all gone. I shifted back and snuck in through a side door. I crept up the stairs as quickly as I could. I squealed when I reached my room. The door was closed and all three scents were incredibly strong. Were they in there? I peeked under the door. I sighed in relief and went in.

I put on my clothes. My clothes smelled like Alex. They had been here. All of them. Recently. Their scents were heavenly. Every single item of clothing and every book smelled like Alex. The bed smelled intensely like Calix. Felix's scent was concentrated near the door. They knew. That's the only thing that would have led them to my room. They enjoyed teasing me, but in the last nine years, they had never set foot inside my room, not once.

I went back to the kitchen to find a seething party planner. Ronda was furious at me for taking off. The Triplets' scents were here too. They probably had not noticed her skimpy outfit. I laughed to myself as I worked alongside her. I was incredibly jumpy, expecting the Triplets to return at any minute. I dared not ask Ronda where they had gone. The time passed by quickly. Before I knew it, it was four o' clock. The party started at six in the evening, and I needed enough time to get ready.

I was walking up the stairs when the Luna spotted me.

"Oh! Hey, I'm so sorry but one of the servers called in sick, so we'll need you to help out with the serving? Okay?" She asked, though it was not really a question. It was not like I could refuse. I did have one condition though.

"That's fine, but I'm not wearing a uniform," I said, laughing.

She laughed too, as if she had not even considered it, but I bet she would have made me wear one if I had not brought it up first. Every pack member would be here soon. Thankfully, the pack house was huge with a sprawling living room. The DJ was setting up in there now. All the decorations were hung, and the lights were dimmed. I wondered if I would have to watch the Triplets dance with their girlfriends. They would obviously be at the party. I sighed. I needed to stop feeling entitled to being with the Triplets. They were my mates, but they hated me, and I hated them.

I showered methodically. My muscles ached. I knew I would pay for that long run. My skin no longer looked sallow though. It was golden and had a healthy glow. The dark circles under my eyes were still there though. My body needed some rest, but I was always working or studying. I sighed. My hair looked shiny. I left it down. Mina and Tina thought my dark blonde curls were my best feature. I put on the outfit they had picked out for me, a black sequin mini dress and high heels. I did my makeup the way they had taught me. I was pleasantly surprised with the result. I spritzed on some perfume and ran downstairs.

People started arriving early. I greeted them and took their coats. Everyone called me "Charity", genuinely thinking that was my name. It was too late to correct them. I would be leaving this place in a matter of months. My inner wolf growled at me. I noticed when Sandra, Tonya and Avery all arrived together, holding hands, and looking disgruntled in their mini dresses. Their eyes were red. They approached me to talk for the first time ever.

"Hey... uh... Charity," said Sandra, tossing her flaming red hair back.

"Hey girl!" Tonya said. She had long straight black hair and olive skin.

"Nice to see you again," Avery said with a smile. She had shoulder-length blonde hair.

"Hey girls, welcome, please help yourselves, feel free," I said, awkwardly motioning towards the refreshment tables.

"Have you seen the Triplets today?" Sandra asked, narrowing her green eyes at me.

"No," I said honestly, in the most innocent tone I could muster.

Chapter 4: Dangerously Cute

"Okay, well, here's the thing..." Tonya paused, exchanging glances with the other two.

"The guys broke up with us!" Blurted out Avery. The other two glared at her. "Well, it's true," she said to them.

My heart was pounding.

"I'm so sorry to hear that," I said stiffly.

"They said they found their mate," Sandra added tensely.

I felt lightheaded. I stumbled backwards but caught my balance, leaning against the wall.

"They brushed us off. They said we'd only been together six weeks," Tonya said, folding her arms.

That was true. The longest relationships the Triplets ever had thus far were all about two months, so the girls were only missing out on two more weeks.

"So, since you live here, we figured you'd know who she is," said Avery. "Their mate."

I braced myself against the wall. I felt nauseated. The Triplets had already ended their relationships... for me? They would've ended them anyway, but I felt awful for the girls. Did that mean the Triplets wanted me? Like right away? They had wasted no time breaking up with their girlfriends. I did not answer the girls' question.

"Please, excuse me, girls," I said feebly.

I went into the kitchen. What was I going to do when the Triplets arrived?

Third Person

The Triplets were late for their own party after spending so much time bickering at the mall over what to get Chasity. They ended up getting her a whole host of things and getting it wrapped and gift-bagged at the mall. They loaded the stuff out of the car, greeting guests as they entered the pack house. They narrowly avoided a confrontation with their ex-girlfriends. All three girls stormed out together, hand in hand. At least, they had each other. The triplets showered and got dressed in a matter of minutes, all three in matching black blazers, black trousers and baby blue shirts.

"She's not in her room," said Calix anxiously.

"Of course, not," said Felix. "Mom and Dad are making her help with the party"

"Okay, before we do anything else, we need to have a serious conversation with Chasity," said Alex, the Alpha even among Alphas.

His younger brothers nodded.

Chasity

I stayed hidden in the kitchen until the Luna came in and found me doing nothing. She glared at me and handed me a tray of champagne glasses to serve, so that the current Alpha could make a toast to his sons, before he officially handed over the position. My mates would be Alphas in a matter of minutes. I passed out the champagne. Everyone smiled. The pack members were in a great mood. I even got a few thank yous and a few compliments on my outfit. I was a really low ranking member of the pack, but because I served the Alpha and his family, everyone knew my name, or, at least, they knew my cruel nickname.

I refilled the tray with more glasses of champagne. I spotted the party planner in an even skimpier outfit than this morning, if that were possible. I remembered the gift bags she had brought. I had not gotten my mates anything, even though I helped put this party together. I had literally zero dollars and zero cents. I hoped they'd understand that.

I spotted Mina and Tina, grinning at me. I hugged them. They actually seemed to like me now. Our hug elicited a few glares and disapproving looks from older pack members nearby. Mina and Tina were the daughters of rich pack members and some people considered me trash, because my parents were addicts who had borrowed a lot of money from the pack funds and pack members. I had been so little then. I felt it was unfair to blame me, but I was the only one around to blame. I pushed those old memories away.

Mina and Tina wished me happy birthday. I was so happy, I got a little teary-eyed. They were the only ones who had remembered or said anything. They each handed me a sparkly pink gift bag. I was shocked. They had already bought me clothes as part of our deal.

"Girls! Thank you! I'm shocked!" I said, taking the bags.

Chapter 4: Dangerously Cute

"It's nothing!" Said Mina.

"We dropped off our homework assignments during Saturday morning football practice, cause we were so excited!" Said Tina.

"Just like you promised, we aced it! He corrected it right in front of us!" Added Mina.

I grinned. They flipped their hair in unison. They were wearing identical hot pink dresses.

When the Luna caught me socialising, I quickly scampered off to get more champagne. I handed a glass to the Luna, who smiled coldly. The Alpha took a glass and nodded at me.

I almost dropped my tray, when I turned around and saw the Triplets. They looked unbelievably handsome. My inner wolf was howling. Their scents were out of this world. They were staring at me, their expressions unfathomable. I could not be with them but I could not be without them either. I just hoped they would not reject me right away. It was my birthday too, and I just wanted to enjoy it a little, without worrying too much.

I offered them some champagne. Alex took the whole tray away from me, to his mother's chagrin. He handed the tray to an offended-looking Ronda. Calix grabbed my hand, causing tingles to shoot through my arm. Felix put his hands on either side of my waist from behind. My core started to moisten just from that. I bit my lip. Some pack members were regarding us with curiosity. Alex led us up the stairs, with Calix pulling me by the hand, and Felix gently pushing me forwards as he gripped my waist.

They took me to Calix's room and shut the door, locking it. I quickly scurried away from them to the other side of the room, pressing my back against the wall. The spell of seeing my mates for the first time, since I had come of age, had broken, now that we were alone, and they were very real threats.

"Don't be scared, Chasity," pleaded Calix, his blue eyes widening with hurt due to me letting go of his hand. He was using my real name.

"We're not gonna hurt you, Baby," purred Felix, eyeing me intensely.

I was shocked at the pet name. The heat in my lower tummy was back.

"We need to talk," said Alex sternly. "Okay, Chasity?"

At least, they were being respectful for once, and using my real name, with the exception of Felix, who seemed to think I was already his Baby. The brothers sat on Calix's bed on one side of the room. I sat in the chair by his computer desk. The chair had wheels. I spun on it a little. I had never been in any of their rooms at all before, until early this morning, when I had inspected Calix's room. The Triplets cleaned their own rooms. We had lived together, but, emotionally, we were like strangers. I knew the Triplets had to have normal personalities outside of bullying me, because they were certainly admired by everyone else, and I had seen them be good to others with my own eyes. It stung, thinking that they had reserved their venom for just me. What had I done? Besides be born unfortunate? And, just like that, I broke an eight year long promise to myself as the tears streamed down my face without warning.

Alex looked despondent.

"Shh, Baby, it's ok," said Felix softly, handing me a tissue.

Calix grabbed my hand again and pulled the chair, wheeling it over to them. I was within arms reach of all three of them now. My heart raced due to fear and my core moistened at the same time. My body was really confused when it came to them. I knew they could hear my heartbeat and smell my arousal.

"As you probably already know, Chasity," Alex said gently, "you're our mate. All three of us. Triplets tend to have just one mate because…"

"I know," I said, annoyed.

I was probably better at science than them. They were always treating me like I was stupid. Normally, they would glare at me for interrupting them and even curse and complain, but they just stared at me intently. "Because identical triplets are naturally occurring clones, one fertilised egg that split into three so one mate."

"Exactly," said Alex smiling.

I dried my eyes and blew my nose.

"You smell so fucking good, Baby," said Felix. His eyes were black. He reached out and caressed my knee. I shivered.

"Easy, Felix!" Warned Alex, removing his brother's hand from my knee. Alex sighed.

"We're so so so sorry, Chasity," murmured Alex. "The way we've treated you is disgusting. We won't make any excuses for it.

Chapter 4: Dangerously Cute

We don't deserve you, but we want you as our mate and Luna. We're willing to spend the rest of our lives making everything up to you."

I was shocked. I had always wanted an apology. Now I had one, I wasn't sure if it would suffice.

"We're so sorry, Chasity," said Calix. "Please, let us love you!"

I blushed. Calix was always so dramatic.

"We're really sorry, Baby," said Felix.

I was pretty sure I would never hear my horrid nickname, *or* my real name come out of him ever again. I was henceforth Baby, as far as he was concerned. I giggled at that thought. That was the wrong move, because it set Felix's wolf off.

"Oh, you're so fucking cute!" Growled Felix just before he grabbed me.

Chapter 5: Happy Birthday

Chasity

Felix grabbed me before Alex could stop him. He pinned me to the wall. He pressed his nose against my neck, inhaling deeply. He bared his canines. He was going to mark me!

"Stop!" I squealed, but Felix's eyes were black. His wolf was in control. I was completely not ready for this. I was not even sure if I wanted to be with them.

In a flash, his brothers pulled him off of me. They pinned him to the other wall.

"Calm down!" Bellowed Alex in his Alpha voice, making the whole room shake.

Felix took a few deep breaths. His eyes slowly turned blue. His brothers walked him back to the bed, and they all sat down again.

"Oh my God," he said, panting. "Chasity!" He said my name! "I'm so sorry, Baby." We were back to Baby again.

"It's... okay," I said slowly. I laughed half-heartedly. "Actually, that's not the worst thing you've done to me by a long shot. That won't even make the top ten."

I laughed at my own feeble joke. The Triplets looked horrified and guilty.

"So after Felix has gone and ruined the scrap of a chance we had left... what do you say?" Said Calix.

Chapter 5: Happy Birthday

That actually made me laugh. The brothers all smiled. I had seven more months until high school was over, and I was still angry as hell with the Triplets, but I was no fool. Rejecting them would mean I would have to move out. I had no idea what I wanted. My wolf craved them. She was filling my head with positions I had not known were possible. I had never even been kissed. If I even decided to be with them, only one of them could be my first kiss. My eyes went instinctively to Calix. He grinned. The other two looked a little jealous, wondering why I was staring at just him all of a sudden.

"I don't know what I want," I told them honestly.

"That's completely fine!" Said Calix.

"Take your time," said Alex.

"All the time you need," added Felix, who had pinned me to a wall a few moments ago to try to mark me as his mate forcibly. Yeah, sure.

"Okay, that brings us to the second part of this discussion," said Alex.

Huh?

"Happy birthday, Chasity!" Said the Triplets in unison.

I smiled. They pulled a lot of gifts out from under Calix's bed. I squealed, and then I felt guilty. I bit my lip and frowned.

"Baby, what's wrong?" Asked Felix quickly.

"I had thought about getting you something, but I really couldn't. I had literally no money," I said apologetically, feeling ashamed.

Felix laughed. "Baby, we know you have no money. That's ok."

"You never let me forget it," I muttered.

Felix frowned. They started prompting me to open my gifts. There were so many. It was so awkward for me. I had not gotten a single gift in nine years until today. Mina and Nina gave me gifts and now the Triplets had bought the whole mall. I wanted to open all my gifts later in the privacy of my room. I had already put the bags from Mina and Nina in there.

"Alex, Felix, Calix," I said.

They all reacted to their names. They all looked so gleeful.

"I want to open these later okay, when I'm thinking about stuff," I said.

"We wanted to see your face…" pleaded Calix.

"It's not about what we want," interrupted Alex.

31

I smiled.

"I'm just going to put the gifts in my room. Thank you so much!" I said.

I approached them shyly. We had never hugged before.

Felix snatched me up first, just as I expected. He squeezed me tightly, lifting my feet off the ground. I giggled. He let me down. Calix bent down to hug me gently, massaging my back soothingly with his hands. Alex lifted me by the waist and spun me around like I was a little princess. He put me gently on my feet. I started carrying an armful of gifts to my room.

"Wait!" They all said.

"You can't stay in that room. It's too small. We will organise the best guest room, and turn it into your room," Alex said.

This should have made me happy but it actually made me angry suddenly.

"So this room isn't good enough for me now, but it was good enough when you didn't give a shit!" I snapped.

I immediately regretted saying that. I waited for the huge argument to start. They were quiet.

"If you're not ready for your new room yet, that's okay, but I'm very uncomfortable with you staying there. It's not even a bedroom, and it's a complete disgrace that my parents put you there," said Alex.

We did not talk anymore as we moved the gifts to my room. We went downstairs, where everyone was still waiting impatiently for the birthday boys.

"Boys!" Said Luna Ronnie, narrowing her eyes. "Where have you been?"

She seemed shocked to see me coming down the stairs with them.

"Do another lap to see if anyone needs more champagne," she ordered me.

Ronda handed me a fresh tray filled with glasses. The party planner had a smug look on her face. Alex took the tray from me again and put it on the floor this time.

"Alex!" Said Ronnie to her eldest son.

"Let's start the toast!" Said Alpha Romeo.

Chapter 5: Happy Birthday

The pack members cheered. Everyone gathered around the grand staircase, and Alpha Romeo stood a few steps up, so that everyone could see him. The Triplets pulled me with them to the same step as Alpha Romeo. The Luna, who stood next to her husband, was eyeing me suspiciously. I was pretty sure she was putting two and two together, or, in this case, one and three together. Alpha Romeo began his speech. It literally started with him meeting his mate, the Luna, their love, their wedding, honeymoon, childless years, having the triplets, their childhood, their teenage years and now, their manhood and ascension to Alphas. It made absolutely no mention of me, despite me being there for the past nine years since the triplets were twelve. The Alpha and Luna truly viewed me as a servant, so I knew I should not expect to be mentioned. A lot of people kept glancing at me, wondering why I was there in the limelight. I tried to descend the stairs a few times, but Alex kept grabbing my wrist. Felix put his hand absentmindedly on my behind. I stifled a gasp. He squeezed it and rubbed it gently. I started to cream my underwear. I glared at him, and he blew me a kiss, which many people noticed.

"I present to you, Alpha Alex, Alpha Felix and Alpha Calix Thorn, the Triplet Alphas," boomed former Alpha Romeo, officially using his Alpha voice for the last time.

The pack members cheered. Their screams were deafening. Many girls shrieked and squealed over the Triplet Alphas. The Alpha Triplets went around the room to be congratulated by important pack members. They dragged me with them. No one asked about me, but everyone's eyes darted to me. Finally, the Luna could take it no more. She marched her sons, me and the former alpha into the kitchen. The party planner nosily followed us.

"Since when are you three so close with Charity?" Asked the Luna.

"It's Chasity, Mom," said Felix.

"Sorry," said the Luna.

People truly thought my name was Charity, so I never held it against them.

"She's our mate," said Alex, getting straight to the point. There was utter silence.

"And you've accepted her as your mate?" Said Romeo.

I felt a little offended. "Of course," said Calix. "We want her more than anything."

My cheeks burned. Felix started massaging my butt again.

"And has she accepted?" Asked the Luna.

There was more silence.

"I want to finish high school, while I think about it," I said.

The Luna laughed. "She wants to live here for as long as possible before she rejects you the day after she graduates high school, and then goes off to search for her gambling drug-addicted parents."

"Mom!" Said Calix, the Luna's favourite.

She stared at him. "Honey! I..."

"Chasity has not been treated well here, and you know it!" Said Calix.

The Luna sighed.

"She's our mate, and things around here will reflect that," said Alex firmly.

The eavesdropping party planner was looking at me with so much envy I actually feared for my life a little.

"She hates you three, you know," said Ronda, the party planner. "She thinks you're all arrogant overrated snobs."

I paled. I looked at the Triplets, half-expecting them to turn on me. Calix had not even been listening to her. He was still pleading with his Mother with his eyes. Alex was looking at the big birthday cake, and Felix was still massaging my behind and looking at me, smirking. Felix was definitely going to try to sneak into my room tonight. I felt really warm thinking about it.

"They're old enough to decide," said Alpha Romeo.

"Let's cut the cake with Chasity," said Alex.

Ronda wheeled the huge cake out to the guests. Everyone began singing happy birthday and snapping pictures. I knew people wanted me out of the shot. They wanted pictures of the identical triplet alphas and birthday boys, but the guys would not let me go. Calix grabbed one wrist and Alex grabbed the other. Felix was standing behind me, squeezing my waist. This was the first time all three of the Triplets had their hands on me, and I felt like fainting. I was so overwhelmed. What was I going to do when they all *really* got their hands on me? I had thought I did not have to worry about that anytime soon, but, looking back on it, I should've worried more

Chapter 5: Happy Birthday

because all three brothers snuck me into one of their rooms that very night.

Chapter 6: Good Night

Chasity

I had always wanted the Thorn family to give me a proper bedroom, but now that the Triplets wanted me to leave my little room, I stubbornly did not want to. Too much was changing too fast. The Triplets were really annoyed that I would not stay in any of their rooms or in a guest bedroom. I went to my room and shut the door locking it. It was after midnight. I had actually used Alex's bathroom to shower because he did not want me using the ground floor one because then I'd have to walk around in my robe to get back to my room which is what I'd done for the past nine years. I was exhausted but I was curious about my gifts.

Mina got me a designer sparkly baby pink party dress and Tina got me a designer sparkly baby blue party dress. I smiled. The Triplets had gotten me an iPhone, an iPad and a Mac book. I was shocked. I knew they liked apple products a lot but I had never gotten any technological stuff before. This was my first cell phone at eighteen. I'd need their help to set it up. They also got me a proper Winter coat, a baby blue one. It was so pretty! One of the gifts was a small envelope with a bow on it. It was a credit card with a note from the triplets with the pin, saying to use it to shop for whatever I needed. There was a pair of winter boots, also baby blue. I wondered how they knew my size but then I remembered Alex's smell on all

Chapter 6: Good Night

my clothes and smiled. There was a proper backpack for school. I honestly did not have one and would hold all my books or use a canvas grocery bag. I felt a little teary-eyed thinking about that. I had never really let myself notice all the normal things I did not have. I wiped my eyes hastily in response to a knock on the door. Felix?

"Come in," I said.

Alex.

"You're driving me crazy," he said.

Huh. He scooped me up and carried me out of the room bridal style.

"Thanks for all the gifts. They're really thoughtful and wonderful," I said softly.

I kissed his cheek. He grinned. Calix and Felix were standing at the entrance of Alex's room. Alex carried me into the room and put me on the bed. Calix shut the door and Felix locked it. My stomach clenched.

"Where's my kiss for the presents?" Asked Felix, pointing to his cheek. I jumped up, eager to get away from the bed, and kissed his cheek.

He grinned. Calix tapped me on the shoulder. I giggled and he bent down so I could kiss his cheek.

"Let's get some rest. I couldn't fucking sleep with this one in that room that's really just a cleaning supplies cupboard," said Alex to Felix who snickered.

Hey! It was true though.

"Time for bed," said Calix, moving to turn off the light.

"I always sleep with a nightlight!" I said quickly. I was afraid of the dark and had begged their parents in tears for that nightlight.

Calix quickly fetched it from my room. I kept waiting for them to make fun of me for being afraid of the dark but they were arguing amongst themselves. Only two of them could get to sleep next to me at a time.

"I'm going on *two* nights no sleep cause her scent in my room was driving me crazy!" Insisted Calix.

"Ok, so definitely Calix," said Alex.

Felix glared at his brothers.

"You rushed her today in all fairness, Felix, so tomorrow, when you're in better control, you'll definitely be one of the two, okay. Tonight, it's me and Calix," said Alex.

"What about what she wants?" Felix asked.

They looked at me.

"I'm really tired," I said, not wanting to get in their argument.

I was still really confused and a little nervous around them. I wanted to talk about the time they hit me and put me in the ice-water but I couldn't even think about it without getting too upset. I turned on the nightlight and turned off the bedroom light. I climbed into the middle of the huge bed. It dawned on me what was about to happen. I was going to be sleeping in the same bed with all three of my mates. My inner wolf was so excited, hoping that they would put their hands all over me. The human me was really nervous and unsure.

Calix climbed eagerly into bed. "Spoon me," he said. "And Alex will spoon you."

"Spoon?" I asked.

Alex got in on my other side. Felix spoke from the corner next to Alex, "Awww, she's so innocent. That's why she needs me next to her to corrupt her."

The brothers all laughed. "Can I *please* show her what spooning is and then I'll go back to the corner?" Pleaded Felix.

"Fine," said Alex and Calix in unison.

Instead of coming over to me, Felix's hands reached out and snaked around me, pulling me to him. He pulled my back against his front and curved his body around me, putting his arm over me to snuggle me. It was so comfortable. I immediately started to feel sleepy.

"That's me spooning you," he told me. "Now spoon me!"

He turned away from me. He was much bigger than me but I snuggled into his back and put my arm around him.

"She gets it. Now, bring her over here," said Calix.

I was lifted and placed between Calix and Alex. I was not even sure who had lifted me which made me kind of excited. My inner wolf was howling in delight again. I spooned Calix now that I knew what that was, and Alex held me, his nose near my neck.

"You smell really good," Alex whispered in my ear.

Calix's and Alex's body heat was overwhelming. Being sandwiched between them, I could hardly keep my eyes open. I wanted to hate them. All three of them. I wanted to use this opportunity to break their triplet hearts but my body craved them. I had to fight to *not* feel happy as Alex whispered to me. He seemed to have a lot he wanted to say to me now that we were lying here in the dark.

"You're *so* beautiful," he whispered. I was glad he could not see me blush. "I've always thought that you know."

I could not let that one slide. "As if," I said, getting annoyed with him again.

"Yes, I have," he insisted. "I've always loved your hair. I've always pulled on the curls. You know that."

I considered that part of their bullying.

"I stole this before I knew you were my mate," said Alex, showing me the hair tie he had put in his pocket the other day.

I gasped. They had took my hair tie because they thought my hair was pretty? Guys were so weird.

"Good night, Chasity," Alex whispered.

"Good night, Chasity," said Calix.

"Goodnight, baby," said Felix.

"Good night, guys," I said.

"Can I kiss your neck?" Alex whispered so softly I almost missed it.

"Um, Ok," I said.

Alex kissed my would-be marking spot. The tingles that shot through me made my whole body feel extra warm and I drifted off into a deep peaceful sleep.

Chapter 7: Good Morning

Chasity

Everything that happened yesterday felt like a dream: Mina and Tina befriending me, all the presents, and the triplets' confessions. I was actually afraid to open my eyes in case I found myself in my cot in the cleaning supply room and the triplets hated me again. However, I felt extremely warm, too warm to be in a bed alone and too comfortable to be in my cot. I moaned, stretching out. It was only about five o' clock in the morning but that was my usual wake up time to start making the family's breakfast. I did not want their parents to despise me even more now that I might be interested in their sons. I wondered if I could sneak downstairs and start breakfast. The Triplets did not wake up until noon on Sunday, but the parents would be up by seven. I tried to extricate myself from Alex and Calix. Alex woke up, groaning, and pulled me back to him.

"What're you doing? Do you have to use the bathroom or something?" He asked groggily.

He looked really cute with ruffled hair. I did not have the heart to lie to him.

"This is the time I usually wake up," I said softly. "I have to make you guys' breakfast."

Calix laughed and yawned. "We wake up at like noon, don't we?"

Chapter 7: Good Morning

"Yeah, but your parents wake up at seven," I said.

"They'll fend for themselves, don't worry," said Alex, tightening his grip on me.

Felix stirred. He snatched me from Alex and Calix when their grips slackened.

"Hey!" Calix protested.

Felix draped me across his chest which was quite comfortable. His hand found my behind again, and he started to squeeze my cheeks. This is what I was afraid of and yet, my core started to soak my underwear. I moaned.

"What're you doing, Felix?" Asked Alex suspiciously.

"I'm bonding with my gorgeous mate," said Felix.

I remembered Felix eating the last pancake and telling me I was fat. I winced at the memory. Felix noticed my strange movement.

"Sorry, Baby, am I squeezing you too hard?" He asked.

"You think I'm gorgeous?" I said.

"You are," he said simply.

"The other day you called me fat," I said.

Felix stiffened. From the silence, I could tell that Calix and Alex were uncomfortable too.

"And you took the last pancake. I literally ate nothing that day. I spent the whole day organising stuff for you guys," I said.

The memories flooded back.

"Shh, Baby, I'm so sorry," whispered Felix, kissing my forehead.

"Don't touch me!" I screamed. I jumped out of bed.

The triplets all sat up.

"Felix, you fucker, what did you do? She wasn't scared before," yelled Alex.

"YES I WAS!" I screamed so loudly that all the triplets jumped, and their parents ran into the room.

I burst into tears, sobbing uncontrollably. I was so confused. The Triplets rushed to comfort me.

"NO!" Bellowed their father, still powerful, despite making them the new alphas.

They sat back down.

"What is she doing in here?" He asked quietly. His tone was dangerous.

"I can't sleep with her in that cleaning supplies room. I can't stand it," said Alex, taking responsibility.

"Then why did you not put her in a guest room?" Asked Romeo.

Their mother was quiet, letting their father handle this.

"Um," said Alex.

"Look, Dad, everything was good, wasn't it Chasity?" Asked Calix sweetly.

"It's my fault," said Felix, sounding truly broken. "I've been pushing her a lot, and I'm sorry. She was literally so happy up until she came over to my side of the bed, which was five minutes ago."

I felt sad for myself, but now, the stupid mate-bond was making me want to comfort Felix.

"Felix, we're ok right?" I asked softly, my inner wolf needing reassurance. Since when was I so weak?

"*Always*, Baby, I fucking love you, Chasity," he said. His brothers looked shocked.

My eyes widened. Did he mean that? It sounded so real. My inner wolf told me he did. I was not expecting Felix to fall the hardest and the fastest. He had been the meanest!

Romeo ignored Felix's confession of love for me.

"Chasity is very young. She is eighteen. You boys are still young. You are twenty-one. You have had numerous girlfriends in swift rotation," said Romeo.

Major shade from their Dad.

"As far as I know Chasity cleans, cooks, and studies, and that's about it. You can't sneak your very inexperienced mate in here at night. There's three of you, and you all hated each other day before yesterday. It's too much for her," said Romeo.

Whoa. Did Romeo actually care about me? He definitely loved his boys. Maybe, now that they had been fated to me, he had to salvage what remained of my wellbeing.

"We really didn't do any... mating stuff though," Calix said.

"Maybe in your eyes, Honey," cooed Calix's Mom, "but in Chasity's eyes, it may seem different."

The Triplets were looking crestfallen and I desperately wanted to comfort them. I was wholeheartedly regretting my outburst. I wanted this awkward moment to be over.

Chapter 7: Good Morning

"Let me start on breakfast. It's already late," I said, turning to leave. Felix rushed at werewolf speed, closed the door, and stood in front of it.

"I know I already fucked up this morning but while I'm ahead," Felix shrugged, "Over my dead body, Princess."

I stared at him.

"I am still one of the Alphas of this pack and whether you wanna be with me or not, you will never lift a finger in this house again." Said Felix, narrowing his eyes.

"Hire a maid and a cook again. Two each if it's too much for one person," Felix directed this at his parents.

They looked annoyed but Felix was an Alpha.

"I agree," said Alex, nodding.

"Same," said Calix, winking at his Mom so she would not get too mad.

She ruffled Calix's hair and left with Felix opening the door for her.

"Before today is over, sort out the bedroom situation, and decide which guest bedroom will become Chasity's," said their father. He left.

All the Triplets were once again sitting on the bed with me standing nearby.

"Baby, I'm sorry for all the times I called you fat," said Felix. "What I meant is your ass is fat and that's a good thing."

I was so shocked, I actually laughed.

Alex rolled his eyes. "What my idiot brother meant was you're beautiful and you do have a really nice ass."

I blushed. I realised Alex had never actually called me fat. I remembered him claiming to have always had a crush on me. I wondered if that were really true.

Calix was the only one who had ever complimented me *before* the mate bond. He would be the easiest to forgive.

I went over to Felix, put my arms around him, and climbed into his lap. My wolf was screaming at me to do it. I decided to give in. Alex and Calix looked shocked.

Felix nuzzled my nose with his. I realised Felix's wolf had been calling to mine. I realised something else.

"I've never seen any of your wolves," I said.

The Triplets grinned. They were wide awake now.

Chapter 8: Running with Wolves

Chasity

The Alpha Triplets undressed, standing barefoot in the snow like it was no big deal. I turned away. I was not ready to see them. I caught a glimpse of Felix's though by accident, and even in the freezing cold it was extremely thick and long. They were *identical* triplets so I was worried for myself. They shifted much more quickly than I did. It took them barely ten seconds to break their bones and grow fur becoming wolves before my very eyes. They were shiny black wolves reflecting their hair colour. They were huge. I hid behind a nearby snow-covered tree and undressed. They gave me my privacy. Shifting was still painful for me. It took me about five minutes. I trotted out to show them my sandy wolf. They playfully circled me. I was half their size.

We ran through the snow. I could tell them apart in wolf forms by their mannerisms. Felix bounded. He had heavy steps. He snarled and growled playfully a lot. Alex was often in the lead and had the most fluid movements. He slowed his pace to run beside me, watching over me protectively. Calix was extremely playful. He was the first to nip me. He tackled me gently and we rolled around in the snow. Then, he ran circles around me, showing me how fast he could go. We must have spent hours playing as our wolves even though we were adults. I wondered why we had never played together as children in our human forms.

I ran behind my tree to shift back and dress myself. The boys shifted back and dressed, following me as I walked inside.

"We need to talk," I told them. They looked mortified.

"Get used to us having talks," I told them.

They were Alphas and I was their future Luna if I decided to be with them. They were three of them, and only one of me, so I had to learn to be firm with them. I wanted respect. We went to Felix's room, the only room I had not seen yet. He had artwork covering the walls, which was completely not what I was suspecting.

"Who drew all of these?" I asked.

"I did," said Felix, grinning.

Felix? A sensitive artist? What parallel universe had I entered?

The drawings and paintings depicted wolves. I recognised the triplets in their wolf forms in many of the drawings. I noticed one with five wolves. The other two must be their parents. There were random sketches of items and portraits of family members and some of their school friends. Felix did not seem to have any artwork of Tonya or his other ex-girlfriends which made me relieved. I spotted one painting of a girl. I gasped. It was me, sitting on the porch steps, looking out at the snow. All of his artwork was dated. The painting of me was from about a year ago. I looked at Felix, waiting for an explanation.

"I told you," he said simply. "I think you're gorgeous."

I blushed.

"You're giving me anxiety, Chasity, let's have this talk, come on," encouraged Calix.

We all sat on the bed. Felix and Calix were sitting so close to me. Their entire legs were pressed against mine from hips to knees. I felt really warm. Alex was sitting behind me. He got up on his knees and put his hands on my shoulders. He started massaging my scalp, neck, shoulders and back. Felix and Calix grabbed an arm each, massaging my fingers, palms, wrists, forearms, elbows and upper arms. I was so lost in all of this, I momentarily forgot what I wanted to talk about.

"Talk, Chasity," said Alex in my ear.

"Right, um, so I have a question," I said. The triplets waited for me to ask it.

"Why did you hate me so much growing up? And please, really think about it, and give me a real answer, not something dumb like we were boys...we were stupid...those aren't good reasons. I've always wondered why we could never be friends," I said, sighing. "Is it just cause I'm poor and burdensome in your parents' eyes? What was it?"

The triplets continued massaging me in silence. Were they trying to make me forget about the talk.

"In my case..." said Felix. "You...frustrated me."

Huh.

"I thought you were a cute little girl when I was a little boy. You came to us after a tragedy and I did not get that. You were sullen and cried all the time and I was also just a little asshole at that age," said Felix.

His brothers laughed.

"I liked teasing you but it got out of hand and the dynamic continued. I didn't know how to fix it. Also, you would be on my mind *a lot* and I was angry that I couldn't get you out of my head. It makes sense, now that I know you're my mate, but back then, I'd be annoyed every time I saw you. Sometimes I'd be making out with whoever my girlfriend was at the time..."

I flinched and Felix kissed my fingers, soothing me. He kissed my wrist.

"...and I'd be thinking about you obsessively. Sometimes...never mind," said Felix.

"No! Tell me!" I insisted, fascinated by his transparency.

"Sometimes, I'd call a girl Charity by accident," he said, mentioning my nickname. "Sorry for that nickname. That was rude. There's no shame in being poor. I can't believe I acted like that."

Felix sighed.

"It's so close to my real name, it really stuck. Most pack members think Charity is my name," I said, smiling.

Felix frowned. "I'll fix that myself, and soon," said the Alpha.

I wondered what he was going to do. I did not want to be reintroduced to the pack as their future Luna. I still needed time to make up my mind.

Alex went next. "I always thought you were cute too but our parents hated your parents. They'd racked up so many debts from gambling and their drug habit. You'd always talk about how great your parents were and how mean mine were. I started to think you were ungrateful but now I realise that... if my parents were gonna treat you like that, then you might as well have gone to an orphanage. There's really no excuse, Chasity. I'm sorry," said Alex.

Calix took a deep breath. "I just went along with everything. Mom also said you were here to repay a debt not to be a playmate. There were a lot of things I liked about you, and I should not have picked on you. That was totally wrong. I'm so sorry."

I sighed. We had to talk about the incident. It was bothering me.

"Last night I was a little afraid being in bed with you three," I admitted.

"Because you're a virgin," said Felix. "Baby, I know I've been grabbing your ass a lot but I really am not gonna rush you to mate us."

"No, not that. I kept thinking about when Calix insulted me and said my parents were dead druggies and I broke his nose. Then you guys..." I paused, shuddering. This was really hard to talk about.

All the triplets stiffened, their faces pale.

"Then, you each slapped me then you put me in the ice fishing hole until I went unconscious. I screamed for my life that day when you were dragging me to that hole. I really thought you were going to kill me. I could've died," I said, holding back tears.

The triplets were silent.

"You don't ever have to forgive us but just be ours anyway," said Calix.

"For what it's worth, we really weren't trying to drown you. We just wanted to scare you. But even before the mate-bond, I would feel sick when I would think about that day. That was a heinous act and I'll never forgive myself," said Felix.

"If you had drowned we would never find our mate and not know why. We would be searching for someone already lost to us. We would deserve that, but you, Chasity, after all you've fought for... you deserve the best life imaginable. Please, let us give you that life," said Alex.

"Please, Chasity, we're so sorry," said Calix.

I sighed. The Triplets were all still massaging me. I could get used to this. They were all looking at me with hungry eyes.

"Have you ever kissed anyone?" Asked Calix suddenly.

"No," I said, blushing. The triplets exchanged glances.

"We wanna kiss you," Felix said.

I bit my lip nervously.

"I'm not sure if I'm ready yet," I said.

"That's ok," said Alex.

My inner wolf was howling at me to kiss them.

"Were you guys disappointed when you realised I was your mate?" I asked.

"No! Of course not!" Said Alex.

"I went inside your room and lay on your bed," Said Calix.

I remembered Calix's scent on my bed and smiled.

"I went through your things," said Alex sheepishly. "Sorry, it just hit me how little you actually had so I wanted to see what you needed me to buy you."

I nodded. Alex was the practical one.

"I freaked out because I thought you'd reject us because I knew we'd been horrible to you," mumbled Felix.

He was not entirely wrong. I had considered leaving.

"I realised what was up when I came back from my first shift and smelled something amazing and it was each of your rooms," I explained.

The Triplets grinned.

"So, I went into Calix's room to investigate. I was too terrified to go in either of the other two rooms in case you guys got pissed. I was least afraid of Calix," I admitted.

Calix smiled. Alex and Felix stiffened uncomfortably.

"Then, I was not sure what to do. I tried to avoid you all for as long as possible while I worked out some of my feelings. I thought you guys would reject me actually," I said.

"What?!" Said Felix, laughing. His eyes widened.

"Never," said Alex.

"We've been waiting for our mate three years since we shifted," said Calix.

"So how come you always date random girls?" I asked.

"We're men. We have needs," said Felix simply. His brothers glared at him but did not say anything to the contrary.

"When I was setting up the party, I thought I'd have to watch you three slow-dancing with your girlfriends while I served drinks," I said, chuckling sadly.

Their jaws literally dropped. The Triplets looked aghast. I giggled at their expressions.

Felix's blue eyes darkened a little. I remembered how I had to be careful with my giggles around him and his wolf. He pulled me into his lap. Tingles shot through me.

"I wanna take you on a date, Baby!" Felix said, his voice husky.

"Um… sure," I said weakly.

Chapter 9: Date Night

Chasity

After a late burnt brunch made by the former Alpha and his Luna, I went around the house with Alex to choose my new room. I had cleaned all of these guest rooms and their adjacent bathrooms before. I knew exactly which room I wanted but not because of the bedroom itself. It had a bathroom with a huge bathtub attached. I had always wanted to soak in that tub. Sometimes, I would lie in it and take a nap in the midst of cleaning. I used to be too afraid to try to use it in case someone realised and I got in trouble. The room was on the ground floor though, and Alex was disappointed.

"I want you on our floor," he said, sighing.

"I want to bathe in that bathtub," I admitted. Alex laughed.

He grumbled to himself. "Sure, I guess it's temporary. Eventually all four of us will sleep in the same room anyway. We can each keep our separate rooms to work in," Alex mused to himself.

Alex seemed so certain that I would stay and become their Luna. I felt guilty. Maybe, I had not been clear about how conflicted I was.

Felix and Calix were off somewhere.

"Our date is at seven," Alex informed me with a small smile as he moved stuff to my new room. He did not want me carrying anything and got grumpy every time I tried, so I was lying on my new bed while he arranged my stuff, according to my instructions. This was a departure from the norm: me relaxing, the eldest Alpha triplet working.

"You need to have respect for your Alphas, Charity," Alex said, using my awful nickname.

The memory hit me out of nowhere. I sat up so quickly, panting a little. Alex dropped what he was doing and rushed to me.

"Chasity, what's wrong?" He said, holding my shoulders and scrutinising me.

"Just a memory," I mumbled, without thinking. Alex winced. I felt his guilt as if it were my own. I felt his regret and shame too. I had to get away from him to breathe a little bit. I had nothing to do now that my day was not filled with the upkeep of the huge pack house.

"I'm going for a walk," I said.

He looked upset but he did not try to stop me. I ran out the front door. The wind tossed my curls about, tangling them. It was freezing. The snow was crunchy and deep. It was dark already despite being early in the afternoon. There were not any other houses for miles. It was about a mile walk to the nearest bus stop but no buses worked here on Sundays. I sighed. I wished I had a car but I did not even have my license. I looked at the five cars parked in the driveway, one SUV for each triplet, one for the former alpha and one for his luna. I knew the triplets would get me a car and teach me to drive if I asked, but we had not discussed finances properly yet. What about all the money my parents owed their parents? I was no longer working off my debt and the triplets had bought me so many expensive things for my birthday, it seemed like I was incurring more debt. I knew those were gifts but what if I decided to leave in seven months? Would they turn on me and want their money back?

I was so lost in my thoughts I walked right into Felix. He caught me. He was bundled up in his coat and boots. He was furious. I assumed it was towards me. He scooped me up and ran inside, slamming the door. Calix appeared.

"What the fuck was she doing out there like that, Alex?" Bellowed Felix, stomping back into my new room with me in his arms to confront Alex.

Felix threw me on the bed. I bounced a little. I yelped not expecting that.

"Felix, what the fuck?" Yelled Alex, referring to how he had tossed me.

"Sorry, Baby," said Felix, quickly running his hands all over me looking for bruises. We both knew there were none. My inner wolf was purring. Felix was her favourite because he was the most in touch with his lupine side. Felix was definitely not my favourite. I scampered away from him, coming to my senses.

"What was she doing out there, by herself, no coat, no boots, in the snow?" Snapped Felix, glaring at Alex.

Alex folded his arms.

"I thought you were watching her," Felix added.

I was not a child. I had been taking care of the family a few days ago. I had more responsibilities than them before they became Alphas.

"She wanted to go for a walk," Alex said simply.

"And you let her go like that?" Felix snarled.

Alex sighed. "Yeah," he said softly.

"She was thinking about some difficult memories and she was a little panicked. I could tell she needed to be away from me, from all of us, for a little while," Alex added.

I was surprised he had understood me so well. Calix sat on the bed and pulled me to him while his elder brothers talked. He breathed in my scent. He groaned. He started kissing my neck, licking and biting the skin without breaking it. I was trembling but *not* out of fear. He focused on a spot. I knew he was giving me a hickey on purpose. Tomorrow, I had school where there were a lot of unmated males. Females who had found their mates, but were not marked properly yet, usually had hickeys. It was an unspoken thing, a "don't touch" sign. I had never seen hickeys on any of the triplets' ex-girlfriends. Alex and Felix stopped their argument, noticing what Calix was doing.

The other two Alphas climbed the bed, their eyes lustful and hungry. I shivered. Calix handed me to Alex who started peppering my neck with kisses until he found a spot he liked. He sucked on it, relishing the way my skin tasted. Calix was taking my shoes and socks off. The youngest Alpha started massaging my feet, soothing me. He could tell I was anxious. Alex gently gave me to Felix who immediately latched onto my neck. Felix's hands roamed my body. I tried not to get excited but my inner wolf was going crazy and Felix could tell. He released me, panting. I quickly jumped off the bed, hyperaware that they were looking at the three fresh hickeys on my neck with great satisfaction. They got up to leave.

"Don't forget date night," Calix reminded me cheerfully on the way out.

I realised I had been holding my breath and exhaled as the door closed. I was excited to soak in the huge tub. I sat in the water, thinking. I had always wanted to bathe in this luxurious tub as though the elegance of it would solve all my problems. Now I had the tub and a whole host of other problems. Money would no longer be an issue for me as long as I remained in the Triplets' good graces. I knew I could hold them at bay for a while but I had a feeling they planned to mark and mate me *before* my last seven months of high school were up as collateral so I would not be able to easily leave. Once properly marked, they would be connected to me and able to find my location through the connection. It was a protective thing between mates. Also, with three Alphas, the chances of me conceiving were astronomical, and I knew myself well enough to know I could not bear to leave them if I was pregnant for one of them. I had been robbed of my parents and no child deserved that. I sighed. My head hurt.

After my long bath, I sat on my new bed in a robe and tentatively put on the television. I had not watched television in years outside of random movies every now and then during school. I felt like I should ask someone's permission to watch it. In the past, I had not been allowed to "increase the electricity bill" because my parents owed the former alpha and his luna so much money. I found a show about a teenage witch. I was getting really engrossed in it when I noticed it was already six o' clock.

I wore a baby blue sweater and matching mini pleated skirt over black stockings. The outfit was from my Mina and Tina makeover. I put on the baby blue winter coat and boots from the Triplets. I met them downstairs. They all looked so handsome. My heart raced and my skin flushed. Felix insisted on carrying me to the car, saying the snow was deep. I rolled my eyes, I had shovelled that snow myself before.

Alex was driving us in his car. Felix was in the backseat with me. Calix was in the passenger seat. He kept looking back at me to check on me as well as shooting warning looks at Felix. Felix smirked at his younger brother. He raised his hands to show they were not all over me but they resumed roaming my body as soon as Calix turned frontwards again. I honestly did not mind. It was an amusing game.

The Triplets took me to a restaurant that the family frequented. I had never been there before. The staff all seemed to know the brothers well and regarded me with curiosity. They were the pack's Alphas so I should get used to all the attention. The restaurant was called *Winter Moon Snack* after our Winter Moon Pack. I thought it was clever but I also did not get out much. I sat in a booth between Calix and Felix, and Alex begrudgingly sat facing us. My stomach rumbled. I was used to not eating for prolonged periods of time but the Triplets were anxious to get some food in me.

A blonde, pale waitress in her forties approached us in her white uniform. I looked at my menu.

"Do you want me to order for you, Baby?" Purred Felix in my ear.

"No!" I said stiffly. My wolf promptly made me feel guilty for the hurt in his eyes at my tone.

"No, thank you... Baby," I said hesitantly. Felix's face lit up like a Christmas tree. He began massaging my shoulders while I looked through the menu. He described everything he had already tried to me which was *everything* on the menu.

The waitress, whose name tag said "Martha", was glaring at me, the envy in her eyes blatant.

I knew a lot of girls in the pack fantasied about being the triplets' mate. They were handsome, rich Alphas, and there were three of them. Once word spread that I was theirs, I would have a lot of animosity to deal with. However, I was used to my life being shitty so who cared if it was differently shitty? The Triplets did not seem to notice her dislike for me.

"Hey boys," she said. "My new *Alphas*."

"Hey, Martha," said Felix, grinning.

"Hey!" Said Calix.

"Speaking of Alphas, meet your new Luna," said Alex, nodding towards me.

Chapter 9: Date Night

Martha's suspicions were confirmed. She looked crestfallen but immediately recovered. I had never been more uncomfortable.

"Luna Charity! I've heard of you," Martha said, smiling.

"It's *Chasity* and make sure everyone here knows that. That's an order, okay," said Felix tensely.

Martha nodded fervently.

"What does *Luna Chasity* want to drink?"

"A cookies n' cream milkshake, please," I said.

"In this cold weather?" Martha said.

The triplets laughed.

"How about a hot chocolate?" Asked Felix.

"No!" I said, truly angry this time.

The triplets stopped laughing and placed their orders.

As soon as Martha was out of earshot, I could not help myself.

"Stop bossing me around, Felix! How is now any different from before with you telling me what to do?" I snapped.

Alex and Calix glared at Felix. The mate bond was so powerful, it actually trumped their bond as identical triplet alphas, considering they could easily be made to fight due to me. I felt powerful for once, and then I felt gross.

"Okay?" I said softly to a hurt looking Felix.

"Okay, Baby," he said.

My inner wolf wanted to kiss him. I would not let her have his lips so I kissed his cheek. He grinned. Then, I kissed his jaw and his neck. He growled a little. What had come over me? Calix nudged me. I started to suck on Calix's neck, leaving my own hickey. That caused a lot of commotion because then Felix and Alex demanded one each. I latched onto Felix neck. He groaned at my enthusiasm. Alex waited impatiently across from us. I climbed over Felix, instead of asking to be excused, and got into Alex's side of the booth. He grinned, anticipating the interaction.

Martha came over with our drinks: three hot chocolates and my milkshake.

"Food's coming right up, boys," she said.

She had probably known them for years. There were so many parts of their lives I was not privy to. Alex tugged on my sleeve. I planted open-mouthed kisses on his neck, enjoying the taste of his skin, until I found a spot I wanted. I sucked on it. His hands were under my skirt, squeezing my thighs which was very unlike Alex. I broke away from him and looked at my handiwork, satisfied. My wolf was satiated for now.

My milkshake was delicious but it did make me feel cold. Alex hugged me to him. The food was incredible. The Triplets had rare burgers but I did not like rare meat, despite being a werewolf, so I ate chicken cordon bleu which I was shocked to find on the menu. I had seen it on a cooking show when I was little. It was delicious. The Triplets refused to leave until I took at least one bite of a dessert so I ate a bit of a warm brownie topped with vanilla ice cream. It was good so I stuffed myself with a few more bites.

I hadn't been this full in years. I felt sleepy instantly. I must have actually fallen asleep on Alex's shoulder. When I woke up, Alex was carrying me to my room with Felix and Calix on his heels. I pretended to fall back asleep so they would leave but they tucked me in, took off my coat and boots, and sat on the edge of my bed, talking softly.

I peeked at the time. I had a clock on my bedside table. It was ten o' clock. I had school. I felt overstimulated by them and annoyed for some reason. My hormones were really making me crazy. I was usually not allowed to have mood swings anyway as a servant so maybe this was all that pent-up emotion.

"I have school tomorrow, guys," I said, startling them.

"I really wanna sleep here," whined Calix, fixing his baby blue eyes on me.

"No, Calix, come on!" Said Alex firmly. "Good night, Chasity," Alex said softly, kissing my forehead and cheeks.

Calix kissed the tip of my nose and looked at me with sad eyes. "Good night," he said, pouting.

Felix stroked my hair absentmindedly. "I'll leave my door unlocked if you need me for anything," he said.

Never in a million years, I thought, but my inner wolf heard that, and she was already flashing me pornographic images of what I would need Felix for. I started to blush and Felix saw it, smirking.

"You're such a mean mate," he said to me. WHAT?! ME?! "You won't let me kiss your lips," the Alpha explained.

I shook my head no. He chuckled and sighed. He kissed the corners of my mouth slowly and carefully, lingering at each corner, as close as he could get to my lips without touching them.

"Don't you wanna wear your pyjamas?" He said.

Chapter 9: Date Night

"I can dress myself," I insisted but he began pulling my stockings off and my inner wolf practically tackled me mentally. I literally could not speak as the triplets slowly undressed me. I could not believe this was happening. I was in my underwear, hugging myself to cover my breasts as Calix had just taken off my bra. Felix was massaging my legs and my underwear was literally soaked from all the stimulation. I knew he could smell it. They all could. They were trying to entice me, to make me break and ask to be mated and marked. Alex found a nightgown in my drawer.

"Raise your arms so I can put it on you," He said, feigning innocence.

The other two grinned. If I raised my arms, they would see my breasts. I got up still hugging myself and approached Alex. He seemed taken aback. Felix and Calix were behind me now, so they could not see.

"Close your eyes," I commanded.

Alphas could not be commanded but Alex wanted to please me. He obliged and closed his eyes. I quickly slipped the nightgown over me. I could hear disappointed noises from Calix and Felix behind me.

"You can open them now," I said to Alex.

He opened his eyes. His eyes trailed over my form. He smiled slyly and left. Felix and Calix followed him.

I shut the door, locking it, in case Felix and his wolf came to check on me. I got into bed. I expected to fall asleep easily in this comfy bed but I tossed and turned all night, missing the intense body heat and tight grip of the triplets. Ugh. They tormented me even with their absence.

Chapter 10: School?

Chasity

I woke up at the crack of dawn. Old habits die hard. With no Alex to pull me back into bed, I went downstairs. I did not know what to do. I wanted to eat breakfast but I was not allowed to make it. I had more than enough respect for Felix. He was the last triplet I would disobey, and he had forbidden me from cooking and cleaning, but the new maids and cooks had not been hired yet. My wolf knew what to do, and as always, she had a crazy idea.

Felix really had left his door unlocked for me like he'd said. He looked so sweet and innocent asleep. Every feature was perfectly carved. I took a deep breath. Things were different now. There was no need to fear him. He had explicitly said I could wake him if I needed anything.

"Felix," I whispered.

My wolf snarled at me. She wanted me to climb into bed with Felix. She said our scent would wake him. I got closer. I sat right next to him. He scrunched up his face a little. I leant towards him. A curl brushed his face. That did the trick. I was pulled under the covers without warning. Felix enveloped me in his arms, nuzzling into my neck. He planted kisses on my neck and found the hickey that was his. He started deepening it. I moaned.

Chapter 10: School?

"I knew you would come," he murmured.

He had not been wrong. Was he talking to me or my wolf? My wolf was ecstatic.

"Felix, I don't know what to do," I said sadly, pouting for full effect.

Felix kissed my cheeks. "What's the matter, Baby? I'll fix it."

"I'm hungry but you banned me from cooking, and the new cook isn't hired yet," I said softly.

It sounded ridiculous now. I half-expected him to scoff at me, and say he had not meant I could *never* cook and to get out of his bed and stop bothering him. None of those things happened. Felix scooped me up and groggily walked down stairs carrying me. He put me on a chair near the kitchen counter and went to the fridge.

"What do you want to eat, Baby? I can make you pancakes and then I'll drive you to school," he suggested, rubbing his eyes.

I was shocked. Felix? Nurturing?

"Pancakes are good," I said softly. He owed me one actually. He started on the batter.

"I wonder if I should wake up Calix and Alex?" He said more to himself but looking at me.

"They might be pissed at me, keeping you to myself. Hmm, but you came to me. You're a big girl. You know what you want," he said, grinning.

I tried to stop loving his dimples so much but my heart fluttered.

We ate together. The food actually tasted good. Felix had made chocolate chip pancakes with bacon and eggs. I got ready for school. It felt weird having a regular backpack and a proper coat and boots on.

"Where do you think you're going?" Asked Felix.

He had showered and dressed in a black T-shirt and black jeans. His hair was still damp. He looked so handsome! I snapped out of it. What was wrong with me? I fixed him with a determined stare.

"I usually walk to the bus stop," I said.

"I said I was driving you after breakfast. Didn't you hear me?" He said, grabbing his keys.

I did hear him. He swung me over his shoulder like a sack of potatoes before I could protest. I squealed. Felix put me in the passenger seat and buckled me in. He drove me to school in silence. He was smirking, and I was fuming. A lot of teenagers recognised one of the Alphas driving me to school. A couple girls screamed. I rolled my eyes. Felix would not open the door on my side. Almost two dozen students were staring. I looked at him pointedly.

"Thank you," I tried.

He pointed to his cheek. "Where's my kiss?" I blushed.

He turned the engine off and sat back, scrolling through his iPhone to let me know he had all day. The number of students steadily increased. I launched at him and swiftly kissed his cheek.

"I barely felt that," he teased.

I glared at him. Felix was the same, teasing and taunting me, but now, he craved me so the nature of his antics were different, softer. He wanted to take pleasure for himself but he also yearned to give it. I kissed his cheek softly.

"I'm gonna miss you, Baby," murmured Felix. "What time to come get you?"

"Four," I said, actually looking forward to being picked up by him.

He opened the door for me and watched me walk into the school while students gawked at me.

Mina and Tina were at their lockers. They screamed when they saw me, noticing the three hickeys on my neck despite my attempts to cover it with makeup.

"Oh my God!" Said Mina, pausing between each word.

"I'm surprised you can walk," said Tina. Both girls screamed again.

I blushed furiously.

"You're so lucky! You get the triplets *and* you get to be Luna," whined Mina.

Tina nodded fervently.

"Okay, so who was the best in bed?" Asked Mina.

"I didn't sleep with them!" I said indignantly. I did but it was real sleep.

"What are you waiting for? Haven't you known them years?" Asked Tina.

I realised I had never told a single soul about how awfully the former Alpha's family had treated me and how the triplets had bullied me. I did not feel like talking about it now.

"She's playing hard to get, obviously, to enhance their feelings. Boss move!" Said Mina, nodding.

Chapter 10: School?

Tina grinned.

I giggled.

The whole day was like something from someone else's life. Everyone was nice and respectful towards me. Suddenly, people knew my name was Chasity not Charity. Ashton gave me my hair tie back and apologised. I had forgotten he had taken one. I thought of Alex keeping my other hair tie. I stared at Ashton, who was fidgeting nervously. Did he have a crush on me? He definitely did not want any trouble with three Alphas. He was probably afraid I would tell them he had my hair tie but I was not petty like that, even if I had remembered. I put my hair up in a high ponytail so I would not lose the hair tie. I was wearing a pleated black skirt over black stockings and a pink sweater.

Guys looked at me, eyeing the hickeys on my neck, like I was suddenly desirable because I had been spoken for. I was relieved at four o' clock to scamper out of school. I was tired of all those eyes on me after years of being invisible. The only one who treated me the same was Mr Johnson. He stopped me on my way out.

"Everything okay, Chasity?" He said in a low voice.

I smiled and nodded. Mr Johnson was big enough to be an Alpha.

"You're really young, and you're a bright girl. I know you live with your mates but don't let them rush you, okay," he said, looking at my neck.

I was mortified.

"I won't, Mr Johnson," I promised.

"I'll walk you out," he insisted.

He walked me to Felix's car. Felix smiled when he saw us.

"Hey, squirt," said Felix like I was his little bratty sister or something and he usually picked me up.

Calix and Alex were in the backseat.

"Hey Coach," the Triples chorused.

"Hey, my star players are my Alphas now!" Boomed Mr Johnson proudly. "Be very careful and gentle and patient with this girl" He said sternly.

My face burned. My cheeks were so flushed. The Triplets nodded.

"Don't think I can't still whip you into shape," joked Mr Johnson.

"Bye Coach," the Triplets said.

I got in the passenger seat and Felix started to drive.

"I didn't know Coach liked you," Calix said.

"Yeah, he's also the math group's coach too," I said.

The Triplets laughed.

"What's so funny?" I asked.

"I just can't picture Coach like that," mumbled Calix.

Alex was directly behind me. He sniffed my hair and stiffened.

"That's not the hair tie I gave back to you! It smells like another male!" He said angrily.

Felix stepped on the breaks and the car screeched to a halt. I squealed.

"You scared me!" I protested.

"Sorry, Baby," said Felix quickly. "Who touched you?" He asked, staring at me from the driver's seat.

"No one," I whined.

"Then why does your hair smell like a different guy? Tell us the truth, Chasity!" Said Calix.

I was livid. They had had six girlfriends each year for the past five years.

"Why? What are you gonna do to me?" I yelled.

"Nothing, Baby," grumbled Felix, who started driving again. "We'll just have a talk with the guy. Tell him to watch his hands if he wants to keep them."

"You're ours," said Alex sullenly.

I sighed.

"A boy who stole my hair tie before my birthday gave it back today *because* he didn't want any trouble," I said.

"Smart boy," commented Calix.

Alex relaxed. He took the hair tie off and rubbed it in his palms, annoyed with its smell. He put it in his pocket. He started massaging my scalp. I was seething but it felt amazing. Felix was driving one-handed so he put his other hand up my skirt between my thighs. I gasped. The Alpha started rubbing me. Thank goodness, I was wearing underwear and stockings, but even through two layers, I could feel his caresses. My core started to get wet. Calix smelled it and started massaging my shoulders. The Triplets would be the death of me. It was only a fifteen minute drive to get home but that was a long time with five hands on me. I was thankful Felix had to keep his other hand on the wheel. He was the most devious. He definitely made his one free hand count with what he was doing to me between my legs. I started to moan. He parked the car. We were home.

"Let's take her to my room," said Felix.

"I have homework," I insisted. They looked annoyed.

"I'll do it for you," said Alex.

I knew all the triplets had been straight A students but so was I, and sometimes, I got 100% especially in Mathematics. I wanted to do my own work. School was so important. I was always grateful that growing up poor had not robbed me of my education.

"I wanna do it. It won't take long," I told them.

I took my sweet time, purposefully doing my homework slowly, and then taking a long bath. I put on some new pyjamas that the Luna had gotten me. She was still technically acting as Luna because the triplets had not marked and mated me. This was the first time she had ever gotten me anything. She told me to think of it as a late birthday present. They were soft as butter. She got them in a ton of different colours. I put on the dusky pink ones and went upstairs because my wolf was giving me a headache. She wanted her mates. I found them in Alex's room. I blushed, remembering how we had slept in here together. They were going over some alpha thing with a map of their territory lines. I did not even know who was their Beta or Gamma. I should find out those things. They put their work away though when they saw me.

Felix pulled me into his lap on the bed.

"You had her all morning!" Protested Calix.

"That's because she *came* to me and woke me up. She wanted her Felix," said Felix matter-of-factly.

I blushed.

"Do you have a favourite?" Asked Calix.

"Calix, that's childish, don't ask her that. She's all of ours. Don't make it weird," Alex said.

"You're scared it's me," said Calix smugly.

Alex and Felix rolled their eyes.

"I love how... sweet Calix is," I said. Calix beamed.

"I love how tough Felix is," I said.

Felix replied, "You're my weakness though, Baby."

"And I love how responsible Alex is," I said. Alex smiled.

"We love everything about you, now let's fuck," said Felix quickly, catching me off guard.

I realised he was joking. I rolled my eyes and his brothers laughed. They weren't completely joking because after that the mood changed.

"When will you let us kiss you?" Said Alex softly.

It was not the kissing I was afraid of. It was how heated things tended to get. If I gave them an inch, they took a mile.

"I'm afraid if we kiss, things will escalate," I said.

"That's the general idea," murmured Felix.

"No!" Said Alex sharply. "A kiss is just a kiss."

I thought about it. My wolf was fighting me to take control. I had not slept that well without them last night.

"Will your parents be furious if I sleep with you guys tonight. It's easier to fall asleep next to all of you," I said softly.

"We're the Alphas. You're our mate. They can't stop us. They just don't advise it, that's all," said Alex.

That night I was between Felix and Calix. Felix had promised to be on his best behaviour. Alex was on the other side of Calix near the edge of the bed. Felix was between me and the wall. He had been spooning me for a few minutes when he slipped his hands down my underwear. My eyes snapped open. My inner wolf was howling in delight and did not want me to stop him. I was young and hormonal and curious about sex. I wanted to see what he would do. He stroked the folds of my pussy, gently parting them, and searching for my clit. I knew that was where all the nerve endings were. He found it, the little tender area. He caressed it in a circular motion. It felt heavenly and I stifled my moans.

I knew Alex and Calix would either chastise him or join in and I was afraid of both him stopping and him getting reinforcements. Calix stirred, smelling my arousal. He put his hand in my underwear too but he squeezed my butt cheeks instead. I could no longer hold back my moans. Alex saw what they were doing to me. I thought he would make them stop but he added a third hand to my already crowded underwear. He found my entrance and put one and then two fingers in me, pumping me. I whimpered. The triplets worked me into a frenzy. I was about to come but then...

Chapter 10: School?

I woke up between Felix and Calix with Alex on the end. I had dreamt that. They really were behaving. I was a little... disappointed.

Chapter 11: Christmas Cometh

Chasity

I continued to avoid the topic of kissing the Triplets, and they were being exemplary in their patience. They had begun to insist I tell them exactly what I wanted for Christmas. Holidays were a sore spot for me. I had missed out on years of gifts and love. I usually had to work extra hard during Christmastime to decorate the house to the Luna's standards, and to help prepare Christmas dinner. I remembered watching the Triplets open the most extravagant gifts year after year while the Alpha and Luna looked on proudly, their arms around each other, and cups of eggnog in hand. I was not given anything.

This year would be an entirely new experience. The new cooks and maids had been hired, two of each, all women in their forties or fifties, and all fascinated by the handsome triplets. The new maids, Patty and Fanny, constantly reminded me of how lucky I was to have such wonderful mates. The Triplets beamed whenever they heard this. Yvette and Marlene, the new cooks, agreed with these sentiments, and thought it a travesty that I did not "care for the triplets" by doing the cooking and cleaning. I was furious. I had done that for nine years without so much as a thank you. Before I could give the cooks a piece of my mind, Felix chimed in.

Chapter 11: Christmas Cometh

"I have forbidden my bride from cooking and cleaning, ladies," Felix said warmly.

The cooks smiled. His bride?

"She is preparing for her future as my trophy wife," Felix added, grinning.

I rolled my eyes.

December had finally come and I was on Winter break. The pack house had been decorated in silver, white and icy blue. There were wreaths and garlands hung everywhere. There was a huge Christmas Tree that the Triplets had decorated themselves. The tree ornaments were all so cute: gingerbread men, elves, Santa, Mrs Claus, reindeer, snowmen and even yeti. I had never noticed how beautiful everything looked with twinkling lights strung up everywhere.

We were having breakfast one morning when I decided to discuss an important topic.

"How much money do I still owe you guys exactly, Alpha Romeo and Luna Ronnie?"

I did not feel comfortable addressing them any other way though the Triplets were now the Alphas. The Triples stiffened. Romeo and Ronnie looked surprised. The cooks and maids were eavesdropping nearby.

"Nothing," barked Alex, glaring at his parents. "You owe them zero dollars and zero cents."

"No, you still owe a lot," said Felix, surprising me. "But I'm the Alpha now, and I accept kisses as payment."

I rolled my eyes. Calix laughed.

"I really want to know, please," I said.

Romeo sighed. Ronnie looked at me.

"Your parents owed us about a quarter of a million dollars," she said.

"Two hundred and fifty thousand dollars, okay, and how much have I worked off?" I asked.

"We would have paid you about $500 a week," said the Luna.

"So that's $500 times fifty-two weeks a year for nine years cause I never took my vacation or sick days," I said, laughing awkwardly at my own silly joke.

The Triplets were not laughing.

"That's $234 000!" I said. Wow, I had almost paid them off. The Luna smiled.

"To pay off the remaining $16 000, I'd have to work thirty-two more weeks," I said.

"That's about eight months. If I kept working, I'd be almost totally done when high school is over. I'd just have one more month to go," I explained.

"Great math, Baby," said Felix. "But you won't be working anymore. I've already told you this. Please, don't defy me."

I sulked. I was happy to be free of working but what if I wanted to leave after high-school, and they suddenly wanted their money? I was not working under the assumption that I would marry the Triplets, and therefore, *be* family so all debts were forgiven.

"What if I left after high school, and went my own way, would you still feel the same about me not working?" I asked hesitantly.

The Luna was looking at her sons in an "I told you so" sort of way.

"Yes, I would," said Felix, shocking me. "You're done working here. You're not obligated to be with us but your housekeeping days are over. I told you that already, and I don't like repeating myself. I'm only humouring this conversation because you're my mate. You can ask my brothers how I act with pack members who defy me. You think you've seen the worst of me but I've went soft on you your whole life, trust me."

Felix was even gruffer with pack members who defied him? What did he do? Kill them?

Breakfast continued awkwardly. I got up without asking to be excused and just stormed out of the house, still in my pyjamas. I heard Felix roar and I knew he was coming after me. I was crunching through the snow when I was lifted suddenly. Felix swung me over his shoulder and carried me to his room. He tossed me on the bed.

"I hate you!" I screamed.

"I love you," he said softly.

We stared at each other for a few moments. I got up and went to him. He embraced me warmly. I sighed.

"You don't owe us anything," murmured Felix. "Not money, and not even love."

I was crying in his arms but my tears of frustration turned to tears of relief.

"You should have never been made to work for us. Who asks a little girl to work off her parents debts? It never made any sense. It was wrong, and I'm ashamed of it. I'm struggling, Chasity. I've always thought of my parents as good people but they wronged you. That's not the kind of Alpha and Luna I want us to be. I hope you'll stay, Baby. I need you. The pack needs you," Felix said.

I felt my something damp on my shoulder. Felix was crying! I kissed his tear-streaked cheeks, and then I pressed my lips against his. He lifted me up, and I wrapped my legs around his waist. He kissed me with reckless abandon. We could taste each others' tears as they continued to fall. I was soaring, and though my wolf was elated, I did not do it for her. I kissed him for me. I was out of breath when I pulled away. Felix pressed his forehead to mine. Our noses brushed. Felix was panting.

"Stay," he whispered.

I could not say yes yet but I knew I was in deep. I just held him.

That night the pack house hosted a Christmas party to which everyone was invited. I wore a red velvet dress Alex had gotten me. It was so pretty. I slow-danced with Calix. I had never been asked to dance before. We had not danced on our birthday with all the commotion. I felt beautiful being held and twirled by Calix under the twinkling lights. He walked me out to the porch after and pointed up. I knew what was up there before I even looked. Mistletoe. I smirked at him. He smiled back, raising his brows. I nodded.

Calix pressed his lips to mine. His movements were slow and gentle. His lips felt soft and warm. He cupped my face in his hands. I had my hands on his shoulders. Warmth coursed through me despite the freezing winds and falling snow surrounding the porch. We broke apart. Calix was grinning from ear to ear, and so was I.

I noticed Alex was missing from the party so I went to look for him. He was not in his room. I found him in my old room, sitting on the cot. It was such a surreal sight. I crept in, shutting the door. He looked at me sadly.

"You don't know how sorry I am," he said softly, but I did, because my wolf was whimpering in response to the depth of his remorse.

These guys were going to make it impossible for me to say goodbye to them. I remembered my parents leaving me, dropping me off at the pack house. My heart shattered that day. Is that how the Triplets would feel if I left them? Alex pulled me to him and buried his head in my torso. I hugged him. He pulled me onto the cot. It was so cramped. He was too huge to fit on it. I laughed.

"I love hearing you laugh," Alex said.

I was quiet, my head resting on his chest.

"Look at me," Alex said.

It was not a command but I obeyed. Alex's lips came crashing down onto mine. I was not expecting this kind of urgency from him. His hands roamed my body. I moaned into his mouth, and he slipped his tongue in mine. He caressed my tongue with his. Goosebumps sprang up all over me. He tilted my head back so he could get better access to my mouth. He sat up, never breaking the kiss, with me straddling his lap. He rocked me back and forth on his lap. I could feel how hard he was, and my core moistened in anticipation of him. I broke the kiss, panting, and swiftly gave him another peck when I saw him frown. He smiled.

"Stay smiling like that," I told him. "That's an order!" I said, laughing.

Chapter 12: Merry Christmas

Chasity

Christmas Eve was peaceful. The slow snowfall outside made it seem like the house was inside a snow globe. I had added my presents for the triplets under the tree. I had used the credit card they had given me to buy them. I had also begrudgingly bought presents for their parents out of respect. The Triplets grandparents visited us. Their maternal grandparents were notorious snobs who were scarcely able to hide their horror at me being the triplet's mate. Their paternal grandparents mostly just ignored me.

The triplets insisted that I slept in their room that night. According to Calix, "waking up to me was the greatest gift". He was so dramatic but his lines never ceased to amaze me.

I snuggled up to Alex. Felix was behind me. Calix was on Alex's other side. I could not believe I had kissed all three of them. I wondered if they had told each other about that. Since my first kiss with each of them, I had been keeping my distance out of sheer shyness. Now, I was enjoying their body heat.

"Do I get a goodnight kiss?" Whispered Felix in my ear.

I turned around to face him. The Alpha kissed me, relishing the moment, wrapping his arms around me tightly. He nipped my lower lip, making me gasp and granting his tongue access to my mouth. I moaned as he climbed on top of me and settled himself between my legs, grinding against me, all the while never breaking the kiss. His hands rubbed my sides, squeezed my waist, and finally tangled in my hair, lifting my head closer to his. I pulled away, breathless, and Felix grinned.

"You were very much worth the wait, Baby," he whispered, brushing his nose against mine.

I smiled. I had found out they were my mates on our birthday, November the eleventh, but I had not kissed them properly until late December. I started to feel sleepy. Felix spooned me. I felt so warm and comfortable. He was whispering to me as I drifted off to sleep, telling me I was beautiful, that he loved me, that his brothers loved me, and that he could not wait for me to bear his mark and his heir. Sleep embraced me before I could hear the rest.

I woke up to find that the Triplets already awake, lying in bed talking, waiting for me to wake up.

"You guys never wake up early," I said sleepily.

"Except on Christmas Day, sleeping beauty," said Calix.

Alex kissed me, his lips moving gently against mine. He sucked on my bottom lip and nibbled it. It felt so good. He pulled away and smirked at me. Before I could move in for another kiss, Calix hopped over and pressed his lips to mine with an urgency I was not expecting, lighting a fire in my lower belly. I was breathless when he was done. Felix pulled me to him, kissing me eagerly and tangling his hands in my hair. While we kissed, I felt Alex's mouth on my neck, planting hot open-mouthed kisses down to my shoulder. He nipped my shoulder, making me squeal and granting Felix's tongue entry to my mouth. Calix's and Alex's hands were both roaming my body, squeezing my most tender areas. Felix broke the kiss and pushed me down flat onto my back in the middle of the bed. Three pairs of hands were now caressing me. My wolf thought it was a Merry Christmas indeed. The triplets did not undress me. They knew I was not ready for that but they massaged every part of me they could reach. Felix kneaded my breasts, while Alex was squeezed my thighs and my butt, and Calix rubbed my sides and my core through the thin fabric of my pyjamas. My underwear was soaked in no time. I was panting.

"Merry Christmas, Baby," said Felix huskily, reaching down nibbling my lower lip.

Chapter 12: Merry Christmas

"Merry Christmas, Chasity," said Calix as licked and nipped at my ear.

"Merry Christmas, Luna," said Alex, raising my top and planting kisses on my tummy.

I giggled but quickly stopped in case it made their wolves go crazy. They were looking at me hungrily. I quickly extricated myself from them before things got out of hand. They followed me to the living room. Their parents were already up, holding their mugs, and cuddling together. I was immediately transported back to Christmases of the past, recalling how horrible and alone I had felt watching the family shower each other with love while I cooked and cleaned. No one used to even say "Merry Christmas" to me let alone gift me anything. My first Christmas with them at age nine when I had not known any better, I had made gifts for the triplets in arts and crafts at school: little paper dolls. The Triplets had cast them into the fireplace.

I stopped dead in my tracks. The fireplace was ablaze. Felix immediately pulled me to him, sensing I was tense.

"Mmm, Baby, talk to me," he said, tightening his arms around me.

"Chasity!" Called Alex, gripping my chin and trying to make me look at him.

"Look at me when I'm talking to you!" Demanded a sixteen-year-old Alex on Christmas morning.

I had overslept, crying myself to sleep, dreading another awful Christmas where I felt unwanted. I missed my parents. They had been junkies but they had always tried to surprise me with things. They had been like children themselves, and the three of us would have fun and laugh when they were not too high to notice me.

"Are you even listening to us?" Asked Felix, grabbing my hand.

I had not made breakfast yet, and the triplets were already done opening their gifts.

"What's the point of you being here if you're not going to work off your debts?" Asked the Luna. "It's almost noon and no breakfast!" She rolled her eyes.

Felix pulled me by my hand out into the snow. I remembered when they had dipped me in the ice-water. I started to scream and struggle against him, fearing a repeat of that.

"Ugh, I'm not going to do anything to you. I'm just putting you out of the house! If you're not gonna earn your keep then maybe you'd rather be out here," snarled Felix.

Felix released my hand and went back inside, shutting the door on a thirteen-year-old me. I hugged myself, shivering in the biting cold. Alex glanced at me from a window then shut the window. I thought I would be out there forever.

I was leaning against the house in a nook, trying to stay warm, when Calix found me. If I were human, I would have been hypothermic by then.

"There you are!" He said.

I flinched and looked up.

"Look, hurry up, my brothers are napping after lunch. Go to your room and lock the door," said the youngest triplet.

Calix led me inside, tiptoeing. He waved his hands in the air. I made a run for my room, where I hid for the rest of the day.

Calix waved his hands in the air, snapping me out of my flashback. I launched myself at him like he was a raft in the middle of a treacherous sea. I clung to him and burst into tears, sobbing bitterly.

"Baby, Baby, talk to me," pleaded Felix, rubbing my back.

"Little Luna, don't cry, I can't take it," said Alex softly, running his hands through my hair.

"No!" I whimpered, shrinking against Calix. Calix lifted me into his arms and kissed my forehead.

"It's okay, Chasity. No one is going to hurt you. Ever okay! I'm sorry, I'm here, don't worry," Calix whispered.

"Why is she mad at us all of a sudden?" Felix said.

My wolf whimpered at the pain in his voice. She wanted Felix. She always wanted Felix. I shuddered, trying to make her understand.

"What did we do? Everything was fine," Alex asked, sounding broken.

My wolf whined, wanting to go to him too.

"Did we rush you too much just now. You seemed into it. We're sorry," said Felix.

"It's not that. Calix was there just now too but she wants him," Alex said softly.

Chapter 12: Merry Christmas

"Calix, take me to my room," I pleaded.

Calix did as I asked. His elder brothers tried to follow.

"Just Calix!" I whimpered.

They stopped in their tracks. I looked at their heartbroken faces over Calix's shoulder. I had ruined what was supposed to be my first truly merry Christmas in years. Calix shut my door, and we snuggled together in my bed. I had meant my tiny old room when I had said take me to my room but that was my old life. Calix would not carry me to the my old makeshift room. I needed him so badly all of a sudden. I straddled him. He raised his eyebrows. Maybe, I could separate him from the other two. He was the easiest to forgive, and my heart and mind were too fragile right now. My wolf was furious at the thought of trying to just have one of the three. She was determined to have all of her mates. She would not feel complete without them. I pushed her to the back of my mind.

I moved my hips, rubbing myself against Calix. He groaned, immediately getting hard.

"Oh God, Chasity," he murmured. "Fuck."

I smiled. He gripped my hips eagerly and sat up with me straddling him. He thrusted against me although we were still clothed. He kissed me deeply, moaning against my lips. He broke away.

"Tell me what's going through your head, please. Why are you mad at Alex and Felix? Do you just want us one at a time?" He suggested.

"No, what if I just want one only?" I said

"Huh," he said.

"What if I only want you, and we forget about your brothers?" I asked, instantly remorseful. I could not believe I had just said that out loud.

Calix looked conflicted. "You're my mate, Chasity, my Luna. I was built to do anything for you once the mate bond hit the day you came of age. I would do whatever you asked of me and so would Alex and Felix. I don't have it in me to deny you but that would break my brothers. We're linked. We're like one Alpha in three different bodies. We're identical triplets, Chasity," he said, his eyes pleading with me.

"We can have more alone time, as much as you need," he offered.

"Please don't shut out my brothers forever," he said. "That's a request, not an order. I can't order you. You're my equal."

I pulled away from him. He would let me have my time with him but he would keep making a case for his brothers.

"Just go, Calix. Never mind," I said.

"*Please,* please, tell me what you're thinking," he said.

"You thinking about the times I hid you?" He said.

I looked at him. "Yeah, when I was thirteen and you guys were sixteen, Felix... put me out in the snow for oversleeping and not making breakfast in time on Christmas Day. Alex was angry too. He agreed with that punishment."

Calix sighed. His eyes went dark and I knew it was not lust. He was mind linking his brothers. Ugh. There was a knock on the door.

"Baby, you can put on a dominatrix outfit and spank the shit out of me just don't ignore me," called Felix from the other side of the door.

I smirked initially, and my wolf wagged her tail but I quickly frowned. Alex spoke next.

"Chasity, I'm sorry, I love you, I'm *in* love with you, and I've never felt that way about any girl. I've had like... thirty girlfriends which is something I completely regret. Every couple of weeks, I cast them aside like it was nothing. Maybe, this is my karma. I've never even given that a second thought, but, every night, I think about you. I think about every single day you spent here, every time you cried, and everything that was denied you, and my heart breaks all over again. You break my heart every night, Chasity, and you mend it every morning. It beats only for you. I live for you. Please, let's talk," said Alex, sounding close to tears.

I gasped. It was the first time Alex had said he loved me. Felix had been saying it since the day after my birthday. I opened the door. Alex literally got down on his knees. Felix did too.

"How do you wanna do this, Baby, with a whip and a gag or freestyle?" Felix said.

I rolled my eyes. I embraced Alex to Felix's chagrin. The eldest Alpha stood up and lifted me easily. I wrapped my legs around him, my hands on his face. He crashed his lips to mine, kissing me like he had not seen me in years. He left me breathless. Felix snatched me from Alex. I fixed Felix with a glare.

Chapter 12: Merry Christmas

"Are you gonna tell me that you hate me again?" Said the fiercest of the Alphas.

I didn't hate him. I never had, actually.

"Maybe," I said, brushing my nose against his.

Felix pressed his forehead to mine. "I'll never forgive myself, and you never have to forgive me either. You can hate me, but you're not going anywhere. If you leave, I'll follow you. If you hide, I'll find you. I'm never letting you go. I'll never force you to show me love but I'll never stop loving you. I'll never stop trying to win you over. Chasity, I've won every fight I've ever been in, and I'm not losing this one. You're the most important fight of my life," said the Alpha, taking deep slow breaths.

I kissed Felix because he drove me and my wolf crazy. He was rougher than ever, pinning me to the wall. He kept his hand behind my head so it would not hit the wall. Before I knew it, he tossed me on the bed and lunged at me, crashing his lips against mine, his hands gripping my hips. The heat in my stomach was so intense. His tongue explored my mouth. I was so breathless, I was lightheaded. I managed to pull away from Felix only for Alex to claim my lips again. He brought me to him, making me straddle him as he knelt on the bed. I felt heat all around me. All the Triplets were pressed against me. Calix pulled me from the eldest Alpha, pushing me down gently onto my back. He settled himself between my legs as his lips coaxed mine open so his tongue could caress mine. I tangled my fingers in Calix's hair, sighing happily. After what felt like an eternity of Calix, the longest kiss yet, I extricated myself from the triplets and got to my feet, completely breathless and panting. Felix neared me but I put my palms up, giggling a little.

"You're ready for your presents then, Baby?" Asked Felix.

I nodded weakly and Felix carried me to the Christmas tree, cradling my head to his chest. Alex and Calix followed closely behind. Their parents looked at us strangely. They probably thought we had the most dramatic relationship ever. Felix nibbled on my ears and rubbed my shoulders while I opened one of the gifts from the triplets. It was a small baby blue box with a silver bow. I looked inside and found a set of keys. I looked at them weirdly.

"I don't want you to feel trapped. Trust me, I'll come after you if you run off but you should be able to get around if you need to," said Felix, rubbing the back of his neck.

Huh. I looked at the keys again. They were car keys! I ran outside. There was a sixth car parked in the driveway, a baby blue one with a silver bow on it. I did not know anything about cars but it was so cute.

"It's a Range Rover," said Felix.

I had heard of that before. They must have spent a lot. I felt guilty for how I had behaved earlier but they had a lot to make up to me still.

I kissed Felix, enjoying the warmth of his lips and embrace, as the cold air whipped my curls about. I kissed Alex and then Calix. Calix tasted like chocolate. I noticed a mug in his hand. My tummy grumbled and the Triplets took me back inside. Alex bundled me up in a warm blanket in his arms, and Calix force-fed me hot chocolate, while Felix set up a plate of food for me. My other gifts included a diamond tennis bracelet, a diamond necklace and diamond earrings. I gasped.

"I know you're not ready for an engagement ring yet," said Alex, "but I wanted you to have diamonds." All the triplets insisted on being kissed after the opening of each present.

I found a really thin gift and unwrapped it. It was an envelope. Inside, there were four plane tickets and a brochure for a five star hotel! I read the tickets. They were for the Triplets and me to go to the Caribbean for the rest of Winter Break. I had never left the pack lands before.

"I want to take you away from here. Maybe, the memories here are too painful. Maybe, a change of scenery will help you heal and help us bond," Calix said tentatively.

I kissed him. His kiss was slow and sweet. My first *real* kisses were with Felix, then Calix, and then Alex, but there was more to the story.

I hated New Year's Eve almost as much as Christmas at the Alpha's house. A fourteen-year-old me was sulking. I was hiding in my tiny bedroom, listening to the celebratory noises of the pack downstairs. I was supposed to be working as a server, passing out champagne, but the hired help had taken pity on me. She was an older lady, possibly in her late sixties. She had told me to "go, rest, Muffin." I sighed. Kindness was so rare in my world. The seventeen-year-old triplets were being fawned over by every teenaged girl in

Chapter 12: Merry Christmas

the pack except me. I was tired of rolling my eyes at the girls tossing themselves at the future Alphas. They changed girlfriends like they changed socks.

I heard the Luna's voice. "Where is that girl?"

I quickly revealed myself, stepping out of my room. She fixed me with a glare.

"You know you're supposed to be helping downstairs," she said.

"I heard the housekeeper send her on a break," said Felix, actually defending me. "She didn't just run off like usual."

Felix had begun to stare at me more and more the older we got. Sometimes he'd be cuddling with a girlfriend on the couch but his eyes would follow me as I cleaned. I saw him take a picture of me once, when he thought I wasn't looking, and smile at the image he had captured. When I had glared at him, he had glared back, hastily putting away his cellphone.

Alex was looking at me up and down. He was always pulling on my curls and grabbing my chin to make me look at him. He always said I needed to have respect for him and look at him when he spoke to me. I had been allowed to borrow one of the Luna's old dresses so I wouldn't embarrass them by looking shabby. The dress immediately became the prettiest thing I owned. It was a silvery baby blue dress with a defined waist and a flared-out skirt.

"I like this colour," said Alex, looking at the dress.

"Yeah, me too," said Felix, actually reaching out and touching the material.

I recoiled at his touch. He smirked.

Calix came over. "Chasity, I have work for you to do," he said.

That was really unlike him. He asked the least of me. I followed him. I was curious. It was minutes to midnight. We went to the backyard away from prying eyes. I looked at the frozen river in the distance, feeling afraid. They had dipped me in it once. I shivered.

"Here," said Calix absentmindedly, putting his blazer around my shoulders.

I heard the pack members counting down to midnight. They reached number three and Calix said, "Baby blue suits you."

I shrugged. The pack inside screamed "Happy New Year."

Calix swiftly and lightly pecked me on the lips. I jumped and put my fingers to my lips. He ran away. I spotted him inside. His current girlfriend whined, "I missed my kiss at midnight. Now I'll have bad luck all year."

Calix spotted me eavesdropping. I thought he'd kiss her passionately to show me I was nothing but he pushed her away and shrugged at her complaints. He stared at me a lot throughout the rest of the party. I noticed his eyes were mainly on my lips.

Calix's lips were still on mine but he could tell my mind was far away.

"Mmmm, I'm gonna make this trip really romantic for you, Baby," whispered Calix.

"We all will," said Alex, smiling.

"It'll be really hot and you'll be sweating a lot, but it won't be because of the weather," warned Felix, his eyes lustful.

I shivered.

"I wanna take Chasity bikini shopping the day after Boxing Day," Felix declared.

Bikini shopping?! I was nervous but thrilled to leave this place.

"We'll all go with you to help you pick out some swimsuits," said Alex, winking.

"Or we could just skinny-dip the whole trip," said Calix, waggling his eyebrows.

I giggled.

"So fucking cute," said Felix before he captured my lips with his while his brothers started caressing my body. Their parents promptly left the room.

Chapter 13: Bikini Babe

Chasity

I took a deep breath as I looked at the floor-length mirror in the dressing room of *Fierce Bikini Babe,* a store at the pack's largest mall. I had wanted a one piece or a tankini but the triplets had begged to see me in a bikini. It was a high-waisted light blue bikini. I looked... good. It suited me. I tried to push all the times Felix had called me fat out of my mind as I slowly walked out of the dressing room to face my eager mates.

Their faces lit up. Felix growled playfully. Alex blew me a chef's kiss. Calix held up a piece of paper with a ten written on it. I giggled and blushed which set Felix off.

"Careful or you won't be wearing even that much longer," warned Felix cheekily.

They wanted to see me try on almost every colour of bikini, and they had over-the-top reactions to each. They saw me in red, hot pink, baby pink, yellow, black, white, silver and gold. They bought every single one. I insisted on getting some cover-ups.

"You don't need cover-ups," grumbled Felix. "That's what towels and blankets are for. That and wiping you off. You're gonna be all wet and sticky."

"Felix!" Warned Alex sternly.

Felix seemed to be certain that I would lose my virginity on this trip. He always talked like that but he had turned up the heat recently. Ever since I started kissing my mates, things were getting heated just as I'd predicted. This was what I had been afraid of yet I still found myself often seeking out a particular triplet so we could make out. Calix was sweet and gentle, taking his time with me. Felix was hot and heavy, his rough hands working me into a frenzy. Alex was passionate and methodical, taking me a little further every time I sought him out. I could tell they were anticipating our trip. They were also frustrated again. I was too inexperienced to know exactly why. I had a general idea but I was not entirely sure I understood. Felix was the first to be blunt with me one night when Alex and Calix had walked in on us making out and had promptly gotten in on the action. I stopped them from taking my night gown off despite the fabric being bunched up around my waist with my underwear and bare legs visible. Felix groaned in frustration.

"We want to make you come 11, Baby!" He growled. "We want to hear your screams and see how your face looks when you have an orgasm."

I was trembling. I had had orgasms before. I had touched myself before but those climaxes were feeble. The pressure I felt inside my body when the triplets started to get sexual with me was so intense I was afraid of its release. I had heard of girls with multiple mates passing out because their orgasms were so intense. Mina's cousin was the mate of identical twins and she had spared me none of the dirty details, saying the twins insisted on *both* being inside of her at the same time and thrusting until she squirted. She said her cousin was the happiest girl she knew but I was nervous. I had *three* mates. Just one of their huge members was enough to make me clamp my legs shut. On our trip, would they all push inside of me? Could I handle that? I felt faint just thinking about it but the animalistic side of me wanted that badly.

I had just finished packing for the trip, zipping my new baby blue suitcase up. Alex came into my room to get my suitcase and carry it to the car. Romeo was dropping his sons and me to the airport. I sat in the backseat between Alex and Calix. Felix was in the passenger seat. The triplets had already said goodbye to their mother, each hugging her and kissing her cheek. She had nodded stiffly to me as a goodbye. It still bothered me how strained the relationship was between me and the Luna. The former Alpha was seemingly indifferent towards me. The triplets bear-hugged their Dad goodbye at the airport and he also nodded as a goodbye to me. I was so excited to leave the pack house and all its dreary memories that I did not care if my mates' parents disliked me.

Third Person

When Chasity went to the bathroom, the triplets had a chance to go over their plan. They were sitting waiting for her in a diner in the airport with a stack of pancakes in front of each of them and a stack waiting for Chasity.

"Her dream has always been to leave the pack house behind," reiterated Calix to his brothers. "Taking her away on vacation to a totally different climate, tropical, sunny, will bring out a totally different side of her than the sad girl from the snowy pack house."

"And when that side comes out, you really think she'll relax enough to want to mate?" Asked Felix.

"She hasn't gone into heat yet. I really hope she does on this vacation. The timing would be great. If she goes into heat at the pack house, that'll be too emotional for her and yet another bad experience at the pack house," said Alex.

"Trust me, she'll be frisky, with or without going into heat," said Calix, chuckling. "Also we need to find out what her main worries are. She's a virgin and there's three of us. That's intimidating. She might be self-conscious too."

"Yeah, thanks to Felix for always calling her fat," grumbled Alex.

Felix had the decency to look ashamed. "Even if we don't go all the way, I'd just like to go further than before," said Felix.

Chasity

I walked over to the triplets and saw they had a stack of pancakes waiting for me in a booth at the airport's diner. I grinned and pecked each of them on the lips. Felix was last and followed the peck up with a proper lingering kiss. The pancakes were so light, fluffy and sweet, I was actually able to finish my stack.

"Your appetite has improved so much," complimented Felix.

I could not help but wonder how he seemed to want me to eat so much when he had acted like I was too heavy before. I knew I was healthy but Felix, Calix and Alex always had such skinny girlfriends.

"Guys, all of your ex-girlfriends have always been so thin like size zero," I said. "Nothing's wrong with that, but, you know, I'm like a size four maybe even in a size six in clothes. It's not plus sized but it's not model thin," I said, immediately regretting my words. I sounded like a broken record, always bringing up the past, but I was a little nervous to wear nothing but bikinis around guys who had once made fun of me.

"You're gorgeous, Baby, but you don't believe my words, so let me show you with actions," Felix said.

"How are you gonna show me?" I asked, smiling.

"I'm gonna tickle your belly button from the inside," said Felix.

Alex sighed exasperatedly. Calix laughed. I covered my face with my hands to hide my red cheeks.

We were in first class on the plane. I sat next to Calix while Alex and Felix were opposite us. I slept on Calix's shoulder. It was a long flight. When we arrived, Calix gently shook me awake. The island was beautiful. The stars seemed so close to us here. The moon was so bright. The air smelt spicy and was cool not chilly. The roads were lined with palm trees and coconut trees. Everywhere I turned, I saw colourful buildings and lush green vegetation. I could hear the roar of the waves and smell the salt of the sea. A hired private taxi took us to where we would be staying, the Pointed Crowne Hotel's presidential suite. My jaw dropped at how extravagant it was. There was a full kitchen with a stove, dishwasher, cupboards and a fridge. The living room had a huge flatscreen television. There was a dining room with a table for six and a balcony that overlooked the sandy white beach and the salty sea. There was a jacuzzi on the balcony, a huge bathtub in the master bathroom, and a huge bed in the master bedroom. Images of snuggling with my mates in bed and taking bubble baths with them flitted through my man.

Chapter 13: Bikini Babe

It was about seven in the night on the island. I put on a light pink bikini while the triplets ordered room service. They popped a bottle of Champagne and I had a few sips. The triplets were eyeing my bikini. The hotel food was delicious. All of the triplets were shirtless in their swimming trunks, their perfect abs and muscled chest on display. They wanted to take a dip in the jacuzzi. I was feeling so alive all of a sudden.

"I have an even better idea!" I said.

"Yeah, Baby?" Asked Felix.

"Let's take a bubble bath!" I said, downing my glass if champagne.

Alex poured me another glass, and we all went to the master bathroom. Alex ran us a bubble bath. The tub was huge enough to comfortably fit all four of us. I giggled as Felix tickled me, pulling me onto his lap amidst the bubbles. I relaxed, leaning against Felix. It felt so good to be away from the pack house. I would have never imagined life would turn out this way, and the triplets would be catering to my every whim, rather than making my life miserable. I pushed those old thoughts away. It was easier to do on vacation. Felix was playing with my bikini top, and Alex and Calix were looking at me hungrily.

"You are so sexy, Baby!" Said Felix in my ear. "Aren't you gonna reward us a little for this awesome trip."

"Mmmm," was all I could say.

Felix's thumbs were tracing my nipples through the fabric of my bikini top, and it was making them erect and making me moist. I sighed happily.

"Baby, give us a little peek," whispered Felix, licking my earlobe as he continued caressing my breasts.

Alex and Calix put their hands on my lower body. Alex was rubbing my most sensitive area through the fabric of my bikini bottoms, and Calix was untying the side straps of the bottoms.

"How about this," whispered Felix, "I'm going to take your bikini top off so I can see your pretty little nipples and suck them. Calix is gonna take your bikini bottoms off and hold your legs open so Alex can finger your pretty little pink pussy until you come."

I shivered and moaned, picturing everything Felix had just described. I nodded feebly not able to resist any longer. My body wanted a release so badly. Felix slipped my bikini top off, tossing it onto the bathroom floor, releasing my breasts. The triplets groaned as they took in the sight of my breasts and erect nipples. I blushed. I felt so sexy because of their reactions. The triplets changed things up. They did not do exactly what Felix had said. At the sight of my nipples, Alex and Calix came towards me, mouths open and eager. They each latched onto a nipple and I squealed. Felix ripped off my bikini bottoms from behind. His hands rubbed my lower tummy before descending to my most sacred area. He gently explored my folds. It tickled as we were in water. Alex's hands had found my throat, wrapping around it, and squeezing extremely gently while his mouth sucked my nipple mercilessly. Calix's hands were squeezing and massaging my thighs while he nibbled and nipped at my other nipple. I felt like I was losing my mind. Felix found my little love button, my clit, and pinched it gently.

"I wanna eat you out, Baby," whispered Felix. "Let me eat that pussy for dinner. Ride my face please."

"Okay," I said shakily.

I put one of my arms over Felix's shoulder and the other arm over Alex's shoulder. They they easily supported me while Calix grabbed my ankles. The Triplets carried me from the bath tub to the shower this way. They tossed their swim trunks onto the bathroom floor. I tried not to stare at their monster erections while their six hands washed the soap off of me. They bundled me in a towel, drying me off in the master bathroom. We were all completely naked, sitting on the large bed. I noticed my suitcase was not in the room.

"Have you guys seen my suitcase? I need my clothes," I said softly.

"You don't need your clothes, Baby. It's a crime to cover that body," said Felix, his voice husky.

I had promised to sit on his face. I bit my lip. Felix lay flat on the bed, and Alex and Calix supported my weight, lowering me onto his face. My shaky knees were on either side of Felix's head as I felt his tongue lick my folds for the first time. An electric current shot through me. I moaned and tried to move my pussy away from his tongue but his brothers held me in place so Felix could lick my folds to his heart's content as I whimpered and pleaded. The pressure in my belly was so intense. Alex and Calix were helping me move my hips, guiding me, making me ride Felix's face as his tongue penetrated me. A scream escaped my lips as he latched onto my clit sucking, licking and nibbling it. Many unintelligible sounds were coming out of me as Felix pushed me higher and higher, and Alex and Calix began pinching my nipples, gently squeezing my neck, kneading my breasts, and slapping my ass. I was caught of guard when a particularly hard slap from Calix made my butt cheeks quiver. I had not expected any aggression from him. I was feeling lightheaded but Alex and Calix held me up. Felix was eating me out sloppily now, his saliva all over my pussy. I rocked my hips against his gorgeous face. He gently inserted one and then two of his fingers into my pussy, pumping me, preparing me for later.

"Oh God, I love you, Felix," I cried as he sucked my clit so hard and pumped me so fast, I was pushed over the edge.

I screamed, coming undone. My juices gushed onto Felix's face and into his mouth. I heard and felt him groan happily against my clit. The brothers put me to lie on my back, and Felix sat up, his face wet with my fluids, his eyes bright and excited.

"I know you love me, Baby! I love you!" Felix said, french-kissing me to make sure I tasted myself.

I was spent. I felt sleepy already but they were far from done with me.

"Me next," said Alex, parting my legs, kissing my inner thighs, working his way up. My legs trembled. Felix and Calix were laying on either side of me, stroking their huge cocks as they watched Alex eat me out. I screamed until I was hoarse but Alex was merciless, sucking and licking and nipping my already swollen pussy. I was a shaking mess by the time he was satisfied. I rode his face until I came, soaking the sheet underneath me. Alex leant in for a wet kiss. I tasted myself on his lips.

The edges of my vision blurred as Calix crept over, instructing Alex and Felix to each grab a leg to hold me wide open, spread-eagled for him. Calix used three fingers to pump me while his tongue worked magic on my tortured little clit. I was good at riding faces now. The triplets seemed proud of how quickly I learnt. I rode Calix's face and touched my breasts, enjoying all six lustful eyes on me. Calix licked and sucked my folds and my clit, relishing my taste. He nipped down on my clit, and I came screaming. He crawled upwards for a tender kiss. I was used to my own taste now.

"All right, little Goldilocks, you're all grown up now, and your three wolves have eaten, so it's time for us to feed you," growled Felix.

Three huge cocks neared my face as I lay naked surrounded by muscled horny Alphas.

"Time to learn how to suck cock, Baby," said Felix.

Chapter 14: Hungry Wolves

Chasity

My stomach clenched in anticipation. My mouth watered. Felix was closest to me. I put my hands on his huge erection. It was much too thick to hold with one hand. He groaned and his eyes darkened as I ran my fingers and nails lightly up and down his shaft.

"Good girl," he murmured.

Alex was squeezing my butt cheeks, and Calix had started to finger me. I shivered, my legs trembling. I kissed Felix's large member, planting kisses along the shaft. I licked the tip.

"Now, try to take it in your mouth, Baby," said Felix.

I took as much of his erection as I could into my mouth. I choked and spluttered. He seemed to enjoy that. He was smirking. He smoothed my golden curls back and gripped it like a ponytail to help guide me as I sucked his dick. Sucking him made me even wetter which was something I had not been expecting. Felix started thrusting against my mouth's movements, gently at first, and then he was fucking my face. I spluttered, and my eyes watered. Tears streamed down my cheeks as he came in my mouth, his warm cum hitting the back of my throat.

"Swallow," he instructed in a raspy voice. I obeyed, gulping it down.

His cock left my mouth and was quickly replaced by Alex's monster erection. I tried to keep up with Alex's thrusting, sucking the eldest Alpha as hard as I could. I tasted his pre-cum and locked eyes with him. He mouthed 'I love you, Chasity' as he quickened the pace. He moaned, shutting his eyes tightly as his orgasm hit. Cum splattered the back of my throat, and I swallowed it eagerly, already anticipating Calix's huge cock.

Calix moved agonisingly slow in my mouth, teasing me, a sly smile on his face, while his brothers' hands roamed my body. Calix's cock was so smooth. I enjoyed the feel of it on my tongue. He moved slowly enough for me to savour the taste of his cock and his pre-cum. My pussy was gushing as Alex licked and sucked my clit and Felix eagerly fingered my entrance. I had lost count of what number orgasm I was on. My vision blurred a little again as Calix grunted and started to thrust into my mouth quickly. I matched his movements until my jaw tired, and then, I just let him fuck my mouth roughly as I spluttered on his smooth humongous cock. He locked eyes with me as he came down my throat. I gulped down his cum, swallowing like Felix taught me. I was panting. I had never been so breathless in my entire life.

The triplets were panting too and grinning, looking at me in awe.

"Should we stop?" Asked Calix, his blue eyes anxious as they gazed at me.

I shook my head. I was soaked down there, and I felt…empty. I wanted Calix.

"Only one of us can go first," said Calix slowly and softly.

They all looked at me. I felt a little nervous, hoping no one would get upset at my choice. I loved all of them.

"Calix," I whispered so low that, had they not been werewolves, they would not have heard me.

Calix's eyes lit up. He settled himself between my trembling legs, while his brothers massaged my sides and kept their baby blue eyes on my face anxiously.

"Be really gentle," instructed Felix softly, glancing at Calix.

"Take your time," whispered Alex to Calix.

Calix nodded eagerly, his eyes never leaving mine, an excited grin forming on his face. I loved his dimples! I cupped his face in my hands, and he leant towards me, forehead to forehead, nose to nose, eyes locked. I felt his gigantic throbbing cock at my entrance.

Chapter 14: Hungry Wolves

I was surprised he recovered so quickly from his orgasm, getting hard again in a few moments. I was in for an intense vacation.

"Ready?" he whispered.

"Ready," I answered.

"I love you more than anyone else in this world, Chasity. I'm so in love with you and I'll make you my Luna if it's the last thing I do," whispered Calix, his blue eyes meeting my brown ones, as he pushed inside of me swiftly but gently, breaking my hymen. I winced. He paused. Alex and Felix continued massaging my sides gently.

"You okay, Baby?" whispered Felix anxiously in one ear.

"You okay, Luna?" Asked Alex softly in the other ear, concern evident on his face.

"Yes, Felix. Yes, Alex," I murmured. They grinned in response to their names.

"Calix," I said softly, locking eyes with him again, as the pain faded.

He slowly rocked his hips, pressing his full, soft lips to mine. I deepened the kiss as he slowly thrust into me, and pleasure quickly replaced the pain. The pressure in my tummy was back, and it was building deliciously.

"Mmm," I murmured.

The triplets all grinned.

"Mmmm," they chorused, copying me, smiling. I giggled.

Felix groaned in response to my giggle. Alex's eyes were dark.

"You're so tight, Chasity," groaned Calix softly, as he quickened the pace.

"Baby, move your hips," whispered Felix encouragingly.

I did as he instructed, rocking my hips, meeting Calix's thrusts. I moaned.

"Good girl,' murmured Felix, his teeth grazing my ear.

I wrapped my arms around Calix's neck and my legs around his waist as he started to pound me. I whimpered. The pleasure was so intense. I was shaking.

Calix was nose to nose with me again. "I wanna mark you, wanna make you mine," he whispered.

Countless thoughts flitted through my mind but only one answer left my lips when it came to Calix.

"Yes," I whispered, my pupils dilating.

"Will you be mine too, Baby?" Whispered Felix in my ear.

I nodded. "Yes."

"And mine?" Asked Alex, kissing my knuckles and each fingertip.

I nodded fervently. "Yes, yes!"

Calix was merciless now, pounding my pussy, making me scream.

"CALIX!" I yelled.

He relinquished control, his eyes darkening, as he bared his canines. He looked so glorious and powerful. He found the spot where my neck met my shoulder. I felt his teeth graze me and I shivered. Then, his fangs pierced the skin of neck swiftly, followed by Felix's fangs on one side, and Alex's fangs on the other, all three biting me, and marking me as theirs all at once. I screamed as the intensity of my orgasm made me squirt and see stars.

I must have blacked out. When I came to, all three were looking at my face closely in concern. I had only been gone a few moments.

"You okay, my Goddess?" Whispered Calix. Another nickname. I smiled and nodded.

"You did so well, pretty little Luna," murmured Alex.

"I'm so proud of you, Baby," groaned Felix.

They were licking their marks, sealing them. Alex and Calix switched places. My wolf was anxious for the elder and rougher two. Felix was looking at me hungrily. I could tell he was eager to be the finale. Here we go again.

Chapter 15: Daddy

Chasity

Alex kissed me with unbridled passion, moaning into my mouth. He had settled himself between my legs while Calix and Felix were on either side of me, caressing me gently.

"Lie on your tummy, little Luna," said Alex.

I quickly did what he said. I felt him part my legs, rubbing my weeping flower with his palm. He squeezed my butt cheeks and parted them. I felt his tongue flick out against the tight entrance to my behind. I squealed. The triplets all laughed, and I laughed with them. I felt something cold between my butt cheeks.

"Huh," I said softly. "Alex."

"You're too cute, Baby," said Felix, his voice husky.

"It's lube, Luna. It'll make it easier to do what I wanna do," Alex murmured in my ear.

I felt his cock pressing at the entrance to my pussy while his finger prodded my asshole. He slid into my pussy. I moaned. He started thrusting slowly and deeply into my tight pussy while he inserted a finger into my behind. I groaned. He pumped his finger in and out of my behind, causing pleasure to mix with pain. He quickened the pace of his thrusts into my pussy. I could feel Felix's rough hands on my butt cheeks, parting them, keeping them open for Alex to finger my anus while he fucked my pussy from behind. Calix was kissing the nape of my neck and my shoulder blades to soothe me, while his brothers pushed me to my limits. Alex was pounding into me, his hands now gripping my hips, while Felix took over fingering my behind. My face was buried in a pillow so my screams were muffled. Alex grabbed my elbows and hoisted me up to lean my back against his chest while he continued to pound into me, making my pussy drip.

"ALEX!" I screamed. "Please, please," I whimpered, unsure of what I was even asking for.

He cupped one of my breasts in his hand while the fingers of his other hand began to rub my clit. Calix was able to eagerly lock lips with me, now that I was sitting up. Felix was planting open-mouthed kisses all over my exposed tummy. I was whimpering as Alex worked me into a frenzy. I screamed as my orgasm ripped through me, my pussy contracting around Alex's smooth, hard, perfectly sculpted cock. It felt *so* good. The spasms of my walls around his huge cock triggered his own climax. Alex groaned in my ear as his semen spurted into me. My pussy clung to him, draining him of every last drop of his seed.

Alex let me down gently onto the bed. I lay on my tummy, panting, totally breathless and spent, but I knew Felix would want his turn. My body was already anxious to have his cock inside of me.

"Baby, you're doing so well," murmured Felix. "Turn over onto your back."

I eagerly flipped myself over onto my back, immediately locking eyes with Felix. Felix leant towards me, pressing his lips to mine with a sense of urgency. I moaned as he nipped my lower lip, licking the skin he'd just bitten. My moan allowed his tongue into my mouth. He explored my mouth gently as his fingertips traced patterns on my sides.

"Do you want Daddy to fuck you, Baby?" Asked Felix

"Yes!" I said quickly.

"Yes, who?" Asked Felix.

"Um?" I began.

He slapped my breasts. I squealed. "Yes, Daddy."

"Good, Baby, you learn so fast. Daddy is so proud of his Baby," said Felix.

Chapter 15: Daddy

Felix lay down on his back, and his two brothers helped me to climb onto him, straddling him. Felix was a fan of girl-on-top which was surprising to me. His huge erection was at attention directly qunderneath my dripping pussy. My legs trembled.

"Lower yourself onto me," Felix instructed.

I did as he asked and felt his cock slide deep inside of me. I moaned. Felix gripped my hips, moving me back and forth, showing me how to move, teaching me to ride him. I was enjoying the sensation. Suddenly, Felix sat up with me still straddling him. He brushed his nose against mine and leant his forehead against mine. He was thrusting steadily upwards, making me bounce up and down on his dick. Alex and Calix were watching my breasts jiggle. They licked their lips. Felix put his hands on my throat, squeezing lightly as he pounded into me from below. I whimpered. I had my arms around his neck, clinging to him for dear life, as he quickened the pace and fucked me harder and harder, faster and faster.

"FELIX!" I cried as I came, gushing, my juices dripping down onto his lap and and onto the sheets.

Felix grunted, releasing his massive load into me. Some of it was dripping out of my pussy and sliding down my inner thighs.

I went limp in his arms and he held me, wrapping his arms tightly around me. Felix lay back, taking me with him. He put the covers over me. My skin felt so delicate all of a sudden so I was grateful. I was still lying on top of Felix, my body draped over his. Alex and Calix were on either side of me, lying on their backs, panting and grinning happily. Felix's eyes were on me.

"You did so well, Baby. Daddy is so proud of you!" Felix said.

"Thank you, Daddy." I said softly, my eyes closing.

I was drifting off to sleep when I heard Felix say, "We went easy on you tonight, Baby, but tomorrow, you're gonna have to learn how take more than one of us at once. Okay?"

"Yes, Daddy," was all I could say before I fell into the deepest sleep of my life so far.

Chapter 16: Goddess

Chasity

I woke up, still sprawled over Felix with Alex and Calix sleeping soundly at either side of us. Last night had been surreal. I could not believe my former bullies had spent all night making me cum. I sighed. I was nervous about today. Felix told me I would have to learn to take more than one of them at once. I traced my fingertips over the three marks on my neck. It had really happened. The triplets had marked and mated me. I wondered if I was with child already. I had known this vacation might have been their way of relaxing me into the mating and marking process. I was officially their marked mate and Luna now, whether I ran off after high school graduation or not. Once marked, the bond was permanent until death and even after that, because losing a mate was the worst thing that could happen to a werewolf, leaving them forever changed.

I slowly got up. My whole body ached, and my pussy was sore. Felix got up, kissed my forehead, and started making breakfast: chocolate chip pancakes, bacon, sausages and eggs. He made me a sweet mocha Frappuccino. I sipped it, loving the taste.

"Baby, you have the sweetest and tightest pussy I've ever had," said Felix matter-of-factly, looking at me with soft, loving eyes.

Chapter 16: Goddess

"Mmm, yes, definitely, and the prettiest too," Alex added, walking into the dining area, fixing me with a dreamy gaze.

"Good morning, my Luna," yawned Calix, coming over to kiss my forehead. "You deserve a reward for being such a good girl."

They were making me blush.

After breakfast, all four of us showered together, and the triplets took me to the beach. I was wearing the baby blue bikini that they all liked so much. We were at a gorgeous private beach with the clearest water and whitest sand. Felix carried me into the water. My arms were wrapped around his neck, and my legs were wrapped around his waist. He was holding the backs of my thighs, whilst sitting in the water. He kissed me sweetly at first and then got progressively more urgent. He moaned against my lips as his big erection rubbed against me through the thin fabric of my bikini bottoms. I broke the kiss, needing air. I relished the feeling of the warm water lapping at my aching body.

"Mmm, my brothers and I will take you back to the hotel after our little beach trip. We're gonna strip you naked, and pour warm oil all over your body to massage those sore muscles," murmured Felix.

"You'd like that wouldn't you, huh, Beautiful?" said Alex.

I nodded. "Yes."

"Yes who?" Asked Felix sharply.

"Yes, Daddies!"

"Good girl," said Calix softly.

The other two brothers were enjoying their time in the water, rubbing my shoulders and running their fingers through my hair while I made out with Felix.

"I can't believe I'm really all yours," I said softly.

"Believe it Baby, you're ours," said Felix.

"Yeah, and if you ever run off, pretty little Luna, we *will* find you, and when we do, we're gonna have to punish you for making us worry," said Alex.

"What's the punishment?" I asked.

"Don't break the rules, and you won't have to find out," said Felix simply.

"You won't hurt me, will you?" I asked softly.

"Not at all, Baby, but we will make you scream," said Felix.

"We might have to tie you to the bed," added Alex.

"And blindfold you," said Calix, winking.

"So you won't know how you're gonna get fucked next. We won't take turns, Baby. You'll have to handle us all at once. We'll stretch you to the limit, Baby, if you test us," said Felix.

I knew they definitely were not joking. If I tried to run away from them after I had already allowed them to finalise the bond, they'd be furious. They could not truly bully me anymore because they were deeply in love and in lust with me but BDSM was definitely in the cards.

I was a little worried I had accepted them as my mates too hastily. There was no going back. I wondered what their parents' reactions would be when they saw my marks. I felt smug thinking about it. I held onto Felix tightly as I could not swim. I had never had the opportunity to learn. The triplets were all excellent swimmers. I remembered them coming back to the pack house with wet hair on Saturdays when they were teenagers. They would compete in swim meets against other future Alphas from other packs. Felix carefully handed me to Alex who held me bridal style in the water until our stomachs began to grumble.

We ate at a five star restaurant. The food was out of this world. This vacation was really a feast for the senses with the gorgeous scenery, spicy smells, exotic tastes, Caribbean music, and the caresses of the cool breeze, warm water, and the triplets. I was so exhausted when we got back to the hotel suite. I excused myself, nervously pacing in the bathroom, stalling. Their monster cocks were so thick and long. How would I take them all?

I stepped out of the bathroom. My mates were waiting for me rather impatiently. I had a request.

"I'm really nervous," I said.

"Shh, Baby, don't worry, just think of a safe word. Say your word if anything becomes too much for you, and we will stop," said Felix.

I thought of a word. "Goldilocks," I suggested, chuckling.

The triplets raised their eyebrows.

"You are our little Goldilocks, come to think of it," said Alex, pulling on my curls and watching them spring back into place.

"And we're your three bears," Felix added, pulling me into a bear hug.

"You're my three wolves, my triplet Alphas," I said.

Chapter 16: Goddess

Calix jokingly began narrating a story, "Goldilocks was worried the triplet alphas' cocks would be too big and her pussy would be too small but the fit was just right."

I giggled. The triplets began undressing me. I remembered my request.

"Can I take just two of you down below?" I asked hesitantly, frightened of triple penetration. "I'll take the third cock in my mouth," I offered.

"No problem, Baby," said Felix.

Soon, I was lying on my tummy, completely naked. The triplets started pouring warm oil on me as they'd promised. Felix massaged my back, arms, neck and shoulders, while Calix massaged my legs, and Alex massaged my butt cheeks and reached between my legs to massage my folds. I was trembling. They flipped me over suddenly, making me squeal. They laughed, grinning at my reaction, as they poured more oil on me. Alex massaged my tummy and my pussy, while Felix kneaded my breasts, and Calix massaged the front of my arms and legs.

Felix pulled me up making me kneel on the bed. The oil had made my pussy and my behind really slippery. Felix pulled me onto his lap while I was still kneeling. He lay down, and Alex and Calix helped me lower myself onto his huge cock. I shivered as the feeling of fullness made my core wet itself more. Felix gripped my hips, looking at me hungrily, as he rocked me back and forth. I whimpered. It felt amazing. Alex was behind me. He pushed me down onto Felix's chest. He parted my butt cheeks. I started panting nervously. Calix smoothed my curls and kissed my lips gently, murmuring sweet nothings to me. Alex's gigantic hard cock was poking my behind. He inserted a finger into my behind. I groaned as he pumped my anus with his finger, inserting a second one, and stretching me with more oil. Felix continued to fuck my pussy agonisingly slowly. When Alex was satisfied, his cock slowly entered my anus, stretching it. I groaned loudly as he filled me from behind to capacity. I felt so full! I had two huge cocks in me.

Calix locked eyes with me. He smiled, showing his dimples. He was so handsome! He made my heart flutter. I opened my mouth eagerly and he guided his cock towards me. I licked the tip and tasted his pre-cum, and then I took him into my mouth. He was large in length and girth. Tears ran down my cheeks, and I spluttered on his cock a little but I began to suck it. Calix used my ponytail to guide me as he thrusted into my mouth, while Felix thrusted into my pussy, and Alex thrusted slowly into my anus. I was so overwhelmed. They were everywhere. I felt like I was losing my mind. I wanted to scream in ecstasy but Calix's cock was almost to the back of my throat.

"You're amazing, Baby," whispered Felix, from below me as he massaged my sides and kissed my shoulders.

"You're perfection, Luna," said Alex from behind me as he gripped my waist and licked my ears and neck. I shivered.

"You're our goddess, Chasity," murmured Calix, not one to ever be out done, especially when it came to sweet talk.

I was not sure how much longer I could keep going. I was dripping. I had lost count of my orgasms but I could feel a big one coming as Felix, Alex, and Calix all quickened the pace, switching the angles ever so slightly to hit *just* the right spots. I groaned as I felt it build inside of me. The pressure in my tummy felt so intense. I moaned against Calix's cock as Alex and Felix pumped me a little harder and faster, still trying to be careful because this was all new to me.

I could feel Felix's hot mouth encase one of my erect nipples while his fingers teased the other one. He kept up a steady rhythm with one hand on my waist, helping me bounce up and down on his dick. Alex had both hands on my hips as he thrusted slowly but deeply from behind. He nipped at my shocker and planted kisses on my neck, sucking on my marks. Calix was gripping my curls in his hand like a pony tail, and using that to guide me, as pushed his cock in and out of my mouth. I was whimpering, tears streaming down my face, when Calix pulled out suddenly, and grasped my chin with his hands, tilting my face upwards so our eyes met.

"You okay, Goddess?" He asked. "You need your safe word?"

Alex and Felix paused too which frustrated both my wolf *and* me. I shook my head fervently, and Calix smirked, pushing back into my mouth while his brothers started thrusting rhythmically again, slowly quickening the pace. I was so wet, I was dripping juices down into Felix's lap which he seemed thrilled about.

"The first person to come gets tied up the next time we have sex," Felix announced.

Chapter 16: Goddess

Huh? Obviously, that would be me. I protested but it was muffled by Calix's cock. As if enticed by the promise of bondage, my alphas all sped up, thrusting faster and deeper. The build-up was delicious. I had never felt anything like it. My whole body was trembling. I did not even know whose name to moan. I just whimpered. Felix rocked me back and forth, pulling me down further to grind on him, so that his cock was brushing against my cervix. He was huge. He definitely was making good on his promise to tickle my bellybutton from the inside, whilst Alex's movements were calculated and controlled. He reached down in front of me to find my clit with his fingers and stroke it gently. I groaned spluttering on Calix's big sweet smooth perfect cock. I loved my mates so much, every single one of them. That was all I could think about as they pushed me to the brink and I screamed against Calix's cock. I squirted all over Felix below me. He groaned, spurting into me, filling me up, just as Alex grunted and filled my behind with his load. My legs were trembling, but Felix and Alex were holding me up effortlessly like I was a rag doll. Calix moaned as his cum spurted into my mouth. I swallowed everything, and opened my mouth to show him. He grinned and winked at me, rubbing his thumb against my lower lip. I let my legs give out underneath me, exhausted, but my mates caught me, and put me gently to lie down. Six hands started massaging all my aching parts, and three pairs of lips planted soothing kisses all over me, as I drifted off to sleep.

Chapter 17: Chef Felix

Chasity

I woke up, draped over Alex's chest this time. His hands were in my hair, playing with my curls. He pulled on the golden ringlets and watched them spring back into place. He massaged my scalp. I moaned a little. Calix and Felix were on either side of me. My soft moan had woken them up, it seemed. Felix parted my butt cheeks and began eating my ass. I squealed. I had not been expecting that, first thing in the morning. His tongue darted in and out of my behind, making me tense my butt cheeks. I was leaning across Alex, my mouth pressed against Calix, savouring his taste. Alex bit my neck from under me, making me open my mouth. Calix's tongue dove into my mouth, exploring at a leisurely pace. Felix was now stretching my pussy with two fingers inserted into it while his tongue penetrated my behind. I groaned, wondering if he was stretching me because...

Alex answered my unspoken question, "Yes, eventually, we all want your pussy at the same time, if you can handle that, Princess," he murmured groggily.

My pussy throbbed. It was already deliciously sore. Calix was still kissing me, and I was getting lightheaded from the lack of air. I pulled away breathless. I took a deep breath before Alex claimed my lips, cupping my face with both hands. His kiss was surprisingly gentle. I nibbled his bottom lip. He groaned, tangling one hand in my hair, and grasping my chin with his other hand. He tilted my face upwards, granting himself better access to my mouth. Our tongues caressed each other slowly. Calix was planting kisses down my thighs and calves. He kissed my ankles. He tickled the soles of my feet, making me break my kiss with Alex to giggle. Felix inserted a third finger deep into my pussy, his knuckles at my hilt. I cried out, and the three alphas all grinned. Felix started pounding me with his fingers while his tongue assaulted my sore behind.

"Mmmm," I whimpered, my cries muffled against Alex's chest.

The eldest alpha was now gripping me to him with one hand cradling my head to his chest. Calix started massaging my lower back to soothe me as Felix roughly fingered me until I came. My scream was drowned out by a low grunt from Felix who had gotten off from watching me come. I felt his huge thick hard member slide between my butt cheeks, without penetrating me. He spurted his load upwards onto my tailbone and lower back. I felt it dripping down my sides. Alex and Calix were each stroking their cocks now, watching me with black eyes. Some of Alex's pre-cum had dribbled out and gotten smeared onto my tummy. Calix was leaning over me, stroking his cock. He suddenly flipped me over. I squealed in surprise, and the youngest brother grinned at my reaction as he stroked himself, watching me. I stroked him too with one hand. Alex got out from underneath me and went to my other side. Felix was kneeling between my legs, already hard again. Alphas needed almost no recovery time. I started stroking Alex with my free hand. Felix pressed his huge shaft against my swollen pussy, rubbing his member against my vulva. I shivered at how good that felt. He started stretching me again with his fingers all four of them while his thumb rubbed my clit. I tried to wiggle away but the other two grabbed my waist and pushed me gently back to Felix whose eyes were dark.

I resumed stroking Alex's and Calix's cocks while Felix resumed his delicious torture of my pussy. When he was satisfied, he leant over me, pressing a sweet kiss to my mouth. Alex kissed me then Calix kissed me, lingering a little.

Felix sharply penetrated me, making me cry out. I shut my eyes tightly. I opened them to watch Felix's smirk as he rocked his pelvis against mine, grinding into me. My pussy was already throbbing, and I was a whimpering mess. Alex and Calix moved closer to my entrance.

Calix reached up and stroked my face. "Baby, can we try?" He murmured, kissing my hand and the tip of my nose.

I nodded weakly. Alex position himself and so did Calix. All three of the triplets were between my widely spread trembling thighs. Oh my...

Alex and Calix both pushed in at the same time, joining Felix in my soaked slippery pussy. I was at my limit. My eyes rolled back in my head. They were all still, waiting for me to adjust to the triple penetration.

"You are doing so good, Baby," moaned Felix in his raspy voice, his lust-filled blue eyes, watching my face.

I slowly arched my back, encouraging them to move. They slowly thrust into me, moving in unison, stroking my insides with their cocks. They quickened the pace ever so slightly while their six hands roamed my flushed body. They were bringing me over the edge. I felt it coming. The building of it alone was too much to handle. I was an incoherent moaning mess. Hands kneaded my breasts, pinched my nipples, and caressed my sides and outer thighs, all while the three big mouth-watering cocks filled me.

"Ohhh, yes, yes, yes!" Was all I could say.

The triplets were smirking. They sped up, and I groaned. They started to pound me. I could not bear it much longer. The pressure was way too much. I screamed and squirted, wetting all three of their lower abdomens. They seemed delighted at that as they lost control and spurted into me, three loads of cum coating my insides, splattering into me. I felt faint. My eyes closed. I was sleepy though I had just woken up. They slowly slid out with a squelching noise. I moaned softly, drifting off as my three alphas snuggled up to me.

I awoke again. It was mid-morning. I had woken up early the first time. My pussy was sore, and every time I moved a little, I started getting mini-orgasms in my pussy. I inserted my index finger into myself, moaning at that. I was surprised to find that I was still really tight. I extricated myself from my alphas, put on a robe, and went to the kitchen of our hotel suite.

Oh yeah, I was not allowed to cook anymore.

"Felix!" I called.

I laughed inwardly at how not afraid of that big bad alpha I was anymore. He was more of a lovesick puppy now, and I loved that. Felix walked into the kitchen butt-naked, tight muscles on display and his huge morning wood at attention.

"Felix!!" I chastised him.

He yawned stretching. "You called, Baby?" He said, smirking.

"Put a robe on," I said, blushing.

He walked towards me. I bit my lip.

"Do you really want me to?" He asked with a knowing smile.

I tried to stop my lustful eyes from trailing all over his massive, muscled form. Of course, I did not really want him to. I shrugged, my cheeks burning. Felix started making my favourite, pancakes, instead of ordering room service. He liked cooking for me, it seemed. I had no idea where he had gotten a big fluffy white Chef's hat but he had one atop his ruffled shiny hair. He looked so cute. He grinned at me, deepening his dimples. Ugh! My heart. It was probably unsanitary to cook naked, but Felix and I had put our mouths everywhere on each other already, so maybe that no longer applied. He made enough for everyone, though Alex and Calix remained asleep. I was surprised me calling Felix had not woken them up too.

"Should I go get Alex and Calix?" I asked Felix sweetly.

"Who are those people?" Joked Felix, piling my plate with pancakes. Chocolate chip! My absolute favourite!

"Thank you for making me breakfast, Baby," I said brightly.

Felix grinned at hearing his second favourite word from me after his name: "Baby". He leant in for a gentle kiss, his lips warm and sweet, from the hot hazelnut chocolate coffee he had also made.

Alex walked in just then, wearing his boxers. Calix followed behind him, yawning. Calix was also in his boxers. He laughed at Felix being just in the chef's hat. Alex rolled his eyes but had a smile on his face at his brother's antics.

"Great hat!" Complimented Calix, giving Felix a thumbs-up.

Felix nodded, winking as if to say he already knew how great his hat was.

The pancakes were amazing, and so were all the sides he had made, especially the hash browns. I was still getting used to all the triplets being so... *nice* to me. More than nice. I knew that they really cared now. I knew if I got pregnant, I would not be able to go anywhere.

I did not want to leave them but I did want to track down my parents. I wanted to get my hands on my own money somehow to pay back the former Alpha and Luna. I knew that did not really make sense because I would technically inherit all of that money as the triplet's mate. I was triple marked, and that was eternal. It could not be undone. Rejections of mates were only valid prior to marking and mating. Once both had been completed, a verbal rejection was just a bunch of empty words. Also, leaving a mate, or mates in my case, by whom you had been marked, was excruciating for both sides. The pain worsened with the distance and the passage of time, so it was maddening, and the mates would rush back to each other. Mother Nature really did not play with her wolves and their mates. But... would the triplets let me find my parents? Would they let me work a real job?

"What's on the agenda for today?" I asked.

The triplets exchanged conspiratorial glances.

"Something big," said Felix.

"And unexpected," said Alex.

"And yet, completely obvious," added Calix.

They were all grinning. Huh.

Chapter 18: Surprise

Third Person

Goldilocks was in the shower while her triplet alphas had a
meeting. The topic of discussion was her, of course. Felix,
Alex, and Calix were gathered around the kitchen counter on high
stools, talking in hushed tones so Chasity would not overhear them.

"We never expected to get this far this quickly," Calix said. "But
my idea of taking her away from the site of her painful pack house
memories worked like a charm!"

"Exactly, so we can go ahead and ask her. She's marked. She's
mated. She made her decision," Alex said, nodding.

"It's a bit too soon. Too rushed," said Felix, frowning.

Alex snorted and Calix snickered. "Says Mr 'Baby I fucking
love you' on the morning after we found out she was fated to us,"
said Calix incredulously.

"Yeah, you don't have ground to stand on when it comes to
rushing, Felix," said Alex, promptly agreeing with Calix.

"So what?" Snarled Felix angrily. "She's in a great mood *now*,
away from the pack house. What's going to happen when we
inevitably return to the pack house? What if she starts to regret
everything?"

"She's marked for life by all three of us," insisted Alex.

"Being marked is not the same as happily every after," said Felix. "She could still end up resenting us if we go about it wrong."

"Don't you wanna ask her?" Asked Calix, raising his eyebrows at Felix.

"More than anything," murmured Felix. "I just don't want to blow it."

"We're not gonna blow this, trust us," Alex said reassuringly, patting Felix on the shoulder.

Calix nodded at Felix encouragingly.

"Come on, all for one, and one for all!" Exclaimed Calix, putting his hand on the counter.

Alex rolled his eyes. "We're not the three musketeers, Calix," mumbled Alex.

"Nope, we're the triplet alphas, but the phrase suits us," Calix insisted.

Felix rolled his eyes but put his hand on top of Calix's. Alex added his hand on top of the other two. They raised their hands in unison. Calix was gleeful.

"I almost died of corniness just now," Alex grumbled.

"The cringe transcended me into another reality," muttered Felix.

"You guys are gloomy, that's why I'm the favourite!" Calix said, smirking.

"You're *Mommy's* favourite, not Chasity's," sneered Felix, his eyes darkening.

"Ohhh, someone thinks he's Chasity's favourite," chuckled Calix.

Alex grinned. Felix actually blushed. "Because I am, you two wouldn't get our bond. It's too deep and complicated for either of you. I drive her crazy, and I'm the first name out of her mouth when she needs something."

"That doesn't make you the favourite," Alex said. "And you're both being so childish. Enough talk of favourites. You're not eleven, you're twenty-one, get it together."

And with that admonishment from the eldest, the triplets quieted down.

Chasity

Chapter 18: Surprise

I was relieved to shower alone actually. The triplets could make even a five-minute shower an overwhelming and exhausting experience, after which I had no energy to go anywhere, or do anything. I decided what to wear without their input. They had recently taken to squabbling over what I should wear on mornings. At least one of them was always a bit peeved if their pick didn't get chosen. Having three mates was intense, but they were so adorable.

I put on a cornflower blue puff-sleeved mini dress in a shimmery chiffon material and clear heels with clear straps. I hoped I could walk in these. Felix had a huge grin on his face. He looked so handsome in a baby blue shirt that matched his gorgeous eyes perfectly and slack soft black pants. Alex and Calix were wearing the same thing.

"Where are we going?" I asked.

The triplets glanced at each other. "Pack a nightgown, and a change of clothes for tomorrow, and any toiletries you might need," instructed Alex.

Oh. It was a trip within a trip. Alex helped me pack a duffle bag quickly. The triplets each had a backpack already. Felix held my duffle bag, leading me to the car they had rented to drive around the island.

"I'm so excited," I told him.

He pressed his lips against mine eagerly without warning, leaving me breathless. His fingers traced his mark on my neck and made me shiver.

"You're happy?" He asked.

I knew he meant to ask if I were happy about being marked by them, and belonging to them permanently now.

I bit my lip. It was easier to block out painful memories while I was away from the pack house. "I would like it to work," was all I could say.

Felix's face fell a little. He sort of winced. My wolf whimpered., "I just... I'm trying really hard... I..."

I did not know what to say. I was afraid to get too comfortable with them. I was so scared of being hurt by them now. It was easier to withstand their cruelty when I had been convinced that I hated them. I could not bear any cruelty from them now that I knew I was in love with them.

"Don't give up on me, okay," I said to Felix, my eyes wide, looking up at him.

He seemed surprised. "I would never. Don't give up on us, any of us," Felix added.

Felix tossed my duffel bag in the trunk next to their backpacks. He sat in the driver's seat, waiting on his brothers. I was not sure what they were doing. I sat in the passenger's seat, nervously twiddling my thumbs, sneaking glances at Felix, who was now deep in thought. Why couldn't I have just said "Yes I'm happy" and left it at that?

My wolf was nagging at me incessantly. I could not take her complaining anymore and I genuinely hated hurting Felix, even though he had had no problem hurting me in the past. I sighed deeply. He looked over at me. I climbed into his lap, straddling him where he sat in the driver's seat. He smirked, raising his eyebrows in surprise. He broke into a wide grin. I grabbed his face, and pulled him to me eagerly. He matched my enthusiasm, launching himself at me, kissing me forcefully, nipping at my lips, and making me gasp and moan. We explored each other's mouths with our tongues. Felix was rocking me back and forth on his lap, making me wet. The huge bulge in his pants nudged at my core. My short baby blue dress got hiked up. Felix latched onto my neck, found his mark and bit it, making me moan. He sucked on the area. Without warning, Felix reached under my dress and felt my damp underwear. I heard him unzipping his pants. The sound made me shiver in anticipation. He freed his large member, thick and long with pre-cum dripping from the tip already. He moved my underwear to the side and penetrated me, filling me, stretching me. I groaned loudly, and Felix grunted.

"Baby," was all he could say, his voice husky and his eyes dark, as he thrust upwards into me.

My pussy gripped around him. He stroked my walls, wrapping me up tightly in his arms, cradling me to him, burying his nose and face in my hair. He began to thrust wildly, making my pussy clench around him and weep as he filled it again and again. I could not hold back my moans. His hands found my throat. He was always so rough, and I relished it. He held me by my throat, squeezing slightly, as he quickened his thrusting, making me whimper. He pounded me relentlessly until I was a shaking mess. My orgasm ripped through me, making me cry out and groan, but Felix did not let up. He kept fucking me as I rode out my orgasm, intensifying it. I was almost limp when he finally came and splattered my insides with his load. He kissed my forehead. I was not sure when I fell asleep or when Alex and Calix joined us, but when I awoke, it was sunset and we were boarding a gorgeous yacht.

"She's awake," murmured Calix, lifting me up, from where I had been sleeping in the backseat with my head cradled in Alex's lap as he stroked my hair.

I was momentarily confused. The middle alpha had tired me out. I looked at the beautiful pleasure ship, a glistening white yacht on the shimmering sea. The sun was dipping below the horizon, making the water shine like that. Calix carried me up to the boat. He showed me the emblem on her side since boats were called she apparently.

"We had her name changed! See!" Calix said excitedly.

I rubbed my eyes, blinking in the evening sun. I was still a bit groggy. I peered at the word. I gasped. The yacht was named *Chasity!*

Chapter 19: All Aboard

Chasity

The yacht was named *Chasity*! I giggled. Calix kissed me sweetly. He took me to the bedroom we would stay in on board. It was gorgeous, decorated in rich warm browns, sparkling whites, and creams, with accents of gold. The colour scheme gave the room a homey feel to it despite the luxurious decor. There was a small bar right there in the bedroom. Calix tossed his backpack off to the side of the bed and continued carrying me around like I was a princess. He showed me the master bathroom with its huge tub and shower, the indoor pool, the hot tub, the kitchen, the living room, the dining room, the theatre, and the library. There were other bedrooms and bathrooms but we did not tour all of those.

"Get all dressed up for dinner okay, Goddess," said Calix, kissing my forehead.

I showered and put on the only gown I had brought with me. It was a shimmery white gown with a high slit and a fitted bejewelled bodice. I left my curls down as usual and did my makeup, carefully applying winged eyeliner and a nude-rose coloured lipstick. I put on heels. I was strangely nervous for some reason. My pulse was racing, and I kept fidgeting even though my dress was comfortable. I met the triplets out on the deck. There were fairy lights twinkling everywhere and a table set for four with a violin quartet playing music nearby. The moon hung overhead amidst her shinning stars, casting their silvery glow on the calm sea below.

The triplets all looked so dashingly handsome in their suits. They grinned when they saw me but they seemed nervous too. I went up to them and stood on tip-toe to kiss each of them. Felix's kiss was surprisingly sweet and tender. Calix shocked me by kissing me so passionately, he left me breathless. Alex's kiss was long and lingering. I felt giddy afterwards. They helped me into my chair before they all took their seats.

The meal was being cooked by the head chef of a three Michelin star restaurant.

The food was spectacular but I could hardly eat any of it. I kept waiting for something to happen. I realised my anxiety could be me picking up on my mates' feelings. Maybe, they were anxious about something.

"Chasity," said Alex suddenly, looking at me, his baby blue eyes wide and sparkling in the moonlight. He took a deep breath. Felix was fidgeting a lot on Alex's left and Calix was tapping his foot on Alex's right. I had never seen the cool as a cucumber triplets look so nervous, almost fearful. I waited with bated breath for whatever this big announcement was.

"Chasity," Alex said again, glancing in turn at each brother, "We love you."

"Deeply!" Added Felix.

I grinned.

"Yes, deeply," said Alex.

"Wholeheartedly," specified Calix.

Even though the triplets were identical, Calix's tender-hearted expressions made his face seem softer and sweeter, giving him boyish good looks. Alex's serious nature made him look classically handsome. Felix's bad boy aura made the same features look rugged and sexy. I admired my cute Calix, my handsome Alex, and my sexy Felix quietly.

"And we want to spend the rest of our lives with you," continued Alex, his eyes glistening.

"We don't ever wanna be apart," Felix said, his voice husky.

"We've always dreamed of finding our mate, and we were thrilled when we found out it was you," said Calix sweetly.

"We know that we hurt you in the past," admitted Alex in a solemn tone. "But we've grown up. We have nothing but love for you, and we want to show you that, forever."

"Will you stay with us?" Felix asked softly.

"And make us the happiest triplets in the world?" Calix asked.

I giggled.

"By becoming our wife?" Alex said, brandishing a blue velvet box and opening it to reveal a three-stoned engagement ring.

I gasped. Alex got up and came closer, getting down on one knee in front of me, holding up the ring. Felix and Calix also knelt before me at either side of the eldest alpha. They looked adorable, all wide-eyed and a bit frightened. There was a tiny nasty part of me that saw this as the best opportunity thus far to crush them, to rip their hearts out, and stamp on them. I buried that part of me. The truth was I wanted to be with them. I wanted to be happy. I deserved it.

On closer inspection of the ring, all three stones were identical. How fitting. They were princess-cut light blue diamonds, and the band was white gold. I held out my hand, waiting for Alex to put on the ring. There was a long silence before I realised I had not said yes yet, and the triplets were exchanging worried glances from down on their knees.

I sniffled. "Yes," I managed to say.

The triplets' faces broke into huge smiles. Alex slid the ring on me. It sparkled, seemingly iridescent in the moonlight. The triplets scooped me up into a group bear hug. I giggled.

Before I knew it, I was back in our new bedroom. My head lay in Calix's lap with my lips pressed against his. He was bending over me as I looked up at him, making it an upside-down kiss. His lips were so soft, full, and warm, and his taste and scent drove me wild. I felt Alex slide my underwear off and part my legs. I gasped against Calix's mouth when I felt Alex's tongue lick me, parting my folds. Every broad lick of my vulva parted my folds and made me squeal. Calix had slipped his tongue into my mouth, exploring me gently. My wolf whimpered, wondering where Felix was. I broke apart from Calix and looked around. Alex was sucking my vulva now. I shivered. Felix came into the room, holding more champagne. I extended my hand to him, and he kissed my palm. He tried to hand me the bottle of champagne but I refused that, pulling him to me. He laughed at my enthusiasm.

Chapter 19: All Aboard

Over the next few moments, all of our clothes came off. Before I knew it I was sitting in Calix's lap, facing away from him, his hands reaching down and parting my thighs to explore my pussy. Felix was latched onto one of my painfully erect nipples and Alex was sucking the other. I tangled my hands in Felix's and Alex's hair as they swirled their tongues around my nipples, and I turned my head so I could lock lips with Calix again, savouring the sweetness of his soft slow kisses. I was soaked already. Alex kissed his way down and so did Felix. They were both between my legs, kissing my inner thighs. Calix was still fondling my folds. The triplets made me open my legs wider, giving them all better access to me.

Felix kissed my core, finding my clit and sucking it. I sighed happily. Alex inserted a finger into me, pumping it in and out gently. I whimpered a little. He added a second finger and then a third. Meanwhile, Calix caressed my inner thighs with his rough palms keeping me spread-eagled.

I shut my eyes tightly, lost in all the sensations, listening to the sound of my own ragged breathing intermingling with that of the triplets. The triplets lifted me easily, and I was placed to straddle Alex who was lying down. Calix was still behind me and Felix stood over us. Alex's huge cock was at attention. I lowered myself onto it until it was completely buried in me. I moaned at the intense intrusion. Alex sat up brushing his nose against mine, cupping my face with his hands.

Calix was gently prodding my behind with his long, thick member. I heard a squirting sound and felt something cold between my butt cheeks. Calix slid in slowly, inch by inch. I held my breath while he was penetrating me anally. I felt so full. I cried out as Calix readjusted himself. Alex moved a little and my pussy started to throb.

Felix grasped my chin making me look up at him. He was glorious, perfectly sculpted from head to toe. They all were. I took Felix into my mouth, relishing the taste of his smooth hard thick cock. He thrust gently in and out of my mouth as Alex and Calix started to move. I moaned against Felix's cock. He hissed at the vibration and threw his head back. I sucked him harder, liking his reactions. His breathing was coming faster.

"Mmm, Chasity, my Baby," growled Felix, his voice so deep and raspy.

Alex and Calix were moving, rhythmically filling me again and again. I felt my whole body tremble. I braced myself with one hand on Alex's shoulder and the other hand squeezing one of Felix's butt cheeks. Felix was close, I could tell. I sucked even harder trying to steady myself despite being pounded on both sides. My thighs were shaking. Felix groaned and grunted, spurting into my mouth. I swallowed it all eagerly. Alex and Calix bounced me up and down, faster and faster. Felix was watching them pounding me with lustful eyes. He came over and cupped my face, putting his forehead to mine as I reached my limit. I squealed, coming hard. My pussy throbbed, clenching Alex's length. Alex grunted, and released his seed into me, just as Calix came, filling my behind with his warm load. I sighed, cum dripping out of my pussy and my behind. I went limp in their arms. I felt someone putting me to lay down gently. Someone else was wiping me clean with a towel. Someone was holding me, cradling me to his chest and massaging circles on my back.

"Goodnight, Mrs Thorn," said one of the triplets. I smiled to myself as I drifted off to sleep.

Chapter 20: Secret-keeper Calix

Chasity

I woke up lying against Felix's chest with Alex on my left and Calix on my right. I carefully slid out from under Felix's heavy arm. He stirred a little but did not wake up. They were all sleeping peacefully. I breathed a sigh of relief. I showered quickly and put on a yellow sundress over my gold bathing suit.

I ate at the bar on deck. It was covered so I was in the shade. The refreshing sea breeze whipped my curls about. The world-renowned chef was still on board, and we were still traversing the open seas. The chef was named Chat Chevalier, and was from Chatres, a town in Loire Valley, France, which was in the human realm, not in Wolf Country. He was a tall, lean werewolf with powerful-looking biceps. He had a sleeve of tattoos on his left arm but only one tattoo in the shape of a band around his right wrist. Upon closer inspection, the band were two girls' names in cursive drawn all the way around: *Josephine et Genevieve*. He had dark ash-blond hair, tanned skin and deep brown eyes. His sous chef was a muscular werewolf, just a bit shorter than him, with dark eyes, dark glossy wavy hair and deep olive skin. He was named Sachin Singh and was from Jaipur, India, also in the human realm. He told me he lived near to somewhere called the Pink City. They were both exceedingly handsome, and yet still humble and kind. Of course, I only had eyes for my triplets.

"Chat? Doesn't that mean cat in French?" I asked the head chef sheepishly.

"*Oui, exactement!*" He said (*"Yes, exactly"*).

"*Vous parlez français, Madame Thorn?*" (*"Do you speak French, Mrs Thorn?"*)

"*Je parle un peu de français,*" I replied. (*"I speak a little French."*)

"*Genevieve et Josephine sont ta filles?*" I asked. (*Are Genevieve and Josephine your daughters?"*)

I pointed to the tattoo on his right wrist. Chat smiled.

"Josephine is my mate and wife, and Genevieve is our little daughter," He said in a thick French accent. "They're back home in France. Sachin is my protégé. I'm training him to take over for me when I want family time. He's young. Now is grind time for him!"

Sachin spoke English with a British accent because he had left India to go to a human boarding school in the UK.

"He acts as if he is eighty!" Exclaimed Sachin, laughing.

Sachin looked to be about twenty-five and Chat looked about thirty-five.

"Why did they name you cat?" I asked Chat.

"Because he is sullen and sneaky!" Sachin said.

He was clearly very good friends with his boss as he was allowed to tease him like that. Chat nudged him playfully.

"It's because I am regal, cunning, and proud, like a cat, and my mother loves cats. My siblings are Catherine and Cheshire," said Chat.

Wow, talk about dedication to a theme. I could not help but giggle. I loved cats too. I had never been allowed a pet whilst growing up in the pack house as a second class citizen. I suddenly realised I could get one now.

"You don't like cats, Sachin?" I asked.

"I like cats, yeah. My mate has a black Persian cat named Sphinx. He hates me," Sachin said as he sautéed some mushrooms.

"He's bright!" Chat joked.

"I feed him extra meat to get in his good graces so he won't maul me when I go to her place," Sachin said, tapping his temple to indicate what a brilliant idea that was.

Chapter 20: Secret-keeper Calix

I giggled. They made me a delicious mushroom and onion omelette with truffle fries on the side. I was still taking to the chefs when the triplets appeared, looking a bit grumpy.

"We woke up, and you weren't there," whined Calix.

I gave him a big hug and stood on tip-toe to ruffle his hair.

"We always wait for you when we wake up first," he said, poutinger.

That was true. I felt a little guilty. I kissed his cheek, and he pulled me onto his lap. He started eating some of my omelette, feeding me bits of it every other spoonful.

"Calix needs a lot of love," Felix said, kissing my forehead. "Sachin, how about some cognac?"

"It's ten in the morning," protested Alex.

"It's five o' clock somewhere," said Sachin, pouring the drink, while Felix grinned.

Calix wanted me to come swimming with him in the indoor pool. He scarfed down the basket of truffle fries, took a swig of his cappuccino, and hopped off the high stool, pulling me with him.

Alex and Felix chuckled. I noticed Alex had some alcohol now too, despite his earlier disapproval.

The indoor pool was huge and there was a sun roof at one end so there was a sunlit end and a shady end. The sunlit end was warm and shallow, whilst the shady end was cool and deep. I could not swim so Calix made me practice my breathing by blowing bubbles under the water. Then, he showed me how to doggie-paddle. He put floatation wings on me as a safety precaution. I took them off and wrapped my arms and legs around his bare muscled torso. He grinned and rocked me against him.

"Chasity, I'm sorry," he said suddenly.

"For what?" I asked, leaning against his wet chest.

"For not standing up to my brothers when they went overboard with you when I was younger," he mumbled.

I smiled. I kissed him.

"I would never let them have their way now! Ever! But it doesn't matter now because everything is different," he whispered, his forehead against mine, as he walked, carrying me across the pool.

"I forgive you, Calix, you especially," I said softly, feeling embarrassed, recalling how I'd tried to separate him from his brothers.

"Thank you, Chasity," murmured Calix against my lips. He kissed me with so much emotion I became a little teary-eyed.

I broke apart from him.

"Calix," I breathed.

"Yeah," he said quietly.

"You're your mom's favourite, right?" I asked.

It was commonly believed in the pack that Calix was the Luna's favourite, her little angel, her youngest. The former alpha favoured his elder tougher boys.

Calix smirked. "Yeah, but both our parents love all of us."

I knew that for sure. The parents adored the triplets and were so proud to have produced three alphas in one go. Our pack was famous because of the identical triplet alphas. They had been interviewed on werewolf late night talk shows because everyone in werewolf country was fascinated by them.

"So, you know her really well? Like you guys talk?" I asked hesitantly.

"Yeah, she tells me more than the others. She even comes to me sometimes to talk when her and Dad fight but they hardly fight so that's only every couple of months," Calix admitted.

Bingo. He should know what I wanted to find out then.

"Tell me honestly, why does the Luna dislike me so much?" I asked.

Calix was hesitant. He thought about it for a few moments, seemingly picking out the right words to convey what he wanted to say. He was always the most careful with my feelings and the most gentle physically.

"She had a problem with your Mom," Calix admitted.

An old feud, perhaps.

"Yeah?" I prompted him.

"Maybe, I should have told you this sooner, don't be mad, ok?" Calix said giving me his famous puppy-dog eyes.

Calix had a huge fan club of girls in the pack because of these puppy dog eyes. He was widely considered a sweetheart. Alex was a classic heartthrob and Felix was a bad boy.

My pulse quickened. I could tell Calix was listening to my heartbeat as he quickly tried to placate me by telling me the supposed secret.

Chapter 20: Secret-keeper Calix

"The reason why my parents took you in... was not just to repay the debts... that was a cover... Felix doesn't know this, by the way. Alex knows as the eldest, father handed over a lot of alpha responsibilities to him," said Calix.

Poor Felix was in the dark just like me. A cover? Calix began his tale.

"My mother always hated her step-brother's mate. She felt the girl was a bad influence and she thought his mate was the one who introduced him to drugs. You see, my mother's father married twice so my mother gained a little brother she wasn't biologically related to but loved all the same. He grew up and married this girl my mother hated. My mother and her step-brother became estranged so she never knew what was going on with him. He had a daughter with the girl Mom hated, and when she was a child, the couple got into some trouble with some dangerous people. Mom begged Dad to pay off their debts because she loved her little step-brother so much, even though they'd been estranged since his marriage. My parents paid off the debts but the couple still skipped town because they had made some enemies. They thought a life on the road wasn't good for their little daughter so they dropped her off at the pack house without so much as a phone call or note. They just left the little girl. My mom thought the little girl looked just like her mother and behaved just as wilful. She was not a fan from the get go. Chasity, that little girl was you! My mom and your dad were estranged step-siblings."

Chapter 21: The Worst Memory

Chasity

Calix gazed at me, his eyes filled with worry as he anxiously awaited my reaction. I was trembling. We were in the cool deep part of the pool. Calix attributed my trembling to the temperature and held me close to his warmth. He kissed me, trying to warm me up. I kissed him back instinctively. I broke away from him quicker than he would have liked. He frowned.

"Alex knows about this too?" I asked.

"Yeah," mumbled Calix. "He and I were wondering when we should tell you. We've only known since shortly after becoming alphas after our birthday. We didn't grow up knowing this. We couldn't tell Felix cause Alex knew he would blab or blurt it out to you whenever there was a heated moment, and we wanted to develop a good relationship with you first, and start making you happy. It's been torture keeping this from our brother and you. We're triplets! And you're our mate! The bonds are so intense, but we were waiting for the right time. We didn't want to overwhelm you. I'm sorry, Chasity, for not telling you right away, but I thought it was for the best, and so did Alex."

Calix was pleading with me with his eyes. I was not angry with him, just stunned. So there *was* a real reason for the Luna's hatred of me! She had hated my mother before me. She thought my mother had ruined my father, her little step-brother. I remembered the day my parents dropped me off so vividly. I had tried to block it out but I couldn't. It remained a clear as day memory, visiting me in the form of a nightmare from time to time. Like a red stain on white fabric, it ruined me.

Flashback

My Mommy and Daddy were arguing. Was it my fault? I hugged my teddy bear tightly. "Don't worry, it will be okay," I said to my teddy.

"Chalice, we have to go!" Insisted Daddy, tossing clothes in a suitcase.

"And we can take Chasity with us, Chase!" Said Mommy.

"No! If those men find us, they won't show any mercy! Not even to a little girl! The last person that double-crossed them ended up getting their whole family done in!" Yelled Daddy.

My Mommy sighed.

"Can't we wait a bit and talk about this?" She pleaded.

"No! There's no time!" He said.

"But Ronnie paid them off!" She replied.

He laughed sadly. "But we saw something we shouldn't have."

"We were half gone when we saw it. We were baked," she said, lighting a piece of paper she had rolled up

He snatched the piece of rolled up paper and threw it away.

"Not now! For God's sake, Chalice," he yelled.

"You're stressing me out, ok! Sorry! I won't!" She promised.

She started helping him pack.

"How do we know they won't come for Chasity even at the pack house?" She asked, looking worried.

"They'd never! They're tough but they're not stupid. They fear the Alpha just like every other werewolf. If they broke into his house to get at her, they'd be declaring war on the whole pack, and Alpha would have them killed," he explained.

"Why can't he have them killed now?" She asked.

"I was shocked he even let Ronnie pay my debts. He's not gonna kill for me too unless his family is threatened or insulted," he said.

"What if they hand Chasity over to them?" She said, her eyes filling with tears.

He hugged her. "They'd never do that. Ronnie's not a monster."

"She hates me though! She'll probably hate our little girl," she said.

"Ronnie loves me. She'll make sure Chasity has a fighting chance. She'll make sure she finishes school and has food and shelter. I can't say if they'll be close. Ronnie is a strange one. She hated her stepmother but took care of her for over six months of her being ill. She's cold but she's dutiful," he said.

"I don't like her," she insisted.

"We can't take Chasity. She'll be in too much danger! We'll call every now and then when we get somewhere safe to check up on Chasity!" He offered.

"And when will we get back to her?" She asked, looking up at him, tears falling down her cheeks.

"I don't know," he said, his voice cracking a bit. There were tears in his eyes.

They bundled me up in a warm coat and drove through the snow with me in the backseat of the car. It was night-time. It was dark. I was scared. I hated strangers. I was a shy girl. I had teddy. That was my only friend. I hated school, and I missed a lot of days because Mommy and Daddy would be too unwell to take me sometimes. They would sniff the white powder. It looked like flour. That made them sick. They would smoke rolled up paper and drink stuff that burned. I tried a sip once. It burned my throat and made me sick. Why were they making themselves sick? They had tablets that looked like candy. I liked chocolate but not candy so I did not try those. Those made them happy though. They would dance and laugh.

We pulled up to a huge mansion covered in snow. The snow kept falling like the tears on my cheeks. They walked with me to the front step. They put me on the porch. They hugged me tightly. I asked them to hug teddy. They hugged him, and they cried some more. They blew kisses as they walked back to the car. They had left my suitcase with me on the porch. They gestured for me to ring the doorbell. They got in the car, watching with the headlights on.

I pressed the doorbell. A little boy answered. He smiled at me. I liked his smile.

Chapter 21: The Worst Memory

"Hi," he said. "Are you selling cookies? I want three boxes for me and my brothers."

"No!" I sniffled, annoyed. "I'm supposed to ask for Luna Ronnie."

"My mom?" The little boy asked. I shrugged.

"I'm Calix. My mom is Luna Ronnie. My father's the Alpha!" He said. He was boastful.

I shrugged looking back at my parents' anxious faces. They wanted me to hurry up. Something bad could happen

"Get Luna Ronnie now!" I said. Calix ran off to get her.

"Who is she to you?" Said another boy, who came to the door. He looked the same as Calix. Twins?

"I don't know," I said. I didn't know. I thought Ronnie was Dad's friend or something. I had never met her. I didn't understand the conversation I had snooped on earlier.

"I'm Felix," said the boy.

"Okay, whatever, please get your mother," I said.

Felix looked really angry but huffed away. Their Mother, Luna Ronnie came.

A third similar boy was peeking out. Triplets!

"Alex, go inside now!" She said. The third boy ran away. It was just me and her. She started to cry.

"What's going on?" She sniffed. My father cried harder, looking at her. He started to drive away. The Luna noticed my suitcase.

"Where's he going?" She demanded, crying. I said nothing. I didn't know.

"STOP!" She screamed. She ran into the snow. The car sped off. "Don't leave! I can help you! Please! Don't leave me! Chase! CHASE!!! DON'T GO! LET ME HELP YOU!!!" Luna Ronnie tripped and fell in the snow, sobbing, on her knees.

She stayed like that until the car disappeared in the darkness. She let the snow fall on her. I could see her breath. I was crying too but quietly. A man came outside and ran to the Luna. I could tell he was the Alpha. He picked her up and put her on their feet.

"Where are they?" He boomed.

"They're gone," she wailed, her voice hoarse from screaming and crying. The Alpha spotted me. He was big and scary. I was afraid.

"She can't stay here!" The Alpha said.

I was scared. I knew unwanted children go to orphanages and people treat them badly and no one adopts them unless they're babies. That's what someone told me once when we watched Annie, a human movie about orphans. Annie got adopted though. She was special and a good singer. I loved that movie.

The Alpha walked up to me.

"We'll inform the pack police and they'll organise what to do with her," he said sternly.

"No!" Said the Luna, walking up to the porch. A true Luna could not be commanded, even by her Alpha. I knew that. Every pack child was taught the basics about pack laws.

The Alpha was angry.

"She stays with us, until they come back for her," she said.

They glared at each other.

"She'll earn her keep," he said.

"She can do chores," mumbled the Luna.

"She's not to play with my boys," the Alpha said. "Think of the bad habits she must have."

"She's a little girl..." began the Luna.

"I don't care. She can stay but she's not our new daughter so don't act like she is," the Alpha said.

The Luna looked at me. "She looks like her mother anyway."

"Hmph," said the Alpha. He took my bag inside.

"Chase was a good boy before...he really was...a sweet boy...like my Calix," Luna said.

"Yeah, sure, whatever," the Alpha said near the doorway. "He's not a good boy now. He's a grown man with bad habits."

The Luna walked inside.

I stayed on the porch, crying

"Hurry up!" Said the Luna. "Too much cold air is getting in."

I went inside and she closed the door on my old life.

Chapter 22: Freezing Flashback

Chasity

I extricated myself from Calix's arms, forgetting we were still in a relatively deep area. I went under immediately but only for a split-second. Calix's strong arms grabbed me and pulled me back up. He cradled me to his chest while I spluttered, coughing up water. I immediately began to wriggle in his arms, annoyed.

"Take me back to the pool's edge, *please*! *Now*! I want to get out!" I squealed, feeling panicked.

Calix seemed dumbfounded. He hesitated.

"Take me back!" I shrieked. "Calix!"

He held onto me tightly. "I just want to talk to you, okay. Let's talk about this!"

"Let me go!!!" I screamed.

A memory flashed before me.

I was under the ice, submerged in freezing cold water. I opened my mouth to scream but just gulped down water. The water was so cold, it burned! Everywhere burned! Like I was on fire! I remembered being so shocked that the cold could burn you. I fought and struggled with all my might, but I couldn't get out of the water. I couldn't push my way back out of the ice fishing hole for air

because hands were holding me down in the water. I was terrified.
Was this the last day of my life?

I let out a blood-curdling scream. Calix actually jumped away from me, startled. He had relinquished me finally but, of course, I fell under the water again. I had never learnt to swim, firstly because I had never taken lessons, and secondly, because I had become terrified of drowning after my experience being held under the water by my childhood bullies, the triplets.

I did not stay under for long this time either. Strong arms grasped me again. I looked up, expecting to see Calix, but Felix was holding me, pulling me from the water. He scooped me up, carrying me bridal style, immediately out of the pool. My eyes searched for Calix who was still in the middle of the pool, looking shocked and mortified.

"What the fuck is wrong with you?" Bellowed Felix, glaring at Calix. "Didn't you see her struggling in the water? She was screaming almost a minute now. I ran here as fast as I could. I thought she was alone in the pool or something. Now, I see you're here! What the fuck happened?"

The below-deck indoor pool was on the opposite end of the large yacht from the covered on-deck bar and kitchen area. I was panting, relieved to not be in the water anymore and too tired to protest being held, even though I wanted to be alone right now. My wolf was whimpering at how sad Calix looked as he trudged out of the pool.

"I was trying to grab her. She didn't want to be held by me," said Calix softly, practically wincing at the thought.

He rubbed the back of his neck. His dark wavy hair was drenched and sticking to his forehead. He looked really cute, but I was so mad at him. Why did he not help me back out of the water as soon as I'd asked? He had been holding me and keeping me in the water to talk. I was livid.

"Felix, put me down," I said, close to tears.

They could hear it in my voice from the way they acted. Felix quickly but reluctantly placed me on my feet. Alex came dashing in a second later.

"Chasity!!!" Alex said, rushing over to me. "Calix and Felix both mind-linked me! I didn't hear you, honey! I was near the front of the ship where the wind is powerful. What happened?"

"It doesn't matter," I said, sniffling.

I held back my tears as best as I could but I was shaking. Alex reached for me to embrace me.

"No! Please! Don't!" I pleaded. I did not want to be touched right now.

"Alex, *please*, may I have a separate room from the three of you for the rest of the trip?"

"Baby," said Felix softly, his voice sounding heartbroken. My wolf was upset. She wanted me to forget about the past and just be with the triplets. She couldn't stand the idea of sleeping separately from them.

Alex took a deep, slow breath. "Chasity," he breathed, "You can have whatever you want, whatever makes you feel comfortable, but please, I'm begging you, let's talk about this first!"

I got even more upset. Anger intermingled with my sadness.

"You knew all along!" I said to Alex, my voice shaking. "You knew my father was your mother's stepbrother! That means she probably even knows where my parents are!"

"Wait! What?!" Growled Felix, turning to Alex.

"I shouldn't have kept that from you! I'm sorry! I meant to tell you when the time was right! I've only known since we became Alphas and realised you were our mate, Princess. I wanted you to enjoy life a little bit! Not worry for once! That's all!" Insisted Alex.

I was crying quietly now. Felix was moving towards me really slowly. He hesitantly drew me to him. My wolf purred at the warmth of his body. Calix came up behind me suddenly and hugged me tightly.

"I'm so so so sorry! I shouldn't have kept that from you but I also shouldn't have blurted it out like that! I love you, Chasity! Do you remember New Year's a few years ago when I kissed you. I'd wanted to do that since I saw you on the doorstep of our house!" Murmured Calix.

Calix was hugging me from behind, and I could feel so much of his skin against mine because we were both in our bathing suits. Felix was in front of me holding me against him. They sandwiched me between them, overwhelming me with their body heat. Alex was crying quietly. He played with my damp curls and put his lips against my forehead. I was crying too. Alex licked my tears off of my cheeks, grooming me. I was so furious and upset with them but the skin to skin contact with my mates was making me wet between my legs. I was shivering but certainly not from the cold, not with all their body heat enveloping me. I knew if they tried to convince me to go back to the bedroom and talk, I would end sleeping with all of them. My body ached for that. I halfheartedly pushed at Felix's bare chest, and he pushed back forcefully, making me gasp. He moved my hands away and kissed me passionately, lifting me off my feet. My bare legs instinctively wrapped around his waist, and he held me up with his hands under my thighs.

I returned the kiss until I came to my senses. I pushed gently against Felix's chest and broke the kiss. I extricated myself from the triplets and stood apart from them. I put my hands up, palms facing forwards. I sighed at their heartbroken expressions.

"I won't change rooms if we talk about this. And if you promise no more secrets?!" I said, looking each of them in the eyes.

Felix folded his arms, narrowing his eyes.

"I promise but I never kept any secrets to begin with!" He said, annoyed, glaring at his brothers and then turning back to me. "I don't want to be treated as if we're one person. We're three individual people. And I didn't know about this! So why should I be punished by you too? Is that fair?"

He had a point. I felt a pang of guilt. He was right. They were different.

"When you were mad at Alex and I, you were still nice to Calix at Christmas! So why now that you're mad at Alex and Calix, you don't want me in your bed?" Continued Felix.

Ugh! He was right.

"Sorry, Felix," I mumbled. "You didn't know either."

I walked over and hugged him. He embraced me warmly and tried to pick me up again but I would not let him though I giggled this time and his eyes darkened.

"We're so sorry, Chasity!" Said Calix. "I promise! No more secrets!"

"I did what I thought was best!" Said Alex. "I'm sorry too. No more secrets. I promise."

I gave Alex and Calix a kiss on the cheek each.

"I didn't get a kiss on the cheek!" Complained Felix.

"You got a *real* kiss just a second ago!" Whined Calix.

Chapter 22: Freezing Flashback

Alex rolled his eyes at his younger brothers. He held out his hand to me. I took it.

"I'll tell you whatever you want to know, Chasity, my Luna," Alex murmured in my ear, his lips brushing against my skin. "Let's talk!"

Chapter 23: Ferocious Felix

Chasity

The triplets and I went back to our room. We all sat on the bed. Alex looked determined. Calix had puppy-dog eyes. Felix looked grumpy, clearly annoyed that he had been dragged into this.

"I'm angry too, you know," said Felix, to the room in general. He turned to his brothers. "Since when do we keep secrets from each other?"

Alex and Calix stared at him and then at each other.

"I'm sorry, Felix," said Alex, in a diplomatic fashion.

"Sorry, Felix," mumbled Calix.

Felix was still seething.

"We thought you'd blab to Chasity!" Calix said.

"Yeah, except *you* blabbed to Chasity," Alex said.

"I deserve to know," I said softly.

"Of course, you do," Alex said just as softly.

He pulled me onto his lap. I let him draw me to him this time.

"I wasn't lying when I said I've always thought you were beautiful. I wanted a chance with you. I didn't want to complicate an already horrible situation. That was selfish of me and I'm sorry. Felix, I almost forgot I was keeping it from you and Chasity. I kinda pushed it aside. I just wanted to be happy," said Alex.

Chapter 23: Ferocious Felix

My wolf was completely satisfied with that apology, but she would be satisfied with *any* apology. She was team triplets all the way.

"It's okay, bro," grumbled Felix, smiling half-heartedly.

"Chasity," whispered Calix, pouting and widening his big blue eyes, "Do you hate me?"

"*No!* Calix, I *love* you. And I *love* Alex. And Felix didn't do anything this time but I *love* Felix. I love all of you," I said, looking at each of their faces.

They all lit up.

"That's why it hurts so much," I said, closing my eyes for a bit.

I could feel their smiles falter.

I looked at them. "I want to know where my parents are," I said resolutely.

"I don't know," said Alex, looking me straight in the eyes. I could tell he was being honest.

"We really don't," added Calix.

"Do your parents know?" I asked.

"They might," Alex said. Calix nodded.

"So your Mom really cared about my Dad even though he was just her stepbrother?" I asked, raising my eyebrows incredulously.

"Yeah, she was devastated when he drove away and left you," said Calix. "She thought he was coming back into her life, ending their estrangement, only for him to leave again, skip town, and leave you behind on our porch."

I winced.

"Do you think your Mom hates me?" I asked.

"She doesn't," said Calix. "She's afraid you'll hurt us."

I wanted to roll my eyes. They had hurt *me*.

"She felt as though your Dad, her little stepbrother, was taken away from her and ruined by your Mom," explained Alex, his tone gentle and apologetic. "She was upset when she realised we belonged to you like your Dad had belonged to your Mom. She felt she had let trouble in her house again."

The Luna was not just a snob, who was indifferent to her servant. She had cold calculated reasons behind her dislike of me, reasons she had hid from me my entire life. That made her almost unforgivable in my eyes.

"What does the Luna think my father would think of how I was treated by her and you while growing up?" I asked.

They all squirmed guiltily, including Felix this time.

"Any good father would be outraged but your father isn't exactly a good father, Baby," said Felix.

"What?" I asked, narrowing my eyes.

"Baby, he left you," Felix said softly.

"He was protecting me from something!" I insisted, fighting back the tears and springing up off of the bed to storm away.

"ENOUGH!" Bellowed Felix so powerfully I almost fell over.

Alex stiffened. Calix regarded him with wide shocked eyes.

"You're going to be the Luna of our pack, and you have to grow up, Baby!" Demanded Felix. "Your father and mother were irresponsible. They had substance-abuse problems. None of this would have befallen you or them if they had made different choices. If you're gonna hold us accountable, you're gonna hold them accountable too. Your parents were not a fairytale, Baby!"

His yell had made me sit back down. The tears streamed slowly down my face. Alex was rubbling my back gently. Calix squeezed my hand.

"I can always count on Felix to make sure I never stay the least favourite for long," Calix said brightly, trying to lighten the mood.

Felix rolled his eyes and folded his arms, still standing. Alex was silent.

"I know they were addicts, okay," I said even softer than a whisper.

I knew they had heard me. I crawled to the middle of the bed and got under the covers. They all moved to come cuddle with me.

"Please, I just wanna take a nap, by myself," I mumbled into the pillow. "I won't change rooms but I want to be alone right now."

Alex sighed deeply. He rubbed my lower back and kissed my cheek gently. "Sleep tight, Luna," he murmured in my ear. He left the room. I listened to his slow footsteps.

Calix gave me a bear hug and kissed both cheeks and my forehead. "I'll be back, Goddess!" He hopped off the bed and followed Alex.

It was just me and Felix now. I could sense him. I could smell him. I could feel how tense he was.

Chapter 23: Ferocious Felix

"I shouldn't have yelled like that. Baby... I know you want your parents. I want you to have that chance but don't go running off to do it. I'll help you," Felix said.

I shot up into a sitting position and stared at him. "You mean that?"

Felix nodded. I launched myself at him, wrapping my arms around his neck and my legs around his waist. He caught me and held me tightly in his strong arms. He sighed into my curls and buried his nose in them, inhaling my scent. He rocked me a little.

"There's one condition," Felix said. I stiffened.

"You're not leaving with them, once we find them," Felix said. I relaxed a little, realising I *was* grown up now. I couldn't exactly just redo my childhood. I could get to know my parents as an adult if I could find them.

"What if they're not..." I couldn't bear to finish that question. They just had to be. I needed them to be alive.

Felix sighed. "Well, by find them, I mean find out the story of what happened, even... who did it if they're... you know. And it's no big deal to kill the people responsible."

"What?" I yelped.

Felix chuckled. "Baby, you're mated to three alphas. We have a huge pack to protect from rogues, vampires, wizards, witches, human werewolf hunters. You think we've never killed before. Even baby-boy Calix?"

Calix... kill?

I stared at Felix, remembering him saying he had went easy on me my whole life. Is that because he killed people who crossed him and the pack? In actuality? My wolf was grumbling like I was an idiot. Of course, alphas had to kill sometimes. That was why they were given such strength and speed to protect the pack from rival predators. I felt like I understood the triplets a lot better now. They were cuddly teddy bears with me, compared to how they acted when on pack business. I had just never seen any of that so I had no point of comparison.

"I don't want you killing anyone to avenge my parents if it puts you and my other two alphas in danger," I said. I could not lose my mates. What if my parents were already lost to me? I had contemplated walking away from them many times but now that

Felix was offering this vengeance, I was terrified for his wellbeing and that of Alex and Calix.

"And," said Felix sternly, "Your pretty little ass stays home while my brothers and I do the digging and the dirty work to get to the bottom of everything!"

"Why…" I began.

"That part is not up for discussion," Felix said, his eyes turning black. Rather than feeling afraid or offended, my core got wet, and Felix smirked, enjoying the effect his display of dominance had on me.

He tossed me onto the bed. I squealed but it didn't hurt. I giggled, waiting for Felix to pounce on me.

"I'll leave you to your solo nap, Baby," Felix grumbled.

I pouted.

"It's what you asked for!" He exclaimed.

I curled up in the bed.

"My brothers and I suddenly have a lot of work to do, Baby," said Felix, turning to leave. "See you tonight, Princess."

"The things I do for love!" I heard Felix exclaim dramatically as he walked out into the hallway to go convince his brothers. Would the triplets really track down my parents? Or my parents' enemies? The people who made them leave town? My wedding present might be a hit on some fiend or something. I sighed, lying in the empty bed. What had I just asked Felix to do?

Chapter 24: Investigator Alex

Third Person

"Essentially what you're saying is you promised Chasity that we'd track down her parents, if they're alive, or kill her parents' killer, to avenge their deaths, if they're dead," said Alex, the eldest and most level-headed of the triplet alphas.

"Sounds like a cool movie plot. I like it," said Calix encouragingly.

The youngest alpha was sweet and optimistic as usual but missing the point.

"Yeah, I promised her that because it's what she wants most, and what we want most is her. Until the chapter with her parents has some kind of conclusion to it, she won't be fully present in the relationship," explained Felix, shocking his brothers.

Middle child, reckless Felix had thought this through. He was making a lot of sense but Alex and Calix were not used to this side of Felix so they fell silent.

After a few tense moments, Calix said, "I think we should do it. We owe her that much, but how are we going to get Mom to be ok with this?"

"We don't need to tell her!" grumbled Felix, as though that were obvious.

"We might, yeah," said Alex. "We'll need more information on Chasity's parents, like who their old friends are, where their old haunts are."

Alex was right. They needed leads. The case was nine years old and their mother was the only lead they had right now.

"Calix, are you willing to sweet-talk Mom into being ok with this?" Asked Felix.

"Don't tell her about the avenging their deaths part if they've been murdered! Just tell her about the finding out what happened for Chasity's peace of mind part," Alex explained.

Calix nodded. "I can do that."

"Work in how if Chasity finds out enough about her parents, she'll be content enough to stay, thereby safeguarding our triplet hearts!" Said Felix.

"Good angle!" Commented Alex. "Mom will eat that up!"

"You got this, Calix!" Added Alex.

"Come through, Baby boy Calix!" Cheered Felix.

Calix grinned. Calix put his iPhone on loud-speaker. They were below-deck in a game room that resembled a casino. There were tables for playing cards, namely blackjack and poker, with chips for betting. Their family had hosted high-stakes games here, from time to time, but Mom had put a stop to it, saying the werewolf men got too angry when they were losing. The room also had slot machines and a pool table.

The phone rang just once. "Calix, sweetheart, how are you?" Cooed Luna Ronnie. "Mommy misses you *so* much!"

Felix was stifling a snicker. Alex nodded encouragingly.

"I miss you too, Mom! I'm not good. Mom, I made a mistake," said Calix sadly.

Alex knew his mother could envision the pout on Calix's face from that tone of voice.

"What happened, sweetheart?" Asked Luna Ronnie.

"I... don't hate me okay?" Calix said, his voice shaking.

Damn he was good, thought Alex, making an impressed face at Felix, who nodded in agreement.

"I could *never ever EVER* hate you, Calix!! You are my baby boy! Now tell Mommy what happened?! She's worried sick," said Luna Ronnie.

"I let it slip to Chasity about how your little stepbrother is her father," Calix mumbled.

There was silence. He knew his mother had heard him.

"Calix, you have to be *careful*, hun, ok, especially around *her*," scolded the Luna.

"Okay, Mommy, but she asked something of me and I wanna give it to her," said Calix.

"Okay," said the Luna slowly, prompting Calix to continue.

"I promised her I would help her find out what happened to her parents after that day they drove off and left her at the pack house," said Calix, getting straight to the point.

There was more silence. "Felix and Alex promised too! It was either that, or risk her running away to find out on her own. She could disappear too, Mom, or get hurt or... we couldn't handle losing her, Mom. I can't even think about it. It makes me sick. You know how the mate bond is, don't you, Mom? How would you react if Dad wanted to go off and solve some criminal cold case but it was super dangerous but you couldn't stop him either!" Said Calix, laying it on thick.

"I... I... I would help him," admitted the Luna.

"Exactly, Mom, and we wanna help Chasity. We want her to be at peace with the past somewhat," Calix sticked his landing.

Luna Ronnie sighed deeply from the other end. "Okay," she said, her voice suddenly sounding tired. "What do you need from me?" she said matter-of-factly.

Alex launched into the conversation. "Hi, Mom!"

"Aww, my Big Boy Alex!" Luna Ronnie cooed.

"What were Chasity's parents full names?" Asked Alex, pulling out a pen, poised to write notes.

"They were Chalice and Chase Case," said Luna Ronnie.

"Chase case?" Alex asked incredulously.

Ronnie actually snickered. "I didn't name him," she said, snorting with laughter.

Alex chuckled half-heartedly.

"What was Chasity's Mom's maiden name?" Asked Alex.

"Smith," said Luna Ronnie without any hesitation.

"Did either Chase or Chalice have any close friends?" Alex asked.

"*Yeah*, ummm, Chalice was the social one. She liked a lot of attention, that one." Said Ronnie.

"Remember any of their names," Alex asked hopefully.

"Deirdre and Didi were her two main girlfriends. They were best friends," said the Luna.

"Describe them!" Alex said encouragingly, pen at the ready.

"Deirdre was a tall, statuesque girl. She looked like a model. She actually did some modelling. I wonder what became of her..."

"You mean Deirdre Binx?!" Asked Calix incredulously.

"Yes! That was her last name! I remember now! Tall, dark-skinned, high cheekbones. You could cut cheese with those cheek bones!" Said the Luna, laughing.

"Mom!" Exclaimed Felix. "Deidre really did become a model, an international supermodel. She's retired but she's the real deal!"

Calix googled the name and immediately found countless images of her along with the address of her summer house in the human realm in Los Angeles, California. Wow. Her life looked incredibly glamorous. Alex noted her name and the address listed online.

"Then, there was Didi Torte," said the Luna. "She was a short girl with blonde hair and huge orb-like eyes. She knew everybody's business. A huge busybody!"

"Do you have phone numbers for either of these people, Mom?" Asked Alex.

"Nope, sorry, Hun," said the Luna.

"What about Chasity's father, any close companions?" Alex continued.

"Just one! Chase was a bit of a loner. My stepbrother was shy and sweet," She said wistfully.

"Okay, and this one close companion was called?" Alex prompted.

"Dexter! Dexter Sharpe. He was an aspiring news reporter actually. He was a nervous guy with shifty eyes. Tall and thin, walked kinda hunched over with his fingers wiggling all the time," said Ronnie.

"Where did they like to hang out, Mom?" Alex said.

The Luna scoffed. "Anywhere drugs and alcohol could be found. Bars. There was a bar they frequented called The Serpent's Tongue.

There was a club where people would cage fight called A Fork in the Road and there was a casino they liked…"

The Luna stopped abruptly.

"A casino?" Alex said, perking up. This was it. The best of the leads so far. This could be the place they had incurred that huge dept!

"Yeah, umm, it was called The Lucky Toad," the Luna said.

"A friendly place?" Asked Alex nonchalantly.

The Luna snorted with laughter. "Of course not, the guys there probably eat gravel and drink freshly mixed cement. They were animals! Always getting in fights. The police got called there so many times, they tried to shut the place down but couldn't because the people that owned it had connections."

Wow. The triplets realised they had their hands full as leads went for the next couple days! Their mother had actually helped them to help Chasity. The triplets were filled with hope. There were going to track down all those leads: the retired supermodel, the busybody and the news reporter *and* they were going to visit every haunt that was still standing: The Serpent's tongue, A Fork in the Road, and The Lucky Toad! They were ready to sniff out a cold case to keep their relationship with Chasity smouldering.

Chapter 25: Homecoming

Chasity

I had a great time on the island for the most part. After Felix promised me to help me find out about what had happened to my parents, he convinced Alex and Calix to agree to it. We talked about it once more, and then I put it aside for the remainder of the vacation. I was their fiancée now, and they wanted me to enjoy myself. The chefs cooked amazing meals everyday on the yacht. I got to go into the ocean with Felix holding me tight the whole time. He did not want Calix to hold me to Calix's chagrin. I knew Felix was still upset about the pool incident but that was not actually Calix's fault. It was the bad memory of *all* the triplets trying to dip me in ice water that made me behave like that. Alex suggested something interesting to me.

"Don't be offended ok, my Luna," he murmured in my ear while I sat on his lap on deck, watching the sunset.

"Mmhm," I said, enjoying the cool sea breeze.

I was mesmerised by the kaleidoscope of colours caused by the sun making his way down the sky. He would soon dip below the horizon, making way for the moon and her stars to light the falling darkness.

Chapter 25: Homecoming

"Maybe, you should see a therapist," he said softly and gently. "We'll pay for it of course. I want you to stop thinking of things like you versus us. It's not like that. You are a part of us. You're our mate. It's our responsibility to care for you. You don't owe us money when we buy you things or take you places. Those gifts benefit us too because it helps make you happier," he whispered all of this, snaking his arms around me from behind and rocking me side to side a little as though we were swaying to silent music.

That reminded me of something. I wanted to dance with my father at our wedding but I didn't even know if he was alive. I shut my eyes.

"I'll go... I want to go," I answered.

Therapy was something I was curious about. The rich werewolves and she-wolves at high-school talked about their therapists often. "My therapist said no calling my ex." "My therapist is making me journal." "Ugh! I need to call my therapist!"

"It's nothing to be ashamed of, ok," said Alex. "I love you, Chasity," he breathed, his breath ruffling a few strands of my curls.

"I love you, Alex," I whispered back.

He pressed his lips against mine, coaxing my mouth open so he could deepen the kiss by sliding his tongue into my mouth. I caressed his tongue with mine as I cupped his face with my hands. I broke the kiss and gazed into his eyes. I nuzzled him. He laughed and nuzzled me back.

"You'll protect me from the Luna's wrath when she realises she's getting me as a daughter-in-law?" I asked.

"I'll protect you from everything and everyone that ever tries to harm you for the rest of eternity," he said.

"Are you trying to take Calix's crown? He is the Drama King around here!" I joked.

"Hey! You've cut me deeply, my Goddess," called Calix from the bar.

Felix was behind the bar, getting an impromptu cooking lesson from the chefs. He really was interested in culinary arts. He had on a chef's hat, no shirt, and swimming trunks.

"Felix, aren't you a bit overdressed?" I called.

Felix grinned. The chefs raised their eyebrows. Calix and Alex laughed.

I was sad to leave the yacht, and even more sad to leave the beautiful warm island, and go back to the snowy cold pack-lands. I sighed as we exited the airport. We had just flown back. The former Alpha was picking us up. He bear-hugged his three boys, clapping them each on the back. He nodded politely at me, and glanced at the ring on my finger. I hid behind Calix, who pulled me into him, holding me close to his side and stroking my wrist with his thumb. I sighed.

We piled into the car and drove back to the pack house. I was silent while the triplets talked with their Dad, telling him stories about the island and the yacht. Their Dad had clearly visited that island before, and he had given the yacht, *Luna*, to the triplets which they renamed *Chasity*. We got out of the car and crunched through the snow. We opened the door.

"SURPRISE!!!!"

I jumped. The triplets grinned, their baby blue eyes widening. They looked at their Dad who broke into a huge smile. The whole pack had gathered for a welcome back party. The house was decorated with fairy lights, balloons and streamers everywhere. There was a huge banner that read *Welcome Back Alex, Felix, Calix and Chasity*. I was shocked they had included me in the banner but I figured the Luna knew the triplets would have a fit if they hadn't. Ronda, the party planner, came out from the kitchen wearing a lacy black bralette under micro-mini blue overalls. She had bleached her blonde hair platinum. She really did look good.

"Welcome back, boys!" She said with open arms. All three of them hugged her at once. She was over the moon. She did not say anything to me. I looked at her, daring her to say something to me.

I folded my arms. Thank goodness, I had dressed up a little. I was in a shimmery blue satin dress with black tights and black ankle boots. Ronda was smug because she had gotten a hug. She had her hand on Felix's arm. I put my hand on his chest.

"Baby," I said.

Felix grinned at me and kissed me. I kissed him way more passionately than I should have in a room full of people. When I pulled away, Felix was panting but clearly gleeful. I spotted his Mom, the Luna, watching us with wide eyes. Ronda was seething with jealousy.

Chapter 25: Homecoming

"Felix, Baby," I said breathlessly. "Tell our friend, Ronda, the story of how you three proposed to me! It was so romantic, Ronda, and on a yacht named after me! You should have been there!"

Felix was delighted. He started telling the story to a large group of pack members, including a horrified pale Ronda and the Luna who looked like I had just slapped her in the face. When he was done, he kissed me. Everyone cooed and clapped. Ronda was glaring at me. If looks could kill, I'd be cold and six feet under. She sniffed and walked away. I had not put on that show for the Luna but it had affected her too. She walked over to us hesitantly.

"Mom!" Felix said, grabbing her up in a bear-hug and kissing her cheek.

She smiled but it did not reach her eyes.

"I had thought you three had wanted to wait until Chasity was older. She's only eighteen. She's in high school," Luna Ronnie said.

The former alpha, Romeo, came over and put his arms around his wife. Alex came over to hug his Mom.

"Mom, you knew I had the ring already though," said Alex gently.

"Yeah," said the Luna, laughing humourlessly.

Calix hugged his Mom and she kissed his forehead.

"Mom, I hope you know how grateful I am for all your help," he said, cupping her face. "You're the best, Mom."

She smiled. She had tears in her eyes at Calix's words. She took a deep breath.

"Thanks for the surprise party, Mom!" Alex said.

"Thanks, Mom!" Felix said.

I forced myself to speak. "Thank you, Luna Ronnie."

She plastered a smile on her face. She nodded her head stiffly.

"I guess Ronda and Mom will be able to help Chasity plan the wedding," said Felix offhandedly.

How oblivious was he? I glared daggers at him and he looked confused.

Rhonda hates me and so does your Mom unfortunately, I mind-linked Felix.

But you called Rhonda our friend just now! Said Felix.

I sighed. *I was staking my claim and showing off my engagement ring so she'd back off. She was all over you!*

145

Felix smirked, his eyes darkening. *Jealous Chasity is even hotter than regular hot Chasity.*

I rolled my eyes. Felix grabbed my ass and squeezed it. I squeaked.

Wanna stake your claim some more upstairs and then I can stake mine, Felix suggested.

I blushed and extracted myself from his fondling. He frowned but followed me around the party. I found Mina and Tina. They screamed. I screamed. We all screamed. These were the only two wedding planners I needed. We danced around in a circle like little elves that bake cookies in trees. They gasped at my engagement ring and one of them snapped a quick pic of it with her iPhone.

"I'm gagged!" Said Mina.

"It's gorgeous!" Said Tina.

Felix was grinning at our antics.

"You know Mina and Tina right?" I said to him.

"Um, they're familiar," he said politely.

They squealed. "Are these your bridesmaids then?" Asked Felix.

He was always putting me on the spot but actually...

"Yeah... yeah these are my bridesmaids and wedding planners if they wanna do double-duty," I said.

They screamed. I giggled.

"We love double everything!" Shrieked Mina.

"And triple somethings!" Joked Tina, shimmying and looking at Felix. "You're so lucky, Chasity, and you're gonna be a super cute bride!"

I smiled. At least, there were two people here who were actually happy for me.

Three people! Mr Johnson! He came over and bear-hugged me. He was in a white T-shirt that was straining against his huge muscles.

"Congratulations, Chasity!" He said, looking at my ring.

"Thank you, My Johnson!" I said, smiling.

"You're welcome, *Luna*! Call me Jimmy!" He insisted.

"Thanks, Jimmy," I said blushing. "Then keep calling me Chasity," I said, suddenly a little emotional. He was one of the only people who ever got my name right back when the triplets and everyone else called me Charity.

He pinched my cheek and ruffled my hair. His mate, Mrs Johnson, came over. She was tiny, about four inches or more shorter than me, with long wavy light-brown hair and hazel eyes. She had a few freckles scattered around her nose. She was wearing a loose-fitting tunic and colourful socks with anklets on both feet but no shoes.

"Chasity! Salutations! And congratulations! Whoo!" She said.

She had a bottle of wine in her hand. She was our Art teacher at school and a bit of a bohemian party girl, a sharp contrast to Jimmy who was straight-laced and disciplined. They were both kind though. She seemed a little tipsy already.

"Thank you, Mrs Johnson," I said smiling.

"It's Justice!" She said, raising her hands. "Not like solving crimes and stuff. My *name* is Justine!"

"Justine or Justice?" I asked, confused.

"Justine," she said hiccoughing.

"No, it's actually Justice, not Justine," said Jimmy gently, taking the bottle away from her and steadying her.

I smiled awkwardly.

"Chasity, a minute," said the Luna, coming over with her icy stare.

"Sure," I said and nodded at Jimmy and Justice.

I followed the Luna into the kitchen just like on my birthday. She faced me, folding her arms.

"Calix told you," she said softly.

It was not a question but I answered.

"Yes," I said.

"So you know that your father was my younger step-brother," she said, sniffing and taking a deep breath.

I nodded.

"Our parents, his Mom and my Dad were alcoholics. I raised him you know...like I raised you," she said.

"You didn't raise me," I said.

She looked affronted.

"You gave me a place to stay and food to eat, sometimes, and for that I'm grateful but that's about it," I said.

She laughed coldly. "You're just like your mother, so entitled."

I thought of a million different wicked things to say to her but I just walked away, leaving her alone in the kitchen. I bumped into

Alex. He had been grinning but when he saw me, he stopped. It was only because of his reaction that I realised I had begun crying.

"Hey, hey, shh," he whispered cupping my cheeks and using his thumbs to wipe my tears away.

"What happened, Chasity?" He said softly.

"Nothing," I said, my voice shaky, just as his mother came through the door right behind us.

He glared at her. She glared at me.

"What happened?" He demanded, looking at his mother.

"Nothing," she whispered harshly in a 'not in front of our guests' tone. "I was just trying to talk to her, that's all."

"No more talks without me, Calix or Felix present," said Alex sternly.

His mother looked annoyed at him giving an order but he and his brothers were the Alphas now, and he was the eldest of the three so he naturally led them. She strutted away on her high heels, her hair swishing behind her.

Before I could say anything, Alex pulled me up the stairs, holding my hand. I was shocked when he took me to my old little room and shut the door. He lay down on my cot and pulled me onto him.

"What are you doing?" I said, giggling.

"Trying to make out with my fiancée in the first spot we ever made out," said Alex, playing with my fingers.

He was leaning against the wall and I was straddling his lap. We were face to face. He kissed me slowly, methodically. I kissed back, savouring his taste and his smell. He smelled like cocoa and coffee. I deepened our kiss. He was being passive, letting me take the lead for once. I had my hands pressed against his hard chest. I nibbled his bottom lip and he groaned. I could feel him harden under me. He was pressing against me. I reached for his blazer and pushed it open. He shrugged out of it without breaking our kiss. He had to break the kiss when I tugged at the hem of his T-shirt, and we both lifted it off of him, revealing tight rippling muscles. Tingles ran through me, and heat flared up in my lower stomach. He slipped my dress off over my head. We resumed kissing, enjoying the feel of each other's skin. He unhooked my bra and took it off. He planted kisses on my neck, giving me a hickey although he had permanently marked me there already. I realised something.

Chapter 25: Homecoming

"I haven't marked you! Any of you!" I said softly.

"It's the guys mark on his girl that really solidifies the bond. Your mark on us is permanent too but some she-wolves never mark their mates cause it's not necessary. We're bound already. If you'd marked us, but we hadn't marked you, we wouldn't be bound," Alex explained.

"Then, what's the point of a she-wolf marking her mate at all?" I asked, confused.

"It's a courtesy to the guy and... it's supposed to feel *really really* good, like orgasmic," Alex murmured looking up at me sheepishly.

I smirked and then I bared my fangs and sank my teeth into his neck. He moaned loudly as I pierced the tender flesh there. Alphas were very careful and protective about their throats. That was vital in a wolf fight. Only a mate would ever touch or bite here and only for pleasure. Alex hardened even more, straining against his pants, as I rocked against him.

"Oh, *fuck, fuck,* Chasity!" He cursed, hissing with pleasure.

He was holding me to him extremely tightly. It was almost painful but I liked it. I made sure my mark was deep while he shuddered. I pulled away and licked it, sealing it. He was panting, his eyes dark.

"Stand up!" He commanded.

I stood up on the cot my feet on either side of his thighs. He slid my panties down and I stepped out of them. He tossed them aside. He grabbed my butt cheeks, pulling me forwards. He found my clit by parting my folds. He sucked on it. I was trembling. It was a bit difficult to remain standing while being eaten out but it was a sweet sort of torture. I moaned as he penetrated me with a finger. I heard the sound of him unzipping his jeans. He got out of them and tossed them on the floor. His huge cock was at attention directly below me. He nipped at my clit making me shiver. I had my palms pressed against the wall while I stood with my ankles apart so he could have access to my core. I rocked my hips a little agains his handsome face, moaning softly and taking deep slow breaths.

It was strangely soothing, making love with Alex in my old room. I gripped his silky hair and pulled him away from my pussy. We locked eyes. I got on my knees still straddling him. His huge cock rubbed against my vulva. He lifted me by the waist easily and lowered me onto his cock, penetrating me with it. I groaned. He rocked me on his lap pressing his lips to mine. One hand gripped my hair, tangled in it, and the other pinched both of my nipples, one after the other. His hands moved to my waist so he could hold me steady while he fucked me harder and harder, thrusting upwards into my pussy. I whimpered.

"Chasity," he practically hissed as he fucked me wildly.

I wasn't expecting this kind of savagery from Alex but I loved it. He stood up suddenly. I squealed. He was still inside of me. He bounced me up and down, thrusting forwards now, as he held me up, his hands cupping my butt cheeks. He turned around and pinned me to the wall, grinding against me.

"Aleeeexxx!" I moaned.

He rocked his hips against me and kept going. He had his hand behind my head so it wouldn't hit the wall while he pounded into me. My eyes started to tear up. I held onto him for dear life. His thrusts were incredibly deep and fast at the same time. I buried my face in his shoulder. My arms were limp over his shoulders as I hung from him like a rag doll. I knew he wouldn't let me fall. I couldn't take much more. My thighs were quivering and my brain was foggy. After a few more thrusts and a guttural moan from Alex, I let go, my pussy convulsing around his dick as I came. My whole body shook. He kept thrusting for a few more minutes, intensifying my orgasm. I was a moaning mess. Finally, he spurted into me. I sighed, contented as I felt his warm liquid enter me. He suddenly put me on my back with a pillow under my butt with him still inside me to make sure all his cum stayed in me. I grinned at that. He rocked me a bit more, holding me tightly, pressing me into the cot with his body weight. He made sure every last drop drained into me. I was exhausted and so, so satisfied. I fell asleep with him still inside.

My last waking thought was: *I want to mark Calix and Felix now too!*

Chapter 26: Domino

Third Person

Two of the Alpha Triplets stood in front of the quaint little snow-topped cottage. The wind whipped their coat tails and their hair back and forth. They had not told Chasity they were going to do some investigating today but that was not a secret. They just "forgot" to mention it. They walked up the three steps to the porch. The plaque on the wall outside read: *My home is clean enough to be healthy and dirty enough to be happy.* Alex smiled. Felix frowned. The middle-child alpha banged on the door until the eldest grabbed his wrist and pointed to the doorbell.

"I hadn't seen it," lied Felix.

"No intimidation! Charming inquisitive alphas!" Repeated Alex.

He had said the same thing in the car that they should charm the woman not interrogate her.

A blue eye peeked out at them through the ajar door. It actually *was* orb-like.

"Are you Didi Torte?" Said Felix.

She opened the door. "Alphas?" She said. The alphas smiled.

Chasity

It was the first day back after winter-break. The triplets had acted strangely this morning. Felix and Alex had left early to "run errands" and Calix had dropped me to school a bit early but I didn't mind. I read until it was time for class. I spotted Ashton staring at me while I read in the library. He had stayed clear of me ever since he realised I was fated to the triplets. No one had picked on me, even in the slightest. I spoke too soon.

It was almost time for class so I got up. Before I could gather up my books, Parker Ford, the biggest, meanest football player in the school knocked my books off the desk and onto the floor. I assumed it was by accident. I had not been bullied in so long. I chuckled at him, as though it were all good and went to pick them up, but he kicked them across the room. I stiffened.

"What are you doing?" I asked, confused.

"What am I doing?" Parker mocked me, towering over me.

His best friend Bryan was there. Bryan was about a foot shorter than six-foot-three Parker. Bryan came from an extremely rich family and always wore designer blazers to school with his black hair gelled back neatly. Parker was in overalls, a sweater and combat boots. His tawny hair was tousled. He narrowed his brown eyes at me. Bryan regarded me with apologetic green eyes. Ashton looked like he wanted to help but was afraid. I saw him dash off as if going to get someone.

"Parker, stop!" Muttered Bryan.

"Why?" Scoffed Parker. "It's just Charity Case! Here, look!"

Parker took out a hundred dollar bill and tried to stuff it in my mouth. I squealed. He gripped me by the nape of my neck. I shut my mouth tightly as he smushed the bill in my face. A few on-lookers gasped. I kicked him in the crotch. He yelled and relinquished me. I fell on the ground on my palms and knees.

"That's enough, Parker!" Hissed Bryan. "You don't know..."

"Calm down, Bryan! Don't get your panties all in a bunch! I won't hurt our little Charity Case!" Snarled Parker.

He usually bullied me but he had been away from school for a few months due to a football injury, to my absolute relief and happiness. I had almost forgotten he existed. I felt helpless again.

Chapter 26: Domino

Parker snatched me up, pulling on the hood of my coat. I was at a lost for words.

Is this guy crazy?! Said my wolf. *You're the triplet alphas' mate! Chasity tell him! He probably doesn't even know yet!*

"You wanna earn the money, don't you?" Said Parker with a disgusting smile. "How about a blowjob then, since you obviously like being on your knees!"

The small group of on-lookers gasped.

"FUCK YOU!" I screeched. "How dare you talk to me like that?!"

Parker's face got red with anger. I slapped him, reddening it further. He smacked me back. He had never hit me before. I squealed at the impact but didn't fall because he was gripping my hood with his other hand still.

"HEY!"

Parker looked up. It was Arnold Grey, another football playing senior. I did not know much about sports but he was the star player so girls always swooned over him. He was just as tall as Parker but with olive skin, dark eyes and dark hair. He had dimples like the triplets. He was flanked by two other big football players and they all looked pissed. They had never noticed me before but I knew their faces. They were all very popular at school. Ashton was standing near the doorway. Had he brought these other football players here? Ashton was on the team too.

"What's up, Arnold?" Said Parker, nodding.

"ARE YOU OUT OF YOUR MIND?!" Yelled Arnold, making Parker flinch.

He punched Parker in the face and grabbed me from him. I stumbled but one of the other football players held me delicately to his side. Huh.

"Are you okay, Chasity?" The blonde football player said, grasping my chin and turning my face side to side so he could see the bruise.

His name was Brett I think.

"Shit! That's a death sentence right there! You okay, little Luna?" Said the other brunette football player.

This was Jerald. He had mocha-coloured skin and a chiselled face.

"I'm okay," I mumbled, shaken up, but feeling grateful.

These three had never bullied me. They ignored me mostly. They probably did not know I existed before. Arnold had smiled at me once though, and let me cut in front of him in the cafeteria line. When I had gotten up there, I had realised I was short. I had only had money from a math contest I had won but it was running out. Arnold had paid for me, and winked, putting a finger to his lips, when I had tried to say thank you.

Parker quickly recovered from the punch with a roar of anger.

"How dare you disrespect the Luna like that? What a disgrace!" Yelled Arnold.

Parker stiffened. "What the hell are you talking about?" He said, paling.

"I tried to tell you, man," muttered Bryan.

"Shut up, Bryan!" Snapped Parker.

"Chasity is the mate of Alex, Felix and Calix," whispered Bryan. "Her birthday was the same day as theirs. They became alphas and she became their mate."

Parker stared at me in disbelief. His eyes trailed over me until they landed on my neck where the three silvery marks were. Parker trembled. Arnold cracked his knuckles.

"I would punch you again for speaking suggestively to the Luna *and* hitting her but there's no need. I couldn't possibly outdo whatever the triplets will have planned for you when they see their little mate's face and I'll make sure they *know* it was you along with your address," threatened Arnold.

The crowd gasped. Some people snickered.

"Charity, Charity, we're good, right? We were playing around!" Stammered Parker, trying to playfully punch my arm, but Brett snarled and pulled me closer and slightly behind him.

"Stay away!" Said Jerald, his tone deadly.

The three football players walked me to the nurse's office. Ashton came with us. He *had* helped me.

"I'm fine! Really, I'm fine," I insisted.

Brett lifted me onto the nurse's bunk, and Jerald alerted the nurse. Ashton smiled at me, and I smiled back, relieved. I was shaken up. Parker's temper was the worst of any person I knew. He often beat guys up but I had never seen him hit a girl before today.

Chapter 26: Domino

The nurse gasped when she saw me. She made me ice my face, and she called my guardian. I was praying the Luna did not answer the house-line.

"He's coming to get you," said the nurse sweetly, writing a pass for me to stay home today. "You didn't lose consciousness, so that's a good sign and when I feel your face, there's no significant swelling or palpable fractures."

She gave me some painkillers. I sighed but took them. I hoped the "he" that was coming to get me was not the former Alpha. It was not. Thank goodness.

"Calix!" I squealed and launched myself into his arms. He squeezed me tightly. He swept my curls back, looking at my bruised face. I had never seen Calix so angry. He looked murderous.

"Where is he?" Was all he said to the four footballer players. The nurse had left to see about something.

"He usually skips class around now to go smoke by the bleachers," said Ashton.

Calix walked off. I scurried behind him.

"I'd rather you stayed inside, Chasity!" Said Calix.

"No, Calix, it's okay, you don't have to talk to him. It was a misunderstanding!" I said, feeling a bit panicked.

Calix kept up a steady pace, and the four footballers walked behind him. Parker and Bryan were at the bleachers along with some other guys I did not know.

"Parker, come here," said Calix.

"Aww, come on, man, give me a break, she wasn't spoken for a few weeks ago. I didn't know," said Parker calmly.

All his friends looked pale.

"Did any of them have anything to do with it?" Asked Calix, looking at Ashton.

Ashton shook his head.

Parker stayed put. Calix walked up the bleachers slowly. Parker glared at him.

"I'm not scared of you! Aren't you like the nicest one?" Laughed Parker.

"I am actually," laughed Calix.

Parker laughed again. They laughed together only that was not Calix's normal laugh.

In one swift fluid movement, Calix grabbed Parker by the scruff on his neck and threw him off the bleachers like he weighed nothing. All of the friends scampered away. Parker hit the snow a couple yards down the field. I saw blood soaking into the snow.

Please, don't let him be dead, I thought.

I could not take that kind of guilt although Parker had always been awful to me.

I ran over. He was face-down. I rolled him over with all my might. His arms and legs were at weird angles and his nose looked broken. I checked his pulse.

"He's alive!" I announced to literally no one.

I looked around and saw Calix and the four footballers were already walking back to the school. All the "friends" had fled. They even left their stash behind.

"Should I tell the nurse to go check on him in the snow since Chasity says he's alive?" Asked Ashton

"Do whatever you want," shrugged Calix.

Ashton nodded.

"Thanks," Calix said, nodding to the four of them. They smiled.

"No need to thank us, Alpha," said Ashton, smiling.

"No problem, Alpha," said Arnold.

"You're welcome, Alpha," murmured Brett, as though star-struck.

"Not a problem, Big C!" Exclaimed Jerald, which made Calix laugh.

Jerald bounced knuckles with me.

"Your girl kicked him in the balls!" Said Jerald to Calix. "I thought you should know! I would've been proud of my lady!"

I blushed. I waved bye to the footballers, who were all excited about talking to one of the Alphas as they scrambled back into school. I noticed some kids surrounding them to find out what had happened. The bell signalling the end of first period had just rang so everyone came out of class. I did not think I would have any more run-ins with bullies but I was not quite right about that, though none were violent after this episode.

Calix walked me to his car, and opened the door for me. He got into the driver's seat. He drove away from the school but did not go to the pack house. He drove up to the mountains for about fifteen minutes in complete silence. Our pack lands were a true wilderness with ice, snow, mountainous planes and wild beasts. The Alphas here were known for their incredible strength.

He parked at a spot I had heard about. It was a lookout point with a really beautiful view of the horizon. The sea, hundreds of feet below, had blocks of white ice all over it. The sky was a pale greyish blue. The high school seniors and young adults called this lookout "Domino". I could see why now, because the sea looked black and the blocks of snow-covered ice floating on it were white. Black and White spots like dominoes. I would always hear the popular kids like Mina, Tina, Arnold and his friends talking about taking someone they liked to "Domino". It was a hook-up and make-out point.

I blushed and squirmed in my seat. I had not had a chance to connect properly with Calix since I had freaked out when we were in the pool together. I felt excited about being alone with him now. Calix was always so gentle, leaving goosebumps everywhere. I moved towards him to kiss him, and he stopped me, grasping my chin and looking at my face with a pained expression. Did he think I looked ugly? I had not looked at my bruise yet. I fought back tears at him not wanting to kiss me. Then, why would he bring me here?

"I want to know what happened, Chasity, in your own words, okay? Please, don't lie to me, remember we said no secrets. That works both ways," said Calix, sounding pained and tired.

"Okay," I squeaked, nodding. "I, uh, was in the library, reading. Ashton was there. He's cool. I was sitting alone though," I made sure to say, knowing how jealous all the triplets were.

"It was almost time for the first class so I got up but someone knocked my books over. It was Parker," I said softly. Calix took a deep breath.

"Then I, uh, tried to pick them up but Parker kicked them across the room," I said.

Calix growled. It sounded worse now, talking about it.

"Bryan told him to stop. That's Parker's best friend. Um, Parker called me 'Charity Case' the nickname Felix gave me," I said softly, playing with my fingers.

Calix stiffened. Felix never smacked me about though, except once when he was twelve and I was nine and I broke Calix's nose. I pushed that memory away. I could not handle it now.

Calix was leaning back, seemingly enjoying looking at me, his head resting against his head-rest, his wavy dark hair falling to his shoulders. The triplets' hair had grown a bit on vacation. Calix's gloved hand was behind my head-rest.

"He grabbed my neck and tried to stuff a hundred dollar bill in my mouth. I kicked him in the crotch then he grabbed me, and asked if I wanted to earn the money by giving him… a blowjob since I like being on my knees," I mumbled the last part really quickly but Calix heard it all clearly and looked murderous.

"I said 'Fuck you' and told him not to talk to me like that. I slapped him and he smacked me back. Then, Ashton brought the three big footballers. Ashton had gone for help back when Parker knocked over my books I think," I said, falling silent, signifying that was the end.

Calix groaned. "And after all that Chasity, you don't want me to kill him," Calix said.

"No! Of course not! You've done enough! Thanks!" I said quickly. "I'm satisfied. No one will bother me again, I'm sure," I insisted.

Calix grumbled to himself. "Goddess," he said softly, making me shiver. He pulled me into his lap.

"Would you have even told me any of that if the nurse and the guys hadn't?" He asked gently.

I squirmed. I probably would have edited it. I wouldn't have wanted to say any names. I didn't like causing trouble. I felt like I had caused trouble my whole life when I hadn't meant to.

"I'm sorry, Calix. I just wanted it to go away, so I probably wouldn't have said anything, unless you asked about the bruise and then I would have had a hard time saying it was Parker," I mumbled.

"You're lucky it was me, you know, and not Felix," laughed Calix. I did not even want to think about what Felix would do, seeing as sweet gentle Calix held my bully by his neck and threw him across a field. Felix might have thrown everyone hanging out on the bleachers with Parker whether they had anything to do with it or not. Guilty by association. I laughed humourlessly.

Calix was smelling his own scent on me, on my silvery mark, the one that was his.

"I have a surprise for you!" I said.

Chapter 26: Domino

"Yeah?" Said Calix, perking up, his big blue eyes wide with excitement.

He was so cute!

"Close your eyes!" I instructed.

He closed them. His lashes were long. I kissed his eyelids and he smiled, showing his dimples. I smiled. I found his marking spot, and I bared my fangs. I let them graze the spot. It was his turn to shiver.

"Chasity," he moaned softly, gripping me tighter, encouragingly.

I let my wolf come forward a bit, and I sank my teeth into his tender flesh causing waves of pleasure to course through both of us. I was rocking on his lap. He groaned. I licked my mark to seal it, happy with my handiwork. Calix turned his black eyes on me. He got into the back seat, pulling me with him, and pinning me under him. His lips found mine. I kissed him hungrily, my hands tangled in his silky hair. He reached under my skirt, pulling my tights and my underwear down, not wanting to expose me to the cold too much. He was covering my jaw and neck with hot open-mouthed kisses. His hands roamed my body squeezing my most tender areas. I squirmed under him, and he grabbed my wrists, pinning them above my head in one of his huge hands, while the other hand found my entrance and forced two fingers in. I groaned and rocked my hips. My body relished the intrusion. Calix pumped his fingers in and out, adding two more. I squealed. His four fingers pumped me, knuckle deep, while his thumb massaged my clit. He licked the side of my face from chin to hairline where my bruise was. It stung but my wolf purred with happiness.

I heard the sound of his belt unbuckling and his pants unzipping. No amount of fingering ever really prepared me for the triplets. They were all so huge. Calix entered me with one sharp deep thrust. My cry was muffled by his lips crashing down on mine. I wrapped my legs around his waist instinctively as he thrust into me.

"Fuck, you're so tight, Chasity," he breathed against my face.

I was so *full*. Suddenly he pulled out and flipped me over. I felt cold air on my bare behind and thighs as he raised my skirt up. My underwear and tights were around my knees. I whimpered. Calix parted my butt cheeks and spat on my behind. I felt his tongue lick my behind and enter it. He darted his tongue in and out of my back entrance while my squeals and moans were muffled, my face against the carseat. I felt his weight press me into the seat as his huge erection poked my behind. His hand reached under me, his palm pressing against my vulva and finding my clit just as his dick penetrated my behind. I groaned and he grunted. He kissed my cheek sweetly as he slowly thrusted into me from behind while his fingers massaged my clit. Anal had always frightened me a little but this was heavenly.

"Ohhh, Calix," I whispered as he continuously kissed my cheek and the side of my neck while he deepened his thrusts. My thighs were quivering. I felt his palm rubbing my front. I moaned and he licked my ear, burying himself in me to the hilt. I could not take much more. Just a few thrusts later, I felt myself coming undone. My whole body shook. Calix pulled out of behind and pushed into my pussy, releasing his load in me. My Alphas never let any chance to put an heir in their Luna go to waste. He kissed my marking spot gently as our heart rates and breathing slowed.

"I love you, Chasity," he breathed in my ear.

My wolf was gleeful, two marked, one to go.

Chapter 27: Didi Torte

Third Person

Didi Torte lived with her husband, three sons and three cats. She had huge orb-like blue eyes, rosy skin and lank blonde hair that fell to her shoulders. She was a house-wife and a quiet person despite knowing everything about everyone. She had dreamed of being an investigative journalist but had partied non-stop in her youth, met her mate, cleaned up her act, got married, got pregnant, got pregnant again and again. Now with three rowdy boys, aged nine, ten and eleven, she had no time for anything else. The cats were like her other children. They were all wearing sweaters she had knitted. She had named them Wynken, Blynken and Nod after her sons' favourite poem. They were gorgeous creatures, orange, white and calico respectively. Felix was trying to pet the orange cat who immediately jumped onto a nearby shelf to avoid being petted.

"What can I do for you, Alphas?" Said Didi nervously. "I have apple pie, and ice cream to go with it! I'll fix it right up!"

"No apple pie for me, just ice cream! Thanks!" Said Felix.

Alex made a face at Felix. They were here on a mission!

"Nothing for me, Mrs Torte!" Said Alex politely.

"Oh, please, Alpha, call me Didi!" Said Didi.

She hurried into the kitchen, and they could hear her rummaging around.

There were in a living room with pale blue walls, blue sofas and blue shelves. Even the floor had a bluish tint to the pale wood. They sat on a squishy sofa opposite Didi's armchair.

Didi scurried back in, holding a tray with two bowls: vanilla ice cream alone for Felix as requested, and vanilla ice cream *and* apple pie for Alex who had refused. Felix took both bowls and started eating.

"Should I bring more?" Asked Didi.

"No!" Said Alex quickly.

"Sorry to drop in on you like this out of the blue but it's very important!" Alex began.

Didi nodded.

"I'm told that you were a good friend of a woman by the name of Chalice a while back?" Alex asked.

Didi stiffened.

"What can you tell me about her?" Said Alex encouragingly.

"Alpha, to be frank, I know Chalice is the mother of your mate, little Chasity," said Didi.

Alex sat up a little straighter.

"But I don't know where Chalice went! She just...left," Didi said, shrugging.

"Right, but what happened before that?" Alex asked.

"She was tense leading up to her leaving. We were friends. We partied together. We skipped school together. We even got tattoos together!" Laughed Didi, pointing to her tattoo of a moon with a snake curled around it.

"So Chalice has the same tattoo?" Asked Alex.

"Yeah," said Didi. "Hers in on her ankle though, and mine is here, by my forearm," said Didi. "I was wild back in my day. We liked to gamble at The Lucky Toad. A group of us, me, Chalice and Deidre Binx. We were inseparable at one point. We took care of each other. We had our vices. Chalice had pissed off her dealer *and* the Casino Owner! She owed both of them money!"

"Was she ever threatened by either of them?" Alex asked.

"By her dealer, yeah, not the casino owner, he considered her small potatoes," said Didi.

"Who was her dealer?" Asked Alex.

Chapter 27: Didi Torte

"A guy who went by the name Casper. They used to call him Casper the Unfriendly Ghost," chuckled Didi.

She slapped her knee, laughing wholeheartedly at that. Felix had a blank expression. Alex smiled half-heartedly.

"I didn't know his full name or his real name," Didi said.

"You know if he still deals?" Alex asked.

"Of course! It's a small town," Didi said.

"Got a number or an address?" Asked Felix, speaking for the first time since he finished his snacks.

"I've got both!" Said Didi. She gave them the number and they put it in their phones. She told them address.

"And this Casino Owner? Name and number?" Asked Felix.

Didi scrambled to get her cellphone.

"Here's the number for The Lucky Toad casino. His name is Alexi Franck. I don't have his personal number, but, uh, he's even less friendly than the unfriendly ghost I told you about," Didi warned.

Chasity

I was dreading seeing Alex and especially Felix. After Calix took me home, I went to take a bath, and I saw how obvious the bruise was. I contemplated covering it up with makeup but I was the one who had made everyone promise that there be no more secrets between us. I heard when Alex and Felix got back around noon. I was hiding in my old room so I was on the same floor as the triplets' rooms. It dawned on me that this was a terrible hiding place.

"Chasity is home," I heard Calix say.

"Really?" Said Felix eagerly.

Where was Alex?

"Where's Alex?" Calix asked.

"He dropped me off. He going to a meeting at Beta Keaton's house. We already discussed those pack disputes together so he's just gonna present what we decided. Tomorrow you can go, then me on Wednesday. We'll all go Thursday," said Felix.

Four meetings in a week! Their Beta's name was Keaton. Why didn't I know any of this? I hadn't really taken up the position of

Luna. I had thought of Alpha and Luna as something genetic only, like it wasn't a real job, but it was.

"Why is Chasity home?" Asked Felix.

I could just imagine him checking the time and the way he would raise his eyebrows.

"Because she got bullied at school," Calix said. "A boy named Parker hit her and tried to stuff money in her face. I threw him across the football field. It's handled."

Calix said all of this matter-of-factly.

I heard footsteps and the door rattled. Someone knocked. I opened it hesitantly. Felix. He was frowning. He stepped into my room.

"You're not supposed to sleep here," was all he said.

"I know," I said softly.

He looked at me with a pained expression. He was looking at my bruise. He picked me up, bridal style, and carried me downstairs to the master bedroom I had chosen for myself. He put me on the bed gently and sat next to me. He was silent.

"Are you mad?" I asked, feeling more worried by his lack of a reaction.

"What do you think, Baby?" He said.

"You're mad," I said.

He sighed and lay down pulling me with him.

"Did Parker die?" Felix asked.

"No!" I squeaked.

"Then how is it handled?" Felix grumbled.

"I don't want Parker to die!" I insisted.

"Assaulting a Luna *is* punishable by death," mumbled Felix.

"I'm not Luna yet and he didn't know and..."

"None of those things make it okay!" Said Felix dryly.

"Please, please, don't kill him. I couldn't live with the guilt," I pleaded.

I kissed his cheek and his other cheek and the tip of his nose. He smirked.

"Felix!" I said.

"What?" Said Felix, annoyed.

"Promise me!" I whined.

"There are some things I can't promise you, Chasity," said Felix softly, stroking my cheek carefully.

Chapter 27: Didi Torte

I shut my eyes.

"He's already badly injured!" I said pointedly.

"Well hopefully his injuries kill him before I get to him," Felix said blankly.

"I'll give you anything you want in exchange for his life," I bargained.

Felix chuckled. "Anything like what? Like you'll mark me?"

"No," I said.

Felix's face fell.

"I'm going to mark you today because I'm in love with you. I won't bargain that away," I explained. "Pick something else."

Felix sat up and cupped my face. "You're gonna mark me today?" he said, his eyes wide.

I nodded in earnest.

"You're in love with me?" He asked.

I nodded emphatically. "I.."

Before I could reiterate how I felt, Felix's lips came crashing down against mine. He pinned me underneath him and settled himself between my legs. I instinctively wrapped my arms around his neck and my legs around his waist as he rocked his hips, pressing the growing bulge in his pants against my most intimate area. He nipped my bottom lip, making me squeal so he could explore my mouth with his tongue. I kissed him back just as ferociously, enjoying every sensation as moisture pooled in my underwear. He pulled my cotton shorts and underwear down to my knees in one fluid motion. He freed himself and I felt his huge thick cock rubbling against my already swollen vulva. I moaned and whimpered into his mouth. I was getting a little woozy from the lack of air. He broke the kiss, panting.

He entered me just as I my teeth found his neck. I pierced his flesh with my fangs. He tasted so sweet. They all did. I heard him grunt and moan as his grip on me tightened reflexively. He did not start to move within me until I parted from him, licking the mark and sealing it. Then, he pressed his forehead to mine, as he thrust slowly into me. We were both black-eyed, staring at each other. As my eyes faded to brown and his to blue, he quickened his pace. I moaned his name and he smirked. Faster and faster. The pressure and heat in my tummy built to a crescendo until it overflowed. My scream was muffled by another breath-taking kiss as I came. My pussy contracted around his huge member. He let go too and I felt his seed spurt into me. We stayed entangled afterwards and fell asleep.

Chapter 28: Close Call

Chasity

Dinnertime was awkward. The Luna did not miss the fact that all three of her darling sons were sporting my mark but she *did* seem to miss the fact that I was sporting a huge bruise. She had not said anything when I had marked Alex. She had just gazed at the silvery permanent mark on his neck distastefully. Today, I had marked Calix in the morning time, and Felix in the afternoon, so she came home to find all three spoken for, including her favourite, the youngest, Calix. He usually made animated conversation with her at every dinnertime but it was slightly stunted tonight.

Calix was retelling the dramatic tale of picking me up at school and "handling" my bully. Alex seemed to agree with not killing Parker.

"We don't want to seem too blood thirsty!" Said Alex. "You sent a clear message and you gave him a chance."

"What chance?" I said. The guy probably had half a dozen broken bones.

"He's alive. A life is a chance. A chance to be better. To try again," said Alex in a somewhat inspirational tone.

"You're both nuts. We need to be firm. If someone can get away with stepping to our Luna, then they'll think they can get away with anything. Who knows what he'll do next?" Muttered Felix.

"He won't be doing anything for a while," said Calix matter-of-factly.

He had been given another three months or so at home, healing injuries *not* caused by football this time.

"I'm glad he's alive. Thank you, all of you," I said humbly.

The Luna glared daggers at me. The former Alpha was difficult to read. He seemed distant but not angry about the triplets being marked and engaged to me.

"So Chasity, then you've decided that you're staying, and you wanna be with my boys? You've accepted the ring. You've marked them. Only a crazy person would do all that, and then still run off," she said snidely.

I ignored her vitriol. "I'm so happy to finally make the guys feel as secure as they've helped me feel," I said sweetly.

The triplets grinned at me. Luna Ronnie was not amused. The rest of the meal passed by in awkward silence where everyone could hear the scraping of forks against plates. The Luna began snatching up everyone's plates early before they were totally finished, and giving the plates to the staff to wash. The triplets were livid. The former alpha looked tired.

Go upstairs to my room and wait for me, please, Baby, said Felix over mind-link.

I listened to him, figuring I had done my own thing enough times. I could hear yelling downstairs, and I strained my ears to pick it up properly. Eventually, the curiosity became too much, and I went creeping down the stairs to try to eavesdrop. I could hear the triplets and their parents arguing. They were still in the dining room.

"So basically you're never gonna give her a chance, Mom?" Asked Felix.

"She lives in this house, doesn't she?" Said Luna Ronnie.

"But she has always lived in this house," retorted Felix.

"All I am saying is I can't believe you would all mindlessly let her mark you. Think of the pain you'll be in when she leaves the minute high school is over. It was bad enough you marked *her*. Oh and *proposed*! I was under the impression that ring was for the future..."

Chapter 28: Close Call

The former alpha interrupted his luna.

"Calm down, Ronnie, come on," he cooed.

I could tell he was probably hugging her. I dared not peek by the archway.

"Mom, mom," cooed Calix. "It's okay. You have to believe, just a little bit, when we say that Chasity won't leave us. She *loves* us."

I wondered if I would hear better from my new room. I crept towards the hallway and tiptoed to my new master bedroom. I was moving so surreptitiously that I actually peeked into my own room before I set foot in it. My blood ran cold.

Someone was prying open my window silently. He was climbing in to try to get to me. He had a rag. I smelled chloroform. I gasped and the person spotted me in the archway. It was kind of an instinct at this point though I loved all my boys dearly.

"FELIX!" I screamed.

The middle-child Alpha was in front of me before I could scream anything else. I breathed a sigh of relief.

"A kidnapper," I cried pitifully as Alex scooped me up.

Felix had the guy by the throat. I was not sure what happened exactly but I could hear the noises. Calix zoomed passed us and was in the room also. Alex held me and covered my ears but I still heard it. It was a sickening loud crack like someone's neck had been snapped. I heard a thud as the man's body probably hit the floor. I heard a sound as though the pried open window had been shut. Calix exited the room to the hallway where Alex was holding a shaken me to his side.

"Who is it?" Alex said.

"I have no idea. Don't recognise him. Did you?" Calix said, looking at me, his eyes wide.

I shook my head furiously.

Calix and Alex switched places. Calix held me and rubbed my back soothingly. Alex was assisting Felix with whatever. They had killed him I believed. Shouldn't they have gotten information from him first? The Luna and the former Alpha came into the hallway, and the Luna refused to make eye-contact with me.

"You all right, Chasity?" Asked the former alpha.

I nodded, not trusting my voice.

In a few minutes, the pack house was flooded with activity. A huge man bounded in the house. He had dark olive skin and dark

---

eyes with a strong jaw. He was tall and broad-shouldered and looked to be about in his late thirties. I realised he was Beta Keaton. A few prominent pack warriors were now stationed around the pack house as guards. We were a relatively peaceful pack in a region where attack was difficult because of the extreme cold, but the triplets had taken this threat very seriously and wanted the pack house on lockdown. One of them constantly kept me close to his side though they switched every once in a while. I was a little out of it. Some pack warriors asked me questions. There was a police force in our pack with special warriors and investigators. They interviewed me. There was an ambulance, and a doctor looked at me, which was overkill. The intruder literally had not touched me which was what I kept trying to explain to everyone. I thanked the doctor though. She was nice and was more concerned about the aftermath, in terms of it being a traumatic experience. That made me remember my promise to Alex to go to therapy. I asked the doctor if she knew of therapists in our pack and she gave me a few options.

A whirlwind and a blur later, I was actually back in Felix's room, and the three alphas were talking while I stared at them. I felt close to tears. I motioned for them to all come towards me. They did so eagerly. I was in the middle of their triple bear-hug, enveloped in their warmth. It soothed me a little.

"Don't worry, Baby, we'll get to the bottom of this and figure out who sent the kidnapper. There's already suspects."

It seemed that Felix had snapped the kidnappers neck just a few moments after I had screamed his name.

"Luna Ronnie," I said blankly.

"Huh," said Calix.

"Luna," said Alex disapprovingly. By Luna, he meant me.

"Baby, no, no," grumbled Felix, draping me over his chest.

"We know you heard the arguing," began Calix.

"But it's not like that," continued Alex.

"She would never endanger you. She knows that would destroy us," Felix mumbled into my hair, inhaling my scent deeply, as he made tingles spring up on my skin.

He was grazing my arms and legs very lightly with his claws which he had allowed to spring up. I yawned.

"She wanted it to seem like I ran off like she always said I would," I said.

"No, Princess," cooed Alex, kissing my cheek.

"She's just protective of us. She'd never do that!" Calix said, kissing my forehead.

"She's traumatised. She's shaken up. That's why she thinks that. It happened just as she probably overheard the kind of things our Mom was saying!" Felix said, defending me.

I tightened my hold on him. We had woken up, entangled in the evening. I shivered, remembering each of the markings. I really loved them, and I needed them to believe me. The Luna was trying to make me out to be a runaway, even if she had to pay someone to drag me away, because I had gotten too attached and too comfortable. I had no plans of leaving now. The triplets were trying to help me with my situation with my parents and I was satisfied.

"Please, if you ever look for me, and I'm gone, I didn't leave you, someone took me okay. That's all I want you to remember," I said to each of them, making sure I locked eyes with them each, Alex, Felix and Calix.

"That's all I'll ever believe, heaven forbid that happens," said Felix, his voice husky and surprisingly emotional, like he was going to cry.

Calix nodded and nuzzled me.

Alex sighed. "You're not going anywhere. Even if I have to handcuff us all together so it's not an option to snatch you, I will," said the eldest.

I smiled and kissed him.

"Kinky," commented Felix, and we all laughed.

"I'm not going anywhere by choice," I reminded them as they turned out the light and tried to calm me down.

Three bodies pressed against me as my heart beat frantically.

I'm not going anywhere by choice, I kept whispering to them over mind-link as they surrounded me, six hands, three mouths, my whole body covered in goosebumps. My wolf and I *both* needed them to know.

Chapter 29: Shift Work

Chasity

I woke up entangled with Alex. It was his turn to watch me. The triplets were on a strict schedule. They actually had a shift system while their pack warriors scoured the pack lands for intruders. Alex had decided on three shifts: 8am to 4pm, 4pm to midnight, and midnight to 8am. He was on the midnight to 8am. I had woken up at the crack of dawn which was my body's go-to because of my years of housekeeping. I sighed and buried my head in his chest. I didn't know where Felix and Calix were.

"Try to sleep, okay," Alex murmured.

"You're awake," I said pointedly, smiling slightly.

"I'm in charge of watching you," he said sleepily, his long wavy hair ruffled. He looked so adorable. I crawled up his chest to reach his face so I could kiss him. His lips were soft and warm. I groaned into his mouth.

"Sleep," he instead groggily. I pouted.

"Where are Calix and Felix?" I asked.

"Leading the pack warriors on their search," Alex mumbled, closing his eyes and tightening his hold on me.

"Is that really necessary?" I asked. "The guy is dead."

Chapter 29: Shift Work

"There's no way he acted alone. Someone who acted alone would have to have a personal vendetta strong enough to do so which he couldn't possibly have when none of us knew him. That guy was hired by someone *with* a personal vendetta or a grudge against the pack. Hurting you would weaken the three alphas of our pack and leave us vulnerable to outsiders," Alex said all of this with his eyes still closed.

"What if it's not about hurting the Alphas? What if it's just about hurting me? Or separating me from you?" I asked, looking at him square in the face although his eyes were still closed.

"It's possible," he mumbled.

"Your mom..."

"Chasity!" Said Alex sharply, his eyes opening. "Stop it! That's enough!"

I fought back tears.

"Chasity, why would she wait *years* to suddenly get rid of you?" Alex said.

"For *years* I was a lowly servant. That's a lot different to me becoming her replacement as Luna, her daughter-in-law, marrying *all* of her sons, inheriting everything," I said. I sighed.

"I have school," I said.

"Shit! I knew we forgot something!" Alex said. "Ugh. Not today."

"NO WAY!" I said. It was senior year. The only thing I had ever had to be proud of was my grades. I had maintained straight A's despite being overstretched and bogged down by housework at the gigantic pack house. I had not had *any* significant real emotional support for most of that time. Even my nutrition was meagre. And yet, I had still pushed myself at school It was the only thing I was good at. No one was taking that from me by messing up my grades last minute. What if I wanted to go to college? I could actually afford it now!

My yell startled the eldest alpha. He bundled me up in the blanket and carried me to the bathroom. He was so sleepy but he insisted on helping me get ready.

"What are you *doing*?" I chuckled.

Alex put me on the counter. He found the hem of my nightgown which made me bite my lip. He raised it over my head and pulled my underwear down. I blushed and instinctively covered my breasts.

Her Triplet Alphas

He smirked and leant forwards, demanding a kiss. I happily complied, savouring his taste and his smell. I loved the smell of coffee and cocoa that seemed to emanate from him.

"You smell like a cosy cafe," I told him.

"*What*?!" He said, laughing wholeheartedly.

"You smell like coffee and chocolate or cocoa powder. You have a rich, yummy smell that wakes me up like being in a cafe," I proudly told him.

"That's why you won't let me sleep then," he chuckled.

I giggled.

"I should get some new deodorant and cologne, go for chamomile and hops, nice sleepy smells," he mused.

I playfully slapped his arms, forgetting I was naked and exposing myself even more by removing my arms from covering my top half. I blushed and covered myself again. He raised his eyebrows.

"It's cute how you can *still* be shy around me after everything we've done together," he smirked.

My blush deepened. I wanted to nudge him but didn't. He started drawing a bath for me.

"On mornings, I take showers. I only take baths on evenings," I said, feeling a little odd for specifying like I was being a brat. My wolf chastised me for calling myself a brat, telling me I was a Luna and I could demand things. Alex put the shower on lukewarm. I nodded, hopped off the counter and got in. He dropped his boxers and got in with me. My cheeks were burning. I felt so shy around Alex sometimes. He kissed the nape of my neck as he swept my curls out of the way. Alex insisted on washing my hair for me. I made him use conditioner after. He even wanted to pick what I would wear. He picked something baby blue. He was obsessed with this colour on me. It was a lantern-sleeved dress with a shimmery satin material, really pretty but a bit fancy for school. I obliged him and wore the dress over some stockings and high-heeled black Mary Janes.

He grinned.

"You look so pretty!" He said, then he frowned. "When boys try to talk to you, tell them immediately you're mated to the Alphas."

Everyone probably knew that by now. "Ok," I said, not wanting to argue. Alex made breakfast. He made me an omelette that was really good. So all this time all the triplets could cook. Why had I done all the cooking then? I pushed that from my mind and enjoyed my cheesy omelette and my French toast. Alex was on the phone. He had gotten dressed in a simple grey T-shirt and soft grey sweatpants. How did he make such simple clothing look so good? He was like a walking ad for everything he wore. All the triplets were. Felix and Calix came back from wherever the search party had reached. Our pack lands were huge and icy and rocky. I shuddered to think of anything happening while they searched like an avalanche or the ice breaking underneath them. Felix kissed me deeply and my wolf purred. Calix cupped my face in his surprisingly warm hands and nuzzled me, making me giggle then he silenced me with a kiss.

"Until we get you a bodyguard we feel we can trust, you're not going to school alone," said Felix grabbing a slice of French toast and taking a bite.

"What?" I said.

"Don't pretend you didn't hear me!" Said Felix. "I know you did."

I took a deep breath, narrowing my eyes at him.

"I was thinking, neither of you slept, I can go to school with Chasity, and you guys can sleep," said Alex.

"Nah, we should switch like we said," instead Felix. "Baby boy Calix has already been to school with Chasity so it's my turn!"

Felix at my high school *all* day! I couldn't imagine a world in which there wouldn't be any drama with that premise.

Chapter 30: History

Chasity

Calix wished me a good day at school, and nuzzled me again. I had a tiny bit of an obsession with nuzzling. I missed out on it a lot as a kid, and Calix seemed to realise that. The youngest alpha went upstairs to get some sleep. Felix showered in the blink of an eye, and came downstairs with his long dark wavy hair still damp and hanging in his eyes a bit. All of the triplets said they really needed a haircut but I liked their hair long though. Felix was all in black, his signature. Alex drove Felix and me to school. I was in the front seat and Felix sprawled out in the backseat so he could take a quick nap. Alex stayed in the school's parking lot until it was literally exactly time for my first morning class. This was because he wanted his younger brother to get a little more sleep which was so sweet of him that I didn't protest even though it would make me a bit late.

When Felix and I walked into school, every head turned towards us and every pair of eyes was on us. I blushed and looked down. Felix grasped my chin and made me look up.

"Chin up, buttercup," he said, winking. Even the corniest things seemed cool when Felix did them. Girls glared daggers at me when he wasn't looking, envy practically dripping from them. Mina and

Tina were thrilled. They screamed and hugged us both before scampering off to class, also late.

I remembered I had History with MacDonaldson, the strictest teacher in the school. She was an old, mean-spirited she-wolf who could always find something to give you extra homework as punishment for. She claimed detention was a social event, and therefore, not true punishment. I walked into her class slowly, looking at her sheepishly, knowing she was about to yell at me in front of the whole class and make me write some six-thousand word essay, the standard fee. She rose from behind the desk slowly, straightening her cat-eye glasses and her tweed blazer. Everyone gasped. For one second, I thought it was because I was late and MacDonaldson was going to go Godzilla on me but that was not the gasp-worthy event. That honour went to Felix. Girls were actually swooning. I wanted to roll my eyes. Guys grinned and high-fived, excited to talk to the Alpha. Felix smirked.

MacDonaldson spotted Felix behind me, and her whole demeanour changed. Her face broke into a huge, placid smile. She sat back down and put her hands daintily on the desk.

"Class, the Alpha has graced us with his presence, what do you say?" She said.

"Good morning, Alpha!" Chorused the class excitedly.

"Good morning, class," said Felix, grinning incredulously. "I'm Felix, by the way, in case you can't tell my brothers and me apart. I'm the best-looking one though," said Felix, winking.

Girls giggled and blushed. MacDonaldson was among them, covering her mouth with her hands.

"To what do I owe this honour, Alpha Felix?" Asked MacDonaldson.

Felix took on a grave expression. "Chasity was almost kidnapped," Felix announced to the entire class.

They all gasped. They did not know I existed a few weeks ago. People hugged each other for comfort. Felix nodded.

"The actual kidnapper has been dealt with," Felix said sternly.

"Hell yeah!" Said a football player near the back. His friends nodded. Felix smiled.

"My brothers and I will be taking turns watching over her even at school until the situation is completely handled. A proper investigation has to take place," Felix explained.

177

MacDonaldson lit up like a Jack O' lantern. "We are elated to have you, Alpha Felix!" She practically squealed.

Felix and I took our seats. Felix lifted my entire desk with me in it and put it so close to his that his thigh was pressed against mine from hip to knee. My body reacted of its own accord and my core moistened a little. I blushed deeply, hoping the other guys would not notice my arousal. Felix's eyes went black for a second responding to my arousal but also angry at the thought of other males being nearby while I smelt like this.

MacDonaldson erased what she had painstakingly written on the white board and wrote: *Movie Time*. The class cheered. We only watched historically based movies in her class once a year and we had already seen one for this year. This was an exceptionally rare treat. All the lights were turned off. The movie was *Troy* and all the girls swooned when Achilles and Briseis got together. In the dark classroom, Felix sniffed my hair and my neck. He kissed the spot where he had marked me, letting his tongue slide over it. I shivered. Felix was squeezing my thigh, making me squirm in my chair. I did not want to get so aroused in a class with others. I quickly got up and excused myself to the bathroom. Felix followed me, causing my breath to hitch. I scurried into the girls' bathroom, Felix hot on my heals. I closed the stall door in his face but he banged it open and locked it behind him. My stomach clenched.

"Felix, I..." I began but Felix put one finger to his lips, closing the distance between us and towering over me.

He crouched down and helped me take off my ankle boots. He slid my stockings and my underwear down. I could not believe this was happening. I recalled back when the triplets had attended this school and I was three years below them, they had purposefully ignored me at school though everyone knew we lived in the same house. I frowned. Felix could tell I was suddenly upset about something so he decided to act quickly by picking me up and putting me on his shoulders with my bare pussy facing his mouth so he could eat it. I covered my mouth so I wouldn't moan too loudly as he grabbed my bare butt cheeks under my satin dress and ate me out like there was no tomorrow. He parted my folds with every persistent lick. He found my clit and tickled it with his tongue swirling around it. He sucked on my clit and then he took most of my vulva into his hot large mouth sucking on my folds. I felt my butt cheeks press against the wall. Felix had pinned me there. I was high enough on his shoulders to see over every stall. Thank goodness, we were the only ones here. I was pressed against the wall now as Felix plunged his tongue deep inside me, in and out. He moved back to my clit and used to finger to pump into me while he hummed on my clit. I muffled my own squeal with my hands.

Felix! Oh, Felix, I can't take much more, I pleaded over mind-link.

We're almost there, Pretty Baby, he cooed.

Felix enveloped my vulva in his mouth, sucking on me, while his fingers plunged deep inside of me. I came, contacting around his fingers and stifling my own screams. Felix seemed satisfied, setting me down gently on my trembling legs. He helped me get dressed. I walked on shaky legs to my next class as the bell rang.

"History is *so* fascinating, isn't it, Chasity?" Said Felix as he walked with me to the next class.

The present was more captivating in my opinion.

Chapter 31: A Nauseating Night

Chasity

The rest of the day was more of the same. Felix was stared at by everyone and was incredibly comfortable with this and frankly used to it. I was more used to being invisible and mostly hid behind Felix. Teachers were thrilled to have one of the Alphas grace their classrooms.

At lunchtime, everyone surrounded us, listening intently to Felix talk about anything and everything. They hung off his every word and tried to be extra friendly to me. The four football players who had come to my rescue that day came over to say hello. Felix seemed to know about them helping me. Calix must have told him. They all bounced knuckles with Felix and talked about plays and strategies in football. Felix, Alex and Calix had been the star players back when they were students here, which was only about three years ago. Eventually, we were surrounded by the entire football team and the cheerleaders, as Felix recounted how he and his brothers had been instrumental in winning the championship game. Everyone gasped and cheered during his tale. I ate quietly and kept my eyes downcast on my food. Felix nudged me.

"What's wrong, Baby?" He murmured in my ear.

"Nothing," I mumbled, smiling halfheartedly at him.

Chapter 31: A Nauseating Night

Felix frowned.

He had not done anything wrong, per say, but it was difficult feeling like the only thing that suddenly made me worthy was being mated to the triplets. Almost no one, *including* the triplets, had treated me like a person before I had been mated to the three beloved Alphas. Felix and I were invited to some house party by the head cheerleader, Moxie. I had no intention of going.

"You're not going to this party without proper supervision, okay?" Said Felix sternly.

"I'm not going at all!" I protested.

Felix stopped in his tracks on the way to the parking lot. "Why not?"

He looked concerned. "Why don't you want to go?" Asked Felix, his eyes wide. "If you want to go, one of us will take you, whoever's shift it is will take you, okay?"

I shook my head furiously. "I *hate* parties!" I exclaimed.

Felix looked at me like I was insane.

"*Why*?!" Demanded Felix incredulously.

"Because, I hate dancing and crowds so naturally I don't like something that combines those two," I said simply.

Felix smirked. "Chasity, you're in high school! You should try to enjoy it. Make some happy memories," said Felix encouragingly.

"Okay, sure, good talk," I said dismissively. Felix frowned.

We had reached the car. Alex was here to pick us up with Calix in the passenger seat. Felix opened the door for me and then he got in.

"How'd it go?" Asked Alex as though he'd been worried.

"Perfectly!" Purred Felix.

Alex rolled his eyes but smiled, clearly relieved.

"No more bullies?" Said Calix, looking at me, his eyes questioning me.

"No more bullies," I replied, smiling.

"None, whatsoever," added Felix. "In *fact*, our little Princess Chasity here is loving school and her new friends so much she wants to hang out with them tonight at a party they're throwing!"

Ugh!

"No, I do not!" I said immediately.

"A party sounds like fun!" Calix said brightly. "Why don't we all go?"

"A high school party?" Asked Alex, twisting his mouth in disdain.

"Nah, I know the girl who's throwing it. Her sister is in college. It's a joint thing with high school seniors and college kids," explained Felix.

"That sounds cool," Alex said, smiling a little.

"I don't wanna go," I wailed.

"Why not, Luna?" Asked Alex.

"I just don't," I grumbled.

"*Please*, Goddess, let's go have some fun!" Whined Calix.

"Come on, Baby!" Felix insisted.

Why were they so hell bent on me going to this stupid party?

"Chasity, my Luna, you don't know many of the pack members very well, old and young alike," said Alex gently.

"I know you're shy, Baby, and we're sorry if we're part of the reason you've always been in your little shell," added Felix.

"But this is a good opportunity to, at least, get to know some of the pack members in your age group," continued Calix.

"A Luna is what holds a pack together. She's a mother to the entire pack and the Alpha is the father figure," said Alex.

"Most Lunas try to learn the names and basic info about each member to keep a check on them, see who needs what. You can't help your children if you don't know what their issues are," said Felix.

"A good mother knows what's up with all of her babies. A she-wolf has to keep track of her cubs!" Calix said.

Triple Ugh. I hated when they were right. I squirmed a little bit. Being with the triplets meant I had to be their Luna. I technically already was in a biological sense. I'd been fated to them and they'd mated and marked me. Ronnie was just holding the post for me until I finished high school. I sighed.

"Let's go to the stupid party," I grumbled.

The triplets all grinned and cheered.

Third Person

The triplets were ready early for the party and waiting on their mate, Chasity. They hoped this party would serve two purposes: one, to help their little luna get to know her pack members and two, to help get her mind off of whoever was out there trying to get to her. They had already arranged for several pack warriors to come to the party dressed in plain clothes as party goers just in case they should need back-up of any kind.

The investigation looking into the attempted kidnapping had notified them of something concerning. The kidnapper, whose finger prints had all been burnt off, and who did not seem to have been registered as a pack member, bore an interesting identifier, a full moon with a serpent curled around it. Didi's tattoo. The one she had said Chalice also had. The triplets had not shared any of this with Chasity yet. It was *not* keeping secrets. It was all part of an ongoing investigation. They wanted to present Chasity with something comprehensive and satisfying. They wanted the whole story. What was the connection between the tattooed werewolves: a cult, a gang, a mindless trend?

Chasity

I was so nervous about this party. I really didn't socialise much. I was relieved that Mina and Tina would be there. I had just messaged them to make sure. I wore a sparkly black figure-hugging mini dress and high heels. I left my hair down. I put on red lipstick that I felt suited me. I was thinking about changing as I turned to and fro anxiously scrutinising myself in the mirror when Alex walked in. He raised his eyebrows, flashing them upwards quickly. His lips parted in surprise. He gave me an "ok" sign with one hand. He drew me to him and pressed his nose to my neck.

"You look gorgeous, Luna," he murmured against my skin.

I shivered a little as the cold tip of his nose slid along my jawline. I raised my chin so he had better access to the area and he took that as an opportunity to plant kisses down my neck to my shoulder. He swayed with me back and forth on the spot as though we were dancing. He twirled me and dipped me. As he dipped me, he leant down and pressed his lips to mine.

The triplets and I drove to the head cheerleader's house. She lived in a sprawling mansion almost as large as the pack house. Out front there were dozens and dozens of cars parked in the huge driveway and snow-covered lawn. There were teenagers and young adults in the porch, smoking, drinking, laughing and nodding their heads to the upbeat base-heavy music coming from inside. As I walked up to the porch, I noticed several guys trailed their eyes over me and licked their lips. They quickly looked away and stiffened when they spotted the triplets with me. Felix walked in front of me and Alex and Calix were at either side of me protectively.

The whole party seemed to stop or perhaps slow down as we entered. Every gaze was on us. Girls ogled the triplets, grinning, blushing, swooning and squealing. Guys nodded, bowing their heads slightly in respect and submission towards the Alphas. The crowd parted a little. Moxie was in a hot pink bondage dress and her sister from college, Roxie, was in a similar dress in a dusky pink shade. Both girls had light ash blond hair and big brown eyes. They seemed smug beyond belief that the triplets were at their house and their party.

"Welcome, *Alphas!*" Squealed Moxie. "It's an honour!" Added Roxie.

Felix grinned. Alex nodded but kept his face neutral and Calix smiled sweetly even winking at each sister in turn which annoyed me honestly. Calix caught my expression and grasped my waist. I tried to pull away from him but he latched on to me, pressing his mouth against mine in a shockingly passionate kiss right in the middle of the living room where the thick of things were. All the party-goers, mainly the girls, "oohed" and squealed. The guys "whoa-ed". Everyone cheered when he broke away from me grinning and winking again. I blushed deeply and hid my face in Calix's shirt.

Mina and Tina found me. I threw my arms around them like they were lifesavers in the middle of the ocean. They hugged me back.

"Chasity's first party!" Squealed Tina.

"Let's get drunk!" Shrieked Mina.

"We can't. It's a school night and we really shouldn't drink because..."

An hour and four shots later, I was pretty tipsy. I was on Felix's lap on the living room couch while he chilled with the same four footballers that idealised him and the other Alphas. The entire team and some of their mates joined us one by one, taking up all the couch space. About three dozen people were dancing, mostly just girls grinding on their mates on the dance floor. Calix was winning at beer pong, getting the ball in the right cup of beer every time surrounded by a crowd of admirers. Alex was in the kitchen fetching me some water. He came back. A few girls were edging closer and closer to him, giggling. Ugh, I was so sick of this. I drank the water quickly, feeling a little better. I stumbled away from them when Calix's back was turned, Felix was deep in conversation and Alex was explaining pack laws to the stalker girls. I climbed the stairs. I was out of breath. I had been told by Roxie that there was a bathroom on the landing. I had not been pleased to recognise Roxie as one of Felix's ex girlfriends as soon as I saw her. That was how he had known her sister, Moxie, the current head cheerleader. Roxie, his ex, had been head cheerleader back when he was the star quarterback. How cute. I grumbled inwardly. The light in the bathroom flickered on before I could turn it on myself. There were people around here and there but not as many as in the living room and half of them were passed out on the stairs or maybe just asleep. I realised who had turned the light on before me.

Sandra, Avery and Tonya. The most recent ex-girlfriends of the triplets. I gulped at their pissed-off expressions, their arms akimbo.

"Congratulations on your engagement, *Charity*!" Spat Tonya.

"You know it's funny, girls, I remember a certain *pathetic little girl* who lied to our faces saying she had no idea who the triplets' mate was! Don't you, girls?" Asked Avery.

"Oh, yeah, I remember that. She was a maid one minute and their mate the next. You know without the mate bond *forcing* them to be into you, you'd never be their type, ever," snapped Sandra, watching me up and down.

I hugged myself feeling self-conscious and nauseated from the shots.

"Do you hear me?" Asked Sandra angrily.

"She's ignoring us!" Said Tonya indignantly.

"We're talking to you!" Shrieked Avery.

My stomach burned. The burning shot up my throat. I couldn't help it. I spewed vomit all over three girls who already hated me. I wiped my mouth, looking at my own clean dress. Thank goodness. I glanced at the soiled girls, six coal-coloured eyes filled with anger towards me. I gulped.

Chapter 32: Misgivings and the Moon

Chasity

The three she-wolves blocked my path to the bathroom on the stairway's landing. In the middle was Tonya, Felix's most recent ex, clad in a red dress so tight it looked painted on. She had olive skin, deep brown eyes and long, bone-straight black hair. Flanking her were Calix's ex, Avery, in a blue sequin mini dress with her shoulder-length light blonde hair, blue eyes and pale skin, and Alex's ex, Sandra, with her long vibrant red hair, green eyes and light sprinkling of freckles across rosy skin. Sandra wore a micro-mini dark green velvet dress. Currently all six eyes had turned black and were filled with envy and hatred. All three outfits were splattered with my vomit.

"I'm *so so so* sorry, girls," I said feebly.

"For stealing our boyfriends or for ruining our clothes?" Bellowed Sandra.

"I didn't steal them, they're my mates and they chose to break up with you!" I retorted. "I'm sorry for the clothes!" I specified, my temper rising.

"You little bitch!" Cried Sandra trying to grab me by my wrist. I was furious now too. My wolf was snarling, jealous and threatened and outraged. I snatched my hand away from Sandra and literally growled at her, baring my canines. Something the old Chasity or perhaps, Charity, would have never done.

Sandra recoiled a little. Tonya and Avery glared. "So you think you're hot stuff now, huh, you think you're actually *worth* something now?!" Spat Avery.

"Not a chance!" Added Sandra venomously.

I rolled my eyes.

"You should have *heard* the horrible things they used to say about you!" Said Tonya.

That actually made me a little worried. My eyes widened a bit

"Didn't they tell you all the awful stuff they said about you to everyone including us?" Asked Sandra in mock innocence.

"*Especially* us!" Corrected Avery.

That stung a little. *Had* the triplets insulted me behind my back? They used to do so to my face but this felt worse somehow like they must have truly disliked me. Tonya smirked.

"Felix would go on and on about how *fat* and *pathetic* you were! How your cooking sucks and you always gave attitude as a maid when you should just be grateful that their parents let your poor ass stay in the pack house," snarled Tonya.

"Alex thought you were ungrateful too and that you didn't *deserve* to live in the pack house because you had *no* respect for any of them and were entitled!" Growled Sandra.

"Calix said you broke his nose when you were little but still constantly played the victim as if you were *so* innocent when you were just as vicious if not more!" Hissed Avery.

I took a deep breath, fighting back tears. The girls seemed satisfied.

"Alex, Baby!" Squealed Sandra suddenly, tossing her long flaming red hair. "Look at what this brat did to me!" She shrieked, gesturing towards her dress.

My heart plummeted. For one horrifying second, I thought Alex was rushing up the stairs to comfort Sandra. He would take her in his arms and say she was beautiful right in front of me and then my heart would break. It would shatter. Alex bounded up the stairs and my wolf and I waited terrified. He came to us and snatched me up, enveloping me in his arms.

"Little Luna!" He murmured against my skin, his face buried in my neck. "Are you ok? What happened? Where'd you run off to?"

"I had to use the bathroom," I said softly.

"Did you?" He asked. I shook my head. Alex spotted the open door behind the three she-wolves on the landing leading to a white-tiled bathroom.

"Excuse us, ladies," he said politely but indifferently.

"*Alex*!" Shrieked Sandra. "She vomited on us!" Cried Sandra, disgusted.

"She's sick," said Alex matter-of-factly, "and if you hadn't blocked her way to the bathroom you wouldn't have gotten vomited on."

"You *hated* her! You called her a burden and..." screeched Sandra.

"*ENOUGH!*" Said Alex loudly in his Alpha voice. The three girls stiffened. "*Move, now!*" They were compelled to obey and fled downstairs. Alex took me into the bathroom and locked the door. I made him face the wall while I used the bathroom. I washed my hands and then Alex made me wash my face and sip some water. He patted my head with a cool damp towel. My skin was flushed and my head ached. He carried me down the stairs. He got some ibuprofen for me. I took that.

"How's she feeling?" Came a soft high-pitched voice. I was sitting on the kitchen counter and Alex was holding me firmly by the waist so I would not fall over. The room still swam before my very eyes but it no longer spun round and round haphazardly.

I looked in the direction that the voice had come from: Roxie, Felix's ex girlfriend prior to Tonya. I sighed.

"She's doing ok," said Alex, smiling.

"Could I talk to her for a minute?" Asked Roxie sheepishly. I tried to hide in Alex's jacket.

"I'll be right in the pantry looking for a snack for you. You need to eat something!" Said Alex.

"Help yourself! You know where everything is!" Encouraged Roxie.

Roxie sat on the counter next to me. I looked away from her, focused on siting up straight. Mina and Tina had been driven home after they both drunkenly fell off the porch and into the snow and they had needed to get out of their cold wet things.

"I know Tanya, Sonia and... Avalon," she began, somewhat unsure of herself.

"None of those names are right," I said frankly.

She grinned. "Well you know who I mean, those girls, they were giving you a tough time. That was how it always was when you were dating one of the triplets. Girls would be *so* jealous. They'd be catty, calling me names, messing with my clothes while I was in the gym shower and they even sabotaged my art piece for the fair. They slashed the painting up," said Roxie.

I looked at her my mouth agape. "But, you're popular! You're outgoing! You've always had... friends, money!" I said waving my hands all over this colossal house. "You're pretty," I mumbled, feeling self-conscious.

"None of those things made any difference. Everyone hoped to be Luna and they acted crazily over it. Alex's girlfriend at the time, my friend Clair dealt with the same thing. So did Rosie! She was Calix's girlfriend," Roxie explained. "But people who behave that way aren't worth your time. Any self-respecting girl would let go when a guy meets his mate."

"Why did you and Felix break up?" I asked.

Roxie smiled. "I met my mate, Deacon," she said, her eyes lighting up. "And Felix was *so happy* for me. He really was. He hoped to find his mate soon too! He was never quiet about how much he wanted to meet her."

I had never gotten the point of werewolf relationships where you know you'll have to break up because the person isn't your mate but to each his own. I felt a little insecure that Roxie broke up with Felix and not the other way around.

"Also, the relationship wasn't perfect, we did fight. We'd argue a lot. He called me Charity by accident like twice," she said laughing about it now and shaking her head. "So I'm not surprised."

I blushed and looked away. "You were only seventeen at the time and Felix and I were twenty. We had dated back in high school for a bit when I was head cheerleader and he was the star quarterback. People seemed to like us being together but we weren't compatible. He broke up with me and we both dated other people until aged twenty when we got back together pretty unexpectedly. I was livid that he was like *obsessed* with this little maid girl that lived in his house, no offence. Ugh, that sounds so snobby and awful saying it out-loud like that," said Roxie, covering her face. "He was always either whining about something wrong you'd did or how you looked at him as if he were a monster or how you didn't respect him. Then he would call me by your name sometimes. *Then* I found it!" She exclaimed with such vigour I jumped a little.

"Found what?" I asked, holding my breath for some reason.

"The painting," said Roxie to herself more than to me, her eyes faraway. "The painting of you looking all sullen and forlorn in your hand-me-downs sitting on the pack house porch steps. I mean you were always a pretty girl," admitted Roxie offhandedly making me blush. "But you were *so* sour!" She exclaimed. "But now I get it! Who could blame you? After everything you've been through. Felix was terrified you would reject him as a mate and say no to the marriage proposal. He was scared he'd wake up one day and you'd just be gone no explanation, no note, no apology, nothing."

"Felix told you all of this?" I whispered.

She nodded. "I hope you're not upset. I mean we've been friends for years and years even before high school. I'm Beta Keaton's daughter, didn't you know that?

No, I didn't!

"Beta Keaton seems in his late thirties," I mumbled. He looked too young to have a twenty-one year old daughter.

She laughed. "Oh you know werewolves always look young," she said with a wave of her hand as though it were old news.

I felt a little bit better about Tonya, Sandra and Avery being so jealous and angry but I also felt overwhelmed. The triplets had a whole life that I felt I wasn't privy to. Their time with me was like a private little fantasy world. I sighed.

"You're sobering up," said Alex softly, walking in with a tray of snacks: brownies, chips with dip, soft pretzels and mini croissants some filled with Nutella and others savoury with crab salad.

"Where'd you get all this?" I chuckled.

"Charlista picked some stuff," Alex said.

"Charlista?" I asked.

"Our housekeeper," said Moxie, Roxie's younger sister, who walked into the kitchen at that moment followed by Calix and Felix.

"Chasity! Are you ok?" Calix asked, coming up to me and stroking my hair.

"Baby! Where'd you run off to? What happened? I missed you," Felix said rushing forwards and kissing my forehead over and over again.

"It took you ages to notice I was missing," I said in a small voice.

Felix grinned at me. "Fine. Let me have it then," said Felix, opening his arms wide.

"*What*?!" I squeaked, surprised at his words.

Felix chucked. "Yell at me," he said. "It'll make you feel better."

"No," I said stiffly, shaking my head.

He pressed his forehead to mine. "Chasity," he grumbled in his deep voice. He pressed his lips to my forehead again.

"Come on, little party animal, it's time to go home," said Calix, winking.

Alex carried me to the car holding me bridal style cradling my head to his chest. I sat in the back seat in silence. Alex drove. Felix was in the passenger seat and Calix was next to me.

"So you're not gonna talk to us?" Asked Calix. Felix and Alex looked back at me.

"Don't you have girls to be winking at, Calix?" I said.

Calix frowned.

"And Felix don't you have any more parties thrown by your exes to go to or attended by your exes? I asked.

Felix squirmed a little.

"And Alex don't you have more pack knowledge to share with a crowd of admiring girls while I stumble off by myself at the party you three wanted me to go to?" I said. Alex looked at me through the rearview mirror.

"The three of you were so *furious* when my hair tie smelled like another guy and yet I'm supposed to be fine and dandy with your huge fan clubs. Where are the boundaries? You discussed me with you ex Felix. You talked to her about me being your mate and about you proposing!" I snapped.

Alex was pulling into the driveway of the pack house.

Felix was quiet and so was Calix.

"Aren't you even going to say anything?" I asked.

"You're just a little tip hungover and you're emotional. Let's all go to sleep. Everything will be fine," said Alex.

I opened the door forcefully and hopped out into the snow. I sank into the crunchy snow. It was knee-deep! I shivered. I had on a thin pair of stockings under my mini black dress.

"*Chasity!*" Alex called, upset that I had not waited to be carried but I was already moving as quickly as I could through the mounds of snow and shivering all the way. I climbed the porch steps with some difficulty and went to my room, my downstairs bedroom.

Felix followed. "You *know* you're not allowed in here by yourself since the kidnapper showed up," he said in a no nonsense tone.

"I want to take a bath in my tub that's all," I said quietly.

"There are many bathtubs upstairs, Chasity," said Felix blankly.

"I just need a minute. Just *one* minute," I said. My wolf was angry at me. She felt I was acting childishly. Felix seemed exasperated. Calix seemed indifferent to how upset I was about the winking. Alex was treating me like a petulant child. The Luna hated me and I *knew* she had something to do with that kidnapper. Felix sighed.

"Ok," he said and he left the room.

I was not certain what madness gripped me. Perhaps it was the alcohol, my childhood issues, the triplets' exes harassing me, me being afraid of the Luna who I was made to still live with. I did not know what was the exact cause. It was probably the combination. When I had first come to live with the triplets and their parents when I was only nine, I would go sit on the roof to feel closer to my parents. I felt we were looking at the same moon and thinking of each other. I would go up to the attic and climb out onto the roof to be closer to the moon and thus closer to my parents. I left the bathroom and went up the stairs. There were two pack guards right outside my bedroom door probably put there by Felix. They nodded respectfully to me and I did the same. I crept up the staircase. I could hear the triplets discussing something. I could even differentiate their voices by the intonation.

"She's just stressed, it's all too much for her…" said Alex.

"What do we do?" Asked Calix.

"Can't we take her back to the beach? All this stress isn't healthy for her?" Felix suggested.

"We can't be like runaway Alphas always on vacation. We have so many pack matters to…" Alex's voice faded as I went up to the attic.

It was dusty there. I sneezed. It was spooky with all its ornaments and statues covered in white sheets. I found a light. It flickered on. It was dim but allowed me to see the familiar circular window. I pushed it open. There was a very small balcony there that was more for decor that functionality. I climbed onto it. It was creakier than I remembered. The moon was full. She was so beautiful. My wolf and I felt relieved instantly. I gazed at the beautiful moon surrounded by her silvery stars. I sighed. I got lost in it, the moon and her ethereal beauty. I lost track of time. I heard a sudden series of thud-like heavy footsteps. Felix come to freak out about me being missing for more than five minutes. I smiled. It was cold so I wouldn't mind Felix warming me up. Five minutes and I already missed the warmth and smells of the triplets.The heavy thuds got a little louder. I stiffened. The smell was not like Felix's smell. He smelled of sea salt and coconuts like an island. This smell was sharp, medicinal almost. A slimy colourless liquid dropped onto my shoulder. I recoiled. I turned around slowly and there it was.

A huge wolf crouched on the roof, saliva slipping down its jaw, as its heavy paws thudded on the snow-topped roof. I could see my breath in the cold air. My view grew hazy. I was in no position to shift and this wolf was at least twice my wolf's size. My wolf whimpered. She wanted me to scream for the triplets but I knew if I screamed the very agitated wolf might go for the jugular and rip my throat out. Before I had to make any difficult decision, human arms grabbed me and pressed a cloth to my mouth. Chloroform. Darkness engulfed me as the angry wolf faded from view.

Chapter 33: Chasity?

Third Person

"She's just really young, Felix. She doesn't have as much experience as we do. She's never been in a relationship with someone who was *not* her mate so she doesn't get how different that is. She thinks she actually has to worry about those random girls," explained Alex.

"Well it didn't help that Felix didn't tell her the party was being thrown by his ex!" Snapped Calix.

Felix growled lowly. Calix snarled.

"ENOUGH!" Said Alex, silencing his two younger brothers.

"It also didn't help that you winked at my ex and her little sister in front of Chasity!" Said Felix.

Calix looked guilty. "Those winks mean nothing. Chasity bears my mark. She's my fiancee!" Said Calix defensively.

"That's what Alex is talking about!" Said Felix. "Chasity doesn't *get it*. Tonight made her worried that she's competing with random girls."

"You shouldn't have forced her to go to the party," said Calix.

"*Me!*" Said Felix incredulously. "We all wanted her to go!"

"Yeah, we did," said Alex. "We wanted her to bond with the pack. It wasn't a bad idea in theory but Chasity has too much on her plate right now. Let's hold off on the introduction of her Luna responsibilities for now. After high school, in a couple of months, we'll get married and honeymoon back on the island. *Then* when she's more relaxed, we'll think about her role as Luna."

"Won't Mom be furious having to be acting Luna for Chasity for so long?" Asked Calix.

"No," scoffed Felix. "She'll be thrilled. Mom loves being Luna. Chasity, on the other hand, she's not into stuff like that."

Calix sighed. "Let's go get her. I'm tired," said the youngest, flopping over on the bed.

"She's between Felix and me tonight, right?" Added the youngest, yawning.

"Rub it in why don't you, Calix?" Grumbled Alex.

Felix laughed. "I'll go get her."

Calix jumped up. "We should pamper her. She might be less pissed then. I'm gonna run a bubble bath."

Alex smiled. He loved washing her hair for her. He went to help fix the bath. Felix bounded down the stairs, taking two at a time, feeling lighter now that they had argued it out and were done with it. It was always better to agree as triplets. Very few could understand the closeness among the three. Arguing amongst each other was literally like being at war with oneself. He nodded to the two pack warriors he had placed outside her room. They looked at him strangely when he went into her bedroom and then her bathroom. He came out again.

"Alpha Felix, Chasity went upstairs," said one of the pack warriors.

"I said to watch her," Felix said coldly, his blue eyes darkening.

"She said she was going to you, Alpha," said the other warrior, trembling a little.

Felix sighed. He ran back upstairs. The triplets had been hashing things out in Alex's room but the warrior said Chasity had gone to *him*. Felix smirked. She probably wanted her Felix. He checked his own room for her. It was empty.

"Baby?" He called, his voice husky.

Was she playing a little game with him? She did have a tendency to be a little tease that way. She hoped he would find her in his bath tub as that was what she had been griping about: bathing in some special bath tub. He slowly tiptoed towards the curtain that gave the person in his tub some privacy. He quickly pulled the curtain hoping to startle her and then hop into the tub too. His face fell. The tub was empty, spotless and dry as a bone, not used recently at all. He ran back downstairs ignoring the two warriors. He ran his fingers on Chasity's tub, also dry, not used recently. He checked the pack showers she used to use when she was servant. He looked in her little makeshift room. Empty. Calix's tub. Empty. She couldn't have snuck past them in Alex's room to get to his bathroom.

"Chasity!" Called Felix, getting worried. Her car was in the driveway and she hardly ever used it. She really wasn't the best driver and she had three alphas babying her so she was never without a lift.

"Chasity!" He called, following her smell this time. Alex and Calix came out of Alex's bathroom. They forgot to turn the faucet off for the bath they were running for their Chasity.

Felix felt out of breath, a little panicked.

"What's wrong?" Asked Alex.

"I don't know yet," muttered Felix, running up the stairs.

"Where's Chasity?" Asked Calix sounding as upset as Felix felt.

Felix followed her smell. She had gone up several flights of stairs. Where the *fuck* had she gone? Why was she doing this to him?

"Baby?!!!" Felix yelled. "CHASITY!!"

Alex picked up on her scent too. It led them to the attic of all places.

"Baby, are you hiding, come out?" Asked Felix.

"Chasity, we're sorry! The party was a dumb idea. No more parties until our wedding ok," offered Calix ripping the sheets off of every ornament and statue prompting showers of dust to rise up then fall.

Her scent went towards the circular window. Felix practically launched himself at it. He got onto the rickety balcony. She hadn't fallen, had she?

Oh Fuck! No, no, no, no, no, no, no, no, was all the Alpha could think.

"Felix, careful up there!" Called Alex.

"Chasity was up here!" Called Felix.

Alex quickly climbed onto the narrow balcony and peered downwards into the snow like Felix was doing.

Chapter 33: Chasity?

"She didn't fall, that snow is untouched," said Calix stepping out onto the balcony.It creaked under the weight of three huge alphas. Felix growled suddenly.

"What?" Asked Calix.

"Do you smell that?" Felix asked, his voice deep as his wolf came forwards so he was half-way between beast and man.

"Smell what?" Breathed Calix.

"Another wolf," growled Alex. Calix sniffed the air and snarled. The three turned around. There were unmistakable huge paw prints in the snow-topped roof and they was the smell of the wolf, a male. Felix growled. Alex sniffed again.

"Chloroform," whispered Alex, his eyes tearing up of their own accord. He was terror-stricken now.

Chasity! He tried to mind-link with her but silence. She was probably still knocked out and by the time she came to she would be too faraway to mind-link. Alex roared. The whole night felt it. Bats squeaked, owls hooted, birds flew out from their night perches. The ice cracked and the snow topped mountains shook.

Felix was prowling around on the roof trying to find at what point they had left with Chasity so he could tail them further. Calix was sitting in the snow on the rooftop just staring out at nothing in particular. Felix got frustrated. There was no exit point. He could not decipher where they went from here. He jumped down from the highest floor to the snow below landing on his feet. Alex and Calix followed him.

"We need to put this whole place on lock down. No one leaves or enters the pack lands until we find her!" Felix said, his eyes black.

"What if she just went to Mina or Tina's," said Calix hopefully.

"Those girls were drunk out of their minds," said Alex. "Why would she do that? And how would that explain the foreign wolf smell."

Felix took a deep breath. He snarled. He roared, flipping one of the cars in the driveway over with his bare hands sending it smashing on top of the next car over. The alarms all went off. Their parents and several warriors and staff members ran outside.

"*Felix!*" Cried his mother. "What're you *doing*?"

"Where's Chasity?" Roared Felix.

"How would I know?" Screamed Luna Ronnie.

Felix stalked up to her.

"Felix, calm down!" Said Calix, his eyes turning black.

Felix lay his forehead against his mother's, his nose brushing against hers. There were tears streaming down his cheeks. "Tell me now," he whispered, his voice cracking. "Tell me right now if you have *anything* to do with this. Tell me immediately and give her back to me and I won't be angry. This is the last chance to just admit it if you've done anything," breathed the Alpha.

Luna Ronnie was crying too, shaken although Felix's hold on her was gentle.

"How *dare* you insinuate anything of the sort?" She whispered fiercely back. "I'm not going to stand here and pretend to care deeply about that girl but I love you boys. You are my life and I'd never hurt you. How do you know she didn't just leave?"

"There is a foreign scent on the roof intermingled with Chasity's and the smell of chloroform. She did *not* just leave. We both know that," said Felix softly but ferociously.

Alex was looking at his mother's expressions carefully. He felt his father put his hands on his shoulders. His father pulled him into a hug.

"We're gonna find her ok?" Said the former Alpha.

"Felix, stop it, Mom has nothing to do with this," said Calix grabbing his brother. Felix sniffled. He hugged Calix. Calix could feel the alpha's tears falling onto his shoulder.

"Let's not blame each other, let's just look everywhere until we find her," whispered Calix comfortingly. He felt Felix nod his head. The eldest Alpha, Alex, came over and wrapped his arms around his two younger brothers. They stood like that, huddled together, in the snow for a few moments of relative peace before all the chaos to come.

Chapter 34: Kidnappers

Chasity

Please, this could not be real. I woke up on a hard cold metal floor. I was inside of a van. I could not scream. I had been gagged and bound. I struggled against my restraints. I tried to shift. I could not. There was a pain in my neck. I had a silver choker on, I realised. Tears welled up in my eyes. It burned! The silver! The ropes cut into me.

Felix! FELIX! I tried over mind-link since I could not get any words out with my mouth stuffed with a cloth and tape placed over it.

ALEX! CALIX! HELP ME! I screamed over mind-link. Who knows how far away they were. The marks on my neck were painful. I knew their marks hurt too. We were bonded deeply that way.

Please don't think I ran away. Please don't think I ran away. Please don't think I ran away. I chanted this over mind link over and over like a mantra. They had to know that I did *not* run away. I loved them so much.

The van came to a sudden halt. The door to the back opened. A tall figure loomed over me. A voice. Distinctly male. So deep and gruff. He was barking orders in a different language. I spotted a tattoo on the man's ankle, a snake curled around a full moon. Had this man been the huge wolf or the one that grabbed me?

"You sure this is her?" Said a voice.

"Yeah the triplet's mate," said a higher pitched voice.

"Boss will be so pleased," said the voice.

"I want the full amount before I hand her over," said the higher pitched voice.

"No, half now, half later," said the deeper voice.

"Are you out of your mind? Do you know what I risked to get her?" Said the high-pitched voice. "I want my money *now!*"

After!" Bellowed the deeper voice.

Snarls and growls.

"The other guy before me got his neck snapped by lover boy, the crazy one, her middle alpha. Felix killed him in a matter of seconds. He *died trying to bring her to you!*" Said the higher pitched voice.

Hearing Felix's name thrown around like that made my heart ache. I suddenly felt nauseated. I felt awful. I needed help. I wished I were draped over Felix's chest with Alex and Calix on either side of me. I couldn't stop picturing Calix's dimples, Alex's baby blue eyes and Felix's devilish grin. My heart soared a little even if I was only with them in my imagination.

Heavy footsteps resounded in my ears. I was hoisted upwards. I tried to kick and scream but to no avail. I was bound too tightly. Everything was a blur. Someone slung me over his shoulder like I was a sack of potatoes. I was carried out of the van and into a building. I squirmed in the person's arms until he barked at me, "If you don't hold still, I'll have to knock you out." I went limp in the person's arms. He swung me off his shoulder and onto a cold hard surface that was higher off the ground than I had expected. I was on a table. A wooden dining room table. I glanced around. I was in a high-ceilinged room with stone walls. I could hear the crackling of a fire nearby and felt b]us warmth. I heard the scraping of knifes and forks against ceramic. Someone was eating dinner. I could hear them gulping mouthfuls of liquid, probably wine, and eating food. I smelt steak, medium rare, tinged pink in the middle.The smell upset me. The nausea. I began to thrash about.

"What's wrong with her?" Asked the deep voice.

"She's suffocating!" Said the higher one.

"Do something!" Commanded the deeper voice.

Chapter 34: Kidnappers

The duct tape was ripped off my lips and my gag was removed. My mouth felt grainy and dry. I coughed. The cough sounded hoarse. I was surprised how little power I had in my voice.

"What do you want?" I asked, my voice barely a whisper.

Someone was loosening the ties on me. I was able to sit up. My wrists were still bound behind my back and my ankles were tied. I felt a small amount of relief. I looked at my kidnappers.

The higher pitched voice belonged to a skinny man with a gaunt pointy face, straggly greasy hair and beady eyes. He was human. What was he doing with werewolves? He must have been the one with the chloroform. The other was clearly a werewolf. He was tall, broad shouldered and heavily muscled. He had a sleeve of tattoos on his left arm and a few tattoos on his right. His ankle bore the snake with the full moon tattoo. He had hazel eyes from what I could tell, maybe green, tanned skin and brown cropped hair. His jaw was strong. Something about his demeanour reminded me of Felix, making me think he was tough and even violet yet good-hearted deep down. Deep deep down. He *was* a criminal. I fixed them with a blank stare. There was no need to antagonise them. I had seen tons of movies where the kidnapped person threatens the kidnappers. I didn't think that was smart.

"Hey, I just want to know what you want?" I asked again, still a whisper but clearer. "Money?"

The Felix-like one smirked. He was less cute. I frowned. My heart hurt. Maybe my mind had made up their resemblance as a coping mechanism.

"What's your name?" I asked the Felix-like one. I looked at the human.

"Maurice," said the human. I smiled.

"Shut the fuck up. Shut the is my first name and fuck-up is my last name," said the Felix-like one.

Fuck-up was the perfect name for him but I couldn't insult him. I laughed very feebly. He gave me the weirdest of looks. I looked around at the place. It was a castle based on the design, stone walls, high ceilings, huge brick fireplaces. The kidnappers already had money. Or at least their boss did. I had to ask.

"Are you going to kill me?" I asked nonchalantly. I had to be prepared. The Felix-like one widened his eyes and looked at me like I was crazy. Maurice just stared.

"No, we just have to keep..." began Maurice but the Felix-like one nudged him in the stomach.

Maurice grimaced. "Dante," he groaned. Dante. I smiled, a bit smug.

"Dante," I said.

Dante fixed me with a sneer.

"Listen, you little brat, no one is going to coddle you here like your love-sick alphas do so enough chit-chat unless you want the gag back in," Dante growled.

I blinked at him. I did not think they were hired to kill me. They would not have hastily removed the gag when I was spluttering on it if the end goal was my death anyway. They had to keep me alive for some reason. I nodded to show Dante I understood. He seemed even more upset that I was behaving.

"Should we feed her?" Asked Maurice.

"She'll be fine. One day won't kill her," Dante grumbled.

"May I have some water?" I asked.

There was an empty wine glass on the table. Dante picked it up and dipped it into a murky fish tank nearby that seemed devoid of fish. He offered me the greenish brown water. I did not react to it. I had been through much worse. Dante seemed to think I had spent my whole life being coddled by my Alphas and would crack over some grimy water. He was sadly mistaken. I was convinced he was the huge white wolf. I had gone hungry and been dehydrated before. Dante swung me over his shoulder. We were heading up a walled flight of steps. There was a small room at the top with a cot and a simple bathroom attached. He threw me down on the cot. He took a dagger and cut the ties on my wrists and ankles.

"I'm doing this so I don't have to help you use the bathroom. There are no windows in the bathroom or here in the bedroom. You will be fed periodically. If you rush the door when I open it, the restraints go back on!" Threatened Dante.

I nodded emphatically.

"My name is Chasity," I said.

Dante snorted with laughter. "I would hope so."

"Do you know my parents?" I asked eagerly. I had to ask. I knew it was a long shot but...

Dante's sneer faltered a little but quickly recovered. I caught it though.

Chapter 34: Kidnappers

"When was the last time you saw them?" I whispered intensely.

"Shut up!" Growled Dante, his eyes turning black. I stiffened.

I sighed. I felt drained but unable to sleep. It was cold. I needed my alphas' body heat. I sighed. As soon as Dante left, I scoured the room for any weak point. No windows. Only door was the exit. The door between the bathroom and bedroom had actually been ripped off its hinges. I wondered if we were still in my alphas' pack lands. If the Luna was behind this, would she actually want me dead? Who would her boys marry if she got rid of me? I tried to mind-link again, calling Alex first a few times, then Calix and then Felix. Silence. I was far away or perhaps I had been injected with wolfsbane or something that prevented my lupine abilities from working well. I etched a notch into the bed frame. I sighed. I fell into a fitful sleep. I tossed and turned all night. I woke up to wave after wave of nausea. I vomited and vomited in the bathroom.

"What's wrong with her?" Snarled Dante outside my door. "Is it contagious."

I retched again. I had never felt this way. I groaned.

They went away for a while. The door opened. Dante threw a box at me.

"Pee on it," he said offhandedly.

I glanced at the box. It was a pregnancy test!

Chapter 35: The Lucky Toad

Third Person

The triplet alphas had every pack member on high alert. Every warrior was scouring the pack lands for Chasity. The pack lands were on lockdown. No one could enter or leave without explicit permission from the Alphas. There was a curfew mandated by the Alphas. Beta Keaton was displeased. Something very upsetting had made his way to his desk this morning, the first morning after Chasity's disseverance.

"What is this, Alpha?" Said Beta Keaton, beseeching his former Alpha Romeo handing him the list.

Alpha Romeo scanned the list of suspects. He sighed.

"Roxie and Moxie are suspects!" Whispered Beta Keaton fiercely. "We're friends, Romeo. Our children are friends. Felix and Roxie used to date. They were at her party last night."

"That's why the girls are suspects, Keaton," said Romeo tiredly. "It's nothing personal. The party was the last event Chasity was seen by many at. And *all* of the triplet's exes are suspects. Even the party planner, Ronda, who they never dated! She just kinda envied Chasity."

Keaton took a deep breath, arms akimbo, displacing his blazer backwards.

Chapter 35: The Lucky Toad

"The triplets accused us even," said Romeo.

"You and the Luna?" Asked Keaton.

Romeo nodded sadly.

"Losing a mate is tough. It's... there's nothing worse than that..." said Keaton his voice cracking up. He had had his daughters with his second chance mate. His original mate had met an untimely end.

Romeo clapped Keaton on the back. "They're not real suspects. They'll just be interviewed."

"I *have* a mate!" Snapped Roxie, glaring at the private investigator flanked by pack warriors.

He had brought in because he was the best. His name was Danny Saunders. He was almost as tall as the triples with chiselled features, a five o' clock shadow, an impressive moustache, dark eyes, thick eyebrows, full lips and shaggy wavy brown hair. He was in his mid-thirties. He had been a P. I. For the past decade and a pack warrior for seven years before that, from the day he turned eighteen.

"Ok, Ms Roxie, I know, just answer the question, please," said Danny.

"I would *never* be jealous of Chasity. Felix and I were happy for each other when we found our mates," Roxie said, sniffing.

"The question was did you tell Chasity to go to the landing bathroom knowing full well that Sandra, Tonya and Avery were waiting there to confront her?" He repeated getting tired of this.

"Well... yeah," she admitted.

"And why would you do a thing like that, Roxie?" Asked Danny.

"Because I... I don't know. Chasity was never popular before and now she's like this... superstar or something. It was annoying. I just thought it'd be funny if the girls ruffled her feathers. They were not gonna hurt her. *No violence.* Just bitchy insults. And well she vomited on them so she got them pretty good," Roxie said, snickering.

Danny looked at her like the moron he thought she was.

"Ok, thank you, Ms Roxie, send the next person in," said Danny.

Roxie strutted off in her five-inch heels while Ronda stalked in, on her six-inch heels. Roxie gave her a scowl. Ronda gave Roxie a smirk. Cattiness abounded in this investigation. Ronda sat down, flinging her new platinum hair extensions, gazing intently at the handsome P.I. There wasn't three of him but he was eye candy nonetheless.

"How would you describe Chasity?" Asked Danny.

"She's... great," said Ronda, older and wiser than Roxie. "She's pretty, very smart. She's a bit shy. Can't fault her for that. She's young. She's growing into her personality," said Ronda with a smile.

Danny grinned. "Do you think Chasity loves the triplets?"

Ronda twitched a little. "Yeah... yes... they're all very in love." She took a deep breath rocking on her chair a little.

"Calix called Chasity his goddess, isn't that cute?" Asked Danny.

Ronda narrowed her eyes but quickly smiled. "Aww," she cooed.

Chasity

I had to pee on the stick. I wanted to know too. It had a price on it. I gasped and then a huge smile spread on my face. My kidnappers were amateurs. They did not remove the price sticker which contained the name of the pharmacy they ran out and got this from. *Divine Lupine*. An overpriced store that sold everything: hair and makeup products, snacks, perfumes, feminine products and it contained a mini-pharmacy in the back. There were only two branches of *Divine Lupine* on our pack lands. One was in the main town area. It was super busy with long lines and she-wolves shoving each other over bargain beauty products. I couldn't picture Dante going there. The other was in the more secluded suburbs where rich pack members lived in a mall. The mall outlet was much emptier. No lines really. Friendly staff. No shoving. I was in driving distance of that mall most likely. I highly doubted Dante had a pregnancy test just lying around unless he was a humungous ladies' man and even then a pregnancy test was a stretch. He must have bought it *after* I started vomiting. That meant I *should* be able to mind-link my alphas but I couldn't. Hmm. Had I been injected with wolfsbane or silver or something. Were the walls in here specially designed to prevent mind-linking? Did that technology exist? My head hurt. My pregnancy test was ready.

Chapter 35: The Lucky Toad

I was so nervous. I wished my alphas were here. I pictured them here with me. Felix would pace up and down, anxious but hoping I was pregnant, anything that tied me to him forever was great in his book. Calix would be looking at me with his big blue eyes wide and trying to peak at the test before I was ready to say what it said. Alex would scold Calix for peaking and would tell me to announce it whenever I felt comfortable and whether I was pregnant or not they'd be happy. I almost cried thinking about their would-be reactions. I looked at the test. I sank onto the floor, my back and head against the cold tiles. *We* were kidnapped. I was pregnant. What had I gotten my baby into?

Third Person

Felix broke down the bar nailed to the doubles doors of *The Lucky Toad*, the Casino where Chasity's parents had ranked up a huge gambling debt. He knew they were in there. He and his brothers didn't need back up. They were the triplet alphas. He walked into the place through the double doors, Calix and Alex flanking him. The gamblers stiffened. These were regulars, with bleary eyes and empty wallets. The dimly lit casino held about two dozen people though it seemed shut down from the outside. Perhaps, they knew the alphas were coming.

A lady in a tiny server's outfit came scampering over, teetering over the edge of her platform heels. She had a tray at her side and an elaborate undo, her bleached blonde hair piled on top of her head. She looked mid-forties but she was a she-wolf, she could literally be one hundred and still look like that.

"What can I get you fellas?" She said in a croaky voice that betrayed decades of heavy cigarette smoking.

Felix smirked. "The boss! Get me the boss!" He said, leaning closer to the waitress who recoiled and almost fell over in her high shoes. She scurried away, going up the stairs at the back as quickly as she could. Felix and his brothers sat at the bar. A skinny man with huge eyes and gleaming dark skin stared at them, wiping the same glass with a dish towel over and over clearly nervous.

"I think it's clean, buddy," said Calix, smiling.

The guy dropped the dish towel, and then the glass. It shattered. The guy flinched and hurried to pick it up. Alex looked at the staircase in the back. The waitress was picking her way down carefully. She looked dissolved. Her piled up hair was coming down all around her. Her mascara was running. Her uniform was askew. She'd been manhandled, not badly but still. Alex already hated the boss. Maybe he needed to be manhandled.

"The boss will see you now, Alphas," she squeaked.

They nodded at her and headed up the stairs. There was a long hallway and only one door had a name on it, etched into a gold-plated plaque. *Chance.*

Just one name.

They didn't know. The office was crowded. A huge desk was filled with knick-knacks and papers, some yellowed and coffee stained. There were lucky charms everywhere, the superstitious kind, not the cereal. Although Calix would not have been surprised if there'd been cereal lying about somewhere. The office was crammed with stuff and the floor was dirty and sticky. The alphas were disgusted. They heard squeaking. Mice.

A huge man was behind the desk. He was tall and broad with a huge moustache. He was wearing sunglasses in a dark office in a dark casino. He had salt and pepper straight hair and wore white shirt with a black tie. His blazer was too small for him, straining over his protuberant stomach. He did not evoke a sense of fear or malice or evil. He seemed like a middle school principle or something with a dirty office.

"Chance?" Asked Felix.

"Alpha Felix!" Said Chance as though thrilled.

"Sit!" Said Chance.

"We'd rather stand," said Alex.

Felix immediately noticed the tattoo on the back of Chance's hand. The moon with the snake curled around it.

"What does that tattoo mean?" Asked Alex.

"Snakes shed their skin. The moon waxes and wanes. Renewal. Death and life. Life through death. You have to fall apart, die almost, to be renewed, reinvigorated, reborn," said Chance.

Alex had not been expecting all that.

"Look, you already know why we're here. Chasity is missing. She's our Luna. This is the second kidnapping. The first was unsuccessful. Someone has been after her ever since we started asking questions about her parents who fled town running from someone. All of her parents' old friends and people at their old haunts have that same tattoo. So save me a lot of trouble and just tell me everything you know," said Alex.

"The tattoo is from a... group of like minded individuals. A coven if you will. Werewolves who practice witchcraft. The group is called the Furina Ornata after the moon snake. All members have the tattoo. There's about two hundred members last time I checked. There could be a million reasons why someone would kidnap a Luna. The most farfetched being related to my tattoo. And most importantly, I would never harm Chasity," said Chance, taking off his shades and looking at us seriously. "I'm her grandfather."

Chapter 36: Chance

Chasity

Now that I was pregnant, I had to survive, no matter what. For my baby and for my triplet alphas. I had no idea which of the triplets was precisely the father but was that even possible to figure out? Identical triplets had the same DNA. It didn't really matter. They would all be the father. I sighed. My head was throbbing. I wish Alex were here to massage my scalp. I got up from the tiled floor and a horrifying thought hit me. What did the kidnappers want in terms of my pregnancy? They had gotten me the test. Did they hope I was or wasn't pregnant or did they not care? If the found out I was pregnant would they be easier or harder on me? I hadn't thought this through. I threw the pregnancy test in the toilet after snapping it in half. I flushed it. Thankfully it went down.

Dante came into the bathroom without even knocking.

"Hey!" I said indignantly not able to fake nonchalant anymore now that I was worried for my baby.

He looked impassive. He stared at me.

"Are you or Arne't you?

"What?" I asked.

"Pregnant?!" Asked Dante.

"Does it make a difference?" I asked, trying to gauge his reaction.

"This isn't a game!" Snapped Dante.

A game? A game!

"I'm the one who's kidnapped! I'm the one who's sick and vomiting! Why would I ever think it was a game?!" I yelled, not able to play it cool anymore.

Dante sneered. "Are you pregnant yes or no?

I fixed him with s glare. "When my Alphas get here, they're gonna rip you in half!" I said softly.

Dante glared back. He left the room and slammed the door. I breathed a sigh of relief for the time being.

Third Person

"Chasity's grandfather?" Asked Felix, narrowing his eyes.

The man named Chance nodded.

Felix, Alex and Calix looked at him incredulously.

"So where have you been all this years?" Asked Alex, glaring at Chance.

Who would leave their granddaughter up to chance for so many years?

"I've been *here*," said Chance, gesturing all around the room. "Running the Lucky Toad Casino!" He said grandly, his arms wide and outstretched.

He's insane, said Alex over mind-link to his brothers. *That's why he didn't come to look for Chasity even though he was nearby.*

Calix and Felix looked the eldest alpha and nodded.

"I'm not insane, Alex," said Chance slowly with a wide smile. The triplets recoiled a little. Was that a coincidence?

It's probably just a coincidence! Said Calix.

His elder brother nodded.

"No, it's not, I can hear you loud and clear," said Chance.

The triplets were flabbergasted.

"How is that possible?" Demanded Felix.

"The witchcraft?" Offered Alex. "From the group you belong too?"

Chance nodded. "The Furina Ornata allows each of its members to tap into...special skills...my special skill is being able to listen to any mind-link within a certain radius. I can't explicitly read minds but I can sense the truth and a lie with perfect accuracy and I can listen in on private mind-links," said Chance, smiling.

"Ok, congrats, back to Chasity," grumbled Felix. "You're her grandfather how? Who's Dad are you? Her Mom's or her Dad's?

"I'm Chalice's father. Chalice was Chasity's Mom," said Chance sadly.

"Was?" Asked Alex. "So you know for sure Chasity's parents are...no longer with us?"

Chance sighed.

"My daughter Chalice had her demons. She wasn't perfect. The order of the Furina Ornata was trying to help her. The order helps people with a variety of things including addictions. She was never able to successfully detox. She kept falling back by the wayside. Her mate, Chasity's Dad had better luck detoxing with our order but Chalice's relapses were his relapses since they usually did everything together. Mates can be our saving grace or our Kryptonite, you know," said Chance sadly.

"Ok, we already know her parents were drug addicts," said Felix impatiently.

"Felix," whispered Alex fiercely, nudging his younger brother.

Chance chuckled.

"You're passionate about my granddaughter! I'm glad," said Chance

"This doesn't add up. Where have you been, Chance? Chasity's childhood sucked and I'm sure you knew that if you knew her parents were drug addicts. Didn't you wonder where Chasity was when her parents skipped town?" Calix questioned.

Chance sighed. "When my daughter ran off, leaving Chasity, I followed her. I was trying to track her down and bring her back. I tailed them for a while," said Chance.

"And?" Asked Felix.

Chance looked away from the triplets sadly. "And...unfortunately when I finally caught up to them...they were..." Chance paused to take a deep shuddering breath.

Chapter 36: Chance

"Please, I know it's hard but please tell us Chance. It's not too late for Chasity even if it was too late for her mother," said Alex, gently, pleading with the older werewolf.

Chance nodded, collecting himself. His eyes were filled with tears. He took a deep breath. Calix patted him on the shoulder.

"I found them finally... I caught up to them in a motel miles and miles from here. I remember it so vividly because it was Christmas Morning. You know that song," Chance said, his eyes glazing over.

"Walking in a Winter Wonderland by Dean Martin. It's an old Christmas song. Beautiful. Chalice's favourite. It's so funny... the synchronicity..."said the older werewolf, chuckling sadly. He was motioning everything he did with his hands and his hands were trembling.

"I... I was listening to that song on the radio... Walking in a Winter Wonderland... as I switched off the car and took the key out of the ignition but the song never stopped!" Exclaimed Chance.

What? The triplets were confused. Chance laughed humourlessly.

"The song was still playing on the same radio station but somewhere upstairs in the motel! Chalice! Listening to the same Christmas song as her Dad on the same day at the same time on the same radio station!" Exclaimed Chance, tears beginning to fall down his cheeks.

"That's wonderful," said Calix sincerely, trying to encourage the werewolf. "So you followed the music?"

"Right you are Calix, right you are!" Said Chance.

Chance could tell them apart! The triplets were impressed.

"I followed the faint music. It grew steadily louder. There was an echo to it. The Marigold Motel not the hotel, the seedy motel. I went up the rickety side steps. Found one of the doors to the rooms left open. The music was coming from there. I walked in. The place was small and reasonably clean, nothing spectacular. Minimal Christmas decorations. I followed the Christmas Carol to the radio. I turned it off. I shouldn't have turned it off. The music has been off ever since. When I turned a corner, Chalice and her mate were sitting, staring at the table in the kitchenette. Eyes wide. Just staring. There were fang marks on their necks," Chance said, lost in the story and shaking.

"Vampires?" Asked Felix worriedly.

"Snake bites. Furina Ornata. The venomous Moon Snake. The order has special snakes that are a thousand times more venous than usual," said Chance.

"So it *was* the order! It *is* something to do with the tattoo!" Exclaimed Alex.

"No... not quite," said Chance. The triplets were confused. "We give snake bites on purpose. The venom makes us stronger when administered correctly and under supervision. That's how I got my powers. They were seeking help to get stronger. To fight whoever was chasing them!" Chance explained.

"But?" Prompted Felix.

Chance gulped and wiped the sweat on his brow with a handkerchief.

"But the Furina Ornata member who had come to administer the snake venom was dead on the ground too with a bite bark on the neck. Someone had come upon them and interfered with the ritual. The person or people they were running from interrupted the venom ritual so they couldn't take the antidote and finish it. They died with venom flooding their systems unchecked. The antidote is usually kept in a metal briefcase with our symbol on it. I found the briefcase on the floor open and the antidote missing. Someone took the antidote and ran off. We usually bring many vials of antidote. The person took all, about half a dozen and left. Or people. The administrator of the venom, our member, she was dead on the ground near the empty briefcase with the snake still crawling about," Chance finished his story in hushed tones.

The air was heavy. So Chalice and her mate were trying to get strong enough to fight back whoever was threatening them. Ironically, in the middle of a ritual to get stronger, that someone accosted them, took the antidote, leaving them to die, poisoned with venom but without the life-saving antidote. The person left the snake behind and even the antidote administrator was killed. More questions. The triplets sighed. However they had one big answer for their lovely little Luna Chasity. Her parents really were dead.

"So... what did you do after that, Chance?" Said Calix gently.

"I called the police. They came with an ambulance. I sat there and looked at Chalice staring at me sightlessly. She looked peaceful, hopeful, perhaps about the ritual. She herself had undertaken it successfully once before. We all did, numerous times. The ambulance people couldn't revive them. They were pronounced dead and so was the administrator. The people who were chasing them. I had no ides still who they were or where they went. I buried my daughter and her mate with my own money. I even included the administrator in the funeral. It was a quiet little funeral in Marigold," mumbled Chance.

"Why didn't you tell anyone?" Spat Felix, furious, his eyes darkening.

Chance looked shocked.

"Who was the administrator?" Asked Alex.

"The administrator was Deidre Binx, Chalice's friend, and a fellow order member who used the venom treatments for her skin and whatnot like a beauty regime. She wanted to be a model," said Chance.

Chills crept through the triplets.

"Deidre Binx isn't dead. She *is* a model, *was*. She's a retired supermodel. She's in LA, still schmoozing and again why didn't you tell anyone? Chasity? Our parents? You left her in the dark," Felix said.

Chance stared at him, dumbfounded. "The real Deidre Spinx is dead. I know that with a certainty. I don't know who that woman that models and has her name and looks just like her is. She's not Deidre Spinx. I was never able to catch her and talk to her. She eluded me for years and I grew tired. I don't think she actually killed anyone. Just benefitted from the death of Deidre. Took her spot in the modelling agency. Doppelgängers? I really don't know. It's creepy but my focus was Chalice. I buried her and I did tell your parents. Alpha Romeo and Luna Ronnie. I begged them to bring her to the funeral. I spoke with them on the phone. They hung up. They ignored my letters. I used to show up at the pack house after I got back from Marigold. They got a restraining order against me. Look it's there!" Said Chance, pointing at the wall.

The triplets looked. It was there! Framed! Chance had framed his restraining order. Chance chuckled.

"Your asshole parents. I sent toys and letters and things. Tried to get to see Chasity. They kept returning them. They threatened me. Told me to stay away from Chasity. The Luna blamed me and my daughter for her step-brother's death. I ran my casino and figured when Chasity turned eighteen she'd do her own digging and come back to me. I became... depressed honestly. This room it's filled with stuff they returned. Stuff for Chasity," said Chance, tears in his eyes.

The triplets took a second glance at the room. Alex felt his heart constrict. Many of the knickknacks that he'd mistaken for ornaments were figurines and little dolls. There were teddy bears amidst the clutter, jewellery, clothes even. There were perfumes and antiques that would suit a girl's room. The papers on the floor and on the desk were scribbled haphazardly but he could make out many instances *Dear Chasity* and *I'm sorry* and *See You Soon* and *Merry Christmas* and *Happy birthday* and *Grandpa Loves you.*

Calix had not realised he was crying until he felt the wetness on his cheeks. Felix sat in one of the sticky chairs, breathing deeply. Alex remained standing up, more determined than ever. The eldest alpha would confront his parents about this atrocity. Get the two sides to this story but until then he wanted an Aly in Chance, his grandfather-in-law to be.

"Chance, I am so sorry for everything. I had no idea," said Alex.

Chance just nodded feebly. The gambling debt story? Was that all bullshit? Did Chasity's parents even owe money? Probably not. The casino was a family business.

"But I need you, Chance. We need you. Chasity needs you!" Said Alex.

Chance sat up a little straighter, adjusting his too-small blazer.

"Your ability to tell when people are lying! Your mind-linking reading! Those are amazing! Danny needs you! That's our private investigator. Team up with him, with us, please, for Chasity!" Said Alex.

Chapter 37: A Suitable Guardian?

Third Person

Chance was quiet. He took a deep breath.

"What about the restraining order?" Chance asked.

"We won't let you get arrested if you're with us. No showing up at the pack house without us. And after I have a talk with my parents we can think about getting the order waved," said Alex.

"I wanna help. I wanna help Chasity," said Chance, nodding. "Yes."

Alex and Calix grinned.

"Wait!" Said Felix. "So where is Alexi Franck and who is he to you?"

Chance laughed. He rummaged around in the inside pocket of his too-small blazer. He took out his wallet and brandished a card. He handed it to Felix. It was an ID with a picture of Chance and the name *Alexi Chance Franck*.

"Oh," said Felix. "Oh, it is you! But that doesn't make sense. Our... informant said you were awful and it seemed as though Chalice had a huge gambling dept," said Felix, narrowing his eyes at Alexi Chance Franck.

"She did have a huge gambling dept and I did yell at her a lot. She was a wayward child. I wouldn't say I was awful but maybe she thought so," said the old werewolf, sighing and wiping his sunglasses on his small blazer.

"Being a parent isn't easy," said Chance, with a faraway look in his eyes. "She was angry because I wanted her to straighten up. She was doing drugs and being wild. I tried to get custody of Chasity and after that, she swore up and down the street I was the devil. I wasn't able to get custody. I'm a single man and I own a casino. I probably don't seem like a good guardian either. Chasity stayed with her mother and father till they gave her to the Luna and Alpha and there was no way I would win against them. They run the pack lands."

Calix fidgeted uncomfortably.

"Why would Mom insist on raising Chasity if there was an alternative? Why would she subject Chasity to..." said Calix, looking at his brother, Alex.

"Subject Chasity to what?" Asked Chance.

The triplets stared at him. Felix looked furious. The middle triplet got up suddenly and stormed out of the office.

"What did I say?" Asked Chance.

Alex and Calix got up to follow Felix.

"Wait!" Said Chance. "I wanna help Chasity!" The werewolf scurried after the triplets, grabbing up a few teddy bears and a stack of letters.

Chance followed the triplet alphas to their parked car.

"Felix!" Alex called.

"I need to talk to our parents!" Felix said, getting in the driver's seat. Alex got in the passenger seat and Calix got in the back. Chance got in next to Calix.

Felix sped off, tires screeching. They were at the pack house in no time. Felix stormed in. The Luna and former alpha were with Beta Keaton and a tearful Roxie and an annoyed-looking Moxie.

"Felix! How could you think of me as a suspect?" Cried Roxie, tugging on his sleeve.

"Roxie, I don't have time for this. Get over it! Are you in jail? No. Good," said Felix.

"Felix!" Said his mother.

"Mother!" Hissed Felix. "Do you know this man?"

Felix pointed to Chance who was unsuccessfully hiding behind Alex

Chapter 37: A Suitable Guardian?

The Luna gasped and the former alpha got angry, knitting his eyebrows together.

"What is he doing here?" Bellowed Romeo, the former alpha.

"Yes, he's, he's a... a stalker!" Said Luna Ronnie.

"Is he or is he not Chasity's maternal grandfather?" Growled Felix.

Ronnie opened and closed her mouth like a fish. Romeo glared at his son.

"IS HE?!" Bellowed Felix in his Alpha voice making the whole room shake. Roxie and Moxie quickly left. Beta Keaton stood up to leave.

"Beta Keaton, stay, please," said Luna Ronnie.

"Go!" Whispered Felix fiercely in his alpha voice.

The Beta was compelled to leave, looking back apologetically at his friends.

Calix and Alex were quietly flanking Felix.

"Let's sit down," said Ronnie. "Let's compose ourselves."

"I wanna stand," said Felix, his tone deadly though his voice was soft.

"I'm gonna ask one more time, Mom, Dad, who is this man and what is his relation to Chasity?" Asked Felix, pointing at Chance who was shrinking against the wall.

Ronnie took a deep breath. She sat down in her armchair, hands on her lip, ankles crossed. "He is the father of Chalice and Chalice is..."

"Chasity's mother," answered Felix, laughing humourlessly. "He was telling the truth."

"He was not a suitable guardian," said Ronnie her eyes black.

"YOU WERE NOT A SUITABLE GUARDIAN!!!" Yelled Felix.

"You're out of control!!" Bellowed the former Alpha, flashing his black eyes.

"No! No, I'm not. What is *wrong* with the two of you?" Asked Felix, trembling slightly.

"Ok, let's say you didn't want him to have custody. Did you stop him from bringing Chasity gifts and cards and letters? Did you?" Demanded Felix, looking at them in disbelief.

"We just wanted nothing to do with him," said Ronnie.

"Oh my God, oh my God," Felix said, falling into an armchair and putting his hands over his face.

"Mom," cried Calix. "I don't understand! Why would you do that? Chasity was little. Why didn't you just let her have the comfort of a relative? You never liked her very much," Calix admitted, his eyes watering. "I didn't realise you... *hated her.* "

"No, no," said Ronnie, gulping. "I do not hate Chasity. She's not my cup of tea but..."

"What are you people saying?" Interrupted Chance, speaking for the first time.

Everyone looked at him.

"What do you mean? Are... are you... are you saying that Chasity wasn't happy here?" Asked the older werewolf, wiping his forehead with a handkerchief.

"She was a maid essentially cooking and cleaning to work off debts. Gambling and drug debts that my parents said they paid off," Alex said sadly, looking at the floor.

"We did pay them off!" Roared Romeo. "A quarter of a million dollars worth!"

"I could have paid that!" Hissed Chance, angry for the first time, his eyes black and his face hardening like he was about to shift.

Romeo stiffened. "Your casino is.."

"I know it ain't fancy but it makes money. I have my zombies. They do nothing but gamble. I could've paid that," said Chance, panting.

"Then why didn't Chalice go to you?" Shrieked Ronnie.

"BECAUSE SHE HATED ME!" Roared Chance, dissolving into tears. He flopped onto the couch and sobbed. Calix patted his shoulder.

"Um... uh... don't cry Grandpa. We'll get Chasity back! I promise. She's everything to me. She's my whole life! Then we'll make sure she's happy every single day and we'll dust off those gifts and letters and she'll be so excited to read them," said Calix, smiling with tears in his eyes.

Ronnie smiled at her favourite son, the youngest and sweetest of the triplets. He had a knack for de-escalating things. Chance stopped sobbing. The old werewolf took a few deep breaths. He seemed shocked but pleasantly surprised at being called Grandpa by the youngest Alpha.

Chapter 37: A Suitable Guardian?

"I can see Chasity whenever I want?" Asked Chance.

"Yes, Grandpa," said Calix sweetly.

"And she can stay with me for a bit?" Asked Chance.

Felix straightened up, resurfacing from his hands. "You can stay here for a bit to spend some time together if Chasity likes that idea but my wife doesn't do sleepovers," said Felix in a serious tone.

Chance looked annoyed but nodded.

"So what was it about Chance that made him an unsuitable guardian for Chasity?" Said Alex, his voice controlled but he was seething. His mother had kept Chasity as a main not a daughter and all the while, someone wanted her. Wanted to celebrate her birthday and buy her Christmas presents and treat her like a little girl not the hired help. Alex knew he and his brothers had been little jerks to Chasity growing up but they were children following the terrible example set by their parents. It had been Ronnie and Romeo's responsibility to give Chasity a decent childhood.

Ronnie was silent.

"She thinks I killed my own daughter and her mate, Ronnie's stepbrother," muttered Chance.

"*Prove* that you didn't!" Demanded Ronnie. Romeo folded his arms.

"*Prove* that *YOU* didn't!" Countered Chance, placing the blame back on them.

Ronnie and Romeo sighed. Calix closed his eyes, leaning back on the couch, wanting this argument to be over and wishing he could go cuddle up with his Chasity. He sighed.

Chasity

After I yelled at Dante and refused to reveal whether I was pregnant or not, he and the human accomplice left me alone for a while without water and food. Eventually there was a knock on the door.

"Please, don't rush the door if I open it ok! I'm trying to help you! Dante is in the next room and that's the only way to pass to get out. Flush the napkin down the toilet when you're done and hide the cup!"

The human. What was his name? Maurice!

"Maurice?" I whispered.

"Yeah," he mumbled. He peaked in leaving the door ajar. He threw a rolled up napkin at me. The bundle hit me in the shoulder. It was soft though and I was too tired to dodge it. I unwrapped it. A slice of pizza!

"Water! Please! Please! Please!" I began to say.

"Ok! Ok!" He said, putting his finger to his lips. He had it already. He passed me the small paper cup.

I drank the water in one gulp and looked at him with huge eyes. He took the cup back and shut the door. He returned with a refill. I got him to refill that ridiculously tiny cup three more times so I had five tiny cupfuls.

"That's enough," he warned, eyeing something I couldn't see warily.

"The pizza will make me thirsty!" I said softly.

He shrugged. I ate the slice quickly and flushed the napkin. He let me have two more cupfuls.

"You're the best, Maurice!" I whispered. "I... I won't let my Alphas kill you. I can make them reward you! Let's get out of here! What do you want money... or..."

Maurice cackled softly. "If you think I can fight Dante and win, you're touched in the head, Luna."

I was shocked to be called Luna by him. A human.

"What do you want from me?" I asked curiously.

"I don't know what boss wants," he said.

"Boss is not Dante," I said.

"Boss is Dante's Boss too. He's everyone's Boss," Maurice said.

"Boss is a werewolf," I said.

"I don't know. Probably," said Maurice.

What were these people smoking?

"You don't know what species your boss is?" I asked, my eyebrows raised.

"Boss is just a voice on the phone. And stuff happens as he dictates. He has so many people working for him. He was angry once with another one of us. I heard him on loudspeaker. He said,

"Your time with us is up. Your contract has expired!" Then, the guy was shot in the head with a sniper. Clean. Fell down dead. A few minutes of us being in the next room and the body was gone. Guy's room was cleaned up. No trace!" Said Maurice.

I thought about that. "So won't he know you're helping me?" I asked.

"He wouldn't be mad about that. He ends every conversation saying "Take good care of the Luna." I fed you and gave you water. That's good. Boss will be happy," Maurice said, pleased with himself.

Something about his giddy smiled reminded me of people who are in cults and how obsessed they become with the cult leader.

"Will Boss be mad at Dante?" I asked.

"No," said Maurice.

"But he's being mean to me," I protested.

"Yeah, but Dante is related to Boss, somehow," Maurice said.

I nodded. "Is Boss a man or a woman?" I asked.

"Boss is boss," said Maurice.

Oh, good, grief.

Third Person

"Let's assume neither our parents nor Chance killed Chasity's parents," said Alex with a sigh. "For the time being."

Felix nodded. Calix smiled. The Luna opened her mouth to argue.

Alex put his palms up to signal for everyone to calm down.

Everyone was silent, looking at the eldest alpha.

"We need to work together. We need to find Chasity. No one is here is totally blameless and our focus should be Chasity!" Said Alex.

There was a knock at the front door. A hulking pack warrior opened it to reveal the P. I., Danny. He approached the three Alphas who hired him, his briefcase in hand. The alphas, their parents and older man he had never seen stared at him.

Danny addressed the room, "I have a lead in Luna Chasity's case, Alphas."

Chapter 38: Deidre and her Doppelgänger

Chasity

Have you ever went to bed one place and then woke up somewhere completely different? I have.

I woke up in a bedroom with clean white walls and a cold marble floor. The bed was made of black wood and piled with white Egyptian cotton bedding. I could feel it. It was *so* soft. These were the same sheets my alphas had. The sheets made me even more homesick. The walls were lined with photographs, all of beautiful women, ethically different with varying skin and hair and eye colours but they all had symmetrical faces, high cheekbones and perfectly arched brows. They were familiar. I was looking at framed photographs of supermodels, all of them close-up beauty shots. The one above the head of the bed was the most familiar. What was her name again?

It wasn't as though I didn't like fashion but I had never been able to afford those sorts of things before I became the triplets' mate so I never paid that much attention to it. I wore whatever I had or whatever I was given. How had I been moved from the simpler room in the castle-like building to here? Was this room even in the same place? Had they drugged me so they could transport me more easily?

Chapter 38: Deidre and her Doppelgänger

I thought of the water and the pizza from Maurice. Had Maurice just pretended to "sneak" me the food? Perhaps it was all a farce just to get me to ingest the drug somehow. Maybe even Dante's anger had been a part of the trick. I felt like crying but I had to be strong. I just hoped they hadn't moved me off of the pack lands.

I sighed. The door opened. This sleek black wooden door didn't creak, it just smoothly opened on well-oiled hinges. Dante walked in and threw a plastic bag at me. It hit the bed with a soft thud.

"Where am I? How did I get here? Did you drug me?" I demanded. What if the drug was a substance that would hurt the baby?

Dante stared at me, drinking me in. It was strange. I realised why he reminded me so much of Felix. It was the way he looked at me, like he was agitated that I was there because me being around meant he could focus on nothing else. This was the old Felix though, the one who said I frustrated him but painted me secretly. The new Felix looked at me with intense but softer eyes, openly loving. I understood that sort of look a lot better now. Something was brewing underneath. This did not make sense though. Felix and I had a long history of intense emotions. I didn't know Dante from Adam and he didn't know me from Eve. Unless...

"Did you know Chalice?" I asked.

Dante just stared at me.

"You look at me like you recognise me," I said.

He actually flinched. "Don't ask questions!"

"Ok, Dante," I said softly. He responded to me saying his name with a sharp intake of breath. Something was up. I wanted my alphas and no one else but if I needed to be flirt a little bit to get away I would. I wanted my Alex, my Calix and my Felix. My wolf wanted them too. I wanted to tell them I was pregnant and be babied because of it. I sighed.

Dante sighed too. "Put on these," he said, gesturing to the plastic bag.

I looked inside. It was a simple white dress, knee-length with short sleeves. I was still in the party dress from the night I was kidnapped. My mascara was smudged all over my eyes and down my cheeks. I could use a shower and a change of clothes. There was underwear in the bag too, just a simple white cotton bra and panty. The sizes were all correct.

"Um, thanks," I said.

Dante shrugged. "The bathroom is through that door," he said, gesturing to the only other door besides the exit.

"Ok," I said.

"There's stuff in there for you to use, like soap, shampoo, conditioner, hair stuff, toothbrush, toothpaste. There's even makeup," Dante said. It was the most he had ever talked around me without scowling.

"I know you probably can't tell me what's going on but will I live to see tomorrow?" I asked, thinking of my baby and nervous about the white dress. Sacrificial? Dante had tattoo on his ankle that reminded me of the occult.

Dante flinched again. "Yes, Chasity. Fuck," he said, annoyed.

"Ok," I said sweetly. "Thank you, Dante. I won't hug you to thank you when I'm all gross like this." I watched his reaction carefully. He almost smirked but then caught himself. Gotcha. Was Dante the boss? Maybe he just wanted me for himself but that was insane. Felix would kill him without even asking a question first like he'd done with the other kidnapper. Dante was pretty big. He might be the same size at the triplets but there were three of them and one Dante. Dante did have the build of an Alpha though. Was he an Alpha? From where? There were many werewolves that were just really physically impressive despite not technically being Alphas, Betas or Gammas. There were rogues who were physiologically Alphas meaning if they gathered a pack they could easily be its Alpha but since they were lone they were called Sigmas. Maybe Dante was a really wealthy bored Sigma who'd decided to steal a Luna? That still didn't make sense.

I went to the bathroom and pleasantly found that I could lock the door. There were no other doors or windows in the bathroom. The walls and floors were covered in immaculately clean large white tiles. There was a huge semi-spherical bathtub and a shower. I didn't feel comfortable enough to soak in a tub though I could use the relaxation. I took a quick shower, washing and conditioning my hair. I detangled it. There were a lot of beauty and hair products. I used some of what I recognised and put on the white clothes. I didn't want to put on any makeup. I went back into the bedroom and sat on the bed. Dante came back and nodded in approval. I managed to smile.

He took my old clothes away to my annoyance. I felt cut off from my old life now in these unfamiliar clothes.

"Are you the boss?" I asked Dante.

He raised his eyebrows. "No," he said.

"Do you know the boss well?" I asked.

"Yes," he said.

"Do you..." I began but he cut me off.

"You'll meet her eventually," he said.

"Her!" I exclaimed.

Dante looked impassive. He left the room. A woman had organised my kidnapping. Why? Jealousy? Was she in love with the Triplets? Was it Luna Ronnie? If it was her, she might spare me if she knew I was pregnant with her grandchild. I kept silent about the pregnancy as I had not met "Boss" yet. Truth be told, I hated when employees referred to their superior as "Boss". It was vague. I'd rather reference their title. Whoever "Boss" was, I had no idea what "she" wanted, and I was more confused than ever.

Third Person

Danny addressed the room, "I have a lead in Luna Chasity's case, Alphas."

Flashback

Danny was growing tired of interviewing suspects who were merely catty jealous girls who were eyeing the triplets. That really didn't fit the profile when it came to who would be organised enough to capture the Luna. The next three suspects insisted on being interviewed all together. Sandra, Tonya and Avery. The triplets' most recent ex girlfriends. These girls were allegedly dumped for Chasity.

They strutted into the room on five inch heels. They were all different colour mini dresses. The redhead with piercing green eyes was Sandra and she wore red. She seemed to be the ringleader and was the eldest Alpha's ex. Tonya had olive skin and straight, black hair with deep brown eyes. She wore blue and was Felix's ex. Avery was a pixie-like blond with large blue eyes. She was dressed in yellow and was Calix's ex.

The girls all sat facing Danny. They had defiant looks on their expertly made-up faces. They did not utter a greeting. They just waited for Danny to say something.

"Hey girls, I'm the P.I. and my name is Danny. It's nice to meet you," he said, grinning. The girls nodded feebly and smiled faintly.

"So, were you the triplets' exes?" Danny asked.

"Yes," said Sandra the leader. "I am Alex's ex. Tonya used to date Felix and Avery was with Calix."

"What were the triplets like as boyfriends?" Inquired Danny.

"They were romantic, attentive," said Tonya.

"How long were you dating the triplets?" Danny asked.

"Maybe five weeks," Avery said, eyeing the tape recorder.

"Did you girls know Chasity while you were dating the triplets?" Asked Danny.

"Yeah, vaguely," said Sandra.

"She was just some girl, a servant that cooked and cleaned at the pack house," said Tonya.

"The triplets complained about her from time to time. Also, we had thought her name was Charity with an R not Chastity with an S because the triplets called her Charity," said Avery. The other two girls nodded.

"On the triplets' twenty first birthday, did you know it was also Chasity's eighteenth birthday?" He asked.

They all shook their heads.

"When did the triplets break up with you?" Asked the P. I.

The girls were getting agitated by all these questions and it showed. Good. Danny liked to agitate people a bit. They were more truthful that way. Too emotional to fabricate effective lies.

"They broke up with us on their birthday itself before the party," said Tonya.

"And it was via text!" Complained Avery.

"We had all been together deciding on what to wear for the party and we all get texts from them saying they're sorry but they've found their mate. They refused to say who she was so we were in the dark about their mate being Chasity. We went to the party anyway though we'd been unceremoniously uninvited. Chasity was there doing server work and we asked her if she knew who the triplets'

mate was and that little bitch lied to our faces," huffed Sandra, folding her arms.

"So you were quite upset and weeks later decided to confront Chasity at a different party on the night of her disappearance?" Danny asked with narrowed eyes.

The girls got nervous. "We just talked to her that's all!" Insisted Avery.

"We told her the truth," said Sandra with a satisfied smirk.

"What truth did you tell her?" Danny asked rubbing his chin.

"That the triplets complained about her constantly. How ungrateful she was, how unfriendly she was. She was always in a sullen bad mood. She was fat, poor, a loser," said Tonya.

"They used the words fat, poor and loser?" He asked.

Tonya fidgeted uncomfortably in her chair. "I'm paraphrasing."

"So after you confronted Chasity..."

They cut him off. "She vomited on us!" Blurted out Avery.

"And Alex came and took her away," added Sandra.

"That's it, nothing else happened," said Tonya.

"What did you girls think when you found out Chasity was missing?" Danny said.

"That she'd run off to find her parents!" Said Sandra immediately.

"Hmm so what were you girls doing around the time Chasity was allegedly kidnapped?" Asked Danny.

"We went to a bar, after the party, after we'd cleaned up a bit," said Sandra.

"We needed to destress," added Tonya. Avery smiled.

"Ok, what bar?" Danny asked. He would definitely find out if they had really been there or not.

"The Serpent's Tongue," said Sandra.

Danny stiffened. "That's a pretty rough crowd. You girls were comfortable there?"

Sandra shrugged.

"Anything interesting happened at this bar?" Danny said.

"Yeah!" Piped up Avery and her two friends stared at her. "We met a celebrity, a supermodel! Well, an ex supermodel. She's retired. Deirdre Binx. She was with this young hot guy. All those retired supermodels have boy-toys!" Said Avery with a laugh.

"Did you talk to her?" Ask Danny.

"Of course!" Said Avery. "I asked for an autograph. She talked to me for like fifteen minutes! The model looking boyfriend had left to go somewhere so we all got to chill at the bar with her!"

"Yeah," said Tonya. "We were too shy to talk to her before but we worked up the nerve at the bar."

"Before?" Asked Danny. "What do you mean?"

"Deidre knew the party-throwers' family and she was there at the party for a short time. She was there early! And left before the triplets and Chasity came and the whole vomit incident happened," huffed Tonya.

"What was a big celebrity doing hanging around?" Asked Danny.

"She said she was visiting an old friend," said Tonya.

"Did she say who?" He asked. They shook their heads. Danny knew Deidre and been the best friend of Chalice, Chasity's mother. How interesting that Chasity goes missing on the night Deidre swung into town. He knew who he would be interviewing next.

End of Flashback

The triplets were quiet, listening to the conversation playback on the tape recorder.

"The interesting thing," said Danny. "Is that Deidre was photographed at a Hollywood even that night."

"So the girls were lying about running into her?" Asked Alex.

Danny smiled. "Deidre was seen in LA that night but I also went through social media posts from the party attended by you three and the Luna and Deidre was in the background of one of them. Or at least someone who looked exactly like Deidre!"

The triplets fixed Danny with confused stares but Chance nodded as though it were all starting to make sense to him.

Chapter 39: A Tale of Threes

Chasity

I woke up in the immaculately white room in my spotlessly white clothes. I felt like I was in a weird dream. Everything monochromatic. It was a little difficult to look at. Sharp. It hurt my eyes. The only relief was the colours of photographs of all the supermodels in their vibrant makeup and clothing. I sighed.

I believed it was my third day of being kidnapped but I had become unsure. I felt that Dante or Maurice or "Boss" was putting something in my food. Something to make my senses and perception dull. There was no reason why I should not be able to connect with my three alpha mates if I was still on their territory.

Suddenly, I felt my neck throb. Ow! I felt the marks. The three silvery marks were burning. I rushed to the bathroom to look in the mirror. The marks were angry and red. There was something sticky on them like a salve. I gasped. I grabbed a piece of tissue and wiped off the cream. Someone had put something on my marks! I washed my neck with cool water. That soothed the burning. I kept treating the area and the searing pain slowly subsided. The skin was still irritated but it was just a bit pink.

My golden skin was back to looking sallow after it had begun to healthy. It wasn't gleaming anymore like it did on my trip with the triplets. I was back to shitty eating habits and stress, that's why. And now, I couldn't afford to be unhealthy! I gingerly touched my lower belly. I wondered how far along I was.

Dante came into my room just then and quickly rushed into the bathroom, his eyes wild. He must've thought for a moment that I'd escaped. I stared at him blankly. I was seething but I didn't want to start an argument.

"I'm right here," I said plainly.

"I can see that," he snarled.

Prick.

"Did you put something on my marks?" I asked softly.

Dante fidgeted uncomfortably. It was a very quick almost imperceptible movement but I spotted it. He did put something on them.

"Why would you do that?" I asked.

Dante just glared at me.

"You're a werewolf, you know just as well as anyone else those marks cannot be removed. They're permanent," I said, trying to stop my brown eyes from turning black with rage. How dare he try to remove my mates' marks. That was beyond heinous. I'd never even heard of such a thing.

Dante shrugged. "It was magic. I thought it would work," he said.

I must have lost my mind for a second. Temporary insanity. I lunged at him and tackled him to the ground, canines bared. I wanted to rip him to shreds.

Third Person

"Doppelgängers," said Chance, from where he sat at the booth in the cafe.

The triplets and Danny just stared at him. The triplets were sitting across from Danny and everyone's coffee remained mostly untouched besides the P.I. who was on his third cup.

"Doppelgängers!" Chance said. "Lookalikes!"

Silence.

"Celebrity doppelgängers?" Said Chance.

Chapter 39: A Tale of Threes

"You're not making any sense. Explain what you're talking about," said Alex sternly, knitting his thick naturally arched brows together.

"A doppelgänger is a lookalike, a double of a person..." began Chance.

"Look who you're talking to!" Snapped Felix. "We *know* what doppelgängers are. We get what you mean by lookalikes but so what?"

Felix widened his eyes and gestured to his identical triplet brothers.

Calix tried to be helpful. "Ok, so the retired supermodel who may or may not be dead has a doppelgänger!"

"Almost," said Danny. "Deidre is dead! Chance saw her body and I trust him. The first doppelgänger of Deidre, the first lookalike would be the one who went on to become a famous supermodel after the *real* Deidre died or rather was murdered."

"Good, ok," said Alex, nodding, complimenting Danny's deductive reasoning not the murder.

"So there's a third one then, since you have a pic showing one Deidre at the party we all went to with...Chasity," said Felix, sighing deeply. He had dark circles under his baby blue eyes and his skin was a bit paler than usual. Being apart from their mate had hit the middle triplet particularly hard.

"And you also have a pic showing Deidre at some bar, the Serpent's Tongue, around the same time," Felix surmised.

"So like us, there's at least three identical people," said Calix. "But, one of them is dead and they're all claiming to be the same person. Correct me if I'm wrong but the doppelgängers were probably made *after* Deidre's death. Her death was probably a requirement, a prerequisite to be able to go ahead and make other Deidre's to take her spot. You can't replace a position that's filled."

Alex smiled.

"Look at Baby Boy Calix, figuring shit out," said Felix clapping his younger sibling on the back.

"Someone killed Deidre and took over her life, continued on living as her. Realised all her potential, became a supermodel. The person even took her life's dream," said Alex.

"That's sad," said Felix softly. "The Deidre doppelgänger is better at her life than she was."

"Well, that might be because the doppelgänger is obviously superhuman in some way," said Calix.

"Deidre was already a she-wolf," said Alex. "The doppelgänger has to be using either incredible technology or magic. My bet is on magic. I wouldn't put anything past a witch!"

"Don't hate on witches," said Felix. "Our cousin, Jessie, married one. She made a great Luna. She's kinda hot too."

"I like Jamie. She gave me a snow globe that changes season so when I shake it up, it's snowflakes for winter, flowers for spring and leaves for fall," explained Calix.

"You're missing one," smirked Felix.

"In summer, there's nothing, it's just empty," said Calix.

"Now, *that* is sad!" Said Felix.

"Focus!" Said Alex. Calix and Felix straightened.

"Sorry, Alex, I haven't slept properly in days. It's impossible without Chasity," mumbled Calix, the youngest Alpha.

"The sooner we figure this out, the sooner we can save Chasity and all take a nap," said Alex, ruffling Calix's hair.

"When I get my hands on Chasity, there'll be no napping," said Felix slyly.

Alex nudged Felix sharply in the ribs.

"Hey!" Felix protested. Alex nodded towards Chance, Chasity's grandfather who was glaring at Felix.

Felix smiled at him sheepishly. "Uh, that's because we'll stay up *talking*. We have really long deep chats together. Our relationship is very spiritual, intellectual as well," explained Felix.

Chance's glare remain unchanged.

"All signs are pointing to Deidre. No more stalling. Let's find her and get the truth somehow," said Alex redirecting the conversation.

"First, before we go skipping off to LA, we need to check out the bar, The Serpent's Tongue. Your parents also frequented there in their youth," said Danny.

"You mean Chasity's parents," corrected Alex.

"And yours," said Danny, frowning.

"What?" Asked Felix sharply.

"They double dated there from time to time seeing as your mom and Chasity's dad were step siblings who actually got along," said Danny, reaching into his briefcase.

Chapter 39: A Tale of Threes

He took out a photo and showed it to the triplets. Two girls in embroidered bellbottom jeans and crops tops with billowing fishtail sleeves were standing with two men in pale jeans and plain white tees under jean jackets. The triplets easily recognised the younger versions of their parents as one of the couples. The other couple comprised of a blond man with wavy long hair and a mocha skinned girl with curly dark hair. Chasity's parents. All four youngsters were smiling for the camera and huddled together.

"But, they hated each other? My parents all but admitted it. My mom said she had a problem with Chalice!" Said Alex.

"Not right away," said Danny. "They grew apart after Chasity's parents became more heavily involved in the Furina Ornata."

"The group wasn't supposed to be about partying an drugs," said Chance, defending the group. "But the parties the younger members threw became like that. There were a lot of wild young members. They felt invincible. Maybe it was the snake venom."

Felix sighed. So his parents had even liked Chasity's parents once upon a time including Chasity's mother. That made his parents' mistreatment of Chasity even worse. He wished she were sitting right here, between him and Alex, pondering over her menu, taking forever to order. Her smell would be heavenly as always and she would snap at him for trying to order for her. Then she would feel guilty and be sweet to him. He missed her sassiness.

"Felix!" Said Alex.

"We're going!" Said Calix.

"Where?" Asked Felix.

"To the Serpent's Tongue!" Said Danny.

The serpent's tongue was a hole in the wall of a bar. It was on the outskirts of the parklands, not the ideal location for a business establishment. The indoor heating there was not working well so it was exceptionally cold inside the bar. It was snowing outside. The triplets' pack lands had a six month winter, usually spanning from October to March. During the other six months, it was still quite cold but the snow was gone, the flowers bloomed and the ice melted so the rivers ran and fish swam upstream to spawn.

The triplets were shocked to see a graffiti painting on the side of the bar depicting the full moon with the snake curled around it. There was a latin phrase painted in red letters on the moon: *Iterum vivere.*

"What does that mean?" Asked Danny, snapping a picture of it.

"Live again," said Chance. "It's latin for live again."

The five walked into the cold bar. There were shabby wooden barstools at the bar and surrounding all the high tables. The countertops were all a dark green. The walls were plastered with autographed framed photographs of celebrities. Many of the celebrities had also written lines praising the bar.

*How did the people who own this place get all these high profile people to come here **and** lie on their autographed photos? This place is a dump,* said Felix in the minds of the five.

Calix and Alex nodded. It was suspicious. They all sat at the bar. The bartender was human to their surprise. She introduced herself as Destiny. She was a petite, pale, freckled young woman with vibrant red hair. She encouraged them to all get some beers. The temperature of the place kept all the bottles chilled. There was no need for a freezer really but there was one. Destiny did not seem the slightest bit afraid surrounded by all these werewolves. To the contrary, she seemed one of the most relaxed people there as if she were quite at home in the freezing cold werewolf bar. She was not even dressed warmly. She wore a knee length checkered pink and white uniform with a white apron and pink loafers. Her legs were bare.

"How are you not an icicle by now?" Asked Calix, sipping his beer.

She laughed and put her hand to cover her mouth. Calix glimpsed the snake around the moon tattoo near her elbow. Calix frowned. Had moon snake venom made this human powerful enough to handle the same weather as werewolves. Suddenly, the placid smile slid from Destiny's face.

"Dante!" Said Destiny. "What happened to you?"

Chapter 40: Reminiscent

Chasity

"You're a werewolf, you know just as well as anyone else those marks cannot be removed. They're permanent," I said, trying to stop my brown eyes from turning black with rage. How dare he try to remove my mates' marks. That was beyond heinous. I'd never even heard of such a thing.

Dante shrugged. "It was magic. I thought it would work," he said.

I must have lost my mind for a second. Temporary insanity. I lunged at him and tackled him to the ground, canines bared. I wanted to rip him to shreds.

Dante was so stunned. He actually froze as we fell to the ground with me on top of him. My claws came out as I scratched at his torso and his face. He recovered and grabbed my wrists, squeezing until it was painful. I screamed. He stood up and tossed me back onto my bed. He roared at me, his own eyes turning my black. His canines were pointed and extended to his lower lips. I was panting. Slowly, my eyes lightened from black to their usual warm brown. My nails and teeth returned to normal. My wrists were throbbing. Dante returned to normal too, still glaring at me, now with pink scratches all over him. I stared at him, waiting for the scratches to fade.

"Don't *ever* do that again!" He warned.

I knew he could have killed me if he wanted to. He was much stronger. He was alpha material. I was no match for him really. I doubted he would kill me though. One of my alphas would obviously kill him in retaliation and he still did not know if I was pregnant or not. My eyes filled with tears. It was all so unfair. I hadn't asked for any of this.

Dante's expression softened a little . I curled up into a ball on the bed and cried.

"Chasity," was all he said. He was silent for a long time.

"You need to pull yourself together," he said.

"Why would you try to erase my mates' marks?" I sobbed. "Why must you take everything from me?"

Dante sighed. He sat down, slumped against the door that separated my prison of a bedroom from the rest of the house or whatever it was.

"I'm sorry," he said softly.

"You are," I mumbled.

"I... you... remind me of someone," Dante said.

I stared at him through blurry tear-filled eyes. I blinked, allowing the tears to escape.

"Who?" I asked.

"It doesn't matter... but because you remind me of someone... it helped seal your fate," Dante said.

"Seal my fate?" I asked.

"She asked me to choose," he whispered.

What the hell was he talking about?

"She as in the boss," I said.

He nodded.

"What were you asked to choose? Me?" I asked, horrified. He had picked me out. Who were his other options?

"You were a candidate anyway, but because of... me... she found you the most appealing," he said.

I was fed up.

"Just tell me what you intend to do to me. It's the least you could do if you truly are a bit remorseful about it," I said, sniffling.

He got up suddenly and cupped my face in his hands. His nose was very close to mine.

"Don't you dare," I warned.

Chapter 40: Reminiscent

I belonged to my triplets.

"I'm not going to do anything," he promised. "Your eyes are different than hers but other than that. Yeah. Like a perfect match."

"Congratulations, your reward for the most vague speech in the villain category is on its way," I muttered yanking my face away and scrambling across to the corner.

He snorted with laughter.

"She was funny too," he said.

"Oh, really, did she have hair and a face?" I asked.

I was tired of his bullshit. He was probably making stuff up to distract me from how angry I was about the marks.

"Yeah," he said, grinning. "She had long curly dark blonde hair and a really sweet innocent face."

I glared at him.

"Like a little fairytale character," he said.

I was silent.

"Like Goldilocks," he said.

I rolled my eyes.

"The name Chasity is so... bleh. I'm going to call you Goldilocks for the time being," he said.

"You can call me whatever you like but I'll only answer to Chasity," I said dryly.

He scowled. There was the Dante I knew. "Suit yourself," he snapped, storming out.

Third Person

The five looked up to see a large werewolf, tall and broad-shouldered with a scowl on his chiseled face. The man was covered in fine pink lines, scratch marks. Dante frowned at Destiny, upset that she had made a spectacle out of him. Dante spotted the triplets at the bar. He tried as hard as he could not to stiffen or react to them in any way. He had made an effort to hide her smell when he left the house. He always did. He couldn't risk going up to the bar though. He sat near the wall on the other side of the bar. He hoped Destiny could take a hint.

She came over, leaving the bar, drawing eyes to him. He scowled at her. He sighed and tried to look deeply interest in his menu. The menu had almost nothing on it. He grumbled to himself. He chanced a glance at the triplets who were deep in conversation. He felt a little relief.

"What do you want to drink, Da..." Destiny began.

He flashed her his black eyes and she stopped talking. "A beer, ok," he said softly.

"Ok," she mumbled. She brought of a beer thankfully without asking which one. She opened it for him with the opener on her belt. She looked at him blankly. He usually made small-talk with her. He was regretting that now. She took a deep breath and walked back to the bar. He strained his ears, listening to the triplets. There were two others with them. One he recognised as Danny, the private investigator the triplets had hired to interview the pack members on the suspect list. His boss's informant had found that out, asking questions around the pack lands. Who was the older werewolf? Dante had not seen him around before. Where had he been hiding? Clearly he was important for some reason. He was at ease with the three alphas and the P.I., eagerly contributing to the conversation. Who was he?

"...Deidre Binx..."

Dante caught the name. He was all ears.

Felix was staring at the P.I. with a frown, his eyes narrowed. "So once we're done with all the leads here, you think it makes sense to hop on a plane to LA? What if Chasity is still *here* in the pack lands? We locked the pack lands down remember? She's more likely to be here."

"She could be here or she could be anywhere," Alex said. "The point is to connect all the dots and one of the biggest enigmas here is Deidre Binx and her lookalikes. I don't know whether we should be tailing the one spotted here or the one simultaneously spotted in LA so let's try to track down both.!"

Calix nodded. "Cover all the bases. We need to be on the lookout for other members of the Furina Ornata who might know something. So we should be keeping an eye out for that tattoo!"

"Definitely," said the older werewolf. "Not all members knew each other. Far from it. There were different pockets with different goals. Only the moon snake and the amazing power-giving properties of its venom connected them.

Chapter 40: Reminiscent

Finally the pink scratches were fading. The little she-wolf's scratches had taken surprisingly long to heal. Dante was glad they were finally going away. Dante was also glad he was wearing boots that covered his ankles because one of those ankles bore a tattoo of the full moon with a snake curled around it.

Chapter 41: Scent

Third Person

Calix was preparing to work his irresistible charm on this human bartender. He sighed to himself, making sure she heard him. His mind-linked his brothers to be quiet and let him do the talking. They scowled at him but were quiet. Danny and Chance were on either end of the triplets. All five were leaning on the bar with a beer in front of them each. Destiny, the human bartender, turned to Calix when he sighed.

"Can I get you anything else?" Asked Destiny.

Calix frowned and shook his head. He put his head in his hands. Bartenders were therapists who happened to sell and mix drinks. They couldn't resist the troubled.

"Wanna talk about it?" Asked Destiny.

The last handsome werewolf she had befriended was being a jerk today. She should really stay clear of all of them but she decided what the heck? This one seemed sweet. There was something unassuming about his demeanour, something safe and gentle. He smiled slightly and shrugged.

"I'm all ears," said Destiny, pulling up a chair on her side of the bar and sitting with her chin propped up on her hands.

"I'm trying to find this girl," said Calix.

Chapter 41: Scent

"The Luna, Chasity!" Said Destiny. Everyone on the pack lands knew she was missing. Even several neighbouring packs were aware.

"I *do* want to find my mate but I was trying to find someone I heard was in town but it's probably a stupid rumour," muttered Calix. "You're going to think it's so dumb."

"I won't!" Promised Destiny.

"You see, I'm a huge fan of that model competition show where they pick a couple girls from several packs across werewolf country," said Calix, his eyes lighting up.

Destiny snorted with laughter, covering her mouth. "She-wolf Supermodel Search?"

"That's the one!" Said Calix. He blushed. "I *know*, don't judge me."

"I can't imagine an alpha watching that," giggled Destiny.

"It's Baby Boy Calix's favourite show!" Exclaimed Felix with a smirk.

"He never misses a single episode!" Added Alex.

Calix glared at his elder brothers. He'd asked them both to be quiet.

"Anyway," said Calix. "The retired supermodel who coaches them was in town supposedly."

Destiny nodded emphatically. "She doesn't coach anymore though! She moved on to host a show on the Chomp Network."

"Snack Pack Attack!" Exclaimed Chance. "I love that show!"

"What's that about?" Wondered Danny out loud.

"Pairs of chefs from different packs compete. Every episode they have to make a snack in record time and the judges pick the best one..." began Chance.

"I don't watch that," said Calix quickly. "I *only* watch Deidre Binx's show!" Insisted Calix.

Destiny's eyes lip up. "Deidre Binx!"

"Yeah, that's her name!" said Calix.

"She was here!" Whispered Destiny excitedly, jumping up and down a little.

Calix's eyes widened. "Is she still in town? Do you think she'd sign an autograph for me?"

Destiny paused, thinking about it.

"Her boyfriend or whoever he is...he's moody. He's pretty grumpy," mumbled Destiny.

"Was he mean to you?" Asked Calix.

"He was nice at first but he showed up today acting like a jerk!" Said Destiny.

"Where is he?" Asked Calix.

"Oh, he left," mumbled Destiny, wiping a wet beer mug with a dish towel.

"So if he's in town then Deidre Binx is too," Calix concluded.

"I shouldn't tell you this," whispered Destiny. "But I know where they're staying!"

Calix leant in. Destiny whispered in his ear. A smile slowly spread onto the youngest alpha's face.

This was the address that Destiny had whispered to Calix. It was one of the huge mansions in the same area where Moxie and Roxie had thrown their party. The house was made of grey stone and brick. It stood out against the lily-white freshly fallen snow. The youngest alpha neglected to ring the doorbell. He prowled around the side of the house, checking windows and doors to see if anything had been open. There was no such luck. At least, not on the ground floor.

"Look, Calix," hissed Alex, pointing upwards.

At the side of the huge house, on the first story above them, there was an open window. A *wide* open window. Should they just sneak in? Calix was already climbing onto Felix's shoulders so that he could reach the the open window. Felix hoisted him up through the open window. Calix gave them a thumbs-up from the upstairs window.

"Should we all go through the window?" Asked Felix.

"Calix," hissed Danny quietly. "Let us in one of the doors on the ground floor."

Calix nodded. He pointed to the back. Danny, Chance, Felix and Alex made their way to the back door of the house to wait for Calix to let them in.

The youngest alpha was taking his time exploring the first floor on his way to the ground-floor back door. The mansion had grey stone walls and floors with high ceilings. All of the decor had a medieval feel to it. It reminded him of a castle. He wondered what year the house had been built. Every item in the house seemed like an antique, a relic from the past. A few of the rooms had impressive

Chapter 41: Scent

fireplaces. The ornaments and paintings that adorned the house depicted two things mainly: beautiful women and foxes. The youngest alpha did not notice it at first. He marvelled at the oil paintings and the marble sculptures, impressed by the talent of the artists. After several paintings and sculptures in a row Calix noticed the theme. There were foxes present in almost every art piece especially the paintings. They were usually skulking in the background or peaking out from behind a tree trunk or just coming out of their den. That made sense. Foxes were stealthy. The beautiful women were always prominently displayed, lavishly dressed and out in the open, being admired or fawned over. What an interesting fascination the art collector had? Was it all from the same artist? The styles suggested otherwise.

Calix! What are you doing? Let us in! Demanded Alex, his tone annoyed.

Calix hurried to find a staircase but then he caught a whiff of something. A beautiful scent. Only one person in the world smelled that good to the alpha. It was his mate! He tailed the scent, all thoughts of finding a staircase and getting to the back door forgotten. The aroma actually led him to a staircase. It was stronger downstairs. He found a dining room with a huge fireplace. There was a long table made from very heavy wood, simple and sturdy. There were only two chairs very far apart at the huge table. Her scent coated the tabletop.

CALIX! Felix was impatient. Calix knew how crazy the middle alpha could get about their mate. Calix hurried to the back door through the maze-like mansion. He opened the latch from the inside and let his brothers, Chance and the P.I. in.

I found Chasity's scent, he said over mind-link to the others, in case there were people here although he had no yet encountered any.

The followed Calix to the tabletop where he had smelled Chasity. Felix rubbed the straight bridge of his nose with his index finger.

Something is weird about it. It's different somehow. It's still amazing but there's a new element to it, Felix said over mind-link.

They're using magic to mute the scent and weaken it to hide her better, said Chance, his eyes narrowed in anger.

Yeah, agreed Danny. *Her scent has been watered down. It'll help the kidnappers hide too so you won't smell her on them.*

Felix let out a low growl. Alex shot him a warning look, putting a finger to his own lips.

When I get my hands on the people who took Chasity, I'm going to peal their skin off their flesh, said Felix. The middle alpha was seething.

Calix started showing the others all the depictions of foxes and girls wondering if that meant something. They moved room to room. They came across a bedroom with an adjacent bathroom that smelled so strongly of Chasity that Calix curled up on the bed just to be surrounded by her scent for a little while. Alex patted his back.

We don't have time for this, ok, Calix, we have to keep moving, said Alex gently. *It seems like she was here but isn't now.*

They must have taken her to a second location. I can find out from the real estate company who was leasing this house or who owned it and we can got from there, said Danny.

Something else is different about Chasity's scent though! Fumed Felix, annoyed he couldn't figure out what it was. Yes they were masking her scent but her scent itself was different it was...

Alex's hand shot out and grasped Felix's upper arm. Everyone was startled by the sudden movement.

What?! Asked Felix.

I know why Chasity's scent is different, Alex said. The eldest alpha's heart was racing.

Why's it different? Asked Calix, getting worried.

The eldest alpha looked at his younger brothers, eyes glassy and wide. They needed to find Chasity and get her away from those kidnappers as soon as possible. She would need them more than ever at this time.

The new element is another person...a baby...Chasity's pregnant.

Chasity

I was becoming certain that this chic room with all the beautiful models staring at me from their framed photographs was in a different house. I hoped I was still on the pack lands and within range of my alphas. Dante had not come back since I had scratched him. Maurice had not checked on me today either. There was a knock at the door. I jumped a little. A kidnapper was knocking? A kidnapper who respected my privacy? That seemed contradictory.

"Come in?" I said, my tone very unsure and practically a question.

The door opened. It was a girl. Her skin was as pale as the moon and her hair as dark as the night's sky. She was tall, thin and willowy. She observed me with large round dark brown eyes. She was dressed in all white also, white overalls over a white T-shirt. She was the first woman I had seen and the boss was female according to Dante. My heart was racing and my breathing hitched in my throat.

"Are you Boss?"

Third Person

Dante was fuming. He was angry at her, that little wench, and yet, he was angry at himself for upsetting her. He had pushed her too far. Removing the marks on her neck had not been part of Boss's plan. *He* had wanted them removed. The marks made him uneasy. He needed to secure his position. He still didn't know if she were pregnant. That made him uneasy also. If she were, it would be a huge problem. His heart broke for her. He wasn't sure what boss would do if she found out the Luna was pregnant. He felt guilty. Her being here was partially his fault. Boss had let him decide on a girl. Poor Goldilocks. Her problems were much too big.

Chapter 42: Haute Couture

Chasity

"Are you Boss?" I asked the tall, willowy girl with her almost silvery pale skin and midnight black hair.

She smiled and giggled, covering her mouth with her hands.

"No of course not! I'm not Madame! Madame is out," she said softly.

"Is this a brothel?" I asked, my stomach in knots. Madame? Was this young girl a former kidnap victim too made to work for Madame.

"No, no," said the girl. "I'm June."

"Hey June," I said softly.

"Hi, Luna Chasity," she replied with another faint smile. "This is a modelling agency and a spiritual centre."

Huh?

"What a strange combination," I commented.

"Madame handpicks us to model for her agency but she also acts as a spiritual adviser. Some people in Hollywood *love* her teachings. She has quite the loyal following because if it," said June.

"So she kidnapped me so I can model?" I asked incredulously, feeling as though this situation was even weirder than I had ever imagined. "I'm short," I added as if that would help make them let me go. I had no interest in being a model, especially not for Madame Boss.

June giggled again. "No, of course not! You won't be one of her models but you're very special to her. She told me how special you are and that I have to help take care of you." June explained

I felt so uneasy. June was trying her hardest to be friendly toward me despite my unenthusiastic response. I was so tired of all the vague half answers.

"I want to meet Boss or Madame or Madame Boss," I said simply.

"As soon as possible," I added seriously. To my utter surprise, June opened the door wide, holding it open for me.

I cautiously approached, hoping it was not some trap.

"You're taking me to see Boss?" I asked June. I was hopeful but wary at the same time.

"Eventually," said June. "For now, let's meet the others."

Third Person

The new element is another person...a baby...Chasity's pregnant, said Alex to his three brothers over mind-link.

Felix felt as if a band was constricted around his heart and his lungs. He couldn't breathe properly and there was so much pain in his chest. He knew his brothers felt the same way.

I know she's ok, murmured Felix. *She has to be, she has to be, she has to be,* the middle alpha repeated like a mantra, almost as if he said it enough times, it would surely become or remain true.

We're gonna find her, said Calix confidently. *And once we do, we'll never let her out of our sight again.*

Yeah, we'll find her and the rest of her pregnancy will be spent safe with us, said Alex reassuringly.

Felix could not help but wonder how scared she might be, for herself but also for the baby. Chasity was soft-hearted at times. What if she felt sick? What is she were nauseated, vomiting, in pain? Who would take care of her? Was she being fed enough for two? Was she warm enough at nights? It was always cold on their pack lands even when the six-month winter ended.

Felix, stop torturing yourself with questions. Let's focus on the investigation. The sooner we find Chasity, the sooner we can put this all behind us and make her kidnappers pay!

Felix gritted his teeth. His elder brother was right. After the five had combed and swept every inch of the castle-like residence, they realised it was truly devoid of all people. Chasity was no longer here. They hoped she was still close.

"Find out who owns this house and if they were renting it out to anyone!" Said Alex to Danny.

Danny nodded. "Will do. Also, I'm arranging for us to meet Dexter Sharpe in the interim while we're tracking down Deidre Binx."

"That's the conspiracy theory guy who was friends with Chase, Chasity's father?" Asked Calix.

Danny nodded.

The triplets, Danny and Chance didn't waste any time. They met with Chase's old best friend as soon as he would allow it. Luckily for them, Dexter Sharpe agreed to meet with them the very same day. They met him at his home which was not too far away from the lookout point Domino. Calix smiled sadly as they drove past the lookout point. He touched the mark on his neck. Her smell, her eyes, her hair, her voice. They were all so vivid in his memory and his imagination. He could summon the memories of her so easily. He was terrified of them fading as time passed. It would be like losing her twice. He reminded himself she was not lost forever.

The house was dilapidated. It was a narrow but long one-storey wooden home that had not been painted or perhaps every bit of paint had pealed off. The wood had black spots here and there. Calix peered at it more closely. Black mould! Chance pulled him back.

"Be careful, son, you could get sick!" Warned Chance, tugging on his shoulder. Calix was an Alpha. He was much tougher than that but he just smiled at the older werwolf, grateful for the concern.

"Thanks, Grandpa," said Calix sincerely, moving away from the mould.

Chance beamed.

Felix was already standing on the shaky porch and banging on the rickety door. The door opened abruptly and Felix halted his fist in midair. He grinned sheepishly at the man behind the door as he lowered his fist and put it in the pocket of his coat.

Chapter 42: Haute Couture

"Dexter Sharpe?" Felix said, raising his eyebrows.

The man stepped out a little from behind the door. He was tall and thin with a gaunt face and large watery blue eyes. His hair was thin and brown. He had very fuzzy eyebrows like two caterpillars that had taken up residence above his eyes. He did move his fingers often, wiggling them, as the triplets' mother had described. Alex wondered if he had a nervous system disorder. The man had a strange affect but seemed good-natured enough. Instead of answering Felix directly, he launched into a performance.

"Dexter Sharpe?" Parroted the man. "You are under arrest! You have the right to remain silent! Anything you say may be used against you in a court of law! You had the right to an attorney. If you can't afford one, one will be appointed to you..."

"Ok," said Felix holding his gloved hands up, palms facing forwards, signalling for Dexter to stop.

"Our mate, Chasity, is missing!" Said the middle alpha slowly as though each word was physically painful to utter.

The man stopped his quoting and nodded, his expression grave.

"Time is of the essence," said Felix, pleading with the man with his eyes.

"Are you Dexter Sharpe?" Felix repeated softly.

"Yes!" Said the man. Felix breathed a sigh of relief. Dexter led them into his house. It was crammed from ceiling to floor with tall shelves and each shelf filled with video tapes, cassettes, CDs, DVDs and books.

There was a television on a stand with more books piled around it. There was a living room set somewhere under the piles of media. Dexter moved a few stacks of DVDs off of a seat on the couch. Calix insisted that Chance as the eldest present take the seat. The rest stood.

"We're sorry for any inconvenience if you were busy or anything..." began Calix.

"Oh, no!" Said Dexter. "I am ready for this moment!"

"So you have an idea of why we're here?" Asked Alex.

"It's all over the news! I have all of it recorded! Would you like to watch it?" Asked Dexter.

"No! That's ok!" Said Felix quickly.

"Your story...the triplet alphas...Chasity's disappearance! It's all over the news!" Said Dexter, twiddling his thumbs nervously.

"What do you know about Chasity?" Asked Calix.

"Past, present or future?" Inquired Dexter, gesturing behind him, next to him and in front of him respectively.

"Start at the beginning," instructed Felix.

Dexter shrugged. He looked sad all of a sudden. "Chase was my best friend. My only friend," whispered Dexter.

"I'm really sorry," said Calix softly.

"I'm really sorry! About your mate! Little Luna Chasity!" Exclaimed Dexter.

"Well, she's not dead!!" Said Chance suddenly, the older werewolf clutching his chest. Calix rubbed his back.

"I know, I know. Neither is Chase," said Dexter.

Third Person (Somewhere in LA)

"'Deidre Binx. Supermodel. Fashionista. Mentor. Guru!'"

That's what I want it to say," said the Charles von Charles. He was wearing all leopard print today, everything faux. He wasn't an animal! He supported animal rights. He cradled his white Persian cat, Haute, to his chest. His black Persian cat, Couture, was strutting across his desk at his label, Charles von Charles.

"Do you see how Couture walks!" Exclaimed Charles. "The confidence neigh the arrogance, the I belong here and *you* don't of it all. *That's* how I want the girls to walk in my show!"

His assistant, Soya, was scrupulously taking notes, typing on his iPhone with one hand and writing on a planner with the other. Thank goodness his assistant was ambidextrous. That was the best hiring decision Charles ever made. Except for her. *She* was the best hiring decision Charles von Charles ever made. Soya would have to settle for second. He looked adoringly at the framed photograph of the supermodel on the wall of his office. There were many other supermodels gracing the wall, only the best girls, proficient in runway and in print. He discovered them and he also dressed them.

Haute dashed out of her father's arms and onto his desk to join her brother Couture. Haute was a snobby white fluff ball with blue eyes and Couture was a snobbier black fluffier ball with green or yellow eyes depending on the lighting. They did not work in harsh lighting. They were models too! Charles smiled at his fur babies and then he looked back at his top model. Even retired she made him millions and millions picking and choosing what jobs she still did. Just the mention of her name made clothes and makeup sell.

And to think, Charles had found her soaking wet and confused, standing in the rain, staring into space, seeming ungainly on her long legs almost as if she didn't know her own body. He had made his chauffeur stop his stretch limo for her. Charles remembered it so well.

Flashback

He rolled down his window. Haute and Couture were not even been born yet. Their mother, Avant and her brother, Garde, were in the car.

"Excuse me! Excuse me, Miss!" He called from the window, raising his voice so she could hear him above the wind and the rain.

She stopped in her tracks and turned her large almond-shaped eyes on him. Her skin was the colour of mocha, smooth and perfect. Her eyes were dark chocolate. Her face was oval-shaped, her neck long, her limbs willowy and fragile-looking. She had her hair pulled back but it was falling out of its ponytail. Her simple grey tunic dress was drenched but she made it look like fashion. She was fashion. Charles decided she was.

"What job do you do?" He asked, curious.

"Nothing," said the girl.

"How old are you?" He asked.

"Old enough."

"Do you want to model?" Charles.

*"I want to get **out** of the rain," she said simply.*

Charles' jaw dropped. She was ballsy. She was frank.

*"Then get **in** the car," said Charles, opening the door.*

She got in. Avant and Garde hissed in unison. Charles hushed them and waved for his chauffeur to continue driving. He had found a diamond in the rough or so he thought.

Chapter 43: Body Snatchers?

Chasity

I followed June. I couldn't believe she was letting me out of the room. Should I make a run for it? We walked down a maze-like series of white-walled hallways with marble floors. I gasped when we came to a huge open high-ceilinged area. It was like we had stumbled upon an ancient temple right in the middle of this chic upscale house. There was a huge white stone fox statue right at the far end of the room. It was the centrepiece in an array of artwork. To either side of it were huge intricate paintings depicting colourful forests filled with flowers, girls and foxes. I stared at the white stone fox. It was positioned as though it was about to land gracefully from a jump with one of its front paws just touching the floor. It was steady on a white base. Its hind legs were midair and its tails were pointed upwards. It had two tailed. It was a two tailed fox. I was strangely mesmerised by it. I walked up to it, so engrossed in examining its every detail that I did not realise all eyes were on me.

"Um, Luna Chasity!" Called June.

I looked around. I gasped and actually recoiled a little in surprise. There were several girls sitting on mats in the room as if they were in yoga class. Had they been praying? Exercising? I didn't want to offend anyone. I wasn't in the best position to ask a lot of questions but my curiosity got the better of me.

"What does the two-tailed white fox mean?" I asked, unsure what I meant. I didn't know how to outright ask if they worshipped the fox.

"The fox isn't a deity if that's what you're wondering," said a girl, standing up on her pink mat. She was tall and graceful with long wavy black hair and thick perfectly arched eyebrows. She had dark eyes and an olive complexion. She was wearing all white just like June.

"This is April," said June, gesturing towards the girl who had spoken.

"What happened to May?" I demanded before I could stop myself. I laughed at my own feeble joke. The silence that followed was awkward.

April and June exchanged panicked looks, their eyes wide.

Huh. What *had* happened to May? Had there really been a May? Wow. I was only joking. Were they all named after months?

"What is this place?" I asked.

"This is the Schoo and Spiritual Centre," said April. "Madame teaches us about modelling her. We walk for her and she makes us study the movements of cats and foxes so we will be inspired to move like them on the runway. She gives us spiritual advice too. This particular room is where we meditate."

I wanted to ask if they had all come here willingly but April seemed very pro-Madame and not trustworthy. She seemed deeply indoctrinated. I doubted very much that the only reason for the huge stone fox was as an example of how to be graceful on the runway. Did these girls know that *I* was kidnapped?

Suddenly, there was a series of gongs and chimes. The girls all whispered excitedly, getting up from their so-called meditation mats.

"What's happening?" I asked April and June.

"Madame is here."

Third Person

"Chase was my best friend. My only friend," whispered Dexter.

"I'm really sorry," said Calix softly.

"I'm really sorry! About your mate! Little Luna Chasity!" Exclaimed Dexter.

"Well, she's not dead!!" Said Chance suddenly, the older werewolf clutching his chest. Calix rubbed his back.

"I know, I know. Neither is Chase," said Dexter.

"What do you mean?!"asked Chance indignantly, looking at Dexter as though he were a mad man. Chance narrowed his eyes. "I *watched* him buried. I *found* his body and Deidre's and my own... m-m-my own..."

Chance could not continue. Calix rubbed his shoulder. The older werewolf blew his nose in a tissue, overcome with emotion. He dabbed his eyes.

"I know you found bodies that *looked* just like theirs," said Dexter.

Alex felt a chill creep across him. "What do you mean? Are you saying those bodies were planted there to be found? That those were not them? That they're alive somewhere?" Alex asked a series of questions, eyes narrowed.

Dexter listened to the eldest alpha intently and answered each question one by one. "I mean that magic can easily make one thing look like another. Chance buried three bodies that greatly resembled Chalice, Chase and Deidre. Even perfect resemblances perhaps but was DNA done to ensure this bodies were who we thought they were?" Asked Dexter.

"Yes, I'm saying those bodies were planted there to be found by someone not necessarily Chance. Anyone who would publicise the alleged deaths," continued Dexter.

"No, those were not them. Yes, they're alive somewhere. That is my belief," said Dexter.

Alex was silent. Was Dexter onto some brilliant discovery or was he simply unhinged?

"Where are they then?" Alex asked.

"That I can't tell you but I *can* tell you that the Deidre Binx who became a supermodel is an imposter and the real Deidre Binx *has* to be alive *somewhere* for that type of dark magic to work!" Whispered Dexter.

"Explain how it works," said Calix eagerly.

Was the youngest alpha buying this?

Chapter 43: Body Snatchers?

"I have it all documented... I...," Dexter began to shuffle a huge star of papers.

"No, no, please, explain in words, paraphrase if you must," insisted Felix.

Dexter took a deep breath. "The rich and famous in werewolf country have body snatchers among them!" Warned Dexter.

Alex and Felix were silent. Chance had stopped crying but he did not look moved by this. Danny was looking at a row of DVDs. Only Calix seemed to be listening intendedly. The youngest alpha prompted Dexter to continue.

"The body snatchers are immortal just like werewolves but they have limitations. They need fresh bodies every time the old body wears thin. They are like parasites and the bodies are hosts. They pick bodies that are desirable in someway, maybe the person is beautiful, important or they envy the lifestyle the person has already or what the person has the potential *to* have," explained Dexter.

"They may fake the person's death in one place and carry on their life with that body in another place or they may just carry on living in the same place as them seamlessly. The first step is scouting or vetting," said Dexter. "Meaning they get information about what candidates are out there. The second step is selection. They pick the body they want and kidnap the person. The kidnapping is technically the third step, procurement. So after scouting, selection and procurement, they need to do step four. Preparation of the body for its host. The body must be *empty* spiritually speaking. They take the essence of the person out of the desired body and put it somewhere else."

"Somewhere else?" Asked Calix.

"In an animal, a different empty body, a statue, a doll, preferably in an animal. The next step is transference, transferring the consciousness of the body snatcher into this new host body. The old host body might killed. The new body is now the body snatcher' until the snatcher needs another body!" Warned Calix.

"Ok, thank you," said Felix somewhat impatiently as he stood suddenly to leave.

"So Chalice and Chase and the *real* Deidre are in an animal or a doll or a statue or just re-trapped *somewhere*. It makes sense that Deidre's body could be being used by some diseases out of the way," said Calix, sounding fascinated.

Before Calix could hear the rest, he was being pulled away by his elder brothers. Calix glared at them later in the car.

"Calix, Dexter was filling your head with conspiracy theories and whatnot," snapped Felix. "We didn't come to write a paranormal gossip tabloid rag. We're looking for Chasity!"

"I know, so am I," retorted Calix. "And I believe him. Chasity's parents are alive somewhere and so it the real Deidre Binx. The only person we need to confront next is the *fake* Deidre Binx!"

Felix sighed. Alex was of two minds. "Whether or not this body snatcher thing is true, we *still* need to confront Deidre so we will do that! But first, we need to visit A Fork in the Road cage-fighting club. They scheduled to have fights tonight, and I wanna see whose there. Some of them may have something to do with Chasity or her parents."

The eldest alpha was quite right about that as a certain Dante was fighting tonight.

Chapter 44: Mother

Chasity

I was terrified. I hid behind the group of models. Thankfully, their heights ranged from five feet and nine inches to five feet and eleven inches. At five feet and four inches, I was obscured from view as I crept along behind them, not even daring to peak out from behind someone's shoulder yet. I remembered when I would hide behind my six-foot-four triplets from the Luna. I smiled to myself. One day I would be reunited with them. I had to believe that. I would tell them I was having their baby and hopefully I could marry them before the birth. I wanted the wedding out of the way. I didn't even mind going on honeymoon while pregnant. Someone clapping their hands snapped my out of my daydream.

I gasped. I knew exactly who she was. I had even glimpsed her show a few times when one of the Calix's old girlfriends would obsessively watch it, cuddling with him, while I cleaned the living room. I felt a pang at that. I had to minimise stress for the baby. I pictured myself watching television with Calix cuddling me. Felix's head would be in my lap as he stretched out on the couch. Alex would be on the other side of Calix and eventually I would stretch out and put my head in Alex's lap so he could play with my hair like he liked to do. I sighed.

She was almost six feet tall. She was dressed in a white pantsuit that fit her impeccably well and contrasted with her mocha chocolate skin. She had almond shaped brown eyes, high cheek bones and full lips. Her makeup was expertly done, smoky eyes with nude lips and countered cheeks further accentuating those cheek bones. Her hair had been straightened. It was black, sleek and glossy and hung a little past her shoulders. She raised a perfect eyebrow at the girls. Something about her mannerisms reminded me of a haughty cat. She was very feline for a she-wolf.

"Girls!" Called Deidre Binx, the retired supermodel turned model coach, clapping her manicured hands again. She was wearing thigh high white stiletto boots.

She was boss or Madame.

"Good evening, Madame," chorused the girls. The girls had confirmed it for me.

"We have a very, *very* special new little Sister and I want you to give her a warm welcome. Step forward, Chasity!" Announced Deidre as though we were good friends and this had all been previously discussed.

I stumbled forwards, my mouth agape.

"Welcome, Sister Chasity," said the girls in unison.

"Welcome, welcome, Daughter Chasity," said Deidre softly.

I was so confused.

"Thank you, Mother, for bringing us a new Sister," said the girls in perfect harmony.

"You are welcome, my daughters. Mother is pleased," said Deidre.

I was pretty sure I was looking at them like they were all lunatics.

"I am so glad Chasity is settling in so nicely," commented Deidre. "I have a story to tell you, Daughters. Would you like to here it?"

"If it pleases Mother," said the girls in their sing-song voices.

They all sat on their mats, cross-legged. A male servant in all white brought me a white mat. All the others had colours. Did the colours mean anything? I sat on my mat, cross-legged, at a loss for how else to react.

"When Madame was your age, she had two best friends. We three were inseparable!" Reminisced Mother, I mean Deidre, as she sat on a high stool brought forward by another male servant in white. All of the helpers were men. They seemed to be male models. My heart belonged to the triplets but one glance at each of them and I realised they were all jaw-droopingly handsome like my triplets, all from different parts of the world based on their looks and the snatches of their accents I caught. What was this? A supermodel cult?

"Her very best friend was called Chalice," Deidre said, gazing at me lovingly.

My inner she-wolf growled, sensing falsehood. Deidre did not seem sincere to her. I agreed with my she-wolf. I didn't like hearing my mother's name come out of her mouth. I remembered my mother, her gleaming skin and bright eyes, her laugh and smile. I smiled to myself.

"Chalice had a little girl of her own one day, Chasity," said Deidre.

The girls "aww-ed" at me.

"Alas, my best friend, my soul-sister, Chalice was lost to me forever," murmured Deidre.

What? I yelped inwardly. My inner she-howl let out a mournful howl.

"What?" I said, standing up.

The girls gasped. Deidre looked affronted but she quickly recovered her plastered-on smile.

"You're supposed to say, 'Mother, if it pleases you, may I ask a question?'" Hissed April angrily at me from her mat.

I gave her a look of disdain but quickly turned my attention back to Deidre.

"What are you saying about my mother?" I asked, narrowing my eyes.

"I'm saying she's lost to me…" said Deidre.

My heart was racing.

"Meaning?" I demanded.

I knew what she meant but I couldn't believe it. I just couldn't. I'd waited nine years to turn eighteen and try to find my parents. They couldn't be…

"Dead…Chalice, your mother, is dead, as is your father," said Deidre, looking confused as though shocked I didn't know.

The ground came up to meet me as I fainted.

Third Person

The triplet alphas were on their way to A Fork in the Road, a cage-fighting club. Their page online had advertised someone named Dante the Destroyer was fighting someone named the Blanch the Avalanche. Felix was driving, Calix was in the passenger seat, Alex was in the back and Danny and Chance were meeting them there.

Suddenly the middle alpha pulled over and parked. He was panting.

"What? Felix, what's wrong?" Asked the eldest Alpha, Alex, worried about his younger brother.

Alex stretched over Felix's front seat, gripping his shoulders and giving him a little shake.

"Felix, talk to me," said Alex.

"C'mon Felix, what is it?" Asked the youngest, Calix, who had been giving them the silent treatment previously due to their "narrow-mindedness" about the body snatchers.

"I felt dizzy just now," admitted Felix softly.

Alex frowned. He knew how hard it was for Felix to admit any weakness whatsoever.

"I'll drive," offered Alex.

Felix begrudgingly switched with Alex.

"It's Chasity," said Felix, his voice sounding strained. "She must be giddy. Ugh, my Baby, we have to hurry and figure out where she is. My Baby *and* my baby," added Felix, referencing her bun in the oven and smirking a little.

"Or *my* baby," said Calix.

"Let's call it our baby," Alex said to his younger brothers.

"Felix, you haven't been sleeping much or eating as much as usual. Those are contributing factors probably to the dizziness, I would think," said Alex.

Felix shook his head. "My Baby Chasity is dizzy or something," insisted Felix.

"*Our* Chasity," said Alex, smiling.

"Then how come we aren't all dizzy," said Calix.

"Chasity and I are just attuned to each other," said Felix smugly.

Calix got upset. They were all short-tempered of late. Little to no sleep. Less food. No sex. They were accustomed to having all three necessities taken care of.

"Yet I took her virginity and I was her first kiss," said Calix, just as smug as Felix.

Felix snarled. "You were *not* her first kiss! I was!"

The middle alpha recalled his argument with Chasity before Christmas leading up

To their dramatic kiss then Calix's mistletoe kiss followed by Alex's kiss in the small makeshift bedroom Chasity used to sleep in.

"Nope!" Said Calix. "I kissed her back when she was fourteen and I was seventeen. It was when the clock struck midnight on New Year's."

Felix gave a low growl. Calix snarled.

Alex made the car screech to a halt. "Enough! We're here anyway, A Fork in the Road, cage fighting club."

There was a neon blinking sign above a large one storey beginning. The blinking sign read *Fight Tonight!*

Chapter 45: Throwing Tantrums

Chasity

I woke up back in the chic bedroom. I flew off the bed and launched myself at the door. I tugged on the knob with such force it came off in my hands. I roared in anger. Why?! What did Deidre Binx want from me? She claimed to be a friend of my dearly departed mother but she announced her death to me callously and *kidnapped* me! I started tearing apart the room. I smashed every framed photograph by tearing it off the wall and hurling it across the room or smashing it on the floor. There was glass everywhere.

Dante ran into the room after some initial difficulty with whatever damage I had done to the doorknobs. He was panting, worry evident in his face.

"What the fuck are you doing?" He screamed.

"ME?!" I screeched. "What the fuck are *you* doing? Why are you doing this to me? What do you want from me? Just let me go!!! Please!!" I screamed, tears streaming down my face.

Dante seemed to be at a loss for words. I tried to rush past him out of the door, but he grabbed me, holding my arms still. I kicked and screamed with all my might.

"Please! Chasity! Stop! You're not making this any easier on yourself!" Yelled Dante.

Chapter 45: Throwing Tantrums

"Who are you to Deidre?" I shrieked. "How does any of this concern you?"

"Deidre is helping me," snapped Dante.

"WITH WHAT?!" I screamed.

"With getting my mate back!" He answered, his tone sounded defeated. He was panting. He released me.

I slumped onto the floor. Maurice was standing in the doorway blocking the exit.

"What?" I asked softly. I was totally spent.

"I... I chose you," said Dante.

"What does that mean?" I whispered, my eyes narrowed.

"I chose you because you resemble my mate. I'm *sorry*," said Dante, sighing.

"What happened to her?" I asked quickly, genuinely curious. I was leaning against the bed as I sat on the floor.

"She died," he said softly.

"How?" I asked.

Dante sat on the floor also. His eyes had a faraway look to them.

"Werewolf hunters," said Dante. Tears welled up in his eyes. He quickly wiped them away and took a deep shuddering breath. He shut his eyes tightly causing more tears to fall.

"I'm sorry," I managed to say as my breathing rate and pulse slowed.

"Her name was Georgia but her nickname was Goldie," he said. He put his head in his hands.

"She wasn't very good at controlling herself. She had a short-temper. She shifted once in a human town in the middle of a diner and accidentally killed two people we had gotten in an argument with. One was the waitress and the other was the owner of the place. She wasn't perfect but I adored her beyond words," Dante paused. He took a deep breath.

"The town was tiny human town in the middle of nowhere. I didn't know they had a history of werewolf and vampire hunting," explained Dante.

I stared at him, engrossed in the story.

"We sped away from the scene of the crime basically. These two cars raced after us. Apparently a group of people in the diner had either been hunters or known hunters. I'm not sure," said Dante, sniffling.

"They rained silver bullets dipped in wolfsbane on our car. One hit my Goldie right in the chest through her back. I was just relieved she didn't suffer long. I crashed the car. I was too distraught to focus or to want to live. The car went up in flames. I thought I would die too, but I didn't," he said, his eyes widening.

I stared at him.

"I woke up in the ICU covered in bandages. As fate would have it we had crashed into a tree near a retreat for some spiritual group. The people hosting it organised the ambulance. They were werewolves. My Goldie, my little Georgia, she was already gone. They worked on me till I got better. My burns healed. Everything healed but I had no zeal for life anymore. Not without my mate. The leader of the weird group, the Mother or Madame took an interest in me. She helped me get revenge. We went together with some other members in the group and slaughtered every single one of those werewolf hunters in cold bloodHer mate had died too! And she said I reminded her of him. She said she... changed every fifty years or so," said Dante.

"What?" I said, narrowing my eyes and furrowing my brow. Changed?

"She said she would do for me what I had done for her," Dante said, his voice shaking.

"Which is what?" I asked, confused.

"Replace my mate," said Dante, his eyes shimmering with tears.

It dawned on me. Him trying to erase my marks. Nicknaming me Goldie. He wanted to play house and have me replace Georgia but that was never gonna work. I couldn't replace her.

"I can't *be* your mate, Dante," I said gently. "I'm just *not.*"

Dante sighed. "There's more to it," he said simply.

"I *won't* cheat on the triplets," I insisted.

"That's not a problem. You won't be *you* anymore," explained Dante, still not making sense to me.

What did that mean? Were they going to brainwash me? Erase my memories? What was going to happen to me and my baby? Surely Dante was not that huge of a monster to harm my baby or put my baby at risk.

"Dante, listen , please, I can't replace anyone. I'm so sorry for what happened... but I need my triplet alphas! We're bonded for life.

I marked all three of them and I bear all three of their marks," I said as gently as I could, sincerely feeling sorry for him.

Dante shrugged.

I tried one more time. "Dante, listen, I'm pregnant for my triplet alphas. I'm engaged to them. It's a done deal."

There was a long pause of utter silence. Dante wiped his eyes.

"Engaged is not married. That's not a problem. Pregnant?" He said, nodding. "Now, that would be a problem," he said coldly.

My wolf snarled and I trembled a little. *Triplets wherever you are come get mr right away!* I mind linked hoping someone *anyone* could here.

Third Person

The Alpha triplets were shocked to find *A Fork in the Road* cage-fighting club packed with people, both werewolves and humans. There was even a witch or wizard or two and a sprinkling of vampires. Everyone was cheering and yelling. Most were standing, crowing around the cage where the fight would take place. The cage was cylindrical with a domed roof like a huge bird cage. The triplets noticed everyone was dressed to signify who they were supporting. Red for Dante the Destroyer and Icy Blue for Blanche the Avalanche. The triplets were thankful none of them were wearing red or blue. Felix was in all black as usual, Alex in all grey and Calix in all white. Each triplet essentially work a plain t-shirt with a pair of sweatpants, not wanting to dress up for a place like this. There were bets being placed. The walls were cluttered with pictures and memorabilia from past fights. There were booths lining the walls and these were almost all taken too.

"Get us a booth," said Felix to a short blonde human waitress walking by. She turned to scowl at him then got a proper look at him. Her eyes practically bulged out of her head. She licked her lips looking him up and down. She smiled and said, "Right this way, *Sir.*"

She realised there were *three* of them and fanned herself with a menu.

"Lacey, what are you *doing*?" Said a pretty brunette she-wolf also in a waitress uniform. The uniform was a mini pink dress with short sleeves and a black apron over it. They all wore high-heeled black pumps with their hair in ponytails.

"*What,* Melissa?" Said Lacey, clearly annoyed at being interrupted. Was Mel trying to steal her customers.

"You can't put them back there! These are the alphas," said Melissa in hushed tones though the triplets could hear.

Lacey gasped and glanced the triplets again.

"She's human sorry," said Melissa quickly. "She had no idea."

Melissa motioned for the triplets to follow her. She walked up a few steps leading to a slightly raised platform of booths that seemed as though it were for VIP guests only. The men here were in suits and seemed to be bidding thousands on the fight and ordering bottles of champagne by the bucket-load. Melissa turned to the triplets.

"Please, Alphas, choose where you would like in this section. I'm not sure if you wanna be up front or lowkey?" Said Melissa.

"Up front," said Felix glaring at the cage.

"Lowkey," said Calix, glaring at Felix.

"A comfortable medium would be nice, Melissa," said Alex, reading her name-tag.

She blushed, nodded and put them in a middle booth with a clear view of the cage.

"Anyone else joining you?" Melissa asked.

"Two more, Chance and Danny are their names," said Alex showing Melissa a picture on his phone. "Please, very discreetly find them and bring them to us as soon as they get here," instructed Alex, slipping a hundred dollar bill into her apron pocket.

Melissa grinned. "Yes, Alpha, thank you."

"Chasity would be so pissed if she were here," said Felix sadly.

"About Alex talking to the waitress. It's just business," said Calix.

"Yeah but she gets jealous easily," Felix said smirking.

"If Chasity were here *we* wouldn't be here," muttered Alex, sighing.

They all sighed in unison. Melissa reappeared with Chance and Danny.

"Thank, Melissa, you're a real one," said Calix winking.

Melissa blushed and scurried away but had to come straight back realising she hadn't taken anyone's orders. All five ordered beers for now though no one was particularly interested in the drinks or food right now.

"What's the point of being here when we need to be finding Deidre and questioning her?" Asked Calix, annoyed.

"We said from the beginning that we needed to check out all three people and all three places Mom spoke about when she told us about Chalice and Chase," said Alex.

Felix was looking at the cage. The others followed his gaze. The announcer had a booming theatrical voice. The fans in red crowded one side of the cage and the fans in blue crowded the other.

"Fighting tonight, in this corner, we have six foot six, hard as bricks, two hundred and forty pounds of not playing around, Blanch the Avalanche!!" Bellowed the announcer.

The fans in blue yelled at the top of their lungs.

Blanch was a pale platinum-blond werewolf with icy blue eyes clad in blue shorts. He was missing an eyebrow. He bared his fangs and everyone cheered.

"Fighting tonight, in the other corner, we have two hundred and twenty pounds of lean, mean, fighting machine. At six foot four, let's get him out on the floor it's Dante the Destroyer!!" Yelled the announcer.

Felix snorted at all the cheesy lines.

The fans in red screamed and jumped up and down.

Dante entered the cage, bare torso, red shorts, black eyes.

Felix stared at him. He wrinkled his nose. He got down from the VIP seating platform and walked into the crowd of fans wearing red. His brothers, Chance and Danny quickly followed him. Felix reached the cage and he was certain. Before the announcer could tell the fighters to begin. Felix roared in anger. Dante smelled like *his* mate, *his* Chasity. The alpha was murderous!

Chapter 46: Dinnertime

Third Person

Felix tore into the cage ripping the bars apart. Fans screamed and some scattered, running out of the club. Others cheered wildly thinking it was part of the show or perhaps just loving any form of drama. Dante paled a little and ducked out through where he had entered. His escape was blocked by Calix and Alex. He turned around only to be knocked out by Felix.

Chasity

Ever since Dante had come clean about his involvement in all this, I had been shaking in my boots so to speak. I was terrified. Dante wanted *my form*, my *body*. Literally, just that. I knew girls complained about guys only wanting them for their body, but this was different. He literally wanted nothing else but my shell. He wanted my mind and personality siphoned out somehow and put where? In a jar? He had said I wouldn't be *me* anymore. What did that mean? I had been going through the options in my mind. Brainwashing? Cloning? Maybe there would duplicate and take the clone and train her to have his mate's personality. Did he have his mate's soul somewhere? Was she a ghost? Would they use dark magic and let her possess me? I got chills.

My wolf snarled at me to stop it. I tugged at the silver collar on my neck. It burnt my fingertips. I sucked on the burnt fingertips. Ouch. If I could only shift, I could definitely overpower at least Maurice. I could definitely outrun Maurice even in human form. I would need to shift to outrun Dante. Then, he would shift and I wouldn't get far. Ugh! I looked for another photograph to smash and realised I had already destroyed all of them. Glass was everywhere. I was in the corner of the bed. I hadn't let any glass get on the bed. I was no fool. I deserved some rest at least even though I could barely sleep. I was too terrified someone was gonna wake me up to hurt me or the baby in the middle of the night. Or they would carry me to yet another location during a drug-induced sleep. I sighed. My door opened and I recoiled automatically.

It was Deidre.

She looked nonchalantly at the wrecked room, the smashed photographs and glass strewn all over the floor.

"Feeling better?" She asked serenely, plastering a smile on her face. Her fake niceness towards me reminded me of the Luna. I couldn't tell if she meant if I was feeling better since my fainting *or* if I was feeling better emotionally now that I'd smashed the room up like I was the hulk or something? I was *not* feeling better. What was the point of lying in this weird situation? Did any of them even care how I felt?

I shook my head no but didn't complain any further. I just hugged my knees to my chest. I was tired. I had really exhausted myself with my own antics.

"Perhaps, joining me for dinner would help?" Asked Deidre as if it had only just occurred to her. I was pretty sure almost every event of this kidnapping had been preplanned. I knew her invitation was not truly optional. It was only framed like a question for the sake of feigning politeness.

"I am allowed to say no?" I asked, fixing her with a blank stare.

She drew a sharp intake of breath as if hiding a short temper.

"I think it would be helpful... and enlightening... if we talked," she said, her blindingly white smile widening.

I stared at her.

"Girls, help Chasity get ready for dinner," instructed Deidre.

April and June came in. I stood up suddenly and looked at them threateningly. They hesitated. I could tell by their reactions that they were really mostly models and not warriors or skilled fighters or hardened criminals. I hopped down off the bed.

"Stay away," I warned them. They recoiled a little.

"Further!" I instructed.

They moved back a little one. Something occurred to me. Were any of these people original members of the triplets' wolf pack? If so, they could possibly be compelled to listen to me as I was the fated Luna though I had not officially claimed my post yet. Deidre was one step ahead of me.

"No one here is a member of your pack, Chasity. April and June are just cowards," said Deidre dropping some of the sickly sweet behaviour.

I sneered at her. "So what happened to May?" I genuinely wanted to know because it seemed as though there really had been a May.

"She was too brave," said Deidre softly, turning sharply causing her hair to swish behind her.

I followed her to a dining room where the other models from earlier were all seated. They looked up and chorused, "Good evening, Sister Chasity." Ugh

Third Person

The triplets put the captive werewolf in a cell in the basement of the pack house. These cells were seldom or perhaps never used. He was still unconscious.

"Shake him awake, the sooner he talks, the sooner I can see Chasity," whined Calix.

The werewolf groaned. He was coming to. This was the so-called "Dante the Destroyer."

He stared at them with narrowed eyes.

Alex and Calix stared at him. Felix stepped in front of them, near to the bars of the cell. He spoke to Dante, "I'm going to give *one* chance to talk on your own before I *make* you talk! It's just one, simple question. Where is Chasity?"

Chapter 46: Dinnertime

Chasity

"Good evening," I said stiffly and sat down at the end of the long table. Deidre sat at the head of the table so that we faced each other, many feet apart. All of her drones were at the sides of the table eating kale or whatever green thing was on their plates.

"Chasity, you know, I have to be frank with you, I have reason to believe you're pregnant?" Said Deidre.

The models all gasped, covering their mouths. I rolled my eyes.

"How is that any of anyone's concern?" I snapped.

"Oh, it's my concern surely!" Said Deidre, standing up, her palms pressed against the table, her shoulders hunched.

"It's my body, my business," I whispered.

"*Is* it?" Asked Deidre, laughing. Her canines looked really sharp. Her face was very angular.

I gazed around me. There was a painting on the ceiling with another fox with many tails surrounded by beautiful maidens. It was a masterpiece but I wasn't in the mood for art appraisal.

"What are you?" I whispered, glaring at her.

"Girls, you're all dismissed," said Deidre.

June glanced at me with wide eyes, reluctant to leave but she went with the others. They left their food half-eaten, some plates almost completely full. It was just me and Deidre now.

"What. Are. You?" I asked her. "You're *not* my mother's old friend, that's for sure. You're *not* Deidre Binx!"

"Oh, but I look just like her!" She said, cackling madly. "What am I? Hmm."

She sauntered around the table, coming towards me. As she walked along, she seemed to change. Her features got sharper, her ears pointier.

"I have many names…I live many lives…my people change lives as the years pass…with each new *life*, we grow another *tail!*" She hissed.

A chill crept through me. I stood up and stumbled backwards.

"You've heard of me, haven't you? Your mother must have told you folk tales to scare you at night!" She said and the quality of her voice got lower and lower.

I ran to the door. It was locked. I banged on it. I grabbed the silver collar on neck and used all my strength to bend it. I didn't have the strength of an alpha but I was still a werewolf and I would bare an alpha or three. Maybe my pups gave me strength. I managed to tear the silver collar. I flung it off and shifted just as Deidre burst into another form.

Chapter 47: Adrenaline

Third Person

"**B**y the time you get to Chasity, it'll be too late anyway!" Snarled Dante.

Felix growled impatiently. Calix regarded Dante with black eyes. Alex bared his canines. At that moment, Danny the P. I. And Chance descended to the cellar.

"Do we know anything?" Asked Chance anxiously.

"We will soon," said Felix, taking a pair of pliers out of his tool bag.

"You don't scare me!" Growled Dante.

"We'll see about that," said Felix, shrugging.

"I have nothing to live for anyway!" Retorted Dante.

"Are you seriously trying to make *me* feel sorry for *you*? You have something to do with my mate being missing?" Hissed Felix, his eyes black and his face contorted with rage. "There's no worse pain than that for a wolf!"

Dante chuckled humourlessly. "Think I don't know that? My mate is dead!"

"Then *you* should know *better* than anyone how painful that is! Why would you ever want anyone else to suffer like that? When you already know it's the greatest suffering?" Snarled Felix.

Dante took a deep breath. There was a bruise on his forehead where Felix had knocked him out. He slumped against the side of the cell.

"I just want my mate back," muttered Dante.

"What does that have to do with Chasity?" Asked Calix, exasperated with this whole exchange.

"She *looks* just like her!" Insisted Dante.

In a flash, Alex had entered the cell and was holding Dante by the throat so that his feet dangled in midair.

"You took Chasity to replace your dead mate because they *look* alike?" Roared Alex, tightening his grip on Dante's throat.

"DON'T KILL HIM!" Bellowed Calix. "We'll never find Chasity in time if you do!"

Alex listened to the youngest alpha, dropping the kidnapper onto the floor where he spluttered and gasped.

"They're not gonna kill her! You heard him! She's replacing his mate," snarled Alex.

Dante caught his breath and began to chuckle to himself.

"If you've touched Chasity, I will carve you like a roast!" Said Felix slowly.

"I haven't," insisted Dante. "I want her willing."

"SHE'LL *NEVER* BE WILLING!" Roared Felix.

"*She* won't but Deidre will," said Dante.

"What do you mean?" Asked Calix quickly.

Dante said nothing. He just lay on the floor as if asleep.

"You... you just want her body, don't you?" Whispered Calix.

His two elder brothers were making expressions that showed they did not believe in the bodysnatchers. Dante was fidgeting a little.

"We're not gonna kill her! She'll be fine. Her consciousness will be transferred to something else in the meanwhile!" Said Dante defensively.

Felix gasped. Alex was incredulous. "So it's true?!" Asked the eldest alpha. "You're stealing people's bodies? Bodysnatching?"

Dante sighed.

"Are Chasity's parents dead? Is Deidre dead?" Demand Calix.

Dante shook his head slowly.

"Where are they?" Asked Chance eagerly.

Chapter 47: Adrenaline

"In the bodies of three moon snakes that Deidre keeps in a tank in her room," whispered Dante, cackling madly.

"You've kept them sentient and locked up as snakes for nine years?" Asked Calix, horrified.

The volume of Dante's laughter increased. "Snakes only live about nine years. That's their natural lifespan so I don't know if they're still there. Maybe. They might live a little longer with werewolf consciousness in them," muttered Dante.

A chill crept through Calix. They needed to hurry not just for Chasity but for her parents and the real Deidre Binx.

Chance was shaking and black eyed. "I'll kill you!" He bellowed at Dante and rushed forwards. Alex grabbed him and Calix closed and secured the cell.

"There's no time, Grandpa!" Yelled Calix pulling Chance away from the cell.

"And where are there?! In LA?" Asked Felix, panicked.

"Deidre has a branch of her spiritual model retreat nonsense in LA but she's housing everyone at the branch closer to *home*," said Dante tauntingly.

Felix lit a blowtorch. Dante actually recoiled looking nervous. He walked towards Dante.

"Where are they?" Asked Felix slowly, taking a step with each word.

"You've been there already!" Yelped Dante accusingly.

"WHAT?!" Exclaimed Alex.

Calix gasped.

"The abandoned castle we smelled Chasity in with all the fox paintings isn't abandoned," said Calix.

Dante laughed. He pointed his index finger downwards.

Third Person (Dexter)

At the risk of upsetting or potentially even enraging the alphas, Dexter was driving his somewhat unreliable car over to the pack house. He was almost there. None but the youngest had taken him seriously. He sighed as he raced forwards pushing the old car as fast as it could go. The engine began to splutter. He looked at the meter.

He was on empty. He roared at himself internally as the car came to a halt in the snow.

He grabbed his coat and hastily donned it, abandoning the vehicle for now. He ran through the snow. This would take forever. He hadn't shifted in years. He sighed. This was for Chasity, Chase's only child. He ripped his coat off and threw it back onto the hood of the car. He couldn't afford to rip that one. Hopefully no one came by and "sprang" it. He chuckled remembering the old slang words Chase and him would make up. He pictured his wolf form and he felt the old familiar white hot pain of his bones rearranging.

Chasity

Chasity shifted a lot more quickly than she ever had before almost as fast as her alpha triplets. Perhaps, it was the adrenaline or the pup. She was on all fours, covered in sandy fur. She was a little bigger than she remembered. She had not been a marked Luna the last times she'd shifted. Maybe she was faster and stronger too. She didn't have much time to ponder it as Deidre was twisting and turning into a form before her eyes. Chasity gasped inwardly.

The Deidre imposter became a fox, a snow white fox with two tails. She was beautiful, truly breathtaking, with coal black eyes that contrasted perfectly with her blindingly white fur.

You would've been my third tail! Lamented the Fox.

Chasity knew what she was. She did have many names. In their world, some called this a were-fox, others a fox demon. In Asia, their goodnatured cousins were sometimes called Kitsune. The Deidre doppelgänger was not goodnatured. She was a dark-magic practicing fox demon, stealing life after life, growing a new tail every hundred years or so or in her specific case with each newly stolen body. So she had stolen two bodies before! Deidre and someone before that. She would have approached Dante in her old body, probably as an older woman. Then she became the young Deidre. Now, the retired supermodel needed Chasity's young body but the pesky inhabitant in Chasity's womb wouldn't do. The transfer wouldn't work.

Chasity dove as the Fox lunged at her. The Fox was twice her size, almost as big as an alpha.

Chapter 47: Adrenaline

This is nothing! Hissed the Fox. *If I had gotten my third body, I'd be three times my original size! You should've seen my mother and my grandmother before her. Colossal. Mother made it to seven! Grandmother went all the way to **nine**!*

As she hissed the last word, she pounced on Chasity.

Third Person

Deidre's centre for spirituality and modelling was *underneath* the castle. The triplets ran out the pack house followed by Detective Danny and Chance just as the wolf version of Dexter came galloping up to them across the snow. Felix growled at the unfamiliar wolf but Calix put a hand to Felix's chest. The youngest alpha recognised Dexter's smell. Alex gave Dexter a coat and he shifted back, covering himself.

"I can help! I know you think I'm crazy but..." began Dexter, his tone desperate.

"We don't! Get in the jeep!" Ordered Felix. They all piled in and Felix sped off, flooring the accelerator. The castle was a half an hour drive away but Felix was about to make it in ten minutes.

Chasity

The Fox pinned Chasity's wolf to the ground with a large paw. Chasity whimpered.

Maybe a well placed injury will get rid of the pup but salvage my new body after all! Said Deidre.

Chasity roared with rage. She snapped at the paw and the ankle of the Fox. The Fox yelped and then growled. Chasity darted away. All the doors were locked. Suddenly, one of them opened. April! Of all people! And June standing behind her.

"Let her go! She's with child! You shouldn't take this one! You didn't tell us that! Mother, you *lied*!" Yelled April.

June yelled, "Chasity follow me!"

Chasity scampered towards June just as April leapt into the air and shifted midair, revealing her true form. A jet black fox with violet eyes. Chasity almost stopped to marvel again at the fox's gorgeous forms.

"Chasity!" Shrieked June hysterically, snapping Chasity out of her trance.

Chasity dashed in the direction June indicated.

"Go up the stairs and release your parents!" June called after her.

Goosebumps sprang up under Chasity's fur. What?! Tears formed in her eyes. She saw a winding staircase. It was only a half-level staircase. No windows anywhere in the halls. Was this all underground? Chasity ascended the short flight of stairs and burst through the double doors into a large lavish boudoir.

Third Person

The jeep hurtled through the snow.

"Faster!" Yelled Calix.

"There literally isn't any faster!" Bellowed Felix.

The speed meter was at its limit.

"We can run faster than this! Danny drive Chance and Dexter there as fast as possible! We'll run ahead!" Ordered eldest alpha Alex.

Danny nodded. The car screeched to a halt. The triplets got out and tossed their coats in the backseat.

Danny took the wheel.

"Bring her back, *please*!" Begged Chance.

Alex nodded solemnly and then he shifted into his massive black wolf. His brothers did the same. They raced at inhuman speed across the snowy landscape, twice as fast as the speed produced by flooring the jeep's accelerator. They ran until their breathing was ragged. They spotted the castle up ahead. Instead of finding an opening, Calix dove through a glass window shattering it. His brothers dove in after him seeing the youngest skid and roll across the glass-strewn floor.

CALIX! Yelled Alex across mind-link.

Present! Said Calix, tumbling back onto all fours. His small scratches were already healing.

Felix breathed a sigh of relief.

They searched for a way into the underground.

Chapter 47: Adrenaline

Chasity

Chasity shifted. It was risky but she wanted to reunite with her parents in a form they might recognise. She quickly grabbed a random loose-fitting silk dress from Deidre's wardrobe and put it on. She looked around the dimly lit bedroom. Everything was in mauves and dusky pinks. A huge white fox painting hung over the bed. There was painting of Deidre in her youth and one of another young beauty dressed in vintage clothing. *Her first body,* thought Chasity. She needed to hurry. She spotted a glow emanating from under a mauve sheet on a countertop at the side of the room. She ripped the sheet off to reveal a snake tank. The glow was coming from a heat lamp for the snakes. There was nothing living in this room besides Chasity and these three snakes. Were June and April setting her up? They had seemed completely sincere.

Chasity peered into the tank. One snake remained in the corner. Two of them became very agitated and came up to the glass, staring at her. She had never seen snakes behave quite like this. They were acting like enthusiastic golden retrievers when the family children came hurtling off the school bus. Stranger things have happened.

"Hello!" Said Chasity to the snakes.

They were trying to get out of the tank but there was a lid with holes in it for air but none of these holes were large enough for the snakes. Chasity reached for the lid, feeling strangely drawn to these two friendly snakes.

"NO!" Came Deidre's feral cry. Chasity whipped around. The imposter was in her human form again, clad in a pink silk robe similar to the dress Chasity had threw on. The imposter certainly had an eye for aesthetics. Everything in her word was so exquisitely luxurious it all felt surreal.

Deidre slinked towards Chasity, snarling even in her human form. She was eyeing the tank behind Chasity. Chasity shrunk into the corner but stretched her hand out towards the lid.

"NO!" Came Deidre's inhuman sounding snarl as she leapt at Chasity.

Chasity fell backwards and pulled on the large doily under the tank, sliding it *and* the tank to the edge of the counter. The lid swung open and all three snakes fell out. The one who had seemed disinterested before sprang at the doppelgänger of Deidre!

Chasity gasped at the strange but magnificent site unfolding before her eyes.

Chapter 48: Family

Third Person

The triplets darted through the castle in their wolf forms trying to pick up Chasity's scent or find a way to go down. They returned to the dining room with the huge dining table where they had first smelled Chasity. Calix noticed something. There was a huge printed rug between the dining table and the fireplace. The print was a fox opening its jaws to reveal many beautiful women inside looking forlorn. Calix gripped the edge of the rug with his teeth and pulled. His brothers helped him move the rug. There was a trap door underneath!

Chasity

The snake that had sprung at the Deidre lookalike pierced her neck with its fangs. Deidre shrieked and tried to remove it but the snake was latched onto her neck. The snake become limp but still clung to the supermodel. Deidre lay still, crumpled on the ground for a few seconds before her body started to twitch. The snake fell off of her neck and turned to dust. Deidre's entire form began to glow an ethereal silvery white. I gasped. The other snakes approached me tentatively. I scrambled away from them just in case though they seemed friendly. The glowing Deidre opened her mouth and her eyes. I covered my mouth in shock. Her eyes were stark white, rolled back in her head and out of her mouth coalesced a silvery shimmering white smoke that formed the shape of the white fox. It was not solid though, merely spirit. The essence of the fox. It shrieked as it zoomed away rushing out of sight. The whole place began to quake. Oh no!

Third Person

The three wolves ran through a maze like underground mansion searching for their mate. They came across two wounded girls. Alex shifted so he could talk to them.

"What happened?" He asked the girls. "Do you girls know our mate, Chasity?!"

Alex's eyes were wide pleading with the girls. The girls both blushed averting their eyes from Alex's naked form.

One girl was cradling the more injured one in her arms. The gravely injured one pointed a trembling finger in the direction Chasity had presumably went. The girl holding her badly hurt friend spoke.

"She's in Madame's bedroom. Go out into the hallway and up the stairs. *Please* help us!" Begged the girl.

"We will," promised Alex.

He shifted and ran with his brothers through a long hallway with no window and very few doors. The walls were shaking. Dust was falling from the ceiling. They did not have much time. They found the flight of stairs and ascended them.

Chasity

Deidre was stirring. I recoiled. I wasn't sure of the way out of here. I decided to make a run for it. I darted towards the door but tripped falling over. I looked back. Deidre was grasping my ankle.

"Don't be scared," said Deidre, her voice sounding different.

I yanked her ankle away.

Chapter 48: Family

"Don't leave me and your parents *please!*" Begged Deidre.

I gasped. The fox spirit had fled the body after the snake bit it!

"Are you..." I began.

"The real Deidre! Yes!" Breathed Deidre. "I was trapped in that moon snake's body and Deidre used mine to become famous. Your parents are in the other two snakes. We have to hurry!"

I gasped. My eyes filled with tears. I scooped up the two snakes who slithered onto a shoulder each.

"What do I do? Where are their bodies?" I asked, desperate.

"Here! They work here. Two of Deidre's loyal sycophants took the bodies!" Explained the real Deidre.

"Lead me to them!" I demanded.

"You have to help me! I haven't walked as a human in years!" Cried Deidre.

I let her swing an arm over me. I hoisted her up. She leant heavily on me. I barely made it to the door. The roof started to crumble. I hoped whoever was in my parents bodies had the sense to evacuate. What about June? And April? We were never gonna make it like this! Just as I neared the door, it burst open!

"Alphas!" I screamed. They literally knocked me over, all three of them pouncing on me and licking my face. I giggled.

"We need to get out of here!" I yelled over the sound of concrete breaking.

Felix growled at Deidre. Alex was ready to strike. Calix snarled.

"NO!" I yelled. "This is the real Deidre Binx! These snakes are my parents! There's no time to explain. Please we have to get my parents bodies and go!"

I knew I probably sounded delusional but to my surprise, my alphas looked like they completely believed me. Felix was sniffing my tummy. He was smelling the pup.

Deidre was placed on Alex's back and I was on Felix's back. Calix led the way. We ran into an older werewolf and two other men who were all panting.

"Chasity!" Cried the older werewolf with tears in his eyes. Huh.

Calix whimpered impatiently.

Calix led us through the shaking underground mansion back to the dining room where April lay gravely injured in June's arms.

"No!" I screamed. "April! June!"

I dismounted Felix and ran to them. "We'll help you get out of here!" April and June were hoisted onto Felix's back. I joined Deidre on Alex's back.

"We have to get my parents' bodies!"

"I know where they are," mumbled April, her voice weakening. "Their bodies are inhabited by distant relatives of Deidre. They live down here and help her run the school."

"Mr and Mrs Chalet!" Exclaimed June.

We ran in the direction indicted by April.

"What about all the other girls?!" I exclaimed. "What about Maurice and Dante?!"

Felix growled in response to the name Dante. He was so jealous for everything! He didn't even know Dante!

"Dante's missing. He hasn't been back for a few hours," said June. "Maurice isn't here right now. The other girls all fled as soon as they saw us heading back to the dining room to confront Madame!"

"Are they all Foxes?" I asked.

"Yes! But they don't necessarily want to be *snatchers*. They're not all bad! Trust me," said June. "Madame gave us food and shelter. Many of us come from nothing and actually do want to break into modelling. Madame scouted almost all of us herself, handpicking us, looking for the vulnerable."

April was quiet, her head lulling. I was worried about her. She had fought Madame on my behalf to save my pup. I owed her. She had honour.

We made it to an office of sorts. There was a desk under which two people crouched with their arms flung over their heads, sheltering from the falling dust and crumbling roof. I gasped.

"Mom! Dad!" I shrieked in spite of myself. The snakes hissed and my so-called parents growled at me, recoiling from me and the hissing snakes. My triplets snarled at them. Of course, these were imposters. My parents' minds were still in the snakes.

"Chasity! Let the snakes bite them!" Instructed the nervous, twitching werewolf accompanying my alphas. Who were these three people with my alphas? I listened to him anyway.

"Hurry, Chasity!" Exclaimed the older werewolf.

Chapter 48: Family

"I called for backup while we were on the way," said the youngest of the three men I didn't know. He was still older than my alphas though.

I looked at the snakes and my parents. I didn't know which was which. I guessed. I threw the bigger snake at my father's body and the smaller one at my mother's body. The snakes latched onto their throats and my parents' imposters screamed trying to pull the snakes off of them. Eventually they fell over and the snakes turned to dust. Black smoke unfurled from the mouth of my father until a black smoky fox darted through the air, disappearing. The fox spirit emanating from my mother was grey. It zoomed away with a shriek. My parents moaned, getting unsteadily to their feet. The nervous werewolf helped my Dad and the older one cradled my Mom.

"Mom! Dad!" I screamed. I flung myself at them. My Dad caught me in shaky arms.

"Dad, what are you doing here?" Said my Mom looking at the older werewolf.

He was my grandfather! Where had he been all this time?

My Mom embraced her father as I embraced mine. I hugged my Mom tightly and my Grandpa.

"This is beautiful!" Said the young werewolf. "But let's go!"

We scrambled out of there, barely making it to the stairs. We ascended a staircase that led to a dining room. I recognised the room. I had been laying on that dining table tied up. My first bedroom during the ordeal was nearby and my new location was *right underground*. I had thought those people had taken me far away.

We rushed out of the house. There was an ambulance waiting. They had been called by one of the men I didn't know. They took April, June and Deidre. My parents claimed they were fine. I would make them get check-ups later. We watched as the castle fell through the earth as the underground caved in. Dust filled the air. I began to cough. My alphas shifted and quickly put on cloaks. I ran to them. Felix snatched me up.

"I'm never letting you out of my sight ever again!" He murmured against my ear.

Warmth engulfed me. Calix hugged me tightly. "Chasity I'll never wink at anyone who isn't you! I'll join winkers anonymous!" I grumbled at him. "I missed you, Goddess!" Said the youngest alpha kissing my face over and over again. Alex enveloped me in his arms. "Luna, I was so scared I'd never see you again!" He whispered. Alex! Scared? I nuzzled him and then the other two complained until they were both nuzzled. The triplets and my mother introduced me properly to my grandfather. He cupped my face in his hands. "I have a room filled with presents for you, literally!" He said. I laughed.

The young guy was the P. I., Danny, hired to assist with my missing person's case. I thanked him and he smiled. The nervous guy was named Dexter. My Dad introduced him as his old best friend. I clung to my father. I couldn't believe he was real. I started to cry and my father held me tightly and rubbed my back. My mother patted my head. I had missed out on so much with them. On the bright side, all the time as snakes meant they had maintained sobriety without any choice really for nine years. They said they knew they could keep it up. I told them I was proud of them.

"We're proud of you Chasity, our brave strong girl," said my Mom.

A stray tear slid down my cheek. I felt so loved, like the longest nightmare was over.

"I'm pregnant," I said to everyone though I was certain my triplets seemed to know already.

My father looked horrified. "You were a little girl the last time I saw you," he mumbled.

I blushed. "I'm *eighteen* now Dad! And the Alpha Triplets are my mates!"

The triplets tried to hug my father but he glared at them. It was their turn to have a difficult in-law. My mother hugged the triplets.

"Your mother must have shit bricks when she found out my daughter was fated to you three!" Exclaimed my Mom.

"Mom!" I said indignantly. I forgot how outspoken and honestly a bit crude she could be.

"As if it's not the truth," she said. I sighed. She's been a snake for nine years. I wasn't about to complain too much regarding her frankness.

"Let's go home!" I told everybody.

Chapter 49: Oh Baby!

Chasity

Luna Ronnie's jaw almost dropped to the floor when I walked in with my Mom. My Mom grinned at her. The former alpha was dumbfounded. My father entered the pack house and spotted acting Luna Ronnie, his step-sister. His face broke into a smile and his eyes filled with tears. Ronnie's expression softened. She got up and went to him. She hugged him tightly. She was crying into the collar of his shirt. The former alpha ruffled my hair to my surprise and pulled me into a gentle hug.

"I'm glad you're safe Chasity!" He said. "My boys were a mess without you."

I nodded. "Thank you," I said softly, smiling.

"Dad, I owe you an apology," said my mother to Grandpa Chance. "I should have let you have custody of Chasity back when you asked for it. I was a junkie back then and I wasn't thinking straight. All I could think was how upset I was that you were trying to take my baby away."

Grandpa Chance smiled, teary-eyed. He embraced my Mom.

"Chance," said Luna Ronnie stiffly. "I'm sorry for accusing you of killing my stepbrother and his wife. I was... that was unfounded."

"I'm sorry for accusing you!" Said Chance, sighing. Luna Ronnie smiled stiffly. It would be a long road with her. She still wasn't the biggest fan of my family.

"I'm not sorry for accusing anyone I accused," announced Felix.

"Felix!" Said Alex and the former alpha in unison. Calix laughed.

"I had my reasons," Felix said defiantly. "The important thing is it all led up to finding my Baby, Chasity, who, I would like to announce, is having my baby!"

"Our baby!" Corrected Alex. "Yeah" said Calix.

I smiled and blushed. I watched Luna Ronnie's face closely. She smiled and it honestly seemed genuine. "It would be wonderful to have a baby in the house again," she whispered to the former alpha. "Remember the triplets as babies."

"They were a handful," said Romeo. "We were not ready for that. We were scarcely prepared for one rambunctious child let alone three!"

The triplets chuckled. I needed to take a bath in my bathtub! I was exhausted and had not properly relaxed in a while.

I went to my downstairs bedroom with Felix close on my heels. Alex and Calix followed too. I gasped when I walked in. It. Was. Empty. I screamed!

"You're not to stay down here! You were kidnapped here!" Felix said defensively.

"Where are all of my things?" I demanded.

"In our new room. We got a fourth bedroom on our floor that has all of our stuff," said Alex sheepishly.

"Isn't that cool?" Asked Calix, grinning, not understanding how upset I was.

"Go look in the new bedroom and bathroom! *Please!*" Insisted Felix.

I trudged up the stairs. I was so exhausted. My legs were about to give out under me when Alex lifted me up and carried me bridal style. Felix opened the bedroom door for us. The new bedroom was really pretty, all baby blue, and even a lovely crib in one corner.

"For when you want the pup nearby!" Felix said. "We're working on the nursery, don't worry!"

I nodded sleepily.

Chapter 49: Oh Baby!

They took me to the new bathroom which was also all baby blue. The bathtub was huge! It was perhaps twice the size of the one downstairs I had been obsessed with.

"Tada!!!" Exclaimed Calix.

I leant towards Calix to give him a gentle kiss. Felix kissed me like I was made of porcelain and Alex kissed me afterwards, slowly and methodically. The triplets helped me to undress and ran a warm bath for me. They lowered me into the tub. I pouted when they didn't join me. They were acting like I was *so* fragile. Was it because of the recent kidnapping or the pregnancy?

Felix lathered me up while Alex shampooed my hair. Calix massaged my feet. I sighed. This was heavenly. I must have been in and out of sleep because the next moment I was suddenly in my night gown being spooned by Felix with Calix in front of me. They had claimed the night I had gone missing it had been their turn. Alex had grumbled to himself. I had placated him with a steamy kiss. I squirmed around, rubbing my behind against Felix's member but making it seem coincidental. I really *missed* them. Maybe it was the pregnancy but I felt really aroused and I needed to be sated. No matter how much I wiggled about, my alphas just snuggled me and kissed me gently, planting soft kisses all over my nose, cheeks, forehead and neck. I was really annoyed.

I wrapped my legs around Felix's waist and placed an urgent kiss against his lips. He hugged me tightly to his chest and kissed the top of my head then promptly fell asleep. Ugh! Eventually, thankfully, despite my restlessness, sleep came and carried me off too.

In the morning I decided to complain. I awoke to the sound of my triplets talking softly among each other, trying not to wake me. They were discussing the pup and taking me to a doctor today.

"Alphas," I said softly.

"What it is, Baby?" Cooed Felix, stroking my hair.

"Morning, Luna," said Alex with a huge grin, leaning over to kiss my lips.

"Hey Goddess," said Calix, kissing both of my cheeks over and over again, making me giggle.

"Last night... nothing happened," I said sheepishly.

They were quiet.

"Nothing can happen until you see the doctor," said Alex sternly.

"What?" I yelped.

"You were kidnapped for the beginning of your pregnancy. We need to make sure everything is ok with you and the pup. You both need a proper checkup," explained Alex.

"Yeah," grumbled Felix although he half-wished something *had* happened last night.

"There will be many, many, many nights of passion in your future, Chasity," said Calix, winking.

I blushed.

The triplets insisted on helping me shower for the doctor's visit. They hopped in the shower but we literally just showered. I was not pleased. Alex picked out my outfit and wanted to style my curls but I wouldn't let him. I wore what he chose though, a baby blue maxi dress, surprise, surprise. They bundled me up and carried me to the private place. The clinic was so fancy. Whenever I had been sick when I was younger, I had to go to a public place *except* after the ice water incident when I was taken to a private hospital. The doctor was really nice and surprisingly young. She said everything was normal: mu urine, my blood work and my vitals. My pregnancy test was positive of course. She had wanted to use her more accurate test as I had only used a drugstore one while being held captive. Then she examined my belly and did the ultrasound. She grinned.

"Congratulations!" She exclaimed. "Three future alphas in the making."

The triplets were stunned.

"What?!" I asked.

"You're having triplets! Three pups. If you were human, it'd be too early to tell but as they're werewolves and their momma is a she-wolf, I can see the three of them quite clearly though you're early so they're tiny," she explained.

"They'll be as big as their Daddy, give them time!" Said Felix defensively.

"Their Daddies!" Specified Alex. Calix glared at Felix.

"Is it possible to tell who is the father?" Asked Calix.

"Probably not because your DNA is identical. Identical triplets. Identical DNA. I can try to make an educated guess based on sexual history like who last had sex with Chasity and how that coincides with her last menstrual period to see when she might have conceived..."

"No, that's ok," I said, blushing.

There was very little solo sex so that wouldn't make sense. In future, I did actually want more one on one time with each triplet. I wanted to make each of my future husbands feel special. I smiled at them and they grinned back.

"We love you, Chasity," whispered Calix. He cupped my face and kissed me gently.

"And we missed you like crazy!" Added Felix, massaging my shoulders.

"We're keeping you and these babies on lockdown!" Said Alex, nuzzling me.

"Fair enough," I said, smiling, to their surprise. "I love you you too, all of you, so much! And I missed you! Every second was horrible without you. I thought I'd never see you again!" I started to sniffle. I tried to hold back tears but their came pouring out. I started to sob and all the triplets rushed to comfort me. I knew a little bit of this was hormonal but it *had* been scary.

"Hey!" I said suddenly. "What happened to Dante?"

Chapter 50: Future Family Fiasco

Chasity

Apparently the triplets had held Dante in a cell and planned to do so for as many days as I was kidnapped. He would then be transferred to regular jail. I told them he wasn't the worst honestly. Maurice was dead due to a totally unrelated event. He had choked on a sandwich sitting in his car in the parking lot of a convenience store he had just robbed. He had shot the owner there, a father of five in front of one one the children who'd been helping out in the family store. The father lived as the bullet missed all major organs and major blood vessels but he was still recuperating. The sandwich itself had been stolen. It was kind of a sick poetic justice. Maurice actually belonged to Deidre's centre for whatever and whatever else. I really couldn't remember and I didn't want to. I was trying to blank out some stuff. Due to that membership, he was entitled to boarding and meals which is how Deidre (the old imposter Deidre) kept followers quite easily. However, Maurice had a string of petty thefts despite having buffets available to him. Maybe I was soft but I didn't want to judge him too harshly. Maybe his life had been awful? Alex reminded me *my* life had been awful and I was not someone who would shoot someone over a sandwich when I already had food at home.

Chapter 50: Future Family Fiasco

The triplets were concerned about my sense of justice as I kept reminding them that Dante wasn't so bad in my opinion. They hired me a tutor to teach me pack law proceedings as I was preparing to be the official Luna so Ronnie could stop being acting Luna. I told Ronnie I wasn't in a rush and she seemed secretly glad. Felix had said "Three more months tops!" And Ronnie had frowned. I had smirked to myself. I fully intended to be Luna but I would be more lenient. The triplets were tough. We would compliment each other. Everyone would wait for Luna hearing days instead of the Alpha ones to come for their problems. The triplets seemed to have guessed my plans and Alex and Felix said they would supervise my Luna hearing days for the first couple months. Ugh! I planned to cry in front of Calix about this soon to see what could be done. I didn't want to be supervised.

June and April made full recoveries! They were were-foxes and they did not necessarily need to body-snatch. They could live forever like werewolves once not killed but they would age. Their ageing was a bit faster than werewolves but slower than humans. Deidre's imposter had wanted youth and beauty. This somehow made her body snatching worse. I had thought perhaps she was mortal without the snatching and feared death. She didn't actually need those bodies. Her original body which would be an old woman was already placed somewhere and if her fox spirit got to it in time she would still be alive. That terrified me. The fox body snatchers who were in my parents bodies could also reunite with their original now aged bodies if their fox spirits got to them in time.

I didn't know what the time limit for a fox spirit making it back to its original body was. The girls didn't know either. June and April were from poor families but their fox families never snatched bodies. Their relatives just aged. The girls apologised profusely and were very ashamed due to their involvement. The triplets made them serve short jail sentences in the prison infirmaries as they were accessories to a kidnapping. When they were well enough to be discharged from the prison infirmary, they were released on probation so they were essentially sentenced to time served in a way. June and April wanted to help plan my bachelorette party, bridal shower, wedding, baby shower *and* help the triplets plan my honeymoon!

Mina and Tina were pissed. They told April and June they were not in charge of planning but could be assistants if necessary. Mina and Tina did not trust or like April and June but all four girls had really shown me a lot of loyalty. April who I thought disliked me fought Madame, a much more powerful were-fox, to save me and my pups and June helped me locate my parents. I couldn't ignore those things but I did pronounce Mina and Tina the *Official Ladies in Waiting and Event Planning Committee Heads for the Luna,* a very long name that they came up with after Mr Johnson suggested they apply themselves more. They wanted to be event planners because "being lit came naturally" to them. They also wanted to be makeover experts and start a television show. I would honestly binge-watch a Mina Tina Makeover Show.

Everything was going pretty swimmingly until about a week after I had my first checkup. I heard angry voices downstairs so I slowly made my way down. I was still very early in my pregnancy but the triplets wanted me to be careful around all "dangerous activities" like ascending and descending steps apparently.

"If I had known that you'd brutalise my little girl, I would't have dropped her off here! I thought you would at least treat her humanely if not like your own!" Bellowed my father.

"Brutalise is a very strong word!" Snapped Ronnie.

"And *you* are a very weak person!" Bellowed my father. "Taking out your grudges on a child!"

"You were a DRUG ADDICT! YOU LEFT HER!" Screamed Ronnie.

"I WAS ON THE RUN AFTER CHALICE AND I SAW THE BODY SNATCHERS IN ACTION!!!" Bellowed my father so loudly the house shook. I gasped. He was not an alpha because *his* father had had no pack but his father had been a Sigma Wolf which is like a Lone Alpha. He was physiologically as powerful as an alpha but had no pack to command. Some Sigmas formed packs by gathering rogues. Many snotty packs who look down on rogues actually originated that way. My tutor for pack laws was really good so I was learning a lot. Alex had selected him. His name was Nicolai. He was a brown-haired werewolf with huge brown eyes and dimples. Felix hated him and wanted me to have a female tutor. Nicky had come out to me but I promised not to tell anyone yet. He was going to tell people himself when he was ready. Mina and Tina liked him, especially for his fashion sense. They thought he could be a third expert on the Mina Tina Makeover Show but he wouldn't get his name in the title.

The triplets ran towards the commotion. Calix immediately scooped me up and carried me away from the arguing saying it was bad for the pups. I could hear Felix and Alex talking and they sounded as though they were calmly agreeing with my Dad and apologising. Ronnie was so infuriated by this that she stormed out and drove away. She came back twelve minutes later and sat on the porch fuming. I really didn't like her but she was the grandmother of my babies. I had recently received all the hundreds of things Grandpa Chance had gotten for me over the nine years. That was awful of Ronnie to keep those from me and to return the letters. I sighed. She was such a bitch but I had to fix this somehow. I knew she would actually treat my pups well. I sat in Calix's old bedroom. He was playing video games with me in his lap and he was holding the controller over me. I kept pressing random buttons when he wasn't looking and he was getting frustrated.

"I never got to go to my therapist!" I exclaimed.

Calix paused his game. He looked at me, his eyes filled with concern.

"Let me remake the appointment," he said.

"Make one for a big family counselling session too," I said.

"Ugh, that's gonna be so much drama Chas…"

I glared at him.

"Ok one solo appointment, one family fiasco, coming right up!"

Chapter 51: Family Fiasco and Fainting

Chasity

Doctor Jardine was a psychiatrist *and* a psychologist. She sat across from all of us on a mint green chair. The wallpaper in her office was an abstract swirl of pastel colours that made me feel woozy. I was sandwiched between Calix and Alex with Felix nervously glancing at me every few seconds from where he sat on Alex's other side. We occupied the pastel blue couch. The pastel pink one on our right housed my mother, father and Grandpa Chance. The muted yellow couch on our left was where Ronnie and Romeo sat. Ronnie was sitting cross-legged and was jiggling her top leg nervously. Her Louis Vuitton was in danger of flying off and having its heel enter the wallpaper like a throwing dart.

"So we're all here to iron out any old grudges and seek a greater level of harmony within this family," said Jardine.

"Yes," I responded quickly.

My father cleared his throat. Ronnie huffed.

"Who would like to start?" Asked Dr Jardine.

"I would," said Felix unsurprisingly. I smiled at him and he winked.

"Chasity is my mate, my Luna, the mother of my... our... heirs. But that's now. Before Chasity turned eighteen, she wasn't a part of the family. She shares a birthday with us triplets by the way but my parents chose not to celebrate hers," Felix said, seemingly angry and ashamed at the same time.

Ronnie fidgeted in her chair. My father growled a little but my mother shushed him.

"She came to us when she was nine. My brothers and I were twelve. She was tearful and distraught most days and my parents... they made it worse. I make no excuses for myself. I was a bully. A little jerk but my parents were adults. Chasity was just a child, no birthday or Christmas presents, only permitted to have donated clothes or hand-me-downs. She couldn't eat meals with us. She cooked. She cleaned. She was like a little maid. I'm not sure why we even expected her to ever be in a good mood. We had no right to consider her sullen. What did she have to be happy about? Nothing. And what was the point of my parents treating her so... subpar?" Felix mused more to himself than everyone else.

My father was seething, taking deep breaths, while my mother clutched his hand tightly.

"We didn't get presents for Chasity. She *did* get hand-me-downs. Forgive me but she was treated as though unwanted because she *was* unwanted," said Romeo. My father rushed to get up but my mother and Grandpa Chance held him back.

"It's true!" Said Romeo defiantly. *You* dropped her off!" Snarled Romeo.

My father sat back down.

"How could you expect her to be treated like a little princess. You dropped her off, no discussion, and thus you had no inkling of whether or not we *wanted* to help," said Romeo.

"We *did* want to help," said Ronnie, tears brimming in her eyes, "but no we didn't want to take in anyone. We wanted to help you Chase *out* of your mess!"

I sighed. That stung. I knew Ronnie and Romeo had never really wanted me as their adopted daughter or step niece or anything like that but it still hurt to hear it sad plain as day.

My mother spoke, "No one expected you to treat her like a princess! We would have been ok with *humane* treatment at the very least or a bit of care and friendliness. You treated her worse than a stranger. You made her feel utterly alone on purpose. You made her into a little servant! A child labourer! If the triplets hadn't realised

Chasity was their mate, would the subpar treatment have *ever* stopped?!" Asked my Mom. She was shaking.

"You pushed *your* responsibility on us so yeah we did the bare minimum: food, clothing and healthcare. Nothing less, nothing more," grumbled Romeo.

Now was probably not a good time to mention there were times I was put out of the house in the cold for "misbehaving". I also wasn't allowed to eat quite as much as I liked, only what was allowed me and I ate different meals to the ones the triplets and the former alpha and luna got. I sighed, leaning my head back on the couch.

Calix was squeezing my hand reassuringly and Felix was rubbing my knee very gently with his thumb.

"Ok, I understand the situation was not discussed well," said Jardine. "But imagine someone had to look after the triplets growing up. That someone didn't really want to so they used that as a basis for raising the boys. The boys got no love or affection, no guidance, just food and shelter and healthcare as you say. Would you be angry at that someone or would you understand where he or she is coming from?"

"I would... be mad but I would also never leave my kids in the first place!" Said Ronnie.

"Mom!" Said Alex, his eyes darkening with suppressed rage. "If you weren't going to give Chasity a loving upbringing then why didn't you let Chance take her?!" Demanded Alex.

"I would like to know the answer to that myself," grumbled Chance.

"*Her* mother was estranged from her father, Chance. She said he wanted to steal her baby!" Ronnie said indignantly.

"I did say stuff like that," said Mom, looking incredibly guilty. "I was a junkie and I was paranoid. I was so irresponsible back then. I *should* have given her to you, Dad. I'm so sorry, Dad! I'm so sorry Chasity!" said my mom bursting into sobs that wracked her body.

"It's ok, Mom," I whispered. Alex went over to my Mom and rubbed her back. My father cradled her to his chest. "I'm so sorry too, Chasity and Chance," he said. "We really should have let you two have a relationship."

"I... wish... I would have at least not made Chasity do the housework though I wouldn't have made any fuss over holidays.

Making her do maid work was wrong," said Ronnie softly. "I know that. I... I'm sorry Chasity," said Ronnie as though it caused her physical pain to have to apologise to the likes of me.

"She should not have had to do housework. I agree with that," said Romeo with a sigh. "I... am... sorry too, Chasity," he said slowly as though the words tasted pungent.

My mother pursed her lips and my father glared at the former alpha and luna. Grandpa Chance was dabbing at his eyes and not looking at anyone.

Alex and Calix had been so quiet. Alex came back to my couch.

"Alpha Alex, your thoughts on all of this," prompted Dr Jardine.

"Chasity's parents weren't perfect. Had they been more stable they could've raised Chasity themselves or seen the truth that she would have been better off with Chance. They shouldn't have dropped her off with people who may or may not have held grudges against her but also, holding a grudge against a child is ridiculous and making a child into an unpaid worker is inexcusable. Two wrongs don't make a right but my parents went overboard in my opinion. The only person who was blameless in all of this was Chasity herself. She was just an innocent little girl and it's something that makes me feel sick to think about. We all owe Chasity an apology. I know I've said sorry a lot but there's no harm in saying it again. I'm sorry for making a bad situation worse Chasity, my Luna, by being such a huge jerk to you all the time. You are so sweet and special, Luna. You deserve much better!" Said Alex, his eyes sparkling with tears. He sighed and pulled me across Felix's lap and straight into his arms on the far side of the couch.

"Alpha Calix?" Said Dr Jardine, looking expectantly at the youngest alpha.

Calix's wide blue eyes were staring at the Doctor.

"Chasity was someone who should've grown up our friend and playmate and then the transition from that to mates would have been easier. Smooth even. Our parents didn't set the best example but the older we got, the better we shouldn't have known. There's really no excuse. Goddess, I'm *so* sorry!" Murmured Calix kissing my forehead.

"Chasity," said Doctor Jardine. Me? Me! I hadn't even realised at first how little I'd contributed to the session.

"Um," I said, unsure of where to start. "I was devastated when my parents dropped me off. Going from abandonment straight into a hostile situation for me as a little girl was too much to really process. It's all a blur when I actively try to remember but the memories. The memories come to me though when I'm not expecting them and that's when they're sharp and vivid."

"Chasity," said Dr Jardine hesitantly with look of concern on her face.

"Yeah?" I replied.

"Have you ever considered that you may have Post Traumatic Stress Disorder or PTSD?" She asked.

I bit my lip.

"It crossed my mind once or twice," I said softly.

"That would explain the foggy memory, the flashbacks..." said the Doctor.

Me? PTSD? But that was permanent wasn't it? I felt out control all of a sudden. I was nauseated. Beads of perspiration formed at my temples. I was breathless and lightheaded. I wanted to scream. There was this sense of impending doom.

"Chasity, breath, relax. Focus on the sound of my voice said the doctor. I tried to focus like she had said but I could only whimper as the edges of my vision blurred.

"Chasity!" Yelled Calix, holding me to me. That was the last thing that was said to me before I blacked out.

Chapter 52: Planning

Chasity

When I came to, I was in a hospital bed of all places. Oh no. Many anxious faces were surrounding me. Six to be exact. Alex, Felix, Calix, Mom, Dad and Grandpa Chance. I slowly sat up with the help of Alex who was nearest to me on my right. On my left was my Dad who was relived I was awake but still clearly seething.

"I can't believe my sister. Since when was Ronnie a complete monster like this?" Grumbled my Dad.

Calix growled a little at this insult against his mother, Calix being her favourite.

My father snarled back.

"Stop it!" Said Felix to both of them. "You're stressing my bride out and she's with child."

"Our bride!" Corrected Alex.

"Children!" Added Calix.

"Children?" Asked my father, mother and Grandpa Chance all in unison.

I had totally forgotten to tell them about the multiples. I had been so fixated on preparing myself emotionally for the family therapy session and even after all that preparation, I couldn't handle it. I had fainted. I felt like such a weakling. My wolf reminded me that I had been abandoned at nine years old and bullied from the age of nine years to the age of seventeen years, a time period where I was insignificant. No birthdays acknowledged, no Christmas gifts, no parental figures, no friends, no relatives as far as I had know back then. Then at eighteen, I dealt with finding out my mates were my former bullies. I had managed to forgive them and learn to stop fearing them and to even demand respect from them though there were three of them and one of me. I dealt with bullying at school, at that heinous house party. I was kidnapped after said party and I fought for my own and my pups' lives. I had only even found out I was pregnant while I was a captive. I had freed my parents and Deidre and gotten all their bodies back. I was breathless just thinking about all that. My wolf was happy with me for once. She said I was resilient.

"Mom, Dad, Grandpa Chance, with all the commotion, it totally slipped my mind to tell anyone about it yet. I am having triplets," I announced.

Mom gasped. "I don't envy you, Honey, that's one tough labour of love.

I gulped.

"But congratulations. I love you and I know you can do it. I can't wait to love my three grand babies!" Said Mom.

"Congratulations, Sweetheart, that's wonderful!" Said my Dad looking exceedingly worried and not at all like it was "wonderful."

Grandpa Chance had a thoughtful expression on his face. "I'm here you every step of the way, Chasity. I promise to be a great Grandpa to these triplets!" Joked Grandpa Chance.

Felix groaned.

My Mom shook her head, closing her eyes. My Dad and Calix laughed. Alex was completely stone-faced, looking at my vitals being monitored.

"Get it, *great Grandpa* like the grandfather of the babies' mother and great like awesome!" Explained Grandpa Chance.

Alex sighed, "You scared me half to death, Luna." Alex sniffled. Aww! I pulled him down onto me to my father's chagrin. Alex buried his head on my tummy and tightened his hold on me. "Little Luna, you're my everything."

"Do you guys know exactly what went wrong with me?" I asked.

Chapter 52: Planning

"The doctor says it could have been a panic attack that resulted in a fainting spell. Your blood sugar was normal, your blood work was normal and so were the ECG and CT-Brain," said Calix matter-of-factly.

I was impressed. I stretched over and kissed him gently on the mouth, causing a fire to light in my lower belly. My father narrowed his eyes at our simple kiss. I pulled away. The doctors discharged me the next day after keeping me for a few hours for observation and under seizure watch since I had some head trauma. During the neurology watch, I had not had any strange behaviour or seizure-like behaviour. The pups were fine and all had normal heartbeats. I was so relieved I could cry.

When we got back to the pack house, the atmosphere was tense. My father said Ronnie and Romeo had shown their true colours by not staying to check on me. It was all new to him but for me, this was the way it had always been. Ronnie and Romeo disliked me and there was no use in trying to force them to care. I had enough genuine people in my life especially now that I had been reunited with my parents and my Grandpa Chance.

Mina and Tina came over to discuss my bachelorette party and bridal shower.

"What's the difference between a bachelorette party and a bridal shower?" I Asked.

"A bachelorette party is a celebration of your last night of single hood before marriage. It usually involves alcohol, loud music, strangely shaped cakes, that sort of think," said Tina.

"Meanwhile, a bridal shower is the tamer version like a sit-down meal. Most don't involve alcohol or actual partying," said Mina.

I nodded. "What am I having again?" I asked, smiling sheepishly.

"Both!" Mina and Tina said in unison.

I grinned.

Since the fainting incident at family therapy, we hadn't been back and we had not discussed it properly. My parents and my mates' parents were behaving but they were definitely not acting like a family. My father and his stepsister were behaving icily towards each other. I kept thinking about the day I had been dropped at the pack house. I wondered how much better my life would have been, growing up with my loving Grandpa versus my step aunt who didn't want me and made that very clear. I couldn't help but think that Ronnie and Romeo, despite being pricks, had a point. My parents were aware it seemed that they mightn't want me so why force me on them? They *knew* my Grandpa wanted me but just because he had threatened to fight them for custody due to their drug use, they had refused to give me to him. The more I thought about it, the more furious I became. Ronnie and Romeo were really unkind but Mom and Dad were really unwise.

Mina and Tina showed me the schedule they had come up with. My bachelorette party was on the same night as the triplets' bachelor party. My stomach did backflips. I didn't want girls drooling over them while I was in this delicate state, waddling about and pregnant. Ugh. After these came my bridal shower which would be reminiscent of a tea party. Then came my baby shower and lastly my wedding reception. I knew I wanted to be married before I gave birth. I wanted that sense of stability for myself and my pups. I could scarcely believe I was going from mother of none to mother of three in one shot. Thankfully, I had three fiancés to help me.

On the night of my bachelorette party, my stomach was in knots worried about the triplets having their bachelor party. I didn't want Calix winking at any exotic dancers and I didn't want Alex explaining pack laws to them. Some of the exotic dancers might be exes of Felix's for all I know. I was wearing a sequin gold mini dress and matching heels. Felix spun me around. I giggled.

"No drinking," he said sternly.

"Of course not!" I replied indignantly. I wasn't irresponsible.

The triplets all wore matching blazers, black velvet ones. I ran my fingers along Felix's blazer while he adjusted it in the bathroom mirror. He placed me on the counter. I squeaked because the tiles were cold against the backs of my thighs. Felix nuzzled me slowly. He stayed like that, pressed against me, forehead to forehead, nose to nose, standing between my legs, his lips almost brushing against mine.

"What is it?" I said.

"I'm just relieved you're back. Sometimes I'm scared I'll wake up in the middle of the night and you being back would have been a dream and my real life's a nightmare again," he said.

Chapter 52: Planning

I kissed the tip of his nose. I knew all about having a nightmarish life and I was determined to be strong and to give my pups the total opposite of that.

"Hey, have you thought of any baby names?" He asked me.

"I was thinking you could each name one of the three," I said.

"But then you won't get to pick a name?" Felix replied.

"Who named you Felix, Alex and Calix?" I asked, realising we'd never discussed this before. I had always assumed it had been former alpha Romeo who had named his sons.

"Mom," said Felix smiling.

I smiled back. That woman still disliked me. I guessed I should just accept it. The triplets loved me and that was enough. I certainly wasn't the first girl in the world to have a mother-in-law who didn't like or approve of her. Maybe there was a monster mother-in-laws support group for girls like me.

"Felix," I whispered.

"Yes, Baby," he purred back, getting even closer.

"If you, Alex or Calix do anything tonight that I don't approve of, you won't get anything from me until these pups graduate high school," I warned.

Felix laughed.

"Baby, you have nothing to wrong about. You honestly never did but I don't think you see it," Felix said.

I narrowed my eyes at him.

He kissed me sweetly and gently at first but suddenly increased the urgency of it, pressing himself against me and tangling his hands in my hair. I broke apart, wiggled away and hopped down off the tiled counter. Felix grasped my waist and placed me right back up there.

"Hey!" He protested. A flashback came out of nowhere.

"Thanks for dressing up for us. I hope you wear an even shorter skirt tomorrow," Calix said softly, smirking.

I rolled my eyes. Alex and Felix burst into laughter. I tried to brush past them but Felix grabbed my arms and put my back against the island again. My breath hitched in my throat.

"Did I say you could leave?" He asked, his nose brushing against my nose as he bent towards me. I squirmed in his arms.

I winced, shrinking away from Felix. He noticed it, frowning, concern evident in his eyes. "Did I do something?" He asked softly.

"No," was my soft reply. Truthfully, the flashbacks were a lot less intense nowadays and didn't make me panic anymore. I hugged Felix tightly. He enveloped me in his warm embrace.

"I wish you were coming with us!" Felix murmured.

"To your bachelor party?" I asked incredulously.

"Yeah!" Admitted Felix.

I giggled. "I'd be in the way."

"You'd be on my lap," Felix said.

I giggled and hopped down successfully this time, dodging him.

"Hey!" He protested but I ran down the stairs giggling.

"No running in heels like that! You're pregnant!" Called a voice from the landing. Alex.

"Sure, Daddy!" I called back as I ran to open the door for Mina, Tina, April and June. I was actually really excited about my bachelorette party now that I had a group of girlfriends!

Chapter 53: Jealous

Chasity

I got into the back of a stretch limo that had been ordered for my friends and me. We all squealed. Mina and Tina were in matching baby blue crop tops and shorts and June and April were in similar outfits but they had joggers instead of shorts with their crop tops. I was in my gold dress. I had picked baby blue for my bridesmaids colours because I honestly didn't know what to pick and the triplets seemed to like that colour so I was making it the colour palette for the wedding. Tina put a bridal veil on my head. The girls all cheered. Mine popped a bottle of champagne. More cheers. I couldn't drink.

"I can't drink," I said, shrugging.

"Why not?!" Demanded Mina.

"She's pregnant!" Said April indignantly.

"Oh! Yeah!" Squeaked Mina. "Don't worry! I'll drink yours!" She proceeded to down two glasses of champagne.

"Great save, Mina," complimented Tina.

Mina gave her a thumbs-up.

April rolled her eyes and June laughed.

We went to a club called called *Alpha Appeal*. This place was apparently known for their hunky male exotic dancers. The decor was all black and white with gold accents.

A tall buff guy dressed like a fireman was dancing on the main stage. He actually had a hose that worked and he would spray ladies with it every now and then. The wet ladies were screaming and jumping up and down excitedly. None were the least bit annoyed by their outfits being drenched. No one was spraying me! No thanks!

The fireman who apparently went by the name of *Thunder From Down Under* finished his dance and hopped off stage. Ladies rushed to throw more money at him. He bowed and grinned, picking up armfuls of cash.

A guy dressed as a police officer without a shirt went to the main stage and said into the mike, "Do we have any brides in the house tonight?!" The whole room cheered. I quickly ripped off the veil and hid it. "I am told we have one bride! Chasity!!!! Where are you?!" He spoke like a music DJ announcing the top hit song.

I immediately hid, ducking down. I considered crawling under the table we had been seated at but the girls jumped up and down and pointed to me. Two guys in bow ties and speedos ushered me onto the stage to sit on a pink chair. A guy came out dressed in a tuxedo. A song started to play, soft and slow at first. In one swift move, he ripped the entire tuxedo off. He had boxers on to my relief. The music became upbeat and he danced around my chair while my four friends cheered and got tipsier.

Finally it was over and I scampered back to my chair.

Third Person

Alex, Felix and Calix were at an exclusive gentlemen's club. They had decided to spend the night drinking, gambling and reminiscing with about twelve or so of their friends. They had specified no dancers whatsoever. They couldn't risk that, especially with Chasity being pregnant. They didn't want to stress her out unnecessarily. Besides, they had no interest in that anyway. They were currently playing blackjack. Calix had the winning hand, twenty-one exactly! He pulled all the chips towards himself grinning. The youngest always had the best luck at games. Felix was the most skilled at cards. Alex refused to play. He hated gambling. The eldest was drinking whiskey and telling three of the guys on the couch about a new pack treaty had he come up with. The night passed rather quickly and the triplets were eager to get back to Chasity.

Chasity

There was no way I didn't smell like the guy who had danced for me. I flew into the pack house when the limo dropped me off. Were the triplets back yet?

"Chasity!" Felix. My heart almost stopped at the sound of his voice. I heard his footsteps. I ran upstairs to our room. I spotted Calix in the hallway. His face lit up and I dove into our room. Alex was lying bed. He sat up, smiling. I ran into the bathroom and slammed the door. I could hear all three of them as they congregated by the door. I hadn't done anything. Ugh. But they would go ballistic. I showered as carefully and quickly as possible. They were knocking on the door.I hurtled out quickly, sopping wet, in my fuzzy bathrobe. My hair was drenched.

"Aww," cooed Felix. "I would've showered again with you."

"I'm so sleepy," I mumbled.

"She just wants to get to bed. I can tell," said Alex, drying my hair with a towel.

"May I? Please!" Insisted Alex, picking up my detangling brush. Ugh. I couldn't resist him now with how guilty I felt.

"Yes," I said. He looked shocked but elated and began gently combing my hair.

Calix was drying and massaging my feet. He put warm socks on me. Felix dried me off and put my nightgown on.

"Goodnight!" I exclaimed and crawled under the covers.

They were silent and stood at the foot of the bed.

"You only want one of us next to you?" Asked Alex. Huh. Oh. I was in the corner. I scooted over and they grinned. Alex and Felix were next to me. My heart was still racing. I trembled a little as Felix's nose touched the nape of my hair. He had lifted my hair to smell me. He stiffened. Fuck.

"Chasity," he said.

"Yeah," I replied hesitantly.

"Come with me," said Felix.

I gulped. Felix grabbed me and we went to the bathroom. I could hear Alex grumbling.

Felix shut the door. He looked livid. He folded his arms.

"I'm sorry! The girls organised this weird dancer person. They asked who's the bride and I tried to hide and take my veil off but it didn't work and the dancer person still danced. I refused to let him dance on me or too close to me but I know you have the best nose so…" I was rambling. Felix was shaking in the corner of my eye. I dared it look at him. It was laughter. He was laughing.

"You're so innocent, Baby," he said, pulling on one of my curls. "I don't think I have to worry about you. Remember Roxie?"

I wanted to growl.

"Vaguely," I said.

"She was a major ho, always cheating on me, so I broke up with her," said Felix nonchalantly.

I burst into laughter. "Really, she carefully left that out when she told me all about you guys."

Felix shrugged. "Naturally," he said.

He sighed.

"I'd have preferred no dancers… but you're so young. I know you didn't plan it. Mina and Tina seem the type to take you to a whole club," he commented.

I was at a whole club. Ugh.

"They… did. But that one tuxedo guy was the only person who tried to dance for me. Please don't me mad. I'm sorry," I said rushing into his arms.

"I'm not mad," Felix said. I was shocked. I stared up at him. He nuzzled me.

"I'm not thrilled but I'm not mad. It's over. No more private dancers for you," he said sternly. I nodded eagerly. He nuzzled me again. We walked out to find a pissed-off Alex and a confused and groggy Calix at the door.

"We were just having a chat," Felix said.

"No secrets," Calix insisted.

"As if you both didn't listen at the door," said Felix, rolling his eyes.

Calix grinned. "Strippers, Chasity?"

I hid behind Felix.

Chapter 53: Jealous

"I would've danced for you if I knew you were into that!" Declared Calix who came over to gyrate on me, showing me his dance moves. I giggled and tried to escape, playfully swatting him. Felix started to dance too so I was sandwiched between pretend strippers, Felix and Calix. I covered my eyes but I was grinning. They were so silly and I loved it and I was totally relieved. My relief didn't last long.

We were interrupted by a loud sigh. Felix and Calix stopped dancing. I uncovered my eyes. My grin slipped off my face. Calix and even Felix looked nervous. It was Alex. The eldest was *truly* pissed.

Chapter 54: Daydream Queen

Chasity

A lex was really upset about the dancer at my bachelorette outing. I bit my lip. I had been worried about Felix and his extra sharp nose sniffing me out. I had thought he would be the most jealous but he was chill and understanding. Calix thought it was funny and wanted to dance for me himself. Alex was so furious he walked off and went somewhere else. My heart constricted painfully. My wolf whimpered. I recalled when Austin's smell had been on my hair tie. Alex had been so upset. I had thought some of that was about hair and not about me necessarily as he had such a thing for my hair. I had been a bit daft. He was possessive, but he was an alpha and the eldest so what else would he be like?

Felix stopped me from going after him.

"Please, you're pregnant. Stay here with Calix and don't stress out. I'll talk to him for you," Felix offered.

"No, I need to do this," I said firmly. I gave Felix and Calix both a kiss. They followed me down the stairs. They didn't want me even walking around the house alone. They were a bit traumatised from the kidnapping and so was I. We didn't find Alex anywhere on the ground floor. We looked all over. Eventually we realised he was in the attic. I went up there. He was on the tiny balcony, just staring out, looking forlorn.

"Please come in! Please!" I beseeched him.

He came in and looked at me with sad hurt eyes. I held his hands. I kissed them. He stifled a smile.

"Alex, I would never be unfaithful. The dancer danced and that was it. There was no real interaction and I definitely won't even be going anywhere like that again, especially not when it bothers you. I never wanna hurt anyone, especially not you. I'm sorry," I said softly.

"Give her a break, bro. Mina and Tina took her there. You know Chasity's not like that," Felix grumbled. Alex glared at him.

"If you would have danced for her yourself, Alex, this wouldn't have happened!" Joked Calix in mock outrage. "This is *all* your fault!"

Alex smiled a little at his youngest brother.

"I want a smile for my own, please, thanks," I said.

Alex grinned. He kissed me, rather intensely. "I don't mean to be hard on you. I just... I've wanted my mate my whole life and when I realised it was you, I was so scared you would leave me at some point and then I was scared you'd be taken from you. I just wanna feel like you're here forever and no more worries. Especially not some dancer in speedos or something trying to snatch you away," he said.

I nodded. "That would definitely *not* appeal to me. I only want my alphas," I said.

Alex carried me back to bed. Calix actually *did* give me a lap dance. He was pretty good! He was so cute! He shook his booty in my face which I was completely not expecting. I smacked it and swatted him away. Felix laughed but Alex narrowed his eyes. Exotic dancing was a sore subject. It was too soon.

I straddled Alex and kissed him. He just needed some extra attention. I ran my hands down his chiseled chest and over his rock hard abs. I reached into his boxers to grasp his huge thick length. I sighed contentedly as I felt it harden. Alex hissed in pleasure. He groaned as I squeezed him a little. Felix was pressed up behind me. Calix freed himself and rubbed his smooth cock against my cheek. My mouth went to it instinctively. Before I knew it Alex was in my pussy, bouncing me up and down on his large smooth member. My pussy started contracting around him immediately. Felix pressed lube liberally between my butt cheeks and slowly gently entered my behind. I groaned against Calix's member. I missed them and this. I knew I wouldn't be able to take much more though as they were hitting all the right spots and with incredible vigour. I could tell they missed me too. I was deliciously sore and yet the pressure in my tummy rose and rose until a breaking point. I screamed but it was muffled by Calix's release in my mouth. I swallowed. Alex spurted into my pussy and Felix into my behind. I collapsed on Alex's chest, exhausted and he enveloped me in his strong arms. He and Felix pulled out. I was placed gently on my back. I fell asleep almost instantly.

In the early morning when it was still dark and chilly, I felt fingers tracing patterns on my inner thighs. I moaned, slowly waking up. My alphas were awake and looking at me hungrily. I was surprised to find myself in a nightgown with a panty on. They must have dressed me. I yawned and smiled slightly, looking at them from under my lashes with sleepy eyes. Felix kissed me as though he were ravenous. Our tongues caressed each other lovingly. I felt his hands slip into my underwear, part my folds, find my clit and caress it. I moaned. I was dripping. Alex put his hands in my underwear and squeezed my butt cheeks, parting them and kneading them. Calix stuffed his hands in my panty too so he insert his fingers into my pussy, knuckle deep. I cried out but Alex claimed my lips. This was like my dream from before I'd been mated only it was real. I was awake, sleepy, but definitely awake and six hands were in my panty. Calix kissed me deeply next. I lost count of how many times I came. They were relentless with their caresses and their kisses. They were whispering sweet nothings to me. I heard my name a lot and I moaned their names even more. I couldn't wait to be their wife.

Thankfully our wedding was soon. My dress was picked out. My bridesmaids had squealed with delight and my family members had loved it. I was so excited to see the triplets' faces on our day. I smiled to myself daydreaming about it.

"What're you thinking about?" Asked Felix, his voice husky in my eye.

"My alphas," I told him. "You guys."

Alex chuckled.

"We're right here," murmured Calix, licking my ear.

Chapter 54: Daydream Queen

"No Daydreams necessary," cooed Alex kissing the tip of my nose.

I bit my lip. "But I *love* to daydream," I protested.

They chuckled.

"Then continue," insisted Felix.

Alex nuzzled me. "You're our little daydream queen." I giggled. Felix snorted saying it was corny. Alex grinned.

Calix didn't say anything. He just parted my thighs and headed downwards. Actions really *did* speak louder than words.

Chapter 55: Wedding

Chasity

Tina, Mina, June, April and my Mom stood in a semicircle around me. They were all beaming. My mother's eyes were filled with tears.

"You look radiant, darling! Absolutely beautiful!" She said as she dabbed at her eyes with a tissue and then blew her nose.

"Work, Queen!" Said Mina.

"Slay, Mama!" Said Tina.

June smiled at me with wide eyes. "So pretty!"

"You're such a gorgeous bride, Chasity!" Said April.

I blushed. I would have to get used to all this attention now that I was a Luna to the Alpha Triplets. I was certainly getting used to receiving attention from the triplets themselves.

I looked at myself in the floor-length mirror in the dressing room of the suite we were in. Our wedding would be in this five star hotel. I was nervous but I knew I loved them so much. I was barely showing yet in terms of my pregnancy. The dress was a shimmery satin material. It dazzled me with every movement, catching the light beautifully. It was fitted at the waist though not too tight. It flared out into a full skirt that reached the floor. The dress had a beaded top with a sweetheart neckline and sheer short puff sleeves with floral embroideries and floral appliqués on them. My hair was in loose long blonde ringlets and curls. I had a rhinestone dotted veil attached to a flower crown of white roses. My makeup was done very natural looking with rosy cheeks, nude-pink lips and long lashes and shimmery eyeshadow. I took a deep breath.

"Ready, pumpkin?" Asked my father appearing behind me.

"Ready!" I said smiling brightly.

My Dad looked dashing in his tuxedo. My Mom looked beautiful in a chiffon baby blue dress. My four bridesmaids all wore baby blue too. They were in tea length fit and flair dresses. They looked so cute! The music began to play and we walked out of the dressing room and through a luxurious beige hallway. The hall in which the wedding ceremony was being held had a high ceiling and several arches of white roses. The roses were dew covered and even their leaves sparkled. There were pixies flitting from flower to flower, getting drunk on nectar. They would be raucous and uncontrollable soon. I chuckled. Pixies were always a riot.

I watched my four friends and bridesmaids glide gracefully down the aisle, each one escorted by one of the triplets handsome friends. The guests were all so glamorous. They were the cream of the crop, the who's who of the pack. Here I was, once the shunned lowest ranking member about to marry the famed alpha triplets and become Luna.

I heard the pack wiseman speak. He had an echoey commanding voice that filled the room.

"Please stand for the bride, our Luna Chasity,"he said. Everyone rose from their seats. My Dad walked me down the aisle. I clutched my bouquet of white roses and my fathers arm for dear life. I was so nervous and a little self-conscious but then I looked up and I saw them. Alex, Felix and Calix were standing there in their white tuxedos looking unbelievably handsome. I held my breath. They were gazing lovingly at me and grinning from ear to ear. I blushed. My father gently kissed my cheek and I kissed his cheek. He gave my hand to Alex the eldest symbolically. He nodded at the triplets. They nodded at him bowing their heads slightly as a sign of respect.

My father went to sit with my Mom in the front row. I couldn't help but glance at the former Luna and the former Alpha. Ronnie had a small smile on her face as she looked at her children. Romeo looked proud as he regarded his sons. The pack wiseman was acting as our officiant. We were instructed to repeat the vows after him. The vows had to be aid three times, first with Alex, then with Felix and finally with Calix. Alex was solemn and very serious about the vows. Felix was eager, grinning from ear to ear enthusiastically. Calix was sweet and sentimental. I sniffled the whole way through. The officiant pronounced us husbands and wife. Alex kissed me gently cupping my face. Felix's kiss was a bit rougher, hungrier. Calix kissed me softly trailing his fingertips across my cheeks. The guests cheered. Grandpa Chance was among them, cheering the loudest.

Our reception was held in the same hotel in a huge banquet room. The centrepieces were crystal vases overflowing with white roses. The tables were covered in white satin tablecloths. The pixies had fluttered in flying a bit off kilter. They were tipsy now. I could see their glittery trail as they zigzagged about. The photographers were going full paparazzi on the wedding party. I supposed the alpha triplets were technically celebrities and so was I by association perhaps.

They announced me and the triplets to a chorus of cheers. I walked in arm in arm with Felix and Calix with Alex walking ahead of us. I danced with my Dad. Then I danced with Alex. He held me like I was made of porcelain. He twirled me around and dipped me, planting a gentle kiss on my lips. Felix held me to him so closely while we swayed on the spot. He murmured sweet nothings in my ear. Calix's dancing was a bit livelier like he was doing the jive or something. After all the dancing, I was famished. The food was all superb. The wedding cake was a tall and magnificent as the triplets themselves, with its delicate sugar-spun flowers and tiny pearl-like sprinkles. We cut the cake together with me feeing huge pieces to my guys. The cake was so yummy and decadent. I savoured the sweetness of the cake as well as the sweetness of my new life with my triplet alphas.

Chapter 56: Departure

Chasity

Girls in their formal wear eagerly formed a row, all bending their knees as if they were about to leap. I closed my eyes and spun around in a circle three times with the help of my Mom. I held the bouquet, weighing it in my hands a bit. I threw it over my shoulder. I turned around just in time to see the bouquet soar into the air and then fall as every girl dove for it. Mina and Tina both caught it. I couldn't tell who had grabbed it first and I honestly though they had planned it that way. I watched the disgruntled faces of the other girls and stifled my laughter.

Third Person

The Alpha Triplets were ready to leave their wedding ceremony and set out for their honeymoon with their beautiful Luna, Chasity. At the moment, Luna Chasity was saying a private emotional goodbye to her friends and family. The triplets hugged their father and then their mother one by one. They hugged their grandparents and their best friends who had served as the four groomsmen for the wedding.

One of them was their cousin actually, another Alpha of his own pack, who had flown in for the wedding.

"Maybe Jessie's wife, Luna Jamie, can give Chasity some pointers on leadership skills and developing a rapport with the pack?" Suggested Ronnie to her three boys.

Felix frowned. Calix smiled halfheartedly. Alex had a black expression.

"Um, I'm sure Chasity will get the hang of it without my help!" Insisted Jamie. "After all, Chasity is actually a she-wolf! I had to learn about werewolves on the whole, being a witch and all," explained Luna Jamie who was also the Mother of her own Coven. "But, I'd love to just hang out with Chasity! We're cousins through marriage now and we're both Lunas. It'd be great to be close," said Jamie brightly.

The triplets smiled. Ronnie frowned and changed the subject.

"Jessie, why didn't you bring the little ones?" Said Ronnie.

"They're so adorable," commented Romeo.

"Aww, they'e a handful!" Responded Jessie.

"They're two handfuls!" Said Jamie.

Chasity

I had just told my Mom and Dad goodbye. We wouldn't see each other for six weeks which seemed so long although we'd been apart for nine years before. My parents and my Grandpa Chance followed me over to where the triplets were talking with a few of their family members. My bridesmaids had said their goodbyes to me and went back to the dance floor. I could tell they were all a bit tipsy if not flat out drunk. Mina and Tina had found handsome twins to dance with and had explained to the guys that they were "spiritual twins" because they were "besties". June and April had mates, both were-foxes. The guys had moved to our parklands from June and April's respective home towns as the girls actually loved it here. I decided to dive right into the conversation since Ronnie, my new mother-in-law, seemed to think I needed to be more social with the pack members and what not.

"You have twins right?" I asked Jessie, the cousin of the triplets. He nodded eagerly.

"Jade and Jake. Wanna see some pictures?" Answered Jessie beaming.

Jamie promptly pulled out her phone too as Jessie began scrolling through his phone's photo album. The twins were truly adorable. They were fraternal, a girl and a boy. Fraternal twins would have two separate mates not one like identical twins or triplets. The both had Jamie's golden skin and brown curly hair but they had Jessie's blue eyes. They were half werewolf, half witch or wizard which I found utterly fascinating. What powers would they have?

"Their magic is coming in! Werewolves don't really shift until they come of age but we witches get out powers extremely early. There's even cases of foetuses making objects levitate from inside the womb!" Exclaimed Jamie. Wow. That was cool. I really hoped I would get to see more of Jamie and Jessie. At least, two people from the triplets' family liked me.

"Congratulations, by the way to the new bride and Luna!" Exclaimed Jamie warmly, hugging me.

"Congrats, cuz!" Said Jessie bouncing knuckles with me.

"The limo is here!" Said Ronda the party planner. My Mom and I hadn't taken many of her suggestions wedding-wise but she was still technically my wedding planner. She could barely look at me in my wedding dress. I knew she wished to be me even more than the were-fox who had been inhabiting Deidre's body. There was a crowd of wedding guests spectating as we left. All the people seeing us off were cheering. After one final round of hugs, the triplets and I got into the backseat of the limo. It was incredibly spacious. As soon as we were alone, my alphas began eagerly but gently kissing and caressing me. It was a short ride to the airport but I was breathless by the time we got there. I had been told me were going back to the island.

"I'm so excited to see the island again! I loved it there!" I exclaimed.

"We're not going to the island!" Admitted Alex.

Huh.

"Why not?!" I asked.

"We wanted to surprise you!" Said Calix excitedly.

"So where are we going?!" I demanded, chuckling.

"It's a *surprise*!" Retorted Felix, laughing.

"But I packed clothes for a tropical location?!" I whined.

"Trust me, it'll all be fine, Luna," cooed Alex reassuringly, pulling gently on my curls and watching them spring back into place.

"Yeah, Goddess, we got you covered, don't worry," added Calix, winking at me and trailing his thumb against my lower lip.

"Baby, we've got it all down pat!" Purred Felix, massaging my shoulders.

"If you three say so!" I said, chuckling, giving them each a kiss.

On the private jet, I sat between Alex and Calix. Felix sat opposite us to his chagrin. The plane was basically empty except for us and the plane's staff so I kept going back and forth between seats to keep Felix company too. I was so excited to find out where we were going. Alex had actually covered my eyes while we walked from the limo, through the airpot and to the private jet. The triplets were really hell-bent on this being a surprise. I must have drifted off because when I woke up, Calix was carrying me, bridal style. I blinked a couple times, my eyes adjusting to the light. Once my eyes adjusted, my jaw dropped as I marvelled at my surroundings!

Chapter 57: Honeymoon

Chasity

We were in the middle of an enchanted forest. The trees stretched upwards for miles. Their huge canopies provided shade for the entire landscape. There were flowers blooming everywhere, many of them swaying to and fro. I heard folk music being played on a flute and realised the flowers were dancing to the tune. There were faeries and pixies perched in the treetops. I could see their glittery trails from down on the forest floor. They were responsible for the music. The birds chirped in harmony with them. The forest was cool and peaceful, all the leaves covered in sparkling dew. I looked forwards and spotted a cottage. It was gorgeous with a kitchen garden, flowerbeds and flowering vines growing all over its clean white walls.

"Where is this place?" I asked. I was certainly surprised.

The triplets grinned.

"We're in the Forest of Faded Dreams," said Alex, always ready with information.

I had heard of that! It was nestled between the borders of Marigold and Berryndale. There were no clear lines drawn as to which pack owned the forest but they were very friendly allies so it didn't particularly matter. Both packs made use of the forest on occasion. The triplets' pack also had a good relationship with them as the Berryndale Gamma, Westwood, was another one of their cousins.

"How come Westwood wasn't at our wedding?" I asked, remembering the triplets talking as fondly of him as they had spoken about Alpha Jessie of Ambrosia.

"Westwood's mate is pregnant too and she's on bedrest so she can't travel and he hates leaving her," said Felix.

"Oh," I said, feeling grateful I hadn't had any issues yet but worried about Westwood's mate.

"She's human too!" Said Calix. "So his Alpha always makes special allowances so Westwood can travel seldom or never even if they have treaty stuff to do in a neighbouring place."

"Aww, that's really nice of him!" I said, immediately liking that alpha. I liked when alphas were understanding of their pack members. I had never really seen the triplets in a pack meeting because I'd never attended any.

"Maybe we can visit Berryndale or Marigold?" I said softly. They had good shopping places and nice cool weather like in this nearby forest. I knew that from Mina and Tina. They had mainly talked about the hot guys in Berryndale but they'd also mentioned the shopping. Mina and Tina could find eye candy and good fashion anywhere. They were serendipitous that way.

"Sure, Baby," murmured Felix, turning the key in the lock of the front door.

We walked into the cottage. Calix was still carrying me. The cottage was so cute! It had high-ceilings and hard wood floors. Every piece of furniture looked so cozy. The whole place just made me want to cuddle up with my alphas and take a nap.

They were looking at me anxiously.

"This was totally not what I was expecting... but I *love* it!" I squeaked.

"It's not too..." began Alex.

"It's perfect!" I insisted. "It's not too anything. It's just right!"

Calix set me down gently on my feet. Alex smiled and I stood on my tiptoes to kiss him.

"Ready to see Jamie's wedding present for the honeymoon?!" Asked Calix excitedly.

"Yes!" I said.

Chapter 57: Honeymoon

Felix and Calix began tossing all the adorable pattered plates in the cute kitchen on the floor , breaking them.

"HEY!" I bellowed, my eyes turning black. Whoa. I was definitely becoming a Mom. They were making a mess!

They laughed and my eyes slowly lightened to a warm brown again as I saw all the plates reform perfectly, wash themselves in the sink and stack themselves. The faucet had turned on for itself and the dishtowel had levitated and done its job.

"I. *Love*. Magic." I said pointedly making every word count.

"Who doesn't?" Asked Felix.

"Alex," said Calix.

Alex was in the corner away from the enchanted moving objects.

"It's like it's haunted," Alex mumbled.

Awww. Alpha of alphas Alex. The eldest! Scared of magic!

I went over and cuddled him. He wrapped his arms around me.

"I'm not scared of it! I'm just wary of it malfunctioning, Luna!" Said Alex.

Sure.

"Ok, Alpha," I said, giving him another kisses.

"Alex is getting a lot of kisses," whined Calix.

"Yeah!" Exclaimed Felix. "Did I mention I'm terrified of..."

Felix looked around the room. "Cottages in general.." He tried. I laughed but gave him a kiss anyway.

"And I'm scared of going long periods without kisses," complained Calix, scooping me up again and running upstairs with me. I laughed as Alex and Felix chased after us.

The ground floor had living room with a huge fireplace and tons of cozy furniture, a kitchen with a breakfast table, a dining room with another fireplace, a bathroom and a downstairs bedroom. Upstairs there were three more bedrooms, each with their own bathroom and another small living room with a dining area. Every single thing was adorable. I felt like I was in a fairytale or a dollhouse. Calix hopped into bed taking me with him and making me straddle him. I kissed him deeply, running my fingers through his long silky hair. Felix came up behind me and tickled me. I tried to escape by tickling him back. He was kneeling on the bed and his bare foot was nearby. He had extremely ticklish feet. As soon as I tickled his foot, he surrendered and even retreated. I chased after him.

"Don't run too fast ok!" Called Alex after us.

"He's just afraid to be in a room by himself with enchanted teapots and all those other terrifying things," yelled Calix.

"Ow," said Calix from the other room. Alex must have swatted him.

I stopped chasing Felix. "No hitting!" I said sternly. How was I going to manage three mini versions of them? I resolved to nap everyday of my honeymoon and the rest of my pregnancy. Napping could become a thing of the past with triplet babies. No wonder Ronnie was such a grumpy bitch. I promised myself to not be like her and to give my sons or daughters' future mate a proper chance.

I realised I was still in my wedding dress. I had to pick up my train every time I ran after one of the triplets. I looked out the upstairs hallway window and spotted a little creek with babbling water at the back of the cottage. There was a family of deer and another family of cottontail bunnies all drinking from the rushing water.

"Guys, this place is so beautiful," I said awe-struck. They knew how much I loved animals.

"Jamie said the animals here are enchanted too. They don't fight each other and they're all friendly!" Alex said. Finally a spell he liked.

"Also, there's a hunting ban shell," said Felix.

"Yep," said Calix. "Guns won't fire here and traps and whatnot won't work. Arrows will never hit a moving target that's alive."

I loved that so much.

"It's a tiny sanctuary," I whispered.

"Yep," said Calix grinning. "We did good, huh."

I grinned at them. I went to the biggest bedroom where the triplets had put my luggage. I ran my hands over my tummy. I wasn't properly showing yet. I tried to unbutton the long row of pearl buttons behind me.

"Hey!" Protested Felix and Calix.

"What?!" I replied.

"Undressing the bride is grooms' responsibility," said Alex, waggling his eyebrows at me.

"You'll have to catch me first then!" I said. And with that, I picked up my train and ran down the stairs and outside. I could hear the heavy footsteps of the triplets on the stairs behind me like on that

Chapter 57: Honeymoon

very first day of their birthday week. It's weird how that sound used to give me anxiety. Now, it made me excited. I ran to the back of the cottage and splashed right into the creek. The cottontail rabbits regarded me with curiosity. They scampered away to a nearby patch of lettuce. The deer had left. I looked on the shore to see my three alphas, shirtless, muscles rippling, and stepping into the water.

Chapter 58: Surprise

Chasity

Running was pretty useless. The triplets had only let me outrun them to make it a little more fun for me. I was scooped up by Calix. He carried me bridal style further from the shore where the water was cooler and deeper. I sighed happily, loving the feeling of his strong, warm arms around me. His elder brothers followed us further out into the creek. Calix made me wrap my legs around his torso and fling my arms around his neck. I could feel the bulge in his pants as it pressed against the fabric of my panty.

"We need to take off this wedding dress, Baby!" Felix purred. "It's weighing you down."

I nodded meekly. Felix and Alex began unbuttoning the long line of pearl buttons behind my dress. When they were finished, they helped me pull the dress off over my head. Alex folded it and went to put it on the shore.

My three alphas pressed themselves against me. I giggled as Felix placed kisses from my earlobe down to my shoulder while Alex lifted my hair to kiss from the nape of my neck down to between my shoulder blades. Calix kept my lips busy, kissing me gently but insistently. He pulled away and kissed the tip of my nose. I tightened my legs around his waist, pressing myself against him.

Chapter 58: Surprise

He groaned and slipped his tongue in my mouth. Our tongues danced together as Alex unhooked my bra and Felix dove down into the water to slip my panty off.

Suddenly, Calix lifted me up higher and put me on his shoulders so that my most sensitive area was right up against his face. I tangled my hands in his hair as he licked me eagerly, parting my folds with each lick. He found my clit and enveloped it with his mouth making me shiver. I felt Alex's rough palms parting by butt cheeks from behind. I squealed as his tongue prodded my tight back opening. I wiggled about a bit but both Calix and Alex gripped my waist keeping me equidistant as their tongues drove me crazy. My wolf wondered where Felix was.

Without warning, Calix and Alex put me flat against the water's surface. I shrieked as I fell backwards but Felix was right there. He held my underarms, helping me float. He bent over me pressing his lips against mine while Calix continued tracing patterns on my vulva with his tongue. Alex moved towards my breasts and pressed his thumbs to my nipples, caressing them in circular motions, making them pebble. He took my left nipple into his mouth and sucked on it eagerly, swirling his tongue around the nipple as Calix plunged his tongue deep inside my entrance and Felix's tongue slipped inside my mouth. I couldn't even scream because of the fierce kiss I was locked into with Felix.

I writhed under the three of them which seemed to encourage them. I moved my hips instinctively, rubbing myself against Calix's face. I felt the youngest alpha squeeze by butt cheeks. I groaned into Felix's mouth. Alex had moved to the right nipple while his hands massaged my sides. There was an energy and a heat rising in my lower abdomen. They took me higher and higher and the heat inside me burned hotter and hotter. I could not contain it anymore. I screamed into Felix's mouth as I came against Calix's face. Alex kept rubbing my sides to soothe me as I slowly came back to earth. Felix broke the kiss leaving me so breathless I was a little lightheaded.

My alphas cradled me and carried me indoors. They wrapped me up in a warm towel. The evenings were chilly here. We took a warm bubble bath and then sat on a plush carpet right in front of the fireplace.

Our honeymoon was as sweet as can be. The days blurred into each other. Kisses and caresses in the morning, running through the woods, splashing in the creek, warm baths, deep talks by the fireplace and snuggling together at night, sleeping peacefully.

On the first day of our honeymoon, I had been about seven weeks pregnant. At the end of our honeymoon, I was around thirteen weeks pregnant and my baby bump was showing. I was relieved to be over my first trimester and entering into my second. I had experienced a few nauseated mornings but I had not had actual morning sickness, just a little bit of an upset feeling every now and again. I considered myself fortunate.

We retuned to our parklands. My parents and Grandpa met us at the airport along with the triplets' parents. Even Ronnie seemed happy to see me though I was sure she was mostly excited about her future grandchildren being back home. I wasn't looking to be best friends with my mother-in-law but I decided stay cordial at least.

I started attending pack meetings and even presiding over a few of them. I was definitely a lot more lenient than the Alpha Triplets but it did not make sense to have strict Alphas *and* a strict Luna. My father and his stepsister, Ronnie, stayed a bit distant from each other. Their relationship remained strained. I felt it was my fault though the triplets constantly assured me it was not. We continued going to therapy as a family and I continued going separately. It helped me a lot. I learnt to stop blaming myself and to stop ruminating so much. My flashbacks became few and far in between. At thirty-two weeks, I was only able to waddle from the bed to the couch and back. I couldn't wait to give birth! Carrying triplets wasn't easy. The triplets constantly told me that I was "glowing". I felt like I was just *growing*. The triplets told me to get dressed for a fancy dinner. I put on a loose fitting white maxi dress with embroideries and lace details. It really was a beautiful dress. I kept my hands on my tummy, cradling it, as I walked slowly down the stairs. It was so quiet and dark with all the lights off. A chill crept through me.

"Alex! Felix! Calix!" I called into the darkness.

I quickly moved towards the light switch and flicked it on. I jumped.

"SURPRISE!" Yelled everyone present in unison.

Relief swept over me. The triplets came out and hugged me, kissing lips, my forehead and my cheeks and my baby bump. Mina

Chapter 58: Surprise

and Tina had planned this surprise baby shower, inviting my parents, Grandpa Chance, the P.I. Danny, April, June, my in-laws, Jessie and Jamie, and many of our pack members. Beta Keaton was there with his daughters, Roxie and Moxie. I knew they'd been questioned when I was missing so it was a tad awkward. Everyone made an effort to make me feel comfortable though, even Ronnie who was very excited about being a grandmother even though I wouldn't have been her pick for a daughter-in-law. Ronda was there. She must've snuck in. She eyed my baby bump enviously. I smiled sweetly at her and pulled Alex a little closer to me using his tie. I pressed my lips eagerly against him, eliciting some cheers from several raucous pack members. I spotted Mr Johnson and gave him a big hug.

"Wow!" He exclaimed, looking at my baby bump.

I blushed.

"You look beautiful!" He said reassuringly. I smiled.

His free-spirited mate was dancing with Ronda of all people, both of them a bit tipsy. They'd taken their shoes off and were dancing like they were in a club or something. I covered my mouth to stifle my laughter. Ashton came up to me and congratulated me along with the other football players who had protected me from the bully that day.

The triplets were being really attentive and sweet. They'd been that way for my whole pregnancy. Actually, they'd been making an effort since they had found out I was their mate. I really had forgiven them. There was a hired photographer who usually worked with celebrities. He posed the triplets around me. Alex was sitting in an armchair with me on his lap and Felix and Calix sitting on the armrests. We took a few photos in various poses including me on Alex's lap with the other two triplets on the armrests kissing me.

Chapter 59: Baby Triplets

Chasity

I had been reading a magazine with the *real* Deirdre Binx on the cover, a tell-all exposé on her harrowing ordeal entitled *The Beauty and the Bodysnatcher*. It named me and the triplets as a heroine Luna and heroic triplet alphas. I smiled. I was glad the real Deirdre could benefit off of the fame the doppelgänger acquired, using her image.

I wasn't even thinking about my huge belly today. Suddenly, a sharp pain made me drop my magazine. I felt liquid pool under me. Did my water just break? Alex, Felix and Calix who had all been cuddled up with me in bed immediately felt the wetness and started to panic.

I knew that with multiples there would be a higher chance of a preterm birth, meaning they could come early, *before* forty weeks. I was only an estimated thirty-four weeks when I went into labour. The triplets were freaking out.

"Get my mom!" I shrieked at a hyperventilating Alex who was rifling through the Baby Encyclopaedia he'd been studying looking for L for Labour. Felix scrambled off to go get her and then zoomed back in.

Chapter 59: Baby Triplets

"On second thought, I don't wanna leave you, Baby!" He said breathlessly. "Calix, you go!"

"CHALICE!" Bellowed Calix without leaving the room. In all fairness, Calix was packing my baby bag.

My mom rushed in followed by my Dad and Grandpa, both of whom she promptly put out.

"They were no use when I was in labour with you," she said to me. "So why would they be useful now?" She asked rhetorically, shrugging. I chuckled despite the pain.

At least, I had my Mom here.

"That being said, I don't know about the whole multiples part. Let's get you to the hospital ASAP," she said, helping Calix with the baby bag.

She zipped it up and handed it to him. She went to help me up but Felix insisted on carrying me. Alex threw his encyclopaedia in a corner and rushed ahead of us to open the doors as Felix carried me out of the house. Alex threw a big coat over me before opening the front door. They rushed me into the backseat of the car. Someone ran out behind us.

"I'm coming!" Ronnie said. Ugh. "I've have triplets before! Not many people can say that!" She retorted in response to my grumpy look.

"Fine," I said softly.

Alex drove. Calix and Felix were in the backseat with me. My mom was in the passenger seat and there was a seat between my Mom and Alex where Ronnie sat.

"Are you going to try to push them all out?" Asked Ronnie.

I nodded.

"There's a high chance of C-section with triplets!" She warned.

I shrugged. Whatever was best for my babies. I trusted my doctor and his team. They were prepared to do surgery if necessary. He had already warned me of that possibility in case not all three came out head first. If a hand or leg came out instead of the head, that was called "breach" and they would do an emergency C-section. I'd actually listened to Alex. He read me and the babies passages from the baby encyclopaedia as if those passages were bedtime stories. I smiled at the memory. I caught Alex's gaze in the rearview mirror. He smiled at me. I blew him a kiss, and he grinned.

Alex parked with a screech of the tires through the snow. Felix scooped me up. He ran with me, a whole entourage hot on his heels to the labour ward. I was triaged quickly and they decided I was to stay on the Labour ward. I was placed in a private room as per the triplets' request. It was a really nice room with floral wallpaper and floral carpet. Even the bedding was floral. The doctor came in and checked my vitals chart. He said they were normal. The triplets, my Mom and their Mom breathed audible sighs of relief.

"You're dilated enough! Ten centimetres! It's time to push!" Said the doctor.

"Ready, Chasity?" He asked.

That was fast. I wasn't expecting to have to push so fast. I knew it took a while for the cervix to dilate enough. I was terrified all of a sudden. Calix kissed my forehead.

"You'll be fine, Goddess. Just listen to the doctor," he whispered, stroking my hair. Felix squeezed my shoulders. "Come on, Baby!" He said encouragingly.

Alex was holding one of my hands in both of his. He kissed my hand. "Ready, Luna?"

I nodded resolutely. I pushed as hard as I could. My mom and the triplets mom encouraged me also. The doctor said the first baby was crowning. I was panting. Calix wiped my forehead with a cool damp towel.

"The head is out!" Exclaimed my Mom excitedly.

"That's one!" Said the Doctor as he scooped the baby up in his arms and quickly placed him on my chest as he clamped the umbilical cord. I was already exhausted but my first baby, my eldest, he was so beautiful!

"Congratulations! A healthy baby boy!" Said the doctor.

The nurse smiled. "He's gonna be a heartbreaker one day. He's so cute!"

I pushed with what strength I had left and soon enough the second baby crowned and was born. "That's two," said the doctor, placing this one on my chest. He was just as beautiful as his elder brother.

The third baby came out the quickest as if he'd been in a hurry to be born. He came out crying. The other two had wailed momentarily but calmed quickly. The third one was shrieking at the top of his lungs. I cradled him and rocked him slowly. My youngest was going to need a lot of attention.

"Shh, shh," I cooed at him. He quieted a little. He looked up at me with his baby blue eyes. His hair was a little tuft of blonde curls. They were all identical.

"What are you naming your babies, Mommy?" Asked Felix, kissing my forehead.

"You did so well!" Exclaimed Alex, kissing my hand. "This is the eldest!" Said Alex, showing him to me again.

"Adriel," I said groggily. It just came to me. He looked like an Adriel.

Felix showed me our second son, cradling him to his chest. I called him, "Raphael."

Calix rocked the third son, still hushing him and soothing him. "Tzuriel," I murmured.

"Time for a nap, huh, Goddess," whispered Calix, kissing my cheeks. I yawned. The doctor and nurse saw to me again and cleaned me up. I was able to get the baby triplets to latch on fairly easily. They each drank to their little heart's content. I was exhausted now. My Dad and Grandpa and the triplet's Dad came in and took over holding the babies and rocking them while my Mom and Ronnie hummed a little song. My triplet alphas curled up in bed with me, however they could fit. I felt so warm. They were whispering to each other and to me so as not to wake the babies.

"You guys were so funny today," I whispered.

"We were a little scattered," admitted Alex.

"We were all over the place," grumbled Felix.

"We'll be better prepared next time!" Calix assured me.

"*Next time*?!" I asked incredulously.

"Yeah for the triplet girls. The Luna Triplets!" Said Calix.

I wasn't trying to hear that! I had just given birth! I snuggled up with my three alphas and shushed them. They chuckled and kissed me softly. I soon fell asleep with my triplet alphas watching over me and watching over our little ones.

Chapter 60: Sleepless Nights

Chasity

After three days of observation, the baby triplets and I were discharged. They kept us for longer than usual because it had been a birth with multiples which always carried greater risks. Alex was driving and anxiously glancing in the rear-view mirror every few moments to check and me and the babies. They were all in their carseats and their onesies. I put them in striped onesies: baby blue for Adriel, green for Raphael and red for Tzuriel. They looked so cute. All the onesies were striped with white and my chosen colour for them. I needed to colour code these babies. I was a sleepy Mommy. I didn't want to have to think too hard about who was who.

Felix was in the back with me and Raphael. The middle seat of the six-door SUV contained Calix and Tzuriel and Adriel. Felix was stroking my curls with one hand and patting Raphael's tuft of blonde curls with his other hand.

"Did you guys switch places a lot growing up?" I asked.

They all grinned.

I took that as a yes.

"Did you fool your Mom?" I asked nervously.

I was worried.

"Never!" Said Felix.

"She couldn't be fooled!" Said Calix.

"She always knew! Dad would get confused at first though! Until he learnt to tell us apart by scent!" Said Alex from the driver's seat.

Scent! Of course. I sniffed little Adriel's head. He smelled of Baby powder. They all smelled of Baby powder. I frowned. Alex chuckled, looking at me in the rearview mirror.

"Their individual scents won't be very strong right now. They're a few days old. They'll get stronger over time! By a few weeks or months, they'll probably have slightly different scents," said Alex.

"And by the time they hit late childhood, their scents will be well-differentiated!" Said Felix.

"They won't have full blown scents until they're of age," said Calix.

"Oh!" I said.

We arrived at the pack house and my parents and Grandpa, who had arrived before us, rushed out to help us with the three babies. We got everyone inside and up to the nursery. I put Adriel in the blue crib, Raphael in the green one and Tzuriel in the red one. I was so glad I had picked different colours for everything. The babies were sleeping soundly. My alphas and I tiptoed out of the room.

We curled up in our room next door. The baby monitor had been set up in case they woke up crying. I was between Alex and Calix with Felix in the corner. I couldn't believe we were all parents now. It felt like just the other day we had been arguing after that party. I sighed happily. The doctor had forbidden us from having "intercourse" for a while to allow me to heal properly. I was a she wolf so I would heal pretty fast. He said to come back to him in a week for a checkup. My alphas wouldn't be able to keep me awake tonight!

As if they'd heard my thoughts, all three baby triplets woke up and began to wail! I jumped up.

"No, Baby! Rest!" Said Felix sternly.

"You just gave birth the other day, Luna," said Alex.

"We can handle it, Goddess," said Calix.

"Someone has to stay and watch Chasity!" Said Felix.

"No, I'll come to the nursery! We put a small bed in there, remember," I said.

Calix scooped me up and carried me to the next room. He placed me on the bed and went to the nearest crib. Each alpha was rocking a baby. They were so sweet. I smiled at the three Daddies and three babies.

"Are they hungry?" I asked anxiously.

"I think they're just cranky!" Said Felix.

"Let's try them with the milk though in case!" I said.

I fed Tzuriel. He drank eagerly for a few minutes and then used his tiny hand to push me as if to say he was done. Good grief. Three days old and he already had an alpha attitude. Raphael fed the longest. I switched breasts and he was still feeding. He yawned. Adriel fed quickly and then he was quiet. He didn't fall asleep but he didn't cry. I peaked at him in his crib. Quiet and thinking. A focused expression on his face. He was eldest. He would be head alpha one day. He looked at me quizzically as if to ask why I was staring at him. I giggled and he smiled. They were worth the sleepless nights just like their horn-dog Dads had been. That's how I'd gotten pregnant! The Alpha Triplets were all passed out on the little bed in the corner. The babies were drifting off. I crawled into the tangle of limbs on the cot and fit in somewhere. Someone pulled me onto their chest in their sleep. Felix. Alex was behind me. Calix was sprawled out like a star fish and taking up most of the cot. I finally fell asleep with a huge smile on my face surrounded by my Alpha Triplets and my baby triplets.

ABOUT THE AUTHOR

I write stories about werewolves and witches on Dreame/Stary Writing. I am from Trinidad and Tobago and I enjoy incorporating Caribbean folklore into my fantasy novels. In my free time, I play with my dog and cats, bake cakes, and read horror manga.

I began writing short stories for my own entertainment as a child, and I continued writing into adulthood. Fantasy has always been my chosen form of escapism. I became a Medical Doctor (MBBS) and a fantasy writer for the same reason: to help someone (even just one person) feel better. I have often drawn comfort and courage from books. I hope you can do the same.

You can also visit www.dreame.com for more of my stories.

ABOUT DREAME

Established in 2018 and headquartered in Singapore, Dreame is a global hub for creativity and fascinating stories of all kinds in many different genres and themes.

Our goal is to unite an open, vibrant, and diverse ecosystem for storytellers and readers around the world.

Available in over 20 languages and 100 countries, we are dedicated to bringing quality and rich content for tens of millions of readers to enjoy.

We are committed to discover the endless possibilities behind every story and provide an ultimate platform for readers to connect with the authors, inspire each other, and share their thoughts anytime, anywhere.

Join the journey with Dreame, and let creativity enrich our lives!

Made in United States
North Haven, CT
21 August 2023